WAITING

Claude Delarue was born in Geneva in 1944. He studied at the Academy of Vienna, and between prolonged spells in Vienna, Hamburg, Berlin, London, and a mission in the Near East as Delegate of the ICRC (International Committee of the Red Cross), he worked as musical director for Swiss television in Geneva. For a long time divided between music and writing, he has lived in Paris since 1972 in order to concentrate entirely on his books. He is the author of seven novels, a novella which won the Académie Française prize, a stage play, radio plays, and a biography of Edgar Allan Poe. He is also the literary adviser to a French publisher.

CLAUDE DELARUE

Waiting for War

Translated from the French
by Vivienne Menkes-Ivry

Minerva

A Minerva Paperback

WAITING FOR WAR

First published in Great Britain 1992
by Mandarin Paperbacks
Michelin House, 81 Fulham Road, London SW3 6RB

Minerva is an imprint of the Octopus Publishing Group,
a division of Reed International Books Ltd

First published in France in 1989 by Editions du Seuil
under the title *En attendant la guerre*

Copyright © Editions du Seuil 1989
Translation copyright © Vivienne Menkes-Ivry 1992
The author and translator have asserted their moral rights

The author wishes to thank the
Fondation Pro Helvetia for its support

The author and publishers are grateful
to Penguin Books and Philip Vellacott
for permission to reproduce extracts from
Euripides' *The Women of Troy*,
translated by Philip Vellacott
in the Penguin Classics edition (pp. 88, 263 and 264)

A CIP catalogue record for this title
is available from the British Library

ISBN 0 7493 9910 4

Typeset by Falcon Typographic Art Ltd, Edinburgh
Printed in Great Britain
by Cox & Wyman Ltd, Reading, Berks

For Danielle G.

PART ONE

Stone

. . . I am fifty-one. I studied geology and worked as a geologist for many years, but then deliberately distanced myself from official research and academic circles after publishing a monograph that was criticized by my colleagues as lacking in experimental rigour. They may have been right. But what I had been working on was simply a modest attempt to find a method halfway between reflection as practised by the scientist and contemplation as practised by the philosopher. I was reflecting on what seems to me a key question, though I have never claimed to have found an answer: what is the likelihood that man, that eleventh-hour invention whose conscience and speculative intelligence are both overdeveloped and yet at the same time underdeveloped, will ever be able to apprehend the world outside in its entirety as a dimension of his own being?

I put forward the idea that man may possess a secret memory, an archaic memory that contains the whole of the macrocosm, a type of memory to which we haven't got the key, but which every now and then, during the stases of ordinary memory, communicates the riches it contains to the brain. A love of the world, a love of nature – to put it naively – are a love of self perpetuated in the mind's unutterable hankering after substance.

But what prompted me to apply for the post of secretary and companion is that I feel I have a number of skills that have nothing to do with my academic training, but have been acquired through personal experience. After a severe crisis of conscience I felt the need to withdraw from the world and became an oblate at La Verna monastery near Arezzo, on the very spot where St Francis's stigmata appeared. I spent just under ten years there, seeing to the daily needs of an elderly monk who, like you, had been disabled by a medullary traumatism. It wasn't an easy job, but one from which I derived considerable inner satisfaction . . .

He got off the train on an August day when the sky had that yellow tinge that presages a storm, and stood on the platform, alone in the lowering light. The station clock had stopped. Way beyond the rail line, on a small plain planted with cereal crops, combine harvesters were driving round and round in a cloud of wheat dust. They were making no sound at all and seemed to be transfixed, sunk into torpor like the rest of the countryside beneath the sulphur-coloured sky. The station buildings looked as if they were no longer in use. The train that ground to a halt on the grass-grown track three times a week was a mere ghost train these days. There was no one about as he crossed the track and walked out into a square crammed with military vehicles. They seemed to have been abandoned too. In the far distance he could make out soldiers going through their drill in a field and stopped to watch them for a moment, then set off for the little town.

The road, straight and treeless, bent round following the line of the church belfry, though all that was visible above the sloping hillside was the weathercock perched on top. Further away, veiled by a sheet of rain racing swiftly towards the plain, the foothills slumbered peacefully, their gentle outline wreathed in mist. Yet fierce axe blows and the collapse of ancient peaks had created a jagged landscape cleft with deep gorges, throwing up cliffs and scree made up of black rocks. He tried to make out the fortress perched high up at the top of a ravine, but could see only a chaotic jumble of solid blueish shapes, glittering here and there as the light was reflected in a window pane.

His case wasn't heavy – his prospecting equipment was in

a leather rucksack on his back – and he was able to keep up a good pace as he strode along. Five weeks earlier he'd travelled along this same road, but that time he'd been driven. In the intervening weeks Olga Grekova-Leber had written confirming that she was offering him the post of secretary and – a term that could mean anything – companion. 'After you came to see me,' her letter had explained, 'I interviewed several other applicants, but it was a mere formality. I knew straight away that you were the only one who was just right in every way.' And she had added – La Grekova, as she was still known in theatre circles, apparently didn't go in for hiding her feelings – 'Don't misunderstand me. I'm not taking you on because I like you. You're not what is conventionally known as a nice person – which is just as well.'

By now he wasn't at all sure he could get to the town ahead of the curtain of rain racing towards it. He decided to stop walking, put down his case and waited, standing quite still in the middle of the road. A sighing breath of wind drove the rain towards him and within seconds he was drenched. His whole body was filled with jubilation. Then he strode on. A car drove slowly past, the first sign of movement in a universe that had seemed transfixed. Through the steamed-up window he glimpsed a highly unusual woman's face, her gypsy-like features seeming carved in stone. Below the road, in a dip filled with shadow, the grey houses huddled round the church and the buildings on the industrial estate were lit by a sudden shaft of light, glancing slantingly off their glistening roofs.

The room the innkeeper gave him overlooked a butcher's. But the view at the far end of the alleyway was filled with a small piece of hillside, rife with vegetation in a range of brilliant greens. He undressed and lay down naked on the bed, staring up at the flies flitting to and fro across the wooden ceiling. He had a sense of everything being very beautiful, yet totally unimportant – like his own life, like success and failure. There was very little traffic. He could hear a fountain splashing and the muffled sound of troop movements coming from the large

5

barracks. The solid white body he could see stretched out, headless, on top of the sheet, seemed to belong to someone else, and he thought of all those men lying naked on hotel beds all over the world, numbed by the age-old wait for they knew not what, stretched full out in the primeval layers of their consciousness. And in spite of the flies, he could sense through the thickness of the walls, beyond the rocks and the forest, the towering presence of the fortress. He got up off the bed, dressed and went down to dinner.

The soup was like the soups of his childhood, thick and steaming. He ate it without enjoyment – his childhood memories were full of anguish and bitterness. The dining room was suffocatingly hot, the air stale, filled with the stench of rancid sauce and unpalatable canteen-type food, even though the door had been left open to let in a breath of cool air. He ordered a bottle of wine.

'I remember you. It's not the first time you've been here,' volunteered the innkeeper as he served his meal.

'I went up to the fortress a few weeks ago,' he said.

'You'd answered the job ad, hadn't you? Tanguy came to fetch you. As far as I remember there were two other applicants with you. So you were the one she fancied, were you?'

He smiled at the expression and rephrased it: 'I was the one she appointed, yes.'

The innkeeper sat down astride a chair and, leaning on the back of it, was silent for a few moments, lost in thought. A group of soldiers came noisily into the dining room and settled down round the largest table. A smell of aftershave and leather wafted across.

'I used the word "fancied" deliberately,' said the innkeeper. 'La Grekova only ever takes on men who've managed to catch her eye for one reason or another . . .'

He had barely touched his soup, but pushed the bowl away and asked absently: 'What can you tell me about Samuel Leber?'

The innkeeper seemed disconcerted. He shrugged and fidgeted on his chair. A tall slim woman wearing an elaborate white

6

crêpe hat appeared in the doorway, hesitated for a moment or two, then silently vanished.

'I don't know any more than anyone else,' said the inn-keeper. 'He wasn't born here, but his family came from the town, and his grave's in the cemetery. He was a really top architect, a military architect. They say he built the world's biggest fallout shelters and he was the person the Swiss called in to build their national redoubt. He dreamed up the idea of hollowing out whole mountains and hundreds of miles of underground passages. Apparently it's big enough for the whole population to take shelter in. Just before he died he was in charge of building shelters in Japan, in America, and even in China and Russia. He was a very likeable man, very pleasant. La Grekova's looking after his affairs these days. I don't want to put you off, but she isn't pleasant, or likeable either.'

The chair creaked and he stood up, stunned at having got through such a long speech, then backed away.

After dinner, when the dining room had emptied, he went out and walked around aimlessly, taking deep breaths beneath a clear sky spattered with a few winking stars. Was someone up there watching him as he walked? There was no movement round him; the cycle of days and nights continued interrupted. He was surprised to hear the sound of his own footsteps on the paving stones. He turned round several times, thinking he was being followed. Whenever he stopped walking, for a moment or two he would still hear the footsteps behind him in the deserted street. But then they too fell silent. He walked round the church and found that the iron gate into the old cemetery was open. The local high-ups were still being buried here and he walked from tomb to tomb, reading the names and dates aloud. What was left of the anguish and joys experienced by these eminent citizens? So much pain and so little trace of it now, he thought. Soon he was standing in front of one of those graves that didn't seem old, yet didn't look recent either. It was a plain flat stone of indeterminate age, tilting over to the right where the ground had caved in,

7

as though the dead man had turned over too suddenly in his wooden box.

SAMUEL LEBER
Architect
1919–1977

That's all there was on the marble slab. He felt nothing. He was going to work for the widow of this man, who had once been famous in the vanity of vanities, and whose passionate desire to save mankind had driven him into the grip of an all-devouring obsession. Once again he sensed that there was someone or something behind him. He turned round. At first nothing struck him. Then above the cemetery wall, framed at the far end of a street running straight ahead, he spotted the outline of the fortress, perched high up against the overcast sky. He glanced several times from the grave to the vast and fantastic building he'd chosen as his future home. He'd always been one for making quick decisions. That was the main source of his strength – the irrevocable, equivocal choices he made. But he felt no pride in this. Nothing whatsoever was capable of arousing in him the slightest sense of glorification. In that respect he was already well on the way to achieving a state of impersonality, though he was still far from reaching that place where he would at last be like a mere pebble.

He walked back to the inn and ordered some wine. Another group of soldiers was making merry. This time they were all officers and one of them, already pretty tipsy, was clasping his cap to his chest as he recited some lines of poetry in English. The waitress had gone up to bed and the landlord had taken over.

'What time are they going to pick you up in the morning?' he inquired, eyeing his guest with curiosity.

'They aren't.'

The innkeeper raised his eyebrows, starting to look suspicious.

'You do know, don't you, that you can't get up to the fortress in an ordinary car? You need a jeep. Or haven't you told them

8

you're coming? If so, we can ring them. Tanguy or Varlaam will come and get you.'

'Thanks, but I'll walk up.'

'Walk up? It'll take you a good three hours.'

'That suits me fine. I like taking it slowly when I'm setting off for somewhere that's going to be my new home. I'll start out when the sun's coming up.'

He went up to his room and walked straight over to the window, leaning on the sill. Back in the cemetery he had felt very strongly that there was a thin but unbreakable thread stretching from beyond the grave to link Samuel Leber with his fortress – as though the dead man's will had become immortal and was endlessly being given concrete expression in the building he'd designed. But he himself had no such links or points of reference as he stood alone in this room that seemed to have only a very tenuous link with reality, cut off from the rest of the world by a vast and impenetrable darkness. Staring sightlessly down at the uneven paving stones in the alleyway below, he let the darkness transport him way beyond consciousness, lulled as on the sea by the hours sounding one by one from the church belfry.

When daybreak came he was still standing at the window, as fresh and alert as if he'd just woken from a deep sleep.

He left the world below beneath a cloudless sky. A road pitted with potholes plunged into the moist slit of a ravine. It ran beside a stream whose clear waters trickled over a mossy bed, accompanying it up to its source. But before it reached there, the side of the mountain drew in and a ruined watermill at the entrance to a gorge had almost disappeared beneath a tangle of ferns and brambles. The millwheel was still creaking jerkily round, the sound reverberating in the rushing of the mountain stream like a human voice crying out in despair. At that point the rutted path became a sea of mud, and as the innkeeper had said, impassable for ordinary cars. He stopped near the mill, sat down on a piece of rock and watched the water seething and foaming as it was sucked between the narrow walls of the

9

gorge. The despairing cry behind him began to sound like a prayer. The whole landscape was offering up a silent prayer, and the creaking of the millwheel paddles sounded so frail, so faltering, that it was even more like a human voice. He picked up his case and walked on.

The path climbed up, crossed a rocky spur in a series of zigzags, then dropped down again towards the torrent, which now making a loud rushing sound and had become narrower, bristling with dark slabs of rock with mangy pines clinging precariously to them. From there on the deciduous forest gave way to conifers and he started walking across a plateau dotted with rocks. Then the forest reappeared and the path became a quagmire. Fresh tyre prints showed that some large vehicle had been past there a short while earlier. He leapt up on to the bank and continued on his way, walking on a bed of fir needles. Soon he came out into a clearing where four woodcutters were sitting on logs.

When they saw him suddenly emerge from the forest with his suitcase they started up in surprise. He greeted them with a nod. One of the four got to his feet and walked over to him. He was clutching a sandwich and a bottle of wine.

'Where on earth are you off to?' he asked, his voice hoarse, apparently from lack of use. 'This path doesn't go anywhere.'

I'm going up to the fortress. I'm going to work for Mrs Leber.'

'You're going up to the fortress? On foot? What the hell's that idiot of a Tanguy up to? He could've picked you up.'

The other three were on their feet now and had walked over, curious and sniggering.

'Leave him alone, he can go for a walk if he wants to,' said the shortest of them. 'What's La Grekova going to get you to do then?'

'She needs a secretary.'

A glint of mockery shone in his eyes. One of the others held out a bottle of wine to the newcomer: 'Well, I can tell you something, it isn't exactly going to be a bundle of laughs once you get up there. It's true there's Félicité and Tanguy.

10

But Tanguy's only half human and Félicité's a saint. And the rest of the staff come from far away and can't speak a word of the language.'

A silence greeted these words. Then he was amazed to see the four woodcutters quickly cross themselves.

'How long does it take from here to the fortress?' he asked.

'Oh, an hour and a half, maybe two hours. It depends how fast you walk.'

'He could always go up in the bucket of course,' remarked the only one of the four who hadn't said anything so far, grinning sarcastically.

As he looked puzzled, the man explained that Samuel Leber had put in an electrically controlled cable car, with two open buckets. The idea was that the most fragile of the materials used during the building of the fortress could be hauled up that way, instead of having to be carted up the mountainside each time. Each bucket was big enough to take two people as well, though they needed a good head for heights, as at its highest point the cable was stretched taut over three hundred feet above the torrent.

'Once they'd finished restoring the fortress the cable car was never used, except just once a month to ferry up supplies of food and drink,' the woodcutter told him. 'But then one evening, God knows what got into them, Leber and his wife decided to go down in the bucket. It isn't clear exactly what happened, but the decelerating mechanism must have failed and the bucket plunged downwards. Leber panicked, jumped out as it was falling and was killed as he hit the rocks. The bucket was smashed to bits on the concrete housing of the cab, and so was La Grekova. That's how she lost the use of her legs.'

The others kept quiet, shaking their heads and staring at their feet. Thinking of the accident had drained them of expression. The sun disappeared behind a cloud and there was a sudden chill in the air. He glanced over the row of young trees sawn into lengths with a chainsaw and the antediluvian piece of machinery they were using to dig out the tree stumps.

11

'The cable car's working again now,' the woodcutter added after a silence, staring at him intently.

'I think I'll walk up all the same,' he said with a smile. He picked up his case, thanked them and set off again.

In the limpid morning stillness, without a breath of wind, a sense of expectancy seemed to hang in the air, weighing down the trees from crown to roots, a feeling that the continuity of matter was due to be interrupted by some mysterious upheaval. He wouldn't have been surprised if the ground had suddenly gaped open at his feet, or one of the highest mountain peaks had caved in. This tangible sense of expectancy filled him with a flashing pain, and at the same time with a feeling, elegiac, almost gentle, of being excluded, for it showed that beyond his consciousness, in the humility of his lonely presence amid the galaxies, man is closely involved in everything that has ever come to pass, and will ever come to pass. He closed his eyes but kept on walking, opening them again only when he heard the voice of the shortest of the woodcutters, who was yelling after him.

'There's something you ought to know. Round here no one calls it the fortress. They call it the blockhouse. Best of luck!'

The accident had happened in 1977. He wondered who had dealt with the business of getting the cable car repaired, who had made the decision to do so. The bucket had been secured by an iron chock and the cable running beneath the driving wheel snaked up over the sheer drop of the ravine towards the fortress, as thick as a man's arm. The sun was already high in the sky, bathing the building in a brilliant light. The machinery was in an excellent state of repair – the pulley shiny with grease, the electric winch carefully boxed in to protect it from the elements, the iron chock with its rubber buffers clearly in regular use. It looked as though it was intended for some sort of initiation ceremony, breaking people in to the sensation of swinging above the sheer drop. He leaned over the edge, into the chilly depths of the ravine. Way below him,

12

the slender thread of the stream, spurting out of the bare rock, traced a pattern of silver filigree. He leaned back against the cable car hut and had a good look at the fortress for the first time.

Only the skeleton of the original castle had survived: a keep, a flanking tower clinging giddily to the cliff face, a brownish façade and the odd chunk of rampart or bastion. Samuel Leber had used these medieval ruins as a starting point for his own fortress. The many books and articles on his work stated that right at the outset of his career as an architect he had been convinced that mankind as a species was living on borrowed time. But the true picture was more complex. Leber's detractors claimed that his defensive structures were a way of symbolically sheltering himself from his own death. This was refuted by his supporters: the mark of genius, they said, is a frenetically self-centred outlook, which can sometimes offer the community something so priceless it would be inconceivable in terms of mere altruism.

For over fifteen years, using nothing but a new type of reinforced prestressed concrete, tempered steel and glass, but being careful to fit in with the overall development of military architecture from the Middle Ages down to the work of Louis XIV's engineer Vauban, Leber had pressed his own obsessions and terrors into a matrix of genuine medieval ruins. But did all this meet a true need? Did this piece of ultra-modern infrastructure wrapped round the ancient masonry, this complex and lifeless organism with the summer sun beating mercilessly down on it, express the inner truth of its architect? Was it the product of a tormented conscience or a manic obsession?

He swung his leg over the side of the bucket, which was swaying gently between its chocks. The sun was climbing up the sky and a bright canopy of light was suspended over the ravine. He pushed the control lever forwards. Nothing happened. He looked down and felt suddenly giddy. He beat a hasty retreat, leaping out of the bucket and setting off once again.

A rough chalky track climbed up to the col in a series of

tight zigzags then continued across the side of the ravine exposed to the sun, winding between the forest and the cliff face until it eventually reached the fortress. He didn't feel at all tired. He had been climbing for over two hours by now, but his case didn't feel any heavier. As he climbed higher and the world below sank back into its grey mists his heart grew lighter. Sheets of tarmac were piled up beside the track, which was now as wide as an ordinary road. The odd one was still stuck to the macadam, suggesting that, unlikely as it seemed, there had once been a road with a proper surface here. 'We could never have started work on the fortress if we hadn't first built a real road, with a surface strong enough to take the weight of the various machines,' Olga Grekova-Leber had explained during their first interview. 'But when my husband felt that the work was complete, he gave orders that the road was to be broken up, so that there was nothing left but a track full of potholes – otherwise the whole estate was too accessible. The labourers spent six months breaking it up, without the faintest idea of why they were doing it, and nature took care of the rest.'

When he was still well below the col, he was pulled up short by a tall openwork metal fence that seemed to continue for miles on either side of the path. The gate was shut. Parked up on the embankment a hundred yards or so away was a Range Rover. He walked a little way beside the fence, then tried to force open the gate, but it wouldn't give. At that point a domineering voice made him start.

He turned round. There was no sign of anyone. A sudden gust of wind raced down the col and was swallowed up in the latticework of the fence. The pines spun round, then came to a standstill, and there was a dead calm. He looked round and the voice rang out again, more peremptory this time.

'Don't move! Stay where you are and open your arms wide.'

He hesitated, then put down his case and did as he was told.

14

To begin with there was no sign of anyone. He turned his head to look in the direction of the ravine and the fortress, which was quite near by this time. Nothing stirred, apart from the jackdaws flitting back and forth above the ramparts, uttering their harsh cry. Then a man emerged cautiously from behind a rock and walked over to him.

'I can see who you are now. You can put your arms down,' he said morosely. He was carrying a shotgun, its weight supported on his forearm, the butt tucked into his armpit. 'Why have you walked up? I'd have come and fetched you. You mustn't take the mickey with us, you know.'

'I'm not taking the mickey with anyone, I just happened to feel like walking,' he said irritably. He'd just realized that the man was Olga Grekova-Leber's general factotum Tanguy, who'd once been a forester. Tanguy waved the barrel of his gun vaguely in the direction of the line of the fence.

'That's the Great Wall,' he said. 'There's only two places you can get through – here and about twelve miles further on. I drive along it once a month to check the fencing hasn't got broken.'

He opened the gate, waved him through and shut it behind him. He walked over to the Range Rover. He pushed up the rear door and with an unexpectedly gentle movement slid the shotgun into its leather case. 'You were supposed to be getting here tomorrow. Mrs Leber *will* be surprised. She loathes surprises.'

He vaulted in and opened the passenger door.

'I'll continue on foot, if it's all the same to you.'

He set off without waiting for a reply, passing the Range Rover, whose engine throbbed into life behind him. He heard the doors slam and a short burst of laughter rang out.

'I grovel before you, your eminence!' roared Tanguy, jerking the car into action.

It drove past him, the wheels spinning on the soft chalk, only to reappear and then make an endless series of appearances and disappearances as it hurtled round the hairpin bends

15

until it reached the col, where it shot on to the straight stretch of road running along the sunny side of the ravine to the fortress.

2

Tanguy had warned Olga Grekova-Leber that her new secretary was on his way up and she was waiting for him in the inner courtyard of the fortress, a huge square esplanade surrounded by the buildings housing the living quarters and reached via a postern gate cut into the ramparts. She was at the top of a flight of steps leading to the main entrance, upright and haughty-looking in her wheelchair, wearing a red outfit and with her eyes hidden behind dark glasses, which she didn't take off when he walked over to her.

'I wasn't expecting you till tomorrow,' she said while he was climbing up the steps. 'But it doesn't matter in the least. Welcome to the fortress. Tanguy can go and collect the rest of your luggage this afternoon.'

He couldn't see her eyes behind the dark glasses, but he could sense that she was watching him closely, and he realized he was dripping with sweat.

'This is all the luggage I've got,' he said. 'I don't need much.'

He put his case down, shrugged off his rucksack and mopped his brow. He stole a furtive glance at her wasted legs, which weren't really deformed, but had become very thin and frail, like a little girl's. She wasn't wearing stockings and – something he hadn't expected – he noticed that she was wearing high-heeled shoes, and that she'd wedged the heels against the metal plates on the footrest of the wheelchair, as if her feet were in a pair of stirrups. He put the rucksack carefully down. There was the clinking sound of metal.

'Might one ask what you've got in there?' she asked with unfeigned curiosity. She was slightly stooped, the result of being permanently seated and of having to manoeuvre the

16

wheelchair. She'd adopted the position you often see in disabled people of a naturally active temperament – they always
seem to be trying to stand up.

'It's my prospecting equipment. If I get any time off, I plan
to do some prospecting in the area.'

She pushed her dark glasses up on to her forehead and once
again, as at their first meeting, he was struck by the melancholy
sadness of her expression, which was so much at odds with her
hieratic face.

'Oh yes, of course, you used to be a geologist, didn't
you,' she said quietly, looking him up and down. 'You're
taller and more athletic than I'd expected. Although you're
older, you could soon make mincemeat of Tanguy if you were
more cunning. Cunning gives you the advantage over physical
strength, and sometimes even over intelligence.'

He wondered what she was getting at, but didn't ask. She
pulled a cigarette packet out of a small bag wedged between
her thigh and the arm of the wheelchair and offered him one.
He said he didn't smoke. She nodded approvingly, with a
somewhat mocking smile. There wasn't a breath of air in the
courtyard. His back was aching by now. He felt stiff all over
and his shoulders were drooping with exhaustion. She lit her
cigarette and slowly breathed out the smoke, apparently not
realizing that he'd been walking for very nearly four hours.
He glanced round curiously at the buildings surrounding the
courtyard. They were built on severe lines, in a spare classical
style, and there was no way you could tell that the stone facing
concealed Samuel Leber's indestructible shelter.

'It took fourteen years to restore the fortress. It was the
high point of my husband's career,' she said from her wheelchair, intercepting her secretary's curious glance. 'Fourteen
years. . . . The whole of the time we spent together was taken
up with it, plus a few other similar projects scattered all over
the world.'

She looked up at the sky, as though those fourteen years
were racing past above their heads, like clouds driven on
the wind. Her long hands, the muscles standing out sharply,

17

rested on the wheels of her chair, as though at any moment she was going to go speeding off to the other side of the steps, or career headlong down the metal ramp to the courtyard. She was knocking the ash from her cigarette into a silver box on her lap, fastidiously closing the lid each time. The sun was almost directly overhead now, and the light reflecting off the flagstones in the courtyard was so dazzling he had to shield his eyes before he could look about him. She raised herself up on the armrest of her chair, tossed back a lock of hair falling over her forehead, which was virtually unlined, and seemed to glow with a dark radiance.

'You'll soon realize that everything here is totally abnormal and totally real. The fortress is like an iceberg. The part you can see is barely ten per cent of the whole. When my husband bought it from the Count of Ott it was nothing but a pile of ruins covered with brambles, where he used to play when he was a child, or so he said. He used to insist that while he was running about among these walls he had a revelation that he was going to be an architect. But I never believed a word of it. The fortress is much too far from the town for children to be able to climb up here by themselves. However he probably did come up here quite a few times with his father, and I'm quite prepared to believe that his obsession with ruins started during that period. There was nothing melancholy or romantic about it – Samuel was the least romantic of men – but he had an absolute horror of ruins, they made him feel utterly desolate. It wasn't just a sense of time passing, he saw them much more as symbolizing the long series of violent acts that had been perpetrated there – fires, bloodshed, murder. He thought of stones as living organisms, frail and vulnerable, perpetually under threat of decomposition, just as we are.

'Samuel was undoubtedly one of the world's major architects working in concrete, following on from Le Corbusier and Frank Lloyd Wright, and he had developed theories about concrete. Yet I can assure you that he loathed concrete, precisely because he saw it as totally lifeless, solidity its only true quality, a neutral form of sturdiness, neither dead nor

18

alive – rather apt as a reflection of the spirit of modern man. But concrete is a scientific material, and he felt it should be used as such, because in architectural terms it represents such an exceptional form of protection that medical research will never be able to come up with anything as effective for the human body: it can protect man against his fellow-men.

'My husband wrote several books of philosophy. I'd like you to read them. They'll be essential for your work. As he saw it, although over the last fifty years western man has been making use of science, technology and morality to devise highly ingenious ways of preventing war laying waste his territory yet again, this doesn't mean he's started to see sense, only that he can sense his warlike instinct flooding back. The harder he tries to keep his barbarian side under control, it bursts out even more strongly. He spouts humanitarian sentiments, but inside him someone is thinking, as Tullus Hostilius did: "In times of peace, towns sink into senility." Ah, here's Tanguy! He'll take you to your room. You must be exhausted.'

Tanguy was ambling across the courtyard, the sound of his footsteps bouncing off the walls of the fortress. The flagstones were shimmering in the sunlight and he seemed to be walking on a sea of light. He climbed up the steps without so much as a glance at the secretary and took up his post behind the wheelchair, placing his hands possessively on the handles. In an oddly abrupt movement, forceful and carefully controlled, she propelled the wheelchair forwards and he was left standing there looking foolish, his arms dangling. Up to now she hadn't been looking anywhere in particular as she spoke, but this time she took off her dark glasses and looked thoughtfully at the secretary, her gaze full of warmth.

'It's odd, I scarcely know you, I know virtually nothing about you, and yet I already feel I can trust you completely. Your predecessors never knew why they were here. The sole attraction in the job for them was that it was well paid, and you need more than that to be able to put up with living at the fortress. That's why they made such a mess of it, however brilliant or highly qualified they were. I soon got rid of them, all of them – a whole string of them. I sent them back down to the world below, showing them no pity and feeling no remorse. It's just under ten years since I lost the use of my legs. Over that period I've had twenty-two secretaries, and not a single one of them was really interested in the job. Five of them decided to leave of their own accord, claiming that three months at the fortress was as much as any normal human being could stand. I wasn't sorry to see them go. And I shall never be sorry not to have a so-called normal human being with me here. You can't insist that a person must have an ideal, but you are surely entitled to expect anyone who hasn't got one to be aware of this, and to have good reasons for not having one. Even Tanguy's got an ideal, haven't you, Tanguy? Feeding the wild animals in the forest and helping them breed so we can kill some of them later on.'

The secretary, amazed at this endless stream of words, turned to look at Tanguy, who was standing solidly there, feet wide apart, hands thrust into his pockets, staring stubbornly at the ground. 'The gentleman must be tired,' he said grumpily, looking up. Their eyes met and the secretary was startled at the depth of hostility in his gaze. A brief laugh rippled through their employer's disabled body.

'Yes, of course, do forgive me for rambling on – I sometimes go for days on end without saying a word.'

Exerting pressure on the wheels of her chair, she propelled it to the front door and the two men followed her into a large entrance hall furnished with nothing but an enormous Chinese chest with iron fittings. A staircase with twin flights of steps led up from either side of the room. With its whitewashed walls, it had the look of a bare monk's cell. What was left of the original building was fifteenth-century, and when Samuel Leber had rebuilt the load-bearing walls and the façades, he'd kept the same spare style. Three small round windows let in a little dusty light, and in winter the hall was submerged in a dusky half-light throughout the day.

On his first visit the secretary had been interviewed in a room away from the main building and he had no idea of the overall layout. Olga Grekova-Leber put him briefly in

20

the picture. One of the staircases led up to a gallery linking the various medieval portions of the fortress, which had been almost totally rebuilt on the lines of the original plans. The other went up to the main living quarters. It was here that the Lebers had lived before the accident. But now her rooms were all on the ground floor, and although the fortress had a lift, and a sophisticated system enabling her to get to even the remotest corners of it in her wheelchair, she never went upstairs and spent her time either in her own rooms or in the library. As he was soon to realize, in coming to live at the fortress the secretary was entering a world as complicated as the mind of the man who'd designed it, yet one in which the rationale behind the design was everywhere apparent, as in a piece of theoretical reasoning that is a model of clarity and precision.

She invited him to join her later for lunch. He caught up with Tanguy, who was waiting impatiently at the top of the stairs, but stopped on the first landing for a good look at the whole entrance hall. She hadn't moved and was watching him as he climbed the stairs. He caught a slight movement of her hand on the arm of the wheelchair and felt that she was sending him a secret signal. They looked at each other for a few moments, as though hypnotized. Then a man appeared silently in the hall and walked over to her. He was dressed all in white and had an Indian cast of features. He was carrying a tray piled high with newspapers. The secretary followed Tanguy along a windowless corridor lit by lamps concealed in the panelling. The corridor wasn't built in any particular style, but dozens of little details gave away the ambiguity underlying the whole building. As he walked a few paces behind Tanguy, he mulled over what Olga Grekova-Leber had said as she sat there in her wheelchair, particularly that cryptic sentence: 'You could soon make mincemeat of Tanguy if you were more cunning.'

3

The elements were gathering. They would rise up out of the ravine with the cool air imbued with the scents of water and forest, then seep away with the evening light. Once again he had a sense of how utterly fulfilling their arrival was, like a daily resurrection. His bedroom was in the flanking tower. It was lit by two tall windows, one north-facing, the other looking west, so two different types of light met and merged there. The walls and the highly polished table top shone with a pure brilliance, sober and gentle, cast by this blend of sunlight and north light. Unlike his cell at La Verna, where the unseeing walls made space vanish, this room was suspended in mid-air, like a lighthouse. The tower overlooked the ravine and beyond it came a view of the whole mountain range. When he sat down at the table his knees were only inches from the sheer drop into the ravine. If he stood up he couldn't see anything in the distance except the tops of the fir trees. But if he walked over to either of the windows, the whole of the shady side of the mountain came into view, stretching as far as the torrent, and as he looked down into the deep fault he could still sense the movement of the axe that had cleft the mountain from top to bottom. On the north side the plain dissolved in the haze and he could scarcely make out the little town, which seemed far away, its existence somehow implausible.

'The tower was the only the only part of the fortress Samuel decided not to reinforce,' she'd told him on his second day. 'There isn't the tiniest speck of concrete in its walls, nothing but stone and sturdy old chestnut timbers. Being perched up so dizzily high you're constantly reminded of how fragile it is – none of your predecessors ever fancied living there.'

He spent his first month at the fortress prospecting the rocks in the area, reading Samuel Leber's books and looking at his many unpublished manuscripts. For twenty-five years, along-side his practical work, Leber had toiled away at compiling a whole corpus of philosophical writings on his specialist field that formed to all intents and purposes a moral philosophy of architecture. The manuscripts were in a jumble. Most of them weren't dated and there were thousands of loose sheets covered in handwriting that was very hard to decipher, piled up in drawers and on a long workbench.

'Samuel used to write wherever he happened to be, on any old scrap of paper, and it never occurred to him to put it all in order,' Olga Grekova-Leber explained to her new secretary. 'Part of your job will involve sorting out this huge mass of material into categories, cataloguing everything and putting it into chronological order, then copying it all out so that it's in a fit state for publication in the near future. My husband saw the theoretical side of his work as of lesser importance. He devoted most of his energies to turning his plans into actual buildings, so that as many fallout shelters as possible could cover the globe. For weeks at a time he'd think that war was about to break out and he'd get caught up in a frenzied bout of work. During those periods he'd be happy, full of energy, never writing a word but constantly rushing about from one continent to another. Then all of a sudden, for no apparent reason, he'd convince himself that everything he was doing was pointless, that war would never break out anywhere. So he'd start writing. He constructed the whole of his philosophy during periods when he was prey to appalling doubts. As soon as he stopped being physically active he'd start having misgivings about everything, and the act of writing wasn't enough to calm him down. He'd often say that his thinking, his philosophical reflections, transformed anything concrete he'd managed to achieve into a pale shadow of itself, that contemplation was the worst form of impotence ever to befall a man of action, but it was better than nothing at all.'

When she opened the door to the library he saw why she'd likened the fortress to an iceberg. During the restoration the original buildings had been so thoroughly reinforced that they were the only known example of fallout shelters at ground level, but beneath them, one above the other, twelve floors of dwellings had been carved out of the earth and the rock. Everything had been thought out down to the last detail to ensure the inhabitants' long-term survival. This vast subterranean world made up of acres and acres of dwelling space was left in darkness, waiting. There was no way of telling it was there, and its only visitor was the engineer responsible

23

for the maintenance of the equipment, who did three tours of inspection a year.

'I'd like you to go with him next time he comes. You really do need to be thoroughly familiar with the building that came closest to what my husband was trying to achieve. I've only been down there once myself, not long after the workmen had finished.'

When he was walking across the courtyard he would often pause to stare down thoughtfully at the flagstones, as though the ground beneath his feet had suddenly become transparent, revealing the riddle of this city buried in its innermost depths. He would fantasize that slumbering somewhere in a corner of those pitch-black rooms was a little piece of the soul of the building workers who, on tipsy evenings in the local cafés, would reminisce about the many years of their lives they'd given up to that Herculean task, no longer sure if it had really happened or if it was just the stuff of legend. As he explored the area round the fortress he would keep an eye open for clues on the hostile side of the ravine, to try to see how the work had progressed. But he could never find anything – although he knew nature had been violated, it still seemed virgin territory, the cliff tumbling innocently down towards the torrent, showing no sign of the atrocities that had been inflicted on it.

It didn't take him long to master the way the library worked. Olga Grekova-Leber taught him to use the computerized index. A few startlingly simple keying operations, and the exact position of the item you needed would appear on screen, with full bibliographical details, including where it was published, the language it was written in and any available translations. But the huge gulf between the ease with which you could access the vast mass of information in the system, and the infinite complexity of the material itself, wasn't so much evidence of the way the human mind had mastered matter, as of how utterly fragile it was. Staring at the screen he thought of the large amount of reflection and classification undertaken between the period when the material was first compiled down to the invention of this machine, and of the determination to preserve the fruits of human genius in the most logical sequence that man's intelligence could devise, and he appreciated as never before the extent to which this demonstrated the precariousness of man's consciousness, its uncertainty, rather than its strength, though it clearly was a strength. Backed into a corner by infinity, man was frantically waving tiny banners to indicate his presence in the vast universe, and with no higher aspiration than to go on living a poor existence, was struggling valiantly on at the impossible task of raising his evolution to a higher plane.

'In building up the library, my husband was acting as a cultural Noah.' There was a hint of irony in her words. '"What's the point of saving mankind if you don't save its spiritual inheritance too?" he asked himself. You'll find enough material here to satisfy your curiosity for several decades, maybe several centuries. When he was devising the cataloguing system, he called on the top technical experts, the librarians with the most original minds. This library is your territory, but I've got one thing to ask of you – please agree to have dinner with me whenever I ask you to. It won't ever be more than two or three times a week. I shan't ask you any awkward questions, and if I do, don't answer them.'

4

Dinner with Olga Grekova-Leber often took place in silence. She would lean her forearm on the edge of the table, sit hunched over her plate and tuck greedily into her food, to the exclusion of everything else. Before their first meal together she'd made a point of warning him: 'Don't be shocked, my table manners have been appalling ever since I've been in this wheelchair.' She certainly ate fast, and had an amazingly voracious appetite, but also a fierce delight in food, as though she was getting her own back on her disability. And suddenly a miracle would occur. While she was devouring her food as greedily as if she'd just stolen it and was terrified it might

25

be snatched away from her, the dazzling beauty of her youth would come flooding back.

The first time he witnessed this rejuvenating effect of food he was so fascinated he forgot to eat himself, and instead watched her quite blatantly. She didn't appear to notice, but when she'd scraped her plate clean she looked up at him, her eyes sparkling with mischief, slumped back against the back of the wheelchair and gave a gentle belch that was more like a sigh.

'You don't drink, you don't fornicate, you forget about eating – you really are short on vices, aren't you?' It was the first time she'd tried to rile him. She picked up her glass by the stem, held it between thumb and index finger and twirled it slowly round, admiring the colour of the wine in the candlelight. She drank from it and for a few seconds became magically beautiful, as though the wine possessed some divine property, and she reached the sublime heights of perfection, that timeless moment that occurs a mere second before the radiance starts to fade. Every time he had dinner with her he'd try to catch the precise moment when her face became young again, but he never managed it – she would look up from her plate and the transformation had already taken place.

At the end of one of these meals she became unusually inquisitive: 'Have you ever been interested in money?'

The question didn't embarrass him in the least – it couldn't be classified as specious – but it did take him by surprise. For a few seconds he didn't know what to say.

'I used to have a few possessions, but when I went into La Verna I handed them over to the monastery.'

She pulled herself up on the arms of the wheelchair, leaning forwards as far as she could, as though she was having trouble hearing what he said. Passionate interest was written all over her face and he had the feeling it was the first time she'd really paid any attention to him.

'Tell me about it . . . if you don't mind, that is,' she said softly.

26

'Oh, it's quite a straightforward transaction. A lawyer and the abbey bursar see to all the details. All I had to do was sign a statement saying I was making the bequest and there I was, stripped of all my worldly goods.'

Her expression clouded over and he detected a twinge of irritation.

'I envy you. It's an experience I shan't ever have,' she admitted. Her face was undergoing another transformation, in the opposite direction this time – the radiance of youth was fading, her features were growing harder.

'There was nothing particularly admirable about it – I wasn't attached to my possessions. I had a place in the country, an attractive house surrounded by lime trees, but I hardly ever went there. When I did stay there, I found it quite impossible to think of it as my property. My shirts, my shoes, my furniture – none of it belonged to me. It all weighed on me only very lightly. I felt it could all have vanished in a split second. When it really did all vanish, I realized that it had been a heavier burden than I'd thought. For a while I felt lighter, but then gradually I started feeling the weight of a new burden. Now, apart from my prospecting tools and some books, I haven't got any possessions left, but the burden's come back. You never manage to shake it off completely.'

She signalled an order. The Tamil who was waiting on them emerged from the shadows, opened another bottle of wine, filled their glasses and returned to his post. He was wearing an immaculate white linen outfit and padded around silently on bare feet, like a tiger. His lack of interest was so ceremonial that it reduced the people he waited on to less than nothing. Seven of his compatriots, all of them refugees from Sri Lanka, had been living at the fortress for a number of years.

'I've got pots of money. Samuel inherited a substantial fortune from his mother, which explains why he never had to put up any old building just to earn a living, and why he could concentrate all his energies on his research.' She sounded distinctly weary as she said this.

A middle-aged woman appeared in the dining room. There

27

was something primeval about her as she walked heavily between the halos thrown by the candles. The weird etiquette insisted on by Olga Grekova-Leber stipulated that Félicité must serve the pudding course herself. That evening she was carrying a serving dish with a raspberry jelly on it, quivering gently in the shadowy light, seeming to take on a life of its own. The Tamil servant, Viramanunivar, stood aside to let her pass. (The secretary could never remember his name, however hard he tried, and eventually called him simply Virama.) He was smiling, his teeth shiny white in a childlike face, but this gaiety went hand in hand with an enigmatic formal quality that was somehow disquieting. The Tamils at the fortress were all Shiva worshippers, but Olga Grekova-Leber suspected them of secretly worshipping Kali. The oldest of them, Sarachchandra, a scholarly brahmin, had escaped from northern Sri Lanka ten years earlier. He'd initially lived in exile in India, then moved to Europe, where his younger brother had joined him. Even when Samuel Leber was alive, he'd led the same quiet life of contemplation and reading.

Félicité put the dish down beside Olga Grekova-Leber's wheelchair and served her. A second or two of silence followed, broken only by the clink of fork against china and the occasional creak from the wheelchair. Félicité's soothing, precise movements made the concerns just voiced by her mistress seem very far away. She gulped down her first helping of pudding without even waiting for her guest to be served. The cook walked round the table, taking her time. In a niche in the wall the serving hatch yawned like an open mouth, its gullet plunging deep down into the bowels of the fortress. The kitchen was directly beneath the dining room and the secretary normally ate his meals there, sitting between the huge fireplace, a stove with highly polished brass fittings, and a bottle rack that was so near he only had to reach out and help himself. Along with his bedroom and the library, the kitchen was the part of the fortress where he felt most at home. He would settle down at the table, Félicité's shining face would turn towards him and he had everything he could

28

want – he wanted nothing more. A glorious quietness and stillness enveloped him. He could eat the finest dishes the earth had to offer and drink the finest wines. And anything not on offer was no longer necessary. But he realized right from the very first day that all this emanated from Félicité. With a single gesture she could make this place holy, and even when she was angry, you felt it was only right and proper.

'My husband got to know Félicité in Bogotá,' he'd been told when she was introduced. 'She couldn't find a job. She'd been working for the French consul and now he was leaving and his successor didn't want to keep her on. Samuel gave her a job and got a visa for her. Everyone in her neighbourhood believed she had spiritual powers. Three days before the accident happened – our accident, I mean – she had to go into hospital, so she wasn't there to exorcise the evil that had been festering between us and was suddenly unleashed . . .'

When Félicité had finished serving them both – without removing her pipe, which had gone out but was a permanent fixture – she went back down to her lair and Olga Grekova-Leber stared at her empty plate, panic-stricken. He handed her his portion – he'd scarcely touched it – and she gulped it greedily down. She was a bit tipsy by this time. She gestured towards the block of marble that was used as a sideboard. 'It's a reconstruction of the altar – this dining room was the castle chapel in feudal times,' she said unsteadily. 'It took a huge amount of research for Samuel to trace the earliest plans, but he generally managed to pull off anything he set out to do.' There was an anxious glint in her eyes and she looked agitated as she searched the secretary's face.

'I've already told you that, haven't I? Don't argue, I'm sure I have! You must tell me if I start repeating myself, don't try to spare my feelings. I couldn't stand going senile, I'd hold you personally responsible.'

'You've never told me about the chapel, honestly you haven't,' he assured her.

Virama had almost finished clearing the table. He left the glasses and the bottle and they went on drinking in silence.

For a few moments nothing could be heard beneath the palm fronds of the chapel vaulting but the stealthy sound of bare feet gliding on the flagstones, the clattering of the plates and, drifting in through the half-open door, the hooting of a night bird. She drained her glass, then set the wheelchair in motion, beating out an obsessive rhythm as she moved repeatedly away from the table then back again. When he asked if he might go to his room she stopped her toing and froing and gave him a hunted look.

'Do stay a bit longer – please,' she implored. 'Virama's going to bring some drinks and I'll ask him to leave us alone. I'd like to talk to you.'

He sat down again, slightly irritated, but intrigued. Virama put a tray full of bottles down near them. At that point the secretary noticed that her heart was pounding, and a vein was throbbing at the spot on her temple where her hair started to grow, before tumbling to her shoulders in a soft and heavy mass. He was suddenly discovering that above her dead legs her body was alive and warm, made extra shapely by the constant exercise of propelling the wheelchair. She looked so different that he felt deeply disturbed.

'Money, that's right, money . . .' she went on, as if she was pursuing some obsessive line of thought that she wanted to shake off but couldn't. 'I don't know if I really love money, but that's not the point. Since the accident I've found out that I'm good at anything to do with administration – something I never even suspected before. People often build their lives round a single talent, failing to appreciate all the other things they're good at. If I hadn't lost the use of my legs I'd have stayed on the stage, going on playing Phèdre or Hecuba until the last possible minute. But now here I am in the fortress like someone playing Monopoly, moving pieces about, buying a house here, selling a square there, swapping an avenue for a boulevard. I've got plenty of people to help me, of course, but they're miles away, in America, in Japan, heaven knows where in the world below. But I'm up here, all alone.'

She steered the wheelchair to the edge of the table and

thrust her face forwards into the candlelight – an anxious face, only very lightly made up, still beautiful. But the beauty was on the surface, like a transparent layer of anxiety. She lit a cigarette and he felt as if he was watching her from a distance, acting out a part he couldn't fully understand. Her hands were trembling, her lips were trembling, the cut-glass drops on the chandelier above their heads were vibrating as they set up a tinkling echo beneath the vaulted ceiling.

'I run Samuel's affairs now, as I promised him I would, trying to control this vast machine that went onstream virtually without his knowing about it. Throughout the last three years before he died he'd say over and over again: "Without meaning to, I've given birth to an aberrant system. We simply must make sure we've got it under control. If anything happened to me, you'd have to take over." I've respected his wishes. When he'd put the finishing touches to the first of his planned fallout shelters that actually got built, the last thing he wanted was to make money from the patents. He'd done it to save a tiny proportion of the human race, not to swell his own coffers. But when he realized that the nations he was dealing with directly were subcontracting the work, bringing in businessmen, he had to change his attitude. Yet there was worse to come, much worse . . .'

She closed her eyes. She stayed sitting there for a long time, not saying anything. Thinking she'd dropped off to sleep, he moved the candlestick, which was partly blocking his view of her. She kept her eyes shut, but smiled and said half under her breath: 'Do you realize that if a twenty-megaton bomb were to fall a hundred yards from where we're sitting the wine on the surface of these glasses wouldn't so much as quiver? A quick press of that switch to the right of the door and lead curtains set in reinforced concrete surrounds would be lowered in front of all doors and windows. And have you thought that by coming here, you stand a good chance of sharing that extraordinary moment with me?'

He drained his glass, considered briefly before making up his mind, then eventually plumped for being frank.

'It's certainly pretty amazing. But I don't really believe in that type of scenario.'

This time she did open her eyes and darted a bewildered glance at him. Her whole body grew taut in her wheelchair. Her nostrils seemed pinched and she grew so pale he thought at first she was going to faint. He started regretting that he'd gone further than his position entitled him to by flaunting his scepticism, since it cast doubt on so many things that affected her.

'I see,' she said faintly. And the way she said those two words made him think she might just as easily have fired him on the spot. 'We've had too much to drink and I'm tired. Will you please push me as far as my room, then go and tell Félicité she can come and attend to me.'

Her rooms were on a level with the large corner tower and the parapet walk. They formed a balcony from which she could look down into the ravine, without needing any help to get there. He pushed her, stopping when he came to her door, but not at first letting go of the handles. He was re-experiencing an old sensation and his hands itched to go on pushing her for hours, right through the night, all over the fortress, anywhere, if only it meant he could go on gazing at her thick and fragrant mane of hair and feeling in his hands the weight of her whole body abandoned to his care. Then he opened the door and left her in the doorway. She moved forward a little way into the outer room, then stopped the wheelchair and, without turning round, said in a voice that seemed to come from a long way away, but was clearly directed at her secretary:

'There comes a time when money just goes on making more money, a time when nothing else is being produced except money. Money buying and selling money, money suddenly unable to produce any more money – that's the end of the world too, you know.'

5

At La Verna, Fra Cosimo was always telling him: 'You're already in hell. It's terribly unfair, you don't deserve that any more than anything else.' The old monk believed in earthly damnation but not in heavenly redemption, and when he conjured up the idea of hell, he was referring to the oblate's insomnia – for the last seven years he'd scarcely slept at all. Again and again during the first year he'd summoned death to come to his aid. But death is always more inclined to take you by surprise than take you off, and it was kept at bay by his state of wakefulness, offering him nothing more than the taste of its earthy kiss on his lips and, in his limbs, the torpor of a never-ending embrace. Then, gradually, insomnia had become second nature to him, with a blurring of the line between sleep and wakefulness. Sometimes he would lie flat out in perpetual sleep, busy dreaming he was awake. At others he would be prostrated by boundless exhaustion, yet couldn't bring himself to fall asleep. He didn't want to sleep, he wanted to keep watch, and think, as though he didn't trust the world an inch, and refused to let it out of his sight for a single instant. Night after night he'd lie thinking, and not thinking. We're constantly achieving something, and not achieving anything, he'd tell himself. Reality is a complex web of those vast urges to act that endlessly fade away in their own vastness. Many a time we're happy to come across a tiny desolate island on which our desires can run aground, and that's how we build up the history of mankind. That's the one thing that matters, there isn't anything else. We have to make do with this little island, this desolation, this exile. I'm aware of this, and I too am sometimes happy at the thought of it, he'd think, still up like a horse asleep on its feet in the half-light of dawn – run, run on the burning sands of your little island! And he'd fling himself into the nobility of his daily round as though it had no limits.

One October morning he was dragged out of his insomnia shortly after sunrise by an appalling din. Way beyond the mist-filled ravine the mountain tops were ablaze in the icy sky. The din was getting closer. The mountain with its covering of scree seemed to have started moving. A shadow raced over the sunny side of the ravine. He opened the window and leaned

33

out, just in time to see the helicopter disappearing behind the fortress. Then the noise subsided and he realized it was going to land somewhere near by.

He went out of the room and reached the courtyard when the helicopter was hovering a few feet above the ground. Tanguy was sitting on the steps up to the main entrance, watching it land. Three of the Tamils had shrunk back against the building, screwing up their faces as the rush of air hit them. In the cockpit, its curving windscreen reflecting a view of the whole courtyard, he could make out the blurred white outline of the pilot. The wheels touched down, the noise reached a crescendo, then, in a supple folding movement, the blades came to a standstill and silence spread out round the courtyard, as thick and heavy as a mighty body of water held back by a dam.

The dazed Tamils slowly roused themselves and moved towards the helicopter. The door slid open and the pilot appeared, throwing them a cheerful greeting. He pulled three large butcher's overalls out of the cockpit and flung them in the direction of the Tamils. They pulled them on, laughing. They were too big for them and flapped round their skinny bodies. When they pulled the hoods up, their heads completely disappeared and their laughter was momentarily muffled. Wearing this outlandish gear they hauled themselves on board, with the pilot poking fun at them. The secretary watched the whole scene from the top of the steps, mystified. When the pilot spotted him he jumped down and walked over to him. He was a blond giant with long hair tied back with a ribbon and the face of an archangel. His breezy and good-natured manner suggested he was barely out of his teens, but his expression made him seem older. He was called Varlaam.

'You're the new secretary, aren't you? I've heard all about you. It's good to meet you.'

It was more than just a polite remark – he seemed genuinely pleased, and the secretary took an immediate liking to him. He could see that he was one of those people who have their feet firmly on the ground, who see life as a spontaneous business –

34

the world belongs to them, without their ever needing to stake a claim to it. Olga Grekova-Leber had talked with unaffected enthusiasm about 'her' pilot and 'her' helicopter, saying she'd decided to buy it after Ramanuja had very nearly died of acute peritonitis. It was used for all sorts of things, including ferrying food and post up to the fortress.

'I've heard about you, too. I hear you're the best pilot in the area for mountain flying.'

Varlaam's boyishly smooth face turned pink and he shook his head, dismissing the compliment.

'Have you ever been up in a helicopter? I'll take you on a spin if you like.'

One of the Tamils clambered out of the helicopter and dragged something towards him. It seemed to be extremely heavy. He heaved it on to his shoulders. It was part of a side of beef, with the spine and ribcage standing out.

Walking cautiously, with tiny steps, he lugged it across the courtyard towards the kitchen windows, which were below the level of the courtyard. He was halfway there when the sun suddenly appeared between a pair of chimneys, casting a garish light on the wobbling mass of meat. Virtually nothing of him was visible, except for the occasional glimpse of brown face beneath the hood, as the skirts of the overalls flapped round him and the skinned tail of the carcass whipped against his calves. The stale smell of the meat gradually seeped into every corner of the sunny courtyard. The other Tamils dragged another two sides of meat, even vaster than the first, as far as the door of the helicopter, and with a series of precise movements, as languid as a caress, loaded them on to their backs. In the shadowy recesses of the cockpit other hunks of meat stood waiting. The pilot drew the secretary towards the machine. They both climbed on board. Pools of blood were congealing on the metal floor, giving off a nauseating stench.

'Doesn't the smell put you off when you're flying?'

The young man laughed, thrusting his hands into the pockets of his flying suit.

'My father's a butcher. I worked with him before I sat my pilot's exams, so I'm used to meat.'

His voice was surprisingly supple and high-pitched for someone of his athletic build, and he tilted his head towards his left shoulder as he spoke. He took the secretary over to the cockpit. The morning light was seeping beneath the plexiglass dome as if into the heart of a crystal, its slanting rays lighting up the complex altar of a control panel. The three Tamils were walking back in silence, their progress impeded by their bloodstained overalls. Once they were on board each of them started chattering away nineteen to the dozen in their own language, without stopping to listen to the others, the words rolling out of their mouths like wooden marbles. While they were bearing away the rest of the meat, Varlaam explained what each of the dials was for, then sat down at the controls. After a couple of hiccoughs the helicopter was rocked by a series of convulsive trembling movements that gradually subsided. The engine emitted a muffled humming sound, nothing like the appalling racket it had made before. But then Varlaam pulled on a lever, the blades whirred into action and the noise became ten times louder. The secretary looked up. All he could see was the sky and the sun, both of them seeming darker through the smoked glass of the cockpit. In the courtyard the Tamils, now on their second journey, stopped dead. One of them, dragged along by the weight of the huge piece of beef, toppled over sideways and the other two let go of their own loads. The pilot roared with laughter, waved reassuringly at them and switched off the engine. The three men took a moment to pull themselves together. Then they gave up the idea of carrying the heavy carcasses, dragged them as best they could as far as the kitchen window and tipped them down the chute. Once they'd finished, the coating of brilliant varnish the sun had plastered on the flagstones was stained with three long trails of blood. Varlaam got to his feet and they went to the back of the helicopter.

'It was Samuel Leber who gave me the chance to qualify as a pilot,' he explained. 'If he hadn't paid for my instruction and my hours of flying practice, I'd still be cutting up meat in my father's shop. I've always found it terribly easy. I feel as if I've always known how to fly. Flying's the only thing I know how to do, and it's all I've ever wanted to do.' He kept his eyes on the ground as he spoke and when he stopped, he was pink in the face again. He turned away, glancing in disgust at the floor of the hold and the pools of blood. 'I'm going to have to clean up this filth now,' he said grumpily. 'I loathe meat. Sometimes, when I'm out flying, my own body gives me the shivers. I'd like to be small and skinny like the guys from Sri Lanka . . .'

Heaped up at the far end of the hold were bundles of newspapers, soaked in blood and stained by the sides of beef. Varlaam leaned out of the machine, glanced quickly round the courtyard, then suddenly let out a strident and peremptory whistle. Tanguy, who'd been sitting on the steps all this time, leapt up and raced over to the helicopter. Varlaam grabbed two of the bundles and tossed them in front of the door as though they weighed no more than a couple of pillows.

'Take that and then come and get the other two. Come on, get a move on!' he ordered curtly. Tanguy muttered something and struggled to pick up the papers by the string. While he was tottering off towards the steps, Varlaam pointed to the rest of the bundles.

'Mrs Leber subscribes to an international press service. There's more than a month's worth of papers there,' he said.

'What does she do with them all?' The secretary sounded surprised.

'She reads the financial and political pages, cuts out the articles that interest her and then files them. She started doing it before Mr Leber died.'

They waited for Tanguy, who came back dripping with sweat, with gashes on his hands from the string.

'It's heavy and it cuts your fingers,' he said to Varlaam, smiling vacantly.

'Come on now! How on earth d'you manage when you're battling with the wild boars?'

He shook his head solemnly. His eyes clouded over and he grimaced with pain as he picked up the bundles of papers. But Varlaam had lost interest in him. He was looking at the secretary with respectful curiosity. Eventually he overcame his shyness and asked: 'Were you really a monk?'

Tanguy had stopped halfway to the steps to catch his breath. The jackdaws were fluttering round the chimneys, cawing. The secretary looked at the young man and once again took in the fact that it's virtually impossible to talk about the crucial features of your life – there's no language capable of recreating their enigmatic quality.

'I wasn't a monk. I was an oblate. I never took my vows. I never intended to – I haven't got the necessary faith. It was just that I wanted to withdraw from the world. I didn't know how to set about it by myself, and I wasn't strong enough to do it without submitting to the rule of a religious order. Not that I'm any stronger now, but along with a lot of other things, rules don't have any significance for me any more.'

The sun seemed to be anchored to the roof of the fortress. They were facing towards it, trying to soak up its mild warmth, and although the cold of the night was still lingering in the shadows, a mood of aimlessness was creeping gently over the courtyard. Varlaam nodded, but judging by the blissful expression on his face, his wordless approval was directed more at the sun than at what the secretary had said, and he couldn't think of a reply.

'I can understand that,' he said eventually in an undertone. 'I've felt like withdrawing from the world too. That's why I became a pilot. When I was working with my father I used to do the weekly slaughtering. We'd go to the slaughterhouse and my father would pick out the animals to be killed, then say: "Your turn now." He wasn't brave enough to do it himself.'

He vaulted out of the helicopter, then crouched down and straightened up again several times to stretch his legs and banish these memories. The flagstones with their coating of lacquered light looked like a sheet of ice. The secretary caught up with him.

38

'Would you like me to help you clean up the helicopter?' he offered. 'It'd make a change from the library.'

Varlaam's refusal was emphatic: the pilot must always see to the upkeep of his machine himself if there are no specialist staff around. The young man's face was extraordinarily mobile – you could see exactly what he was feeling. He was clearly one of those people quite incapable of telling a lie, who are aware of this and are naturally truthful.

Before they left the courtyard the Tamils had flung their overalls over the helicopter's tail. Varlaam swept them up all in one go, and although they were revoltingly dirty, folded them carefully before tossing them into the hold and climbing back on board.

'I really must go now,' he said. 'If you fancy a ride in the next day or so I'd be happy to take you. Only I must warn you about one thing – you can't just fly where and when it suits you, there are rules, you know!'

He burst out laughing – a loud, ringing laugh – then disappeared through the sliding door. The secretary could see his blurred outline moving slowly on the other side of the smoked plexiglass. He walked away and didn't turn round until he'd reached the front steps. Tanguy was back there now, sitting on the top step. 'Varlaam's a prince, your eminence!' he called out. His words had a prophetic ring to them.

Then the appalling din shook the air, shattering the stillness of the courtyard.

6

The parapet walk started at the flanking tower and ended at the keep, passing in front of the building where Olga Grekova-Leber's rooms were. It widened out at intervals to form a narrow grass-grown bastion that had once been a gun emplacement – the fortress had never been taken, for the simple reason that no army had ever thought it worth taking. Halfway round, on an overhanging rock suspended like a balcony above the ravine, it formed a formal garden, with little gravel paths and neatly clipped box hedges. This was where the cable car finished up, in a watchtower specially restored and redesigned by Samuel Leber to house it.

She liked taking the air on the parapet walk. Virtually every day, weather permitting, Tanguy would push her along the uneven paving stones, walking slowly so as not to jolt her too much. They would process from the keep to the flanking tower, then from the tower to the keep and so on, sometimes for hours on end. Today, for some unexplained reason, perhaps simply because she wanted to talk to him, she'd asked the secretary to join them there. He caught up with them near the watchtower. Tanguy was sitting on a stone bench, keeping a close eye on his mistress in case she needed anything. She was sitting in the wheelchair near the rampart, her legs decked out in rugs, staring down into the sheer drop between the crenellations in the battlements. He walked up to her and leant over to catch a glimpse of the torrent in the shadows on the shady side of the ravine, running between the brown walls of the gorge. He couldn't really see it, but the whole of the ravine was filled with an infinitely varied sound – thousands of different voices, each following a different babbling note. A gust of cold air raced down the col and whirled round the fortress.

'Mental suffering can tear you apart, but it quickly fades into insignificance compared to physical suffering,' came a voice from the wheelchair. 'My legs hurt. Every single day, every single night since the accident these useless legs cause me real pain, when they're supposed to be dead to all feeling. It feels a bit as if someone was pulling on them, trying to tear them away from my body. I sometimes get the feeling that a pair of instruments of torture have been hooked on to my pelvis, a pair of red-hot artificial limbs. What sin am I atoning for, I wonder? Isn't it punishment enough to be stuck in this wheelchair?'

She asked Tanguy to open the door to the watchtower and push her over to it. A knowing smile hovered on his lips. He did as she asked somewhat condescendingly, apparently failing to notice the secretary. The cable plunged down into the ravine like a ship's anchor chain and sank into the mist.

'This is the last of man's creations Samuel ever entered,' she said. She was speaking almost under her breath, with no trace of emotion or sadness in her voice. 'My husband believed in atonement. Not in the religious sense, but as an inescapable phenomenon that affected everyone, a historical necessity, as it were. In another five, ten, maybe fifteen years the human race will draw on all its learning and skills to wipe itself out completely. Nowadays the essential duty of each and every one of us is not, as it once was, to devote ourselves to furthering knowledge, but to make a humble attempt to save a few specimens of the human race from being wiped out. The age of mere living is over. The age of survival is just beginning.'

She asked the secretary to follow her into the watchtower and ordered Tanguy to wait for them on the bench. He got the impression that the tone she'd suddenly adopted towards the man was too serious, hinted at too many things between them. The grim outline of the nacelle was etched against the sky. He thought of Samuel Leber's tomb – he had a clear view from here of the church and its spire, so the tomb would be visible if you had a good strong telescope. Olga Grekova-Leber had survived that horrifying fall into the half-light of the ravine. And Samuel Leber had atoned. The wheelchair moved forward to the middle of the watchtower. The cold seemed keener in here, more piercing than outside. She draped one of the rugs round her shoulders and sat hunched in the chair, looking tiny, her eyes glittering feverishly.

'Walk forward as far as the bucket, unless you're feeling giddy. It's worth it for the view,' she said.

The concrete platform jutted out over the yawning chasm of the ravine. He walked forward, holding on to the iron nacelle until he came to the far end. He didn't feel in the least giddy. She propelled the wheelchair towards the bucket, struck the metal several times with her fist. It rang like a cracked bell, then a sudden gust of wind banged the door shut behind them. He was standing on the edge of the platform as if it were a diving board – he had no intention of flinging himself down into the sheer drop, but the idea of taking off exerted an irresistible attraction. Behind him, she started humming. Just at that moment he noticed that there was a bit of blue fabric clinging to the bucket, like a scrap of blue sky.

'Why on earth do you go on using this dangerous contraption?' he asked, turning to look at her. She raised her eyebrows, with a look of wide-eyed innocence.

'To bring up materials, of course!'

'You've got a helicopter to do that for you.'

She swung the chair round to face the other way and looked towards the closed door. A boisterous gust of wind suddenly swept into the watchtower, sending the bucket tossing and pitching. It brought in with it a flock of dead leaves, which whirled round on the platform for a moment or two and then were pinned to the floor by another gust. There was a smell of snow in the air.

'You're right, of course, I have got a helicopter,' she murmured. She'd just turned back towards him and seemed to be fascinated by the way the leaves had suddenly come to a standstill.

'Why do you come back here?' he couldn't stop himself asking.

She smiled derisively, taking her time before replying, lighting a cigarette. He noticed for the first time how long and slender her neck was.

'I come back to torture myself, as I'm sure you suspected. But if I didn't come, it would be even worse torture. As you go out of here you'll see that all my windows face the ravine, and I can see the watchtower from my bed. I dithered for ages about whether or not to change my rooms. But it was no good. I just have to see *it*. If you only knew how much I loathe these mountains, this cold, damp ravine, how much I loathe the trees, the forest, the torrent – I go on hearing it in my dreams – the light illuminating it all. I even hate my eyes for seeing them! Every morning, all year round,

I come out on to the bastion, push my chair as far as the parapet walk and try to hate that sheer drop. Don't laugh – I try with everything I've got, I stare and stare into the ravine, for ages at a time, I keep on staring for longer and longer stretches of time . . .'

She pushed the chair back so that she could look her secretary up and down without having to raise her head. 'Will you please pick up one of those leaves?' Her voice sounded almost pleading. They were birch leaves, as delicate as flakes of gold leaf. She held one up to look through it, tracing the veins with a sort of incredulity. Then, pulling a face, she scrunched it up and tossed it away.

'This contraption caused your husband's death and left you disabled,' he said, slapping his hand against the side of the bucket.

Her face darkened. 'Do you really think it's that simple?'

'Why did you decide to go down in the cable car the day the accident happened?'

She stared at him with a defiant expression, as if she was thinking: You've overstepped the mark, we agreed not to ask any questions, but merely left his question unanswered.

The door opened. Tanguy appeared in the doorway, then stopped dead. She turned the chair towards him, made as if to say something, but in the end remained silent. His silent presence in the half-darkness brooded over the watchtower, seeming much more menacing than the alarming closeness of that sheer drop. The secretary caught an expression on her face that betrayed a mixture of anger and fear. She suddenly banged her fist on the arm of the wheelchair.

'Get out, Tanguy! Leave us alone,' she ordered. Her tone was more resigned than commanding and he didn't move.

'Do you know what caused the accident?' the secretary asked, to break a silence that was becoming unbearably oppressive.

She spun the chair sharply round and propelled it towards the far end of the platform with such energy that he rushed after her, thinking she couldn't possibly brake in time. When he caught up with her she burst out laughing, seized both of his hands in hers and squeezed them.

'Goodness me, you *are* attentive!' she said mockingly. 'You wanted to know why the accident happened, didn't you? It was just a technical failure, that's all.'

On the north side of the ravine the blue smoke from a woodcutter's fire rose up through the air, which had grown suddenly still. The delicate ribbon shot straight up like an oracle towards the gods, towards all the gods that nothing had ever managed to banish.

When they were outside again she asked him: 'Do you think a man can go on living in his work?' Then she carried straight on before he'd had a chance to reply. 'Do you remember when Bergotte dies in Proust's *La Prisonnière* and how all through the night, in the brightly lit bookshop windows, his books watch over him, arranged in groups of three like angels with outspread wings, symbolizing his resurrection? Well, I don't believe in that type of resurrection – books swallow up their author until there's nothing left of him, not even a corpse, and they can at last reign supreme, with no one to claim them as his brainchildren. Every day you spend putting together Samuel's unpublished work, you're helping to make sure he'll eventually disappear for good. It's as if you were getting rid of a rival inch by inch – by feeding the jackals who'll share out his carcass and finish off the job. It won't be long now before, thanks to your efforts, we'll be publishing his complete works, and there'll be nothing left of him except paper with sentences on it. Even his name will be just a few typographic signs. That's exactly how you'd set about it if you wanted to cut him out altogether, and make me forget all about him.'

It was his turn to laugh. She drew her travelling rug tightly round her shoulders. Tanguy was sitting with his back to them, perched between two of the crenellations with his legs dangling over the ravine, smoking a cigar. Its acrid smell wafted over to them.

'You're the one who's paying me to finish off the job,' he said.

Her gaze wavered indecisively over Tanguy's back and he thought he knew what she was thinking.

'"Finish off" being the operative words.'

Then, still with one eye on the figure sitting on the ramparts, his head in a cloud of smoke, she propelled the wheelchair a bit further away, until she was sure he couldn't hear what she said, and asked quietly: 'How does Tanguy strike you?'

He had a feeling that she was discreetly pointing out a passageway, a narrow fault she wanted him to squeeze through, to reach the deposit where her secrets lay hidden. But he wasn't at all sure it wouldn't cave in on him once he stepped into it.

'I don't think he cares for me much,' he said carefully. 'Perhaps his hostile attitude will change once he realizes I'm not doing him any harm.'

In some ways Tanguy reminded him of Fra Cosimo. Both of them seemed to embody a flaw that each of us may find in ourselves, in a less obvious form.

'Are you really so sure you won't ever do him any harm?' came the ironic question from the wheelchair. 'Let me tell you a story about him. Ten years or so ago he used to spend a lot of time training a German Shepherd. The dog would follow him everywhere – they were inseparable, and he was the only person who could feed it. For a couple of years he tended it with the sort of loving devotion he'd never have lavished on one of his fellow-men. Then one day Samuel found the dog lying in the grass with its head in a huge pool of blood. Its throat had been cut. Tanguy was there beside it, with the knife in his hand. When Samuel asked him why he'd done it, all he said was: "It was time." After that incident I asked Samuel to get rid of him. But he wouldn't listen because, or so he said – I shall always remember how he put

45

it – the fortress couldn't do without him and he "gave good measure". I'm still wondering what he gave good measure of . . .'

A plump lizard slithered through the gravel between the wheels of her chair and she started. She cast an anxious glance at the ramparts, where Tanguy was still smoking away, taking no notice of them. Instead of reassuring her, his lack of interest seemed to distress her. She sighed, and started biting fiercely on her thumbnail. Noticing these absurd signs of anxiety – Tanguy couldn't hear what they were saying, and if he decided to walk over they'd hear his footsteps on the gravel – the secretary realized that the man crouched night and day in the burrow she'd prepared for him over the years deep inside her.

'Every time I give him an order I wonder if he's going to obey, and he always does,' she went on. 'I'm worn out with struggling against him. Samuel built this fortress so that he could wait for war to break out, but Tanguy and I have always been at war. We wage a cold war, a war that makes no sound, an organic war. We're tearing ourselves apart, without bloodshed. The battlefield is in the darkest recesses of our bodies, as though our entrails were equipped with consciences that have declared war on one another, after silencing our true conscience. It sometimes feels as if several generations of Tanguys and Grekovas are slaughtering one another inside us, feeding on our flesh and drinking our blood, so that they can keep the carnage going.

'When I got back to the fortress after months in hospital and then a long period of convalescence, Tanguy was waiting for me. While I was away he'd acted as estate manager, seeing to everything with staggering efficiency and shrewdness. It was he who took me to Samuel's grave for the first time. In the graveyard he admitted that years before my husband had made him swear to look after me if anything happened to him. Goodness know why! In those days I was in perfect health, going off on tour, acting on stages in London, Berlin and Rome. Why on earth would I have needed someone like

46

Tanguy? One day, without my saying anything, he leaned over the wheelchair, lifted me out and clasped me to him. I smelled his foxy smell, a smell of dried blood and tree bark, and I suddenly realized – it was like a revelation – that if I didn't get rid of him there and then, I'd never ever get away from that smell.'

They heard Tanguy jump down on to the gravel and amble over to them. She held her breath, her jaw clenched. He was taking his time, dragging his feet in the gravel. As he drew closer the smell of his cigar pervaded the bastion. The secretary breathed in deeply, as though he was trying to pick out the smell she'd just mentioned in the foul stench of the dark tobacco.

'Push me, Tanguy, I've been out long enough for today, I want to go in now.' She issued the order in an irritable tone, without turning round. Then, speaking very fast, she said to the secretary: 'Can it really be a coincidence that you answered my advertisement and I took you on?' But Tanguy had already seized hold of the handles and as he walked off between the little box hedges, totally ignoring the secretary, she called out: 'Come and join me in the library this afternoon. I want to talk to you about the Leber Foundation.'

Tanguy crashed the footplate of the wheelchair into the double doors to force them open and they vanished into her rooms.

Aching with hunger, he went straight to the kitchen. There was hardly any warmth in the sun. Nature was growing torpid, like an animal preparing to hibernate. Winter wasn't far off now and was already sending its iron breath throbbing up from the depths of the coombs, pulsing between the rocky walls. The torrent, too, was emitting great breaths like a recently cooled forge, as though as soon as dawn broke the light had started dipping its blades into its seething, incandescent waters. As it wafted over the forests the air drove along with it a musty smell of leaf mould, wild creatures and sodden burrows.

The long kitchen with its vaulted ceiling had been converted from the old stables. Félicité was waiting there,
smoking her pipe. She got up when he came in. He sat
down facing the fireplace and she put a dish of hare pâté
in front of him, its reddish-brown jelly, tinged with gold,
gleaming as brightly as the brass on the kitchen range. The
atmosphere beneath the white ribbed vaulting, in that room
brimming over with earthly sustenance, was one of hushed
contemplation, making it feel like a sanctuary. When she'd
finished serving him, Félicité sat down at the table beside
him and watched him eating. She'd been born deaf and
dumb, but her face did her talking for her and he had a
feeling she could somehow hear with her whole body. She
never showed any sign of being sad, or indeed of feeling
inordinate joy. She seemed to live entirely – and peacefully
– in the present, to have come to terms with a tough past that
she kept well hidden behind an attitude of patience, though
her whole character made you sense how painful it had been.
Her only concern now was to provide lavish hospitality, for
her whole raison d'être was to make others happy. And so
the most frugal meal would take on much of the prodigality
and riches in the generous heart of its provider. She stayed
sitting beside him throughout the meal, filling up his glass
before it was empty, moving away only to stoke up the fire,
uttering guttural sounds forced up from the depths of her
larynx, conducting a dialogue with the flames that meant
nothing to the uninitiated.

When he'd finished his lunch, the secretary took a flat
splinter of rock out of his pocket and held it up to the
firelight. He spun it round a few times between finger and
thumb, then held it out to Félicité.

'I found it halfway up to the col, in a disused quarry.
I prised it out of a collapsed boulder. It's very old – it
goes back about four hundred million years, before these
mountains and valleys took on the shapes we see today.' He'd
slipped automatically into the habit of talking to Félicité as
if she could hear what he said. She probably could hear,

in her own way, because she showed clear signs of having understood. She looked at the piece of stone carefully, still sucking away at her pipe, which had gone out but was still making a bubbling sound. She dusted it on her apron and shook her head several times. Etched on the veined surface was a peculiar pattern that made you think of the skeleton of some sea creature, a cross between a crustacean and a fish. He took it from her and held it up between finger and thumb, well away from her screwed-up eyes.

'This fossil was formed between two ice ages, in marine deposits,' he told her. 'But the sea's over three hundred miles away now. Here, it's a present for you, Félicité. Don't forget now – four hundred million years.'

7

As the weeks went by the world below grew fainter – the world on which, once again, he had turned his back, though with no feeling of hatred. His own memories, even the ones that mattered to him most, seemed like an ice floe vaguely glimpsed through the fog, and if he tried to focus on a specific incident in his youth, or even only a decade ago, he would finish up like a marksman who's staring so hard at his sighting notch that his vision is clouded by tears. And yet behind the fog, behind the cold tears, a figure wrought in bronze stood at the very heart of his being, reminding him that his particular solitude was never being alone. He didn't reject this manifest truth. He accepted that the presence of death constantly tossed him back among the masses he was trying to escape – condemning him to be alive amid the serried ranks of the dead, to be dead amid the serried ranks of the living. Whatever he tried to do, whatever he thought, he was still a representative of the human race as a whole and of its essential transience, just as the lytoceras fossilized during the Lower Jurassic was a petrified bearer of tidings from a species that had become extinct a hundred million years ago.

This gift to Félicité was just the first of a whole collection of fossils, plus a few minerals, none of them particularly rare, and – a more valuable find this time – a flake of biotite he'd come across many miles from the fortress, in a seam of granite. It was brownish-red, with a vitreous lustre, creating an effect of cloudy translucency, It took on a greenish, coppery tinge in the light of the lamp. Despite its sober beauty, it seemed to contain some abstract warning. As soon as he'd prised it out of its granite gangue, he felt somehow that he'd committed an act of sacrilege against the mountain. He didn't give it to Félicité or even show it to her, but put it on his desk in the library, so that the dust of daily life would cover it over again and exorcise this little piece of time preserved in the rock.

Olga Grekova-Leber would sometimes, for no apparent reason, make several visits to the library on the same day. She would race feverishly along the bookshelves, no doubt hunting for something that had nothing to do with the sort of truth enshrined in books, some revelation about her fate that all these hundreds of inmates of the library, standing stiffly to attention, might just possibly have tucked away behind their spines. After one of these fruitless searches she spotted the biotite and pretended to take an interest in it.

'Where did you find it?'

He told her. He realized that she wasn't so much interested in the stone itself as in the fact that he'd shown an interest in it, and had been prepared to walk miles to find it.

'I imagine the places where you do your prospecting are pretty difficult to get to, aren't they?'

'Not necessarily. But you do need some experience of how geological strata are made up. You can find minerals in fractures in sedimentary rocks, on terrain that has experienced recent volcanic activity, in the area surrounding hot springs, or simply in the embankment beside a road.'

'I don't want a lecture. Will you make me a present of this?' Without bothering to wait for his reply, and no doubt wanting to needle him, she crammed the biotite into her bag and said with a smile: 'Everything on this estate is my property.'

She couldn't get at him that way. During his years at the

monastery, Fra Cosimo had taught him how to become as unyielding as the stones he collected.

'It's a present for you,' he said. 'Winter isn't the best time of year to be roaming all over the mountains.' She burst out laughing, burying her face in her hands.

'Oh, I *am* pleased you're here!'

She manoeuvred the wheelchair back slightly. Her disability certainly restricted her movements, but she was adept at loading each gesture with all the significance needed to express her mood.

'Why don't you come with me on my next expedition?' he said suddenly. 'I'll push you. I've had plenty of practice. When I was at La Verna I spent ten years pushing Fra Cosimo over very rough and uneven ground.'

'You must be mad! Listen, it'll soon be three months since you came to live at the fortress. You probably need to get out a bit. Isn't there anyone you could go and see down below? Haven't you got any other interests, apart from collecting stones?'

He stood up and went to stand behind her, placing his hands on the handles of the wheelchair, which moved just a fraction. She was gripping the wheels tightly.

'I did build up a collection once. But I stopped collecting in a methodical fashion a long time ago. I give away anything I find and don't keep anything for myself.'

She suddenly pulled on the wheels, using the full force of her wrists. The wheelchair shot out of his grasp and ran over to the desk. There was a squeal of tyres and, with precision timing, the chair span round on itself through 180 degrees, reared up, then came to a complete standstill facing him. As he was admiring this stylish manoeuvre, clearly the result of hours of practice and demonstrating great virtuosity on her part, she looked him up and down, shrugged her shoulders, gesticulated with her arm in a way that could have meant anything, then crossed her hands on her thighs. Her expression became very serious.

'You walk round the estate a lot, don't you?' She was

51

speaking barely above a whisper, her voice sounding hoarse. 'Do you carry a weapon?'

'A weapon? Why on earth should I?'

'It would be wiser . . .'

At that point something happened that was over so quickly, and was so unexpected, that he failed to react in any way. She let out a shriek and flung herself back against the wheelchair, clutching her left thigh in both hands, just below the groin. Her mouth fell open as though she was gasping for air and she bent double, shaking her head when he started walking over to her, to stop him intervening. This refusal to accept any assistance was so vehement that he stopped dead. By now she was hunched over, her forehead almost touching her knees. For a split second as she doubled up he caught a glimpse of her face through her hair, looking suddenly, terrifyingly, older. Then she straightened up slowly, her hands groping for the wheels. Her lips moved but no sound came. She seemed to be talking to someone hidden inside herself, tormenting her. She looked round, her expression haggard. Her glance went right through him and stopped when it reached the door. As though everything about her had somehow got out of sync, she crossed the library in a series of jerks, then went out without uttering a word. The whole episode had taken no more than a minute.

After this scene he couldn't bring himself to stay in the library a second longer. He collected his prospecting tools and walked away from the fortress.

The sky was clearing over the first of the mountains, but the wind was driving gusts of icy rain from the horizon, sweeping down relentlessly in the murky light. In the far distance the sun was emerging from behind the storm clouds, bringing no warmth. The rain turned into driving sleet, forcing him to seek shelter beneath the fir trees. Thousands of tiny white spheres were bowling along the muddy path and on the grassy embankment, then melting in a flash. The rain stopped abruptly, obeying some peremptory command. He left the path and walked across a meadow strewn with small siliceous erratic

52

boulders overlaid with white limestone. Their porous surface made him think of the scattered remains of some unspecified creatures. He strode quickly down the meadow, then took a shortcut that saved him several zigzags on the path. The ravine suddenly yawned ahead of him, dark and filled with misty cloud.

'Your interest in geology and mineralogy expresses your distaste for history,' Fra Cosimo had said one day. 'But it isn't a healthy interest. It isn't rooted in that positive form of curiosity that leads to an understanding of the origins of all things. It's an escape, a form of regression. I can see you cowering down there in the depths of the millennia, between two ice ages, as if you were in the bosom of a parent mineral. You're afraid, aren't you, *piccolo*?' The old monk was virtually uneducated but possessed the heartless clear-sightedness of the visionary. Yet fossils stood for a world that no human eye had ever gazed on, and the secretary was trying to use them to think himself back into a state totally free from outside influence, where the victory of man's creativeness over time no longer had any meaning, and where it would be possible to exist in a state of maximum humility and clarity.

He found his way back to the path, stood still for a moment and concentrated. Beneath his feet, in a sheet of underground water fed by the melting ice of the glaciers, the torrent already existed, way below its source, in the form of liquid darkness, inseparable from all its constituent parts. He could hear the mocking voice of Fra Cosimo: 'You're going backwards, *piccolo*, you're climbing back down the evolutionary ladder. What are you going to to do when you've got right down to the bottom rung? You'll stay in your cave, surrounded by mosses and bats, totally cut off from any sounds, while up here on the surface of this poor planet of ours, the total destruction of nature and man will take place without you!'

The old monk was an incomparable actor. Olga Grekova-Leber had been a great tragic actress. And both of them had lost the use of their legs, yet continued without flagging on their inner odyssey, along the flimsy footbridges slung across

53

their lives. There is no such thing as true coincidence. We go where a secret will guides us, not knowing our destination. The adventure continues beyond the most dogged schemes, like navigating without instruments, and when we reach harbour it turns out to be nothing more than a mirage – the only true reality is the darkness behind it, casting its unending shroud over all our hopes of achieving something.

Every day he'd spent at the fortress he'd heard a voice asking: 'What were you hoping to find here?' And then once again he'd catch a hint of a reply, in Fra Cosimo's voice: 'You aren't aware of it, *piccolo*, but you love me. If you carry on pushing me, you may end up hating me, but it'll still be a form of love.'

The sky had a stormy look about it as he set off again. Through the gap of the col, looming up out of limbo, he could see the odd mountain top still partly wreathed in mist, seeming very close in the crystal-clear air. It didn't take him long to reach the spot he'd been aiming for. He shrugged off his rucksack, took out his tools, laid his hammer and chisel and specimen boxes on a flat rock. He had his own ritual here.

The quarry faced north, so never saw the sun. While the age of soils is calculated in millions of years and the cooling of the sun – which will bring all life on earth to an end – in billions of years, man's life is so short it doesn't count at all. People dealing with geological numbers and working out the age of the various stratifications of a mountain witness their own physical decay as the days go by, and may sometimes resent it as totally unfair. Since everything to do with man ages rapidly, the quarry – a sandstone quarry worked long before the fortress was restored – seemed much older than the landscape round about. It had the smell of death about it. The death of some human creature had contaminated these rocks, these old wounds that had never healed, where the damp, the lichens, the mosses and all sorts of moulds and mildews had allowed gangrene to set in, spreading the infection. When Samuel Leber had issued that peculiar instruction about breaking up the tarred surface of the road, he'd managed, after a fashion, to make it look much as it had before. No amount of hard labour could ever make this sore look as it once had. The whole place seemed to have been ostracized by its surroundings. It was a stagnant pocket of shame where man's moral baseness was revealed and nature humiliated, in this rejection of a place that had once been exploited. The edges of the upper part of the quarry had caved in. A handful of mangy fir trees, their roots exposed, clung to a crumbling patch of ground miraculously rescued by the laws of gravity. But the impression they conveyed, right down to their lowest branches, was one of utter wretchedness.

The quarry probably dated back to the nineteenth century, to the period when new churches were built in pink sandstone. But much larger deposits of sandstone can be quarried quite close to built-up areas, and he couldn't understand why anyone would want to climb up so high to quarry building materials in this remote spot, when they had to be transported on carts drawn by horses or oxen. The first time he'd come here he'd felt uneasy and hadn't stayed long. But he'd somehow felt drawn to the place and had come a second time, then a third, and then his negative impressions were dispelled, superseded by feverish curiosity.

The quarrying had been done any old how, with no attempt to extract the stone economically, and little skill evident in the way it was cut out. In the middle of the quarry a tall deep fault was honeycombed with geometric drawers. The quarriers seemed to have handled their saws with greater precision here. He came across several dates carved in the stone, covering the period 1862 to 1875 – thirteen years of mysterious quarrying on a small scale. At the far end of the fault, where the quarrying was very uneven, he spotted virtually straight away the first of the many deposits he was later to discover. As the saw of one of the quarriers working here 125 years earlier tore away at the sharp edge of the working face, it had brought to light, inside a flake of quartz, the striated round of a lytoceras fossilized in the sedimentary rock 150 million years earlier. He loosened the whorl of the umbilicus very slightly, then carefully examined the rock across its width for quite a distance. He now felt quite certain that an ocean had once lapped here, bringing with it its own deposits before being engulfed by the land. And now a whole extinct marine bestiary was embedded in the walls of remote country churches.

He was about to go through to the far end of the fault, to the deposit he'd been excavating over the last couple of weeks. His visits to the quarry had been very irregular and he'd only abandoned his work in the library on this occasion because he felt he had to shake off the haunting image of the figure in the wheelchair, writhing with pain. But just then he heard voices. It was a beautiful day now, with the rain-soaked trees and meadows sparkling in the sunlight. But here in the quarry the dominant impression was one of darkness and damp. He walked past the fault and skirted a rock. A little way away, on the edge of the quarry, he discovered two men sitting on a boulder, munching away. One of them was Tanguy. He didn't recognize the other man, but he looked like a woodcutter. His face was alarmingly lopsided, as if it had been slashed in half down the middle, then hastily stitched together again. He clearly didn't feel the cold, as his jacket was hanging up on a miner's bar stuck into the ground beside him. They didn't seem at all surprised to see him and went on eating as if nothing had happened. Feeling vaguely worried, he retraced his steps. As he squeezed into the fault, he remembered Olga Grekova-Leber asking him: 'Do you carry a weapon?' Then he became engrossed in his work, trying to forget that the two men were there.

Wearing goggles to protect his eyes, he worked down at ground level, half lying in the damp on the even, crunchy surface of the quarry. He used virtually nothing but a hammer and chisel set – although the ferruginous sandstone was hard, it surrendered willingly when he tried to burrow into its thousands of years of history. A fair amount of time went by as he hammered away at the rock face with a series of short, sharp yet cautious blows. At regular intervals a lone crow let out an utterly desolate cawing sound. He heard footsteps behind him, at the entrance to the fault, and went on hitting away, his mind totally focused on the fossil, which was starting to look like a living creature fast asleep beneath a curtain of stone. When Tanguy's voice rang out he again didn't move, but his muscles grew taut.

'Just a little game, your eminence. We wanted to ask you to join in a little game of ours. Will you play it with me?'

He didn't answer at once. He was struggling to get a grip on the anger surging through him, and wondering whether Tanguy had his rifle over his shoulder, as he usually did. Eventually he turned slowly round. At first he couldn't make out anything apart from the silhouette of the other man leaning on his miner's bar, his back to the light. He started straightening up, ready to pounce, then saw that Tanguy was standing a few feet away, his rifle over his shoulder and looking at him without a trace of hostility. Before he'd had time to straighten up fully, Tanguy strode rapidly over to his equipment, picked up several of the specimen boxes he'd laid out on a boulder, then retreated a few yards.

'Put those boxes back, Tanguy!' he ordered, walking over towards him.

But he took no notice and went back over to the other man. The two of them pored over the specimens, opening the boxes one after the other and carefully shutting them again. Oddly enough, their attitude didn't seem remotely threatening or challenging. The crow, perched like a weathercock on a scraggy fir tree, let out a caw. The quarry sank into a kind of stupor. The secretary again ordered Tanguy to put the boxes back. Despite the miner's bar and the rifle, he didn't feel a bit afraid. But he did feel as if his will had somehow grown sluggish.

'Your wish is my command, your eminence!' said Tanguy suddenly, putting the rest of the specimens back in the boxes. But instead of handing them back, he lined them up in a row on the ground at his feet. 'They belong to you, of course, but' – he paused – 'why don't we say that if I win this little game I'm going to put to you, they belong to me . . .'

Once again, the way the secretary reacted was a mistake.

Instead of refusing, he let his curiosity get the better of him.

'What's this game you're talking about?'

A long silence followed. The two men gave him a very solemn look, but their faces remained impassive, betraying nothing of what they were thinking. The woodcutter was holding his miner's bar as if it were a shepherd's crook, while Tanguy just stood there, his arms dangling by his sides.

'It's called Looking at the Fire,' he said eventually, with considerable solemnity. 'What happens is this: you and I are going to sit down side by side and we're going to look at the sun. We mustn't look away for a second, or shut our eyes. Mathieu will be watching. The winner will be whichever of us holds out longest.'

The secretary looked up at the sky, way up above the fault. The clouds had drawn back to form a semicircle on the mountainside, leaving a huge blue amphitheatre where the sun waited, a wild beast ready to strike. He looked firmly into Tanguy's eyes: 'All right. Let's give it a go.'

They left the boxes on the ground and walked out of the quarry to find a patch of ground in full sunlight. Tanguy was concentrating hard, looking solemn. They climbed up a few hundred feet and the ravine appeared ahead of them. It had that steely-blue, insubstantial quality of a landscape in the background of a Flemish painting. Beams of light glanced slantingly off the jagged edge of the gorges, leaving the torrent and its wooded banks hidden from view beneath several layers of shadow, except for the odd tangle of bare branches poking up. The secretary bathed his eyes for a moment in these misty depths and when he looked back up at the sky, he knew he was going to lose.

'Let's be having your jacket for his eminence!' Tanguy called out grandly.

Mathieu took his jacket off the mining bar and spread it out on the ground. With much bowing and scraping Tanguy begged him to be seated, then sat down on the grass beside

58

him, legs crossed, very calm and collected. Sitting there, his back straight as a ramrod, his chin jutting forward, his brow furrowed, looking even lower than usual as he frowned in concentration, he resembled a shaman already possessed by the spirits he's been conjuring up. He closed his eyes, asked the secretary if he was ready and told Mathieu to give the starting signal.

The sun had been shining in the distance for four billion autumns. It had given life to the whole planet and would continue to do so for many more billion years. Once man had become extinct, a new race might emerge, in a slow, patient mutation, a race of intelligent beings endowed with different skills and attributes, impossible to imagine, who would themselves one day sink back into the dustbin of time, into molten chaos.

The November sun didn't seem to be a particularly fearsome enemy, but as the minutes went by it weighed the secretary's eyelids down with a heavy mass of thick, black blood that he could hold up only by puckering his whole forehead. The heavenly body above him grew heavier and heavier. Somewhere beyond the earth an abstract glance registered its reflection – a nugget of pure gold – on his contracted pupil, and soon, as though his sight were being granted a special favour by pain, he saw his own eye, and the sun inside his eye. He could sense Tanguy sitting quite still beside him – and he guessed that his eyes were twin steel spheres nestling in the hollow of his sockets, as invulnerable as the fortress would prove in the final conflagration. Black flashes appeared in the sky, minute meteorites proceeding along their trajectory in a dancing movement. At that point he was tempted to cheat, then simply to stand up and climb back down to the quarry. But the sun was in sole command now. He went on sitting there, his eyes wide open, still protected from its fire by a few tears. Every now and then a shadow stirred somewhere below them. It was probably Mathieu crouching down in front of them, but he couldn't be sure because though his field of vision had been quite wide a moment or two ago, it was now hemmed in by a parallax of fire and was completely filled by the sun. He felt as though he could stay like that for hours, until nightfall. But he also sensed that until he turned his eyes away from it, the sun would stay stamped on the same patch of sky.

All of a sudden a burst of laughter crackled on the air and Mathieu's voice rang out somewhere very near him: 'You've had your eyes shut for quite a few minutes! Have you fallen asleep or what?'

He turned towards Tanguy and was surprised to find him gone. Then he spotted him a few yards away, peeing against a tree trunk.

'Aha! He's woken up!' shouted Mathieu. Tanguy turned right round to face them and went on peeing, looking at the secretary, his face expressionless. The secretary got unsteadily to his feet, a black veil obscuring his vision. He rubbed his eyelids, the veil tore slightly, and in his mind's eye he saw that painting by Zurbarán of St Lucy draped in crimson and holding out her eyes on a pewter platter.

'You won, Tanguy, the fossils are yours now.'

Tanguy shook his penis slowly and carefully, spat in his hands, then, without saying a word, without even looking at him, walked past him and set off for the quarry, with Mathieu close behind him. When they'd gone the secretary leaned back against a tree trunk, beneath the canopy formed by its branches, greedily breathing in its resinous scent as he watched them walk away. He didn't feel the least bit humiliated. In fact he was delighted not to experience any sense of humiliation – he realized now why he'd agreed to the contest. There was no question of defeat being better than victory or vice versa. From now on the feeling that he was alive and still vibrantly indifferent to action, which he now saw as futile, would be enough for him. It gave each particle of air the savour of being totally inconsequential, as though all the threads had been cut and destiny had been fulfilled down to the last syllable.

He waited till his sight was back to normal before going back down to the quarry, feeling somewhat dazed. He found the specimen boxes lined up neatly on the ground where Tanguy had left them. There was no sign of either of the two men. He put his equipment away, then combed the quarry, but couldn't find anyone, so finished up sitting on the boulder where the two of them had been eating their lunch. He waited for a long time but no one showed up. Feeling suddenly anxious and dejected, he set off for the fortress.

8

One evening when he was working very late, putting Samuel Leber's unpublished writings into chronological order, Ramanuja, Sarachchandra's brother, knocked on his door. Mrs Leber was asking for him. He followed him out to the courtyard, where she was waiting in the cold in her wheelchair, muffled up to her chin in furs. The façades of the various buildings were illuminated by three floodlights, their orange-tinged light accentuating their structural details and deepening the vistas. She greeted him with relief and seemed unexpectedly delighted to see him.

'I didn't think you'd come. It's really very good of you.' She sounded a bit like a society hostess as she leaned stiffly towards him. Then she turned to the Tamil servant: 'Rama, go and get a chair and the lynx coat.' The secretary waited, intrigued and rather amused. He didn't ask her why she'd sent for him and stayed standing beside her. It looked as though the whole scene had been worked out down to the last detail.

'Here, take this coat, it's a present for you,' she said when Ramanuja reappeared. 'It was Samuel's but he never wore it, and you're about the same height as he was.' Ramanuja helped him into it. It was a pretty impressive mid-calf length garment, and did indeed fit him. The lynx pelt felt soft and warm, and light too. She manoeuvred the wheelchair back so that she could admire him in it, and when she asked him to come and sit close beside her, he found it very difficult to keep his balance on the little folding chair wearing the coat. When they were alone, she stretched her arm over the arm of the wheelchair and felt for his hand, squeezing it impatiently.

'Listen! You must listen . . . Can you hear the screech owls calling?' she asked anxiously. 'Samuel could go on listening to them for hours. Actually they aren't screech owls. They're eared owls. The forest's crawling with them – they like fir trees. He used to say: "I can't bear the idea that one day, before too long now, those creatures will be wiped out. I can't stand it." During the last year of his life, when he'd given up travelling, he used to stay up all night recording their calls on miles and miles of tapes, so that once the disaster had happened, when there was nothing left throughout the land but scorched trees, the survivors crouched in their shelters would still be able to hear the magical voice of the forest. To assuage his passion, he dreamed up the idea of an aviary. That's right, a huge aviary covering acres of forest. As the birds wouldn't be able to get out, he'd be able to go there and listen to them whenever he felt like it. He even drew the plans for this aviary – they were his last drawings. But he eventually gave up the idea of building it, because he realized that the sky is an even larger cage. Listen . . .'

She squeezed his hand more tightly, then suddenly let go of it, pulled her own hand away and withdrew into herself. He thought for a horrible moment she was about to have another spasm of pain, but she started speaking again, her tone calm and even, as though she was reciting a text she'd learnt by heart many years ago and had repeated endlessly, though it still had a spontaneous ring to it.

'That last year before Samuel's death was torture, for both of us. I was desperately worried all the time that he might commit suicide. I imagined all sorts of potential scenarios. I was constantly watching him and following him about wherever he went. One thought nagged at me – he'll kill himself when he's listening to the owls, he'll put a gun in his mouth and pull the trigger. *In his mouth* – that's what I kept on thinking at that point. I could see him sitting where we are now, pulling a revolver out of his pocket and putting the barrel in his mouth, while down below in the darkness the owls would be peacefully calling to one another. I used to wonder whether they'd even be frightened by the sound of the shot. During the last year and a bit of his life Samuel watched as his ideals fell about his ears, one after the other, all his hopes crumbled and his vision of man was transformed into something quite horrific. He refused to admit it, but little by little, having once believed that life is endlessly renewed in the pursuit of perfection, he started loathing the human race. He started loathing himself, and our marriage became a source of silent, unspoken horror.'

Wafting up on the night air, the solemn, lugubrious call of the night birds, somewhat nasal in tone, seemed to convey a message from the remotest of the mountains. Sometimes their responses would continue for a minute at a time, their falling notes rising up to the stars, while way down at the bottom of the ravine, other birds would hoot away in the shadows.

'When I married Samuel he was already a very rich man, thanks to family money. He was well enough off to be able to carry out his expensive experiments and I was completely wrapped up in the theatre, which actually means in Euripides – during that last period I only ever played Hecuba. It was the only part I still felt really passionate about, though at the same time I absolutely loathed it. Hecuba and I were one and the same woman, a single universal cry of despair over the never-ending ignominy of the human race. And the stage couldn't give the necessary resonance to such utter despair, the audience didn't have a strong enough stomach for it. When Samuel came backstage to my dressing room for the first time, he said: "War has stripped Hecuba of everything, but it hasn't destroyed her. She's lost everything – her town, her palace, her husband, her children, her youth. The gods have left her to her fate and slavery is all that's left for her. We're waiting for war, a war that will be infinitely more terrible than the one fought by the Greeks and the Trojans, but we're waiting in a steadfast mood, we're not howling in despair." I realized later that his admiration for man as a species also contained an element of

63

pride at the idea of having snatched away from God his role as sole lord and master of the Apocalypse. He was waiting for war as if it was a natural occurrence, inevitable given the current state of human nature, like a clause in an overall law hanging over the universe. "Man is plunging head first into the chasm he's dug for himself," he used to say. "He metes out death, he accepts death, without ever suspecting that it was he who brought death into existence." He often used to quote St Paul: "The last enemy that shall be destroyed is death."

'Not long after he discovered the new type of reinforced concrete that's been called after him, when he'd put the finishing touches to the techniques of anti-radiation ventilation by means of purifying the contaminated air, and worked out down to the tiniest detail the sociology of the optimum type of existence in what is technically known as a "residential shelter", he set up the Leber Foundation and made an endowment to it of nearly seventy per cent of his fortune. This generous gesture brought him a lot of criticism. Some people accused him of colluding with the various governments as a way of finding an outlet for his "product". That was the word they used – it infuriated Samuel.'

She put her hands on the wheels of her chair, moved it forward a few yards to the middle of the courtyard, then turned round to face him, with the ghost of a smile. He stood up to stretch his legs. It was at that moment that she made the very suggestion he'd given up hope of hearing, since according to the hierarchy that governed life at the fortress it was one of Tanguy's duties, or Félicité's in certain circumstances.

'I'd like us to go for a bit of a walk in the courtyard, but I'm feeling rather lazy. Will you push me? Let's take it slowly – it's a beautiful night.'

He walked over to stand behind the wheelchair, and as he placed his hands on the handles, he noticed they were shaking.

'I haven't pushed a wheelchair since Fra Cosimo's death,'

he said, feeling so weak all of a sudden he wondered if he'd be able to do it.

But as soon as he started pushing he recovered his rhythm and his confidence. The birds were still uttering their piercing monody.

'Don't go too fast. Listen! Can you hear them? The female eared owl makes sounds that aren't really sounds at all. They're known to ornithologists as "silent song". Can you hear it now? She accompanies the others rather than answering their call – her voice is high, a bit mournful.'

Pushing the wheelchair round the courtyard didn't offer much in the way of excitement for anyone used to taking a disabled person out on very awkward terrain, but he felt a great sense of peace flow over him. All he could see of her was her bulky fur hat sticking out on either side of her head, her feet in their fur-lined boots and her slightly stooping shoulders. The furs gleamed in the concealed light from the floodlights and every now and then, when she moved one of her arms, he thought he could see sparks crackling in the air. He pushed her as far as the postern gate. She asked him to take her outside so that she could gaze at the forest by the light of a thin scattering of winter stars, high up in the sky. Then, after a long moment of silent contemplation, she became restless again, returning to the same old obsession.

'Let's go back into the courtyard,' she suggested, as though the words came more easily in that enclosed and familiar space, spurred on by her memories. 'I've been wanting to tell you about the Leber Foundation for some time, but I was afraid of bothering you. But now that we've grown closer, I'd like you to know what's going on.

'The Foundation was originally set up in the European Community with its twelve member states and was officially recognized as being in the public interest. Then Switzerland, Iraq, Iran, the Soviet Union and even Israel took an interest in it. It was a success right from the start, partly because it provided an answer to a form of mass anxiety and to the need to have a clear conscience, partly for less exalted reasons – because a handful of unscrupulous investors were quick to spot its potential as a moneyspinner. Samuel had two co-founders helping him. Then benefactors came flooding in, so that the Foundation's capital, which by now was made up partly of government investment, partly of funds from the private sector, was among the largest anywhere for an institution of its type. Now, a small number of people – it's never been possible to check exactly who they are, but I suspect some members of the board, and also two or three people on the advisory committee, architects, army officers, scientists – set up a tax fiddle by using figureheads to start up companies on the side. In less than three years the initial capital had increased by four hundred per cent – and Samuel knew nothing about it. Although it was completely illegal to touch the capital – endowments and bequests were supposed to be maintained as such, with only the income being used – large sums were placed in share portfolios or invested directly in heavy industry and, needless to say, in the arms industry. Samuel heard about it through a Swiss banker. During that same period the Foundation was setting up offices in Britain and the United States. Samuel called an emergency board meeting, but by then he'd been completely overtaken by events. He couldn't find out exactly what had been going on. However, it was hinted that he'd be well advised to shut his eyes to the Foundation's illegal operations on the side, because high-ups in various governments were involved.

'If he was seen to be asking too many questions – to be too honest – it wouldn't be long before they started boycotting him. After all, his wishes had been respected: huge communal shelters were being built all over the world by this time, without the taxpayers in the various countries – the people who would one day be the survivors – having to pay higher taxes. The Foundation's humanitarian work was continuing, and as they could see their fortune increasing all the time, his co-founders were all the more inclined to accept the situation. It was after that famous board meeting that Samuel started listening to the owls. He returned to the fortress and that same evening, without saying a word, he took a chair and sat down in the middle of the courtyard. He spent the whole night there. I found him the next morning fast asleep, curled up on the flagstones. But there was more for him to swallow . . .'

They went back to where they'd been sitting at the foot of the steps. He reluctantly let go of the wheelchair handles and again did his best to squeeze himself between the tubular steel struts of the folding chair – he was too tall and too bulky with the coat on. The darkness was beginning to seep insidiously into his limbs through the late architect's lynx coat. The cold didn't bother him. It was more that he felt like an old and leaky boat on the edge of a piece of marshland, slowly sinking. She delved into her furs and pulled out a little gold bell, which glittered in the shadowy light. She shook it gently and after barely a second's pause Ramanuja materialized behind them, as though in some magical way he was those crystal-clear notes made flesh. He walked down the steps without making a sound, carrying a tray and two steaming glasses. A heady aroma of cinnamon enveloped them.

'Mulled wine! There's nothing like a nice glass of spiced wine to warm you up!' she said, snatching up one of the glasses with both hands and drinking noisily. He drank too, watching her covertly and remembering that appalling incident in the library – he was constantly terrified it would happen again.

'Believe it or not, this is the first time I've told anyone about all this,' she said, looking down at her glass. 'I didn't confide in any of your predecessors and I've gone over and over it in my own mind so many times I often have my doubts about whether it really happened. And yet it really is true, horribly true. Like most artists and intellectuals who are completely taken up with their work, Samuel didn't know much about how the strings of power are pulled. He was waiting for war to break out, his war, and he didn't pay any attention to the war that has been waged inside each individual, day in and day out for thousands of years. He would often set off on a "mission" – that's what he called the trips that took him to countries fighting a war. He felt they were essential to his psychological well-being. He used to say that nowadays we picture war as something abstract, as less than real, because we're constantly having images of war thrust upon us. The virus of abstraction is killing us. The real world we live in is being created over and over again with each hour that passes. We live in a universe made up of clichés. Before long, abstract concepts will become concrete reality, the world will become totally figurative. And as he sinks into extinction, man will rediscover, through fire, the reality he's distorted. Poor Samuel! That's how he used to speak, carried away by his prophetic visions, and all the time his own life was such an abstraction that he couldn't see those crooks hatching their plots all round him.'

She drained her glass and turned to face him. Her cheeks were flushed from the wine and the expression on her face didn't fit in with what she was saying. 'Have you heard about those anti-ballistic missiles, those atomic "shields" that were banned under the treaty signed by the United States and the Soviet Union in 1972, so that the two great powers were each as vulnerable as the other?' she asked, her solemn tone tinged with irony. 'Well, those missiles that couldn't be used weren't in fact destroyed, and as the enemy knew exactly where they were, they had to be hidden somewhere really safe. Unfortunately the Americans didn't know how to build hiding places where their missiles would be safe from attack. When Samuel went to the States to get hold of the necessary guarantees about setting up the Leber Foundation and to make sure that his shelters would be built on US soil, he met people from the army general staff, various politicians and engineers. The plan was given unanimous approval and within a few months several shelters were under construction, north of New York and Washington and south of Houston. Once he'd made sure of pulling off this victory, he came home.

'It was at that point that they dealt him the final blow. The Americans used the material he'd invented for his fallout shelters to build silos to house their missiles. When Samuel told me about this betrayal, I don't know what came over me, but I couldn't stop myself bursting out laughing – good and evil cast in the same concrete! He never forgave me for laughing. He had a bed made up in his studio, shut himself up in there and started doing the drawings for the aviary. As I told you, he never finished the plans, but they are perhaps the most complex thing he ever designed – a sort of structure in space, an aerial folly that kept him busy for months. But you must understand that it was merely an aviary! One day he came and knocked on my door. There was a wild, hollow-eyed look about him as he said: "I'm tired, Olga. If I could save just one of those birds, I'd be happy . . ."'

She broke off there and was silent for so long he very nearly got up and suggested taking her back to her rooms. But he could tell that she had something else to say and that she wanted to say it out here, in the clear, cold night air. He waited patiently, not asking any questions. He glanced discreetly at his watch. It was gone three in the morning. Ramanuja reappeared, making no noise, and asked in his broken English: 'Would you like to drink something else, Mrs Leber?' He seemed to be available round the clock to see to her needs. She suddenly roused herself from her lethargy and shook her head. Moving as lightly as a ghost, he collected the tray and their glasses and went back in. Once again she reached out over the arm of the wheelchair, feeling for the secretary's hand.

'Please forgive me – I was miles away. But I'm back now,' she said, smiling. 'I haven't quite got to the end. When Samuel stopped attending board meetings I went instead, as an observer. I didn't miss a single meeting over the ten-month period leading up to the accident. I cancelled my stage tours and gave up the theatre altogether to spend all my time learning about how the Leber Foundation worked. It didn't take me long to find out everything that was going on. There were still some real men among the people I was introduced to, but there weren't many of them – the rest only seemed like men. They treated me with suspicion to begin with, but when they realized I didn't want to change anything in the way the Foundation operated they left me alone. Like all idealists and Utopian thinkers, Samuel lived for the future. All the people I met at those meetings were living with a sense of the pressing needs of the present, aware that their names wouldn't live on after the collapse of those ephemeral empires they were hurriedly building, never believing in them for a second. The men sitting in on those meetings with me in a vast office, handling enormous sums of money, didn't realize they were sitting on a crumbling throne in the middle of a field of cinders that had already grown cold. But I did. And now that it's all going on as before, I haven't forgotten either. Ever since the chairwoman of the Leber Foundation board lost the use of her legs, she's handed over her powers every year to a loyal board member – one who's no less dishonest and no braver than the others – and he travels to London three times a year. The fourth meeting, the AGM, is held here at the fortress. Every February the eleven board members come to me, and I entertain them in princely fashion. Samuel started a tradition of laying on a big shoot on the estate to keep them amused once the discussions are over. It goes on for a couple of days, and traditionally even those who don't normally go shooting are expected to join in. But by this time they do all know how to hold a gun, after a fashion anyway.'

The wheelchair was right up against the secretary's chair. They were sitting thigh to thigh, their furs all tangled up. Then the floodlights went out and for a few seconds, until their eyes had got used to the darkness, they sat there in the pitch black. He had the feeling she was squeezing up closer to him, but it might just have been a trick of the darkness. Everything she'd told him was turning over in his brain like a thick, dark liquid, but he felt he'd always known about these revelations, and they made no difference to his feelings for her. He listened out for the night birds, but couldn't hear them. And as though she could read his thoughts, she said categorically: 'It's too late now, they won't call again tonight.'

9

It's morning now, a new day's starting up at the fortress, and any hope of getting some sleep has vanished yet again, he thought. He flicked mechanically through some of the fifteen exercise books piled up in front of him. During the last few months of his life Samuel Leber had filled them with writing that had got tinier and tinier, packed in more and more tightly, and he felt thoroughly disheartened. Then his eye was caught by something written in the margin. He put the large magnifying glass on top of it and the letters stood out more clearly. 'One turning on the evolutionary path that seemed attractive, but in the end always proved catastrophic, involved developing protective armour . . .' he read. The daylight was casting a reflection like clear water on the highly polished table top. He switched off the lamp, stood up cautiously and went over to open the window. Blueish vapour was rising from the forest on the other side of the ravine. A dog was howling with boredom somewhere in the boundless silence of the dawn. He mused on the passage he'd just read and, curious to find out more, was drawn back to the table.

> A living organism can protect itself by hiding, by rapid flight, by an effective counter-attack, by joining forces with other members of its own species to launch attacking and defensive moves, and also by encasing itself in bony plating and spikes.

Both windows were reflected in the convex lens of the magnifying glass. He felt as though the whole setting of his room was embedded in the glass, making it even more spacious than it really was. The architect's text, looking both very close and very far away in the reflected light of the magnifying glass, appeared to be etched on the blank emptiness of the sky.

> This last method was adopted by the ganoid fish of the Devonian, with their shiny armour plating. Some of the large sauria of the Mesozoic were encased in an elaborate shell. And some mammals of the Tertiary era, particularly in America, were huge, peculiar-looking creatures – it would be interesting to know how long it took them

71

to evolve that sort of protective armour. The experiment of developing armour plating invariably ended in failure. The creatures that adopted this method tended to become huge. Their movements would slow down, so they would be forced into eating vegetable foodstuffs and found themselves at a disadvantage compared to their enemies feeding on animal foodstuffs. The long string of failures with protective armour demonstrates that even on a fairly low rung of the evolutionary ladder, the spirit emerges victorious over pure matter. The example of man offers the most sophisticated illustration of this type of victory.

He walked back to the window and leaned out to catch a glimpse of the torrent spurting vigorously between the escarpments of the cliff. The dog was still howling away, but its barks now seemed to express loneliness rather than boredom. 'The experiment of developing armour plating invariably ended in failure . . .' The bedroom was freezing cold by now and he shut the window. But a sudden bout of sadness kept him rooted to the spot, and the prospect of the day ahead made him feel utterly despondent. So that means, he told himself, that Samuel Leber devoted the whole of his life to working out a form of invincible armour plating designed to save the human race from extinction, yet he may well have been fully aware – at least during the last few months of his life, when he jotted down these notes – that developing armour plating invariably ended in failure. He went back to the text to try to find some other explanation, but couldn't find one. He couldn't stand the idea of staying in his room a moment longer, pulled on the lynx coat and went out.

Several of the Tamils and Varlaam were already out in the courtyard. The Tamils seemed upset and as Varlaam didn't speak any English they were waving their arms about, trying to make themselves understood. The secretary joined in and discovered that Sarachchandra, the brahmin, had disappeared during the night.

72

'He can't be far away. He must be wandering about on the estate somewhere,' said Varlaam firmly, once he'd eventually grasped why he'd been woken up so early. He was wearing a brown leather sheepskin-lined jacket over his flying suit, with a red silk scarf round his neck. His hair wasn't tied back today, and was streaming out round his archangel's face in the raw north wind of early morning. His eyelids were still puffy with sleep and he looked somewhat dazed.

'I'm going to fly over the area at low altitude. If you fancy coming with me, I'd be happy to take you.' Then he looked the secretary full in the face, shyly but with obvious concern. 'You look tired . . .'

'I know. I expect you've been told I never sleep, haven't you? It's not entirely true. After all I didn't hear you land. But I'd very much like to come with you.'

Varlaam told him he'd flown up from the south, deliberately not flying over the fortress so as not to wake Mrs Leber: 'You couldn't have heard me. The wind's blowing in the wrong direction and I landed at the heliport.'

He only landed the helicopter in the courtyard when there was something large or heavy to be unloaded. At other times he would put down at the heliport, a circular runway in the middle of the forest, about ten minutes' walk away. The secretary was well aware that Sarachchandra must have had some more complicated reason for walking out on the other Tamils, but he said something reassuring and then followed Varlaam. During the whole of the time he'd been at the fortress he'd only once had an opportunity to talk at any length with the brahmin. He spoke beautifully polished, almost affected French, and during their conversation had mentioned several times that he wanted to take up the life of a *sannyasin* – someone who renounces the world. Both Varlaam and the secretary remained silent until they got to the heliport. The helicopter was waiting in the middle of a stretch of concrete stained black by the rubber on the tyres. A smell of oil hung in the air.

Before climbing on board Varlaam said in a confiding tone:

'I'm glad you agreed to come with me. I've got a secret I want to share with you. We'll look for Sarachchandra and then I'll take you on somewhere . . .'

He broke off there and helped the secretary to clamber into the helicopter and fasten the safety belts. The light filtering through the smoked plexiglass of the cockpit was amber-coloured. The secretary looked round somewhat apprehensively. Varlaam gave him a smile and a thumbs-up sign, put on his leather helmet and switched on the ignition. At first the machine simply gave a jolt, as though someone was giving it a good kick. Then the blades started to rotate silently. The throbbing of the engine got louder and louder, but it seemed to be coming from another helicopter, standing alongside them on the tarmac. The secretary glanced quickly round the ring of trees on the edge of the forest. They seemed very close, so close that the slightest movement off course would send the helicopter crashing against them. Then it rose in a smooth and easy movement and the heliport dropped away beneath them like the bottom of a well. Everything stayed stock still – except that the branches of the fir trees all round them were weaving and tossing about as if a storm was raging.

'Are you frightened?' asked Varlaam, shouting to make himself heard.

He wanted to turn towards the younger man, but the belts kept him firmly wedged to his seat.

'If you mean am I frightened of dying, no, I'm not. I trust you.'

Varlaam's face lit up. He switched on the on-board radio and voices suddenly materialized out of nowhere, filling the cockpit with their nasal tones. The secretary could feel the rocking and accelerating motion of the helicopter being transmitted to his own body, from the stomach to the shoulders. But this physical sensation, both pleasant and alarming, didn't really register in his consciousness. All of a sudden he realized that something quite fantastic had just happened, though he should have been prepared for it – he was hanging in mid-air a few feet above the tops of the fir trees. The helicopter climbed a bit higher, banked sideways, glanced off at an angle and at great speed, barely skimming the treetops, before straightening up and steering a specific course. The earth below them was spinning round like a film on a spool. Varlaam sped along, beaming with delight, performing zigzags for the fun of it, flying low all the time while the landscape raced past.

'Well? What d'you think?' he asked, switching off the radio. But the secretary was too engrossed to reply. He couldn't stop looking. 'We're flying without surveillance – it's a fabulous feeling because it hardly ever happens. There are so many rules and regulations. We're monitored all the time and if I go beyond the boundaries of the Leber estate I run the risk of losing my licence. But here, within a radius of twenty-five miles in the direction of the mountains, I'm on my own patch and I can do as I like – no one can see what I'm up to. I'm as free as air, as long as I don't fly too close to the plain or some of the mountain tops with radar equipment. And now I'm going to show you White Cow Hole.'

The blades were chopping at the air. Their rhythm was like a racing heartbeat, but their gyrating movement was so regular he felt soothed by it. The whole of his body was receiving a message transmitted by the noise itself, so dense as to be almost tangible: the helicopter was working perfectly. Silence meant that it was about to crash. The helicopter lost height, described a wide loop over the forest and all of a sudden he was staggered to see the fortress – he'd thought it was quite a few miles away. He didn't recognize it at first and felt thoroughly confused. The helicopter pulled away, its wheels almost touching the treetops, flew over a clearing, slowed down, then spun on its axis. Varlaam pointed towards the ground. A large stag and several roe deer had been thrown into a panic by the din and were scattering in all directions. One of them, its headlong flight checked by sheer terror, raised its head towards them as though it was giving up the unequal struggle. Varlaam went down lower but the deer didn't stir. It was trembling and they were close enough to see the expression of resigned terror in its lacklustre eyes. Then suddenly, emerging from its trance, it bounded towards the forest and Varlaam burst out laughing.

Soon they were flying over treeless terrain and the forest gave way to a barren and rocky plateau. The helicopter was now flying only tens of feet above the ground. It came to a stop above a hollow that looked rather like the gaping mouth of a volcano, though not as regular in shape – a huge rocky depression with a few dead bushes clinging to it. Varlaam moved the helicopter into position above this exploded crater. There were various hollow openings in its sides and rows of stone steps, descending in tiers, which had caved in, plunging downwards to unfathomable depths. At the far end the secretary could just make out a mossy opening, leading into a black void.

'There's White Cow Hole – it's a swallow hole,' said Varlaam. 'We can't see the whole of its mouth because of the overhanging rocks, but potholers who've gone down it never got to the bottom. Mrs Leber says the Tamils use these caves to worship their gods. Maybe Sarachchandra's gone to ground in one of them. You can get to it on foot from the fortress in a couple of hours.'

'Aren't you going to land?' asked the secretary.

'No. If Sarachchandra's down there and doesn't want to give any sign of life, that's his business. We'll fly back over here later. Can you see that col covered with snow, between the two mountain tops? That's where we're going now.'

Without giving him a chance to object he took the helicopter up higher and flew straight into the sun, which wasn't fully out. The various strata of the alpine landscape unfolded one by one beneath them, taking their allotted place in an abstract and infinitely varied overall pattern. The mountain Varlaam was aiming for was the only one that still looked like a mountain, with its blunt rounded outline, its beauty becoming increasingly bleak the closer they flew to it. A glacier appeared on the left-hand side. The helicopter lost height and the contours of the landscape, which had momentarily levelled off when they looked down on it from high up, now looked mountainous again, endlessly varied and intertwined. They created a feeling of hostility, each of their folds expressing a blunt immutability. Ahead of them, getting closer and closer, a wall of granite reared up, and the helicopter seemed to be racing straight for it. Varlaam was distinctly relaxed as he flew the helicopter, an expression of calm exultation on his face.

'No need to be afraid, I know this part of the mountains like the back of my hand. My real job is rescuing characters clinging to a rock-face and quite unable to get down or go on climbing up. There are the solo climbers too. They set off on climbs that are supposed to be impossible in the winter months. Some of them do manage to get to the top, but then they have to be rescued because they're in a state of exhaustion. You find some of the others dangling on their ropes beside a rocky spine, frozen to death. They've been dead for several days in some cases. And then there's the avalanches. In 1984 I was out flying in the chopper one spring day when I saw a ledge of snow and ice break away from a ridge. A couple of hundred yards lower down there was a party of climbers roped together, making their way up. There wasn't anything I could do. I watched the whole thing – all five of them were killed in that disaster. I couldn't fly for days, and after that, I was frightened to fly too close to the mountains. Then it came back. I've seen lots of dead bodies, all sorts of dead bodies. But there's one that's quite different from all the rest – my very own body. That's who we're going to call on now.'

He turned to his passenger with a facetious smile. Then he suddenly became serious and turned back to his controls, concentrating on the job in hand. They were flying so close to the granite wall it felt as if they could reach out and touch it. The moraine ran at its foot like a river made of stone, the residue – many centuries old now – of a glacier coiling back on itself. The glacier suddenly came into view as the coomb widened out, bathed in sunlight, its blue-tinged face behind the dangerous line of seracs. A living force emanated from it at the point where the flow was strongest and the ice was at least fifty feet thick. They were now flying over a landscape strewn with debris that had reverted completely to its mineral state. The helicopter slowed down and Varlaam pointed to a grassy shelf, quite close to the glacier face.

'I'm going to land there. Don't worry, I've had plenty of practice. I often come here.'

'On your own?'

'Yes. No one else ventures into this coomb, as far as I know. It's of no interest to climbers and you can't use it as a way of getting to any of the passes. The glacier itself is just an insignificant branch. But a long, long time ago, someone did get lost wandering round here . . .'

He broke off to concentrate on manoeuvring the plane. As they flew lower, the place where they were going to land seemed to shrink. The helicopter came to a standstill a little way above it so that Varlaam could take aim. He was whistling under his breath. The secretary clung on tight to his seat and focused his attention on the water trickling out from the bottom of the glacier, hollowing out the moraine. Then he shut his eyes.

When he opened them again the helicopter had landed. The blades were rotating slowly under their own momentum. Then they came to rest and there was silence. They were alone in the world. No one had any idea they were here because the place simply didn't exist.

'It'll be OK. The wind isn't too fierce, but we'll stay near the chopper – you never know,' said Varlaam.

The glacier was of the valley or Alpine type and formed a sharp bend higher up, sliding down like the spine of a saurian, the colour of old bones. Varlaam picked up a powerful pair of binoculars and jumped to the ground, then helped the secretary down. There were turquoise crevasses in the ice, but apart from this translucent colour, which the eye was irresistibly drawn to, seeking to reach down into its depths, the glacier face, the seracs and the moraine made you think of a huge abandoned building site, left to its own devices by nature. Varlaam trained the binoculars on the

78

chaotic jumble of seracs and spent some time peering through them.

'There he is. We'll go a bit closer. I'd like you to see him without the binoculars.'

'See who?'

'Come on.'

The secretary followed him. They climbed down a hundred yards or so, scrambling through awkward scree as far as the lateral moraine. Varlaam turned round at frequent intervals to check on the helicopter. The blades were bending and turning slowly in the silence, driven by the wind. The glacier face seemed to be only a little way away, but the very uneven ground meant that it was a long walk to get to it, through a maze of boulders. Varlaam sat down, again training his binoculars on the seracs. The blackish marl of the terminal moraine was scattered with round, cobalt-blue blocks of ice like cannon balls, the size of a human head. The secretary sat down too, glancing surreptitiously at Varlaam. He felt a sudden surge of friendship for him and longed to seize him by the shoulders and hug him.

'There he is! So he's still there,' said Varlaam, clearly delighted, his eyes still glued to the binoculars. 'Every time I come here I'm amazed to see he's still here – amazed and relieved. If one day I found he hadn't shown up, I wouldn't ask myself how on earth he'd managed to get away, but I think I'd miss him terribly.'

He handed the secretary the binoculars and pointed to a specific spot on the terminal wall, where an old crevasse gaped open. As he peered through the round lens, the figure trapped in the ice seemed amazingly close. It was a man half lying on his side, very close to the surface of the serac, apparently intact. His face had an unhealthy blueish tinge and seemed to be flattened – he looked as if he was squashing it up against the wall of an aquarium so he could see out. A few feet away his ice axe looked as if it was still falling, describing an upside-down Greek letter T as it did so. His left arm was at an odd angle to the top half of his body and his woolly

79

hat was askew, revealing a brownish gash above his eyebrow. There was no sign of any other injury to suggest that he'd come crashing down. He looked as if he'd dozed off on a bench and toppled over sideways in his sleep. But there was one unusual feature – his clothes clearly dated from an earlier period. He'd probably been slumbering there for something like a hundred years, and as the glacier retreated he was slowly coming closer and closer to the surface.

'Hasn't anyone ever reported him?' asked the secretary.

An icy gust of wind raced up the wide embankment of the moraine. Varlaam stood up, zipping his flying jacket right up to his neck.

'No. No one ever comes here. Perhaps I should have told the police about him, but what would have been the point? I've checked the records at the town hall and just in this one small area of the mountains there have been ninety-six climbers who've vanished since the turn of the century, and their bodies have never been found. Anyway, I've got fond of him. I felt I had to show him to somebody and you were the only person who . . .' He tailed off, then added: 'I wonder how much longer it'll take before the glacier spits him out.'

'Several decades.'

'If you were to pull him out of there, it'd take less than an hour for him to putrefy.'

Varlaam had been walking up and down, but now he stopped dead and they stayed there for a moment's silent contemplation, chilled through by the glacier's harsh breath. The sky was growing darker and the countless fissures crisscrossing the moraine were glittering among the black boulders. The secretary heaved himself up from the chunk of stone he'd been sitting on and breathed in the smell of the snow. Banks of mist were moving up the moraine like an insubstantial horde wheeling round to storm the mountainsides, and the glacier was tinged with a blueish-green light. Then it all started to seem threatening.

'It looks as though the weather's turning nasty. We'd better be getting back,' he said.

80

Varlaam was standing quite still. The heavy binoculars were shaking very slightly in his hands.

'Last summer I went right up close quite a few times to have a good look at him,' he said, still studying the glacier. 'To get up to him I had to drive pitons into the ice and carve out steps. The first time I got up on a level with him I nearly came a cropper. I fixed up two snap hooks to steady myself and I stayed sitting there in front of him, suspended by the rope over the sheer drop. There was only a foot and a half of ice between us. I felt sorry for him, with his woolly hat all crooked – I wanted to straighten it for him.'

Eventually he lowered the binoculars and gave the secretary a gloomy look. 'You're right, we'd better get back. We'll soon be surrounded by mist. Winter will cover everything over and he'll be alone right through to next June, under layer upon layer of snow.'

They climbed up quickly, the mist creeping up behind them. By the time they reached the helicopter the wind was buffeting it dangerously and the glacier face was shrouded in mist. Varlaam raced the engine and took off blind. The helicopter climbed and slipped up above the thick wads of cottonwool stealing over the moraine.

'It was such a lovely day earlier on I didn't listen to the weather forecast,' he said. 'We'll return to the swallow hole, then go back to the fortress.'

Soon they were skimming over the plateau at very low altitude, beneath a murky sky with low cloud cover. Smoke from a fire was rising from the depths of the swallow hole. Varlaam switched on the radio and the same nasal, unreal voices blared out. He lost altitude and made a very smooth landing near the swallow hole. Once the engine had been switched off they could hear the crows making a terrible din, their caws reverberating all round the swallow hole.

'Sarachchandra's bound to be down there,' said Varlaam, watching the thin thread of smoke rising straight up in the motionless air. 'Unless it's Tanguy or a poacher.'

They walked away from the helicopter and along the path leading down into the swallow hole. There was a biting north wind and the air was raw.

'D'you need me to help persuade him?' asked the secretary.

'No. I'm sure he won't take any notice, but I'm going to give it a go, just to say I've tried. The Tamils are polite and perfectly pleasant, but terribly obstinate.'

Not wanting to startle the brahmin, he decided to go down into the caves on his own. The secretary was doing his best to shake off the image of the dead man trapped in the glacier. But when he'd eventually managed to do so, another mental picture took its place, and one that was even harder to bear despite the passing of time – Fra Cosimo trapped in the foliage of the felled tree, one of its branches piercing his chest. The dead go on and on being a burden to the living. They climb up on their backs and dog their every footstep. But aren't the living, in putting up with this, doing a spot of double dealing? It was my fault that Fra Cosimo died, he thought. The same phrase again and again, the same complacent lie. Fra Cosimo committed suicide. Yes, there was more truth in that, he thought, but it wasn't the whole truth. 'Before he became a keeper, my father was a woodcutter. I grew up in the forest and I did some tree felling myself when I was in my teens,' the old monk used to say. 'When a beech is being cut down, I can say with absolute certainty which way it's going to fall even before they've got a third of the way through.' The woodcutters had brought the body back to the monastery and he was the one who'd gone to tell the father superior about the accident. He couldn't think of anything else to say except: 'Fra Cosimo is dead, killed by a tree.' Killed by a tree! What about that climber – mightn't someone have pushed him into the crevasse?

He could hear Varlaam's footsteps reverberating in the swallow hole, but he was out of sight now. He walked a few yards down a ledge of rock leading to a very tall but fairly shallow crevice in the shape of an arch, its vaulted roof blackened by smoke from long-dead fires. Beneath him, the slope dropped steeply down towards the hidden opening of the swallow hole, like the broken tiers of seats in a huge theatre. He spotted straight away some stones lying on the sandy ground. He sorted them out, then picked them up. He followed a vague approximation of a path that had been partly washed away by the rain. It led to another arch. This one was smaller, but here again, scattered on the ground and in the undergrowth he found the same type of smooth, waxy stones and stuffed a few into his pocket. He had a good look round at the rocky cirque, its sides honeycombed with a large number of cavities. It had once been a prehistoric settlement and the shades of man's earliest ancestors were still hovering there. He retraced his steps and waited for Varlaam.

There was a brooding atmosphere of ritual murder about the whole place. Lower down, in front of where he was standing, smoke was rising, but the fire itself was out of sight. Soon Varlaam reappeared. There was no one with him.

'Didn't you find him?' the secretary called out when he was still some way away.

'Yes, I did. He's sitting in front of the fire. When he saw me, he smiled and looked at me kindly, but he didn't say anything and I realized there was no point in persisting. I'll alert his brother, they'll sort it out among themselves.'

The secretary pulled the stones out of his pocket and lined them up on the ground in front of Varlaam.

'Does their shape remind you of anything?'

He studied them carefully, then shook his head.

'They were carved by people who lived here something like thirty thousand years ago. You see those three? They're arrowheads. They're somewhat crude, but effective. The two rounder ones have been polished and were probably used as clubs, and the flattest one – it's an obsidian – as an axe blade. There must have been some fierce fighting on the side of this swallow hole, over who was going to have the caves. It's an ideal place for a lengthy stay. It's sheltered, and you can get rid of bodies and waste matter by flinging them down the swallow hole. Those stones have smashed skulls, slashed windpipes, broken limbs, carved up bits of human bodies, hacking them apart.'

He picked up the flints and gave the obsidian axe blade to Varlaam.

'What are you going to do with the others?' Varlaam asked.

'D'you want them?'

'No, it's not that, but . . .'

'Then I'll give them to Mrs Leber – she's waiting for war. They are weapons, after all.'

Shrill laughter spread derisively through the swallow hole and a gust of air eddied against the walls, scattering a flock of jackdaws high into the sky. The slender thread of smoke disappeared for a few seconds as the gust blew through, then a glass cloche came down over the plateau and a lunar hush set in.

'I don't like this place.' Varlaam sounded gloomy.

They returned to the helicopter, leaving Sarachchandra to his solitude, just as they'd left the climber from another age trapped in the ice. Then they flew straight back to the fortress. As they were going their separate ways Varlaam, apparently in two minds about whether or not to ask the question, said: 'Are you happy here?'

The secretary seemed lost in thought for a moment, but actually he wasn't thinking of anything. The question had no resonance for him: it left his mind a blank, quite simply wiping out any power of thought.

'I'm the sort of creature that evolves slowly. I'd need plenty of notice of that question.'

A sharp report rang out far away in the forest and rumbled towards them. And all of a sudden, as though this lone gunshot had shattered the cloud layers to their foundations, it started to rain.

'That'll be Tanguy,' said Varlaam with conviction. 'He's just killed a wild boar. He never fires unless he's sure of hitting his target.'

Olga Grekova-Leber pulled back a series of bolts and opened a door leading into a long room like a refectory in a monastery, but so cluttered that you could only get from one point to another by squeezing through narrow gangways between the jumble of objects.

'None of your predecessors ever came in here,' she said. 'I don't think Samuel came more than a couple of times.' She moved aside to let him in, then, in an exceptionally nimble movement, propelled the wheelchair to the middle of the room, slaloming round dozens of obstacles. There were four desks, each of them in front of a window overlooking the courtyard – some nights he would see light glimmering through the drawn curtains till the early hours. Between the desks were piles of all sorts of newspapers, magazines and journals from all over the world, heaped up so high they looked as if they must topple over, under the watchful eye of three large television sets. On top of them were more piles defying the laws of gravity – this time of files. At first glance the whole thing seemed to be a chaotic jumble, but gradually you could see that there was some order to it, a personal order showing that someone was determined to get it all under control, even though there was clearly still a long way to go – as if someone was slowly recovering the use of logic after a major psychological disorder. A row of metal filing cabinets ran the whole length of the windowless walls facing the ravine, the type used in army offices, with drawers and cupboard doors painted green.

The secretary found his gaze drawn first of all to a large oil painting hanging between two of the windows and surrounded, like a planet with its satellites, by a large number of black-and-white photographs. But he couldn't get any closer to look at them properly, because there were piles of newspapers blocking his way. The painting was a portrait of a sharp-featured man, still young and with a thick head of hair, though it was already grey. He hadn't noticed any photographs or portraits anywhere else in the fortress. Olga Grekova-Leber seemed to live without a past, with no mementoes or keepsakes, as though she had never had any close family or more distant relations whose picture she wanted to have beside her, not a single person whose affection might have followed her when she withdrew into her eyrie. And as he hadn't got any keepsakes of that kind either, it hadn't occurred to him to ask her about it.

He realized straight away that the portrait – a pretty second-rate one – was of Samuel Leber. And orbiting round him were shots of La Grekova playing the part of Hecuba. In some she was with Agamemnon, in others with Cassandra, Talthybius or Helen, and the dates of the various productions appeared at the bottom of each photograph. Apart from his very intense expression, Samuel Leber didn't look like anyone out of the ordinary, and seemed somewhat passive. You got the feeling that the painter hadn't much cared for his sitter, and that the person who'd kept the painting was secretly determined to perpetuate this private grudge.

'I've been working on your husband's papers for four months now, you talk to me about him every day, and this is the first time I've seen what he looks like,' he pointed out absently. 'And I don't know anything about you either. I don't know who your parents were, whether you've got any brothers and sisters, what sort of upbringing you had, if you've ever had children – nothing . . .'

She was sitting in her wheelchair at the only desk that wasn't cluttered up with papers. Instead it was completely taken up with a map of the world, which had pins in every colour of the rainbow sticking into it. As she sat there, stiff and formal, she gave the impression of being in charge of a control post from which she ruled over the whole planet, presiding over the fortunes of the continents and countries spread out before her.

'And you don't want to know either.' Her tone brooked no denial. 'I don't know anything about you either, and I shan't

86

ask. That's what we agreed, surely. As far as we possibly can, let's keep our relationship based solely on what we are as each day comes round, with no reference to what we used to be. Our past is an old sieve – a lot of its holes are blocked up, but something always manages to filter through. I see you're interested in the portrait and the photos. Go on looking at them for as long as you like, then I'll tell you about how the archive works.'

In several of the photos Hecuba was caught in the vertical beam of a spotlight and loomed up out of the darkness like a ghost. The effect was highly theatrical, over-theatrical, thrusting on to the contemporary stage a vanished world that was still highly evocative and was still foisting its ancient prophecies on its audience. All you could see of the Queen of Troy was her face and hands, floating in the darkness that had swallowed up everything else.

On a sudden impulse he said: 'You haven't changed.'

She half turned towards him, then crossed her hands on the map. This position meant she was bent over so far that she looked like a hunchback.

'In a way Hecuba as a tragic figure is timeless,' she said, speaking very softly. 'She talks to herself and to no one else, because she can't find anyone capable of understanding what she's saying, and in the end she's turned into a bitch. In our own time we're all, men and women, being turned into dogs and bitches every single day. Hecuba has to stay on stage – her role is never-ending. But do you think she'll be capable of reaching a pitch of intensity in her lamentations to match the scale of the disaster that's about to befall us?'

At the far end of the room there was a row of calendars hanging on the wall above the filing cabinets. He counted twelve of them, the earliest dating back to 1975 – the page for December showed a lake frozen over and children skating. Pinned up on the side wall, where the rough-rendering was peeling off in wide panels, were various texts written in thick black letters on sheets of cardboard yellow with age. Each of

87

them had been put above one of the metal cupboards, like a label telling you what was in them.

> Look! The land of your birth is a blazing heap!
> Listen! What cry comes from the shore?
> Seagulls robbed of their young?

And on one of the others:

> Lift your neck from the dust;
> Up with your head!
> This is not Troy; the kings of Troy are dead:
> Bear what you must.
> The tide has turned at length:
> Ebb with the tide, drift helpless down.

He read the passages out loud. She hadn't put the light on or drawn the curtains back, but his eyes were getting used to the half-light. The wheels of her chair squealed on the wooden floor. She turned to face him, and this time it was she who recited:

> Up, aged feet; if you can climb so far,
> I will stand here and bid farewell to my poor city.

She laughed, sent the wheelchair hurtling towards one of the filing cabinets, took a bottle of whisky out of one of the drawers and returned to the desk. He cleared a pile of journals off a chair and came over to sit beside her, facing the map.

'I'm afraid there's only one glass, we'll have to make do with that. I wanted to show you my archives, not recite Euripides. Anyone who claims that man hasn't invented anything at all is a fool. Every day, thanks to his inventions, death has a new and more terrible face.' She applied the brake so she could lean forwards. The blue of the oceans was dotted with coffee and alcohol stains and he noticed that on the spot where she leant the top half of her body – clearly in the same place for years on end – the map was torn and crumpled. She filled the glass virtually to the brim, as though it was plain water, drank from it, then handed it to him with a ceremonial flourish.

Every time she moved the arms of the wheelchair banged against the edge of the desk, which was rather wobbly – hence, he realized, the stains on the map. But she didn't seem to notice. She was running her hand over the map at random, taking pins out and then putting them back in the same place, pulling a disapproving face as she did so.

'I came to live at the fortress in 1974,' she said, her voice sounding hoarse, as it always did when she was turning the subjects that obsessed her over and over in her mind. 'It wasn't permanent, of course, but although I never stopped acting now and again until the accident, I didn't take on any more major touring engagements, and my decline dates from that period, when I started giving in to Samuel. He was waiting for war to break out, he wanted me to wait with him, just as all of us want our nearest and dearest to share our tastes and thoughts. But nothing can really be shared, and during that long wait we acted out what Samuel called "a love as invulnerable as my shelters" – which wouldn't actually have lasted more than a season or two if it hadn't been for that sense of expectancy about war being imminent. Round about that time, to keep me amused during the periods I spent at the fortress, I knuckled down to this task, whose fruits you're about to see – I refine the process a bit more every day.'

He glanced round at the chaotic scene of piled-up newspapers and filing cabinets. It was getting dark and for a moment he felt as if he were in an Egyptian tomb that had been robbed several times, surrounded by what was left of the relics of the dead person's life.

'These cupboards and filing cabinets are filled with virtually everything printed in the major western newspapers about the horrors that groups of human beings all over the world have inflicted on other groups and have themselves suffered since 6 August 1945. My original plan was to file away in this room a compendium of everything that had been published on the subject anywhere in the world, from the first atom bomb at Hiroshima onwards. But Samuel put me right straight away: "You mustn't use aberration to deal with aberration, you must use reason." He spent his life standing up for reason, but he never had an ounce of reason himself, that's what I found so fascinating about him – that certainty that he was safely ensconced in the bosom of reason, when in fact, without realizing it, he was somewhere else entirely.

'The pins on the map mark the places where fighting is taking place – wars where one country has declared war on another, civil wars, guerrilla warfare, illicit occupation of territory, and so on. These metal cupboards contain thousands of microfilms and the filing cabinets are full of reports, accounts of war, specialist studies. Ever since 1975 I've been paying people to do research in the major libraries in Europe and America, checking through press cuttings, collecting, photocopying or, whenever possible, putting straight on to microfilm anything connected with armed conflicts, anywhere on the surface of the globe. But that's only one aspect of the work. I've got unofficial agents inside the international organizations, embassies and charities who send me copies of reports and confidential documents, any information they can get hold of on deportations, torture, child murder or genocide. Money makes the impossible much more possible, you know. My money means I can get hold of ultra-secret documents that would discredit our systems of government once and for all, if they were ever to get out from behind the walls built to protect them. New pieces of information plop into my post-office box every single day, and Varlaam brings them up to me three times a week.'

It was completely dark now. The objects cowering apathetically in the room seemed to take on a rudimentary form of life engendered by the darkness itself, just as in the farthest recesses of caves, the darkness is so dense it becomes virtually organic, and the silence becomes that of a hibernating creature. He felt a need for light and asked her to switch on the reading lamp. She appeared in the round patch of light it threw out, hunched in her wheelchair, and the portrait of Samuel Leber on the opposite wall grew taller.

'You may think this room is cluttered, but I've been working single-handed for several months now. We've got the necessary apparatus for developing microfilms, but I don't know how to use it, and the person who looks after that side of things with me, the only person I trust, is seriously ill. It's my own fault – I took on this megalomaniac task, never suspecting for a moment what a huge operation it would turn out to be, and I realized its true purpose only gradually, as the information piled up. What I'd like to do is amass enough material to compile a sort of natural history of evil.'

They heard voices outside in the courtyard. Looking alarmed, she stopped talking and listened. Soon there was silence again, but this sudden sign of human life had aroused some unspecified anxiety. She drank the rest of the whisky, leaned back against the back of the wheelchair and, with a little sigh, looked at the secretary. She looked at him as though she'd just discovered that this man sitting beside her, who she'd been talking to for so long, was a complete stranger.

'I sometimes think that if it weren't for you, I couldn't go on living at the fortress,' she confessed. Her tone was one of reproach as much as of gratitude. 'I want to get up, to join you in your tower, your impregnable ivory tower. But I can't get up! Anyway, what would be the point? What's the point of telling you? I talk, and you sit there in silence. I like your silence, but I must admit that often, when we're having dinner together and I've had a bit too much to drink, I'd dearly love to scratch your eyes out. You're so cold and inaccessible! Incapable of letting yourself go. I dreamt about you last night. There were just the two of us, in the middle of a blank expanse of snow. You were standing right behind me, pushing me, but I couldn't see you. I could hear you breathing heavily, then you started panting and gasping for breath, as if you were making a superhuman effort. The sky was a very dark blue, almost black, light crystals were fluttering all round us, and the wheelchair was moving forward between two sprays of powdery snow. I didn't know how you'd got me there, or why.'

More noise erupted in the courtyard. The secretary got up, clambered his way to the window and flung open the

91

curtains, ignoring her protests. Several ghostly silhouettes bearing blazing torches were moving round the courtyard in a thick mist. The agitated face of one of the Tamils loomed up on the other side of the window and promptly vanished, while the flame weaved around. In the dead of this early winter night the fires were gathering and thick snowflakes were swirling down towards this mysterious ballet. He returned to his chair. She snatched up his hand and he felt her nails digging into his palm.

'They're going to set it alight,' she muttered.

'The fortress is fireproof.'

'But I'm not!'

Someone banged fiercely on the door. It flew open and Tanguy appeared in the doorway, took a few paces into the room, tripped over a pile of newspapers and swore. His hair was dripping wet and hanging over his face as he looked round in amazement. The secretary realized it was the first time he'd been in there.

'I told you never to open that door, never!' she shouted.

He was clearly put off his stroke by the vehemence of her reaction, but he came a few paces further into the room.

'I'm sorry, it's because of the snow,' he growled. 'They don't want to leave Sarachchandra alone in the swallow hole, so they've decided to go and join him.'

She relaxed and her face lost its anguished look. But it was promptly replaced by a look of fury.

'It's quite out of the question! They'll stay here. You can go and fetch Sarachchandra tomorrow with Varlaam. I don't want us all to get into a mess because of that old brahmin.'

'You'll never stop them doing what they want to do. They're stronger than you, and stronger than me too. If they decide to leave the fortress for good, you'll never find anyone to take their place. They're not asking much – just to be allowed to look after the old man.'

Sarachchandra had been living in the swallow hole for four days now. His brother had taken him clothes, blankets and something to eat.

'I'm going to talk to them,' she said, steering the wheelchair towards the door.

But Tanguy was in the way and he didn't budge.

'It's a waste of time.'

'Out of the way, Tanguy, let me get past!'

He still didn't move. He simply said phlegmatically: 'It's pointless.'

It was the first time the secretary had witnessed a direct confrontation between the two of them. Standing there stolidly, his legs apart, his face like a leather mask, tanned and secretive, Tanguy didn't exude authority, but an assurance so overwhelming that she made no more attempts to leave.

'Leave it to me. I'll go with them and I'll see what's the best thing to do when I get there.'

It was a capitulation on Olga Grekova-Leber's part. She retreated and hurtled towards the nearest window, pulling back the curtain and staying there, looking out. The Tamils were now in a silent huddle close to the building and this soundless waiting was a portent of new dangers to come. Without saying a word she returned to her desk and became engrossed in the map, as if that was her only concern. Her expression showed that something was wrong and she seemed to be having trouble breathing. The flames from the torches flickered against the windows. The snowflakes were flying about, floating round the flames and covering the men's shoulders. Tanguy went out and was greeted with excited shouts. Soon the snowflakes were falling on nothing but the deserted courtyard, and the vast night-time darkness of the forests.

'We can't let that man stay down there – he might die,' she said, after a long silence. 'Word gets round quickly and in a day or two everyone will know what's going on here. They'll send the police, journalists and a whole lot of riff-raff that I'd find quite unacceptable. But for the moment, let's go outside. I'd like to see the first snowfall.'

They stayed in the doorway, looking out silently at the snow-covered courtyard. Gusts of wind were sending flurries of snow whirling up to the rooftops, but despite these swirls of powdery snow the night remained utterly peaceful. The shouts of the men and the flaring torches were far away, and any form of violence now seemed quite implausible in the muffled whiteness of the night. Along with the snow came long-forgotten moments of wide-eyed wonder from long ago, a lingering liking for the good life and a vague hope that everything can be transformed by innocence.

11

She appeared in the library shortly after lunch. She was wearing a white roll-necked sweater and a suede waistcoat and looked like a very young woman who happened to be a bit tired because she'd slept badly. Her hair was pulled back in a chignon, leaving her face smooth and naked, as if she was offering it to him. It was the first time he'd seen her like that, without a trace of make-up. Her eyes were sparkling and looked huge. He started up out of his chair when she came in, because the harmonious picture she made was spoiled by one key detail.

'What are you doing with that gun?' he asked.

The look of amazement on his face must have been pretty comical, because she laughed and rested her arms on the gun, which was lying across the arms of the wheelchair. But she didn't answer his question.

'Would you like to come out with me? I really do need to get out and I can't find Tanguy.'

During his months at the fortress he didn't remember seeing her go out more than about a dozen times, and never for long. Tanguy would settle her in the jeep and they'd set off without the wheelchair and be back an hour later, after driving in one direction or the other along the track linking the fortress to the town, or the one via the sunny side of the valley to the plain. Sometimes Tanguy would push her through the meadows to a piece of high ground offering a panoramic view over the forests. But this spot was only a few hundred yards from the fortress. These outings were governed by a ritual that had been

94

strictly adhered to over those ten years, as she couldn't bear the thought of having to submit to the humiliation of being dependent on others out in the open air, though she put up with it willingly enough inside the fortress.

'I trust Tanguy completely. If I asked him to, he'd take me wherever I wanted to go, even if it meant walking for hours,' she'd confided. 'But I don't want to ask him.' So although the secretary was amazed at her request, he experienced a moment of sheer joy when she told him, in a voice that was almost playful: 'There's a place I'd like you to take me to. I haven't been back there since the accident. You can't drive all the way – you'll have to push me the last bit.'

He went to fetch the jeep and parked it at the foot of the front steps. Above the doors at the front there was a special arrangement so that you could hang up weapons horizontally. He secured the gun on the passenger side, as she'd asked him to, then carried her to her seat and strapped her in. The foehn had got up the previous day, the snow had melted, and with the temperature abnormally high for the time of year, the mild air brought a whiff of putrefaction. When they drove off she said, as if to herself: 'If Tanguy were to see us, I wouldn't give much for our chances.'

He drove through the postern gate and continued in the direction she indicated, jolting over rough terrain. After a moment or two he couldn't help asking: 'Have you brought the gun to protect yourself against Tanguy?'

Her expression was very serious as she looked at him, shaking her head.

'Not exactly. You haven't come across any sign of it so far, luckily for you, but these forests can be dangerous in other ways too. He was under orders to put you on your guard, but he deliberately failed to do so.'

'On my guard against what?'

'I'll explain later.'

They were driving along a path that was barely visible and sometimes vanished altogether, though there was always some ghostly trace of it, so he couldn't go wrong. Far away in a

95

milky sky he could just make out the blurred outline of a halo round the sun, looking like an egg yolk floating in some creamy substance. As he drove he had the feeling he was plunging deeper and deeper into the heart of the silent landscape, though against a background of clanking ironmongery – clinking sheets of metal knocking against one another, the engine backfiring and the shock absorbers grating. In the back of the jeep, the wheelchair lurched to and fro, sliding from one side to the other every time they jolted over a bump. A few minutes later they were going along a ride, one that he'd often followed on one of his hikes, though he'd never been right to the end of it. He braked sharply to avoid a tree stump and she jolted about in her straps. She was attacked by a violent fit of coughing that left her exhausted. A hundred yards or so ahead of them the ride disappeared beneath a tangle of brambles and shrivelled ferns squashed by the snow. And just in front of them it was blocked by a fir-tree log lying right across it.

'I see that tree trunk's still there,' she remarked, her voice husky. 'You'll have to push me from here.'

He parked the jeep in front of the trunk, had a good look at the ground round about, then carried the wheelchair up on to the bank beside the path and went back to fetch her. Before he lifted her out of the front seat, she unhooked the gun and kept tight hold of it. It was a double-barrelled gun, with a delicately chased breech. It made you think of the vast open spaces of a beat, hounds racing through the forest, all the rustling sounds of the secret life at bay in the covers, long periods of stalking beneath the dawn sky, a sudden tautening of those slender threads that still link man to barbarity, guiding him towards it via the sunken paths of old, primitive dreams of fire and sharing out the spoils of the chase. She seemed heavier than at the beginning of their outing, and as his hand held her beneath her armpits he could feel through the sweater the place where her breast started to swell, and a roll of soft flesh. When he sat her in the chair he intercepted an expression of fear in her eyes. She looked all round her, at the grass-grown ride with its pools of water, looking reassuringly bright and shining, then at the half-light of the woods that rapidly grew thicker, the trunks furthest away from them mere shadowy outlines in the crypt-like darkness.

'I know it's ridiculous,' she said, 'but I'm frightened. I used to come mushrooming here, and I feel as if something of my earlier self is still roaming about beneath these trees. It's the first time in ten years I've been back to a place well away from the fortress that I used to walk to before . . .' She broke off, then went on: 'I've always refused to return in my wheelchair to the paths I used to walk along before I was disabled. I see the world as being divided into two quite separate realms – one is the realm of movement, but I don't belong there any more, the other, the one I'm supposed to stick to, is a realm without movement. And now, because of you and that absurd fat monk you used to take out into the forest, I . . .' She shook her head, searching feverishly through her waistcoat pocket. The match crackled on the air and the flame shot straight up beneath the branches, as though the forest was holding its breath. 'Do you really think you'll be able to push me over this type of ground?'

He went to stand behind her and took a firm grip of the handles. He was experiencing anew the old mixture of the most altruistic self-denial and a feeling of absolute power, the two blended together in an upsurge of compassion and affection.

'Where would you like to go?' he asked.

'Go to the end of the ride and then keep on going straight ahead into the forest for another few hundred yards.'

The ground beneath the fir trees was dry, covered with a thick carpet of needles. He was finding it easy to push the chair, skirting the felled tree trunks, stopping to thrust aside any dead branches. She said nothing. He could sense that she was tensed up, as stiff as the gun she was holding across her lap. Every now and then they came to a patch of broken ground. The wheels of the chair would grind to a halt and sink in, sending her toppling over forwards before she righted herself by grabbing the arms. The gun fell to the ground several times. When they were crossing a gully, he had to tilt the chair backwards at such an angle that she found herself lying on the back, her legs in the air, her face just below his. For a fraction of a second their eyes clung to one another's with unbearable violence. Her mouth opened to scream but no sound came out.

'There's nothing to be afraid of. Relax and trust me. I spent ten years pushing Fra Cosimo. He was very heavy and his wheelchair had been specially designed for his girth – it weighed a ton.'

She didn't say anything and was still sitting very stiffly. Any stiffness and tension in her, physical or psychological, was expressed physically – she couldn't hide anything now. He stopped, massaging her shoulders and the back of her neck to make her relax. She didn't object and bent her head to make it easier for him. He gradually got the feeling she was letting herself go, that her body was growing limper. Her white neck felt like modelling clay beneath his thumbs.

'You make a good masseur,' she whispered. Then suddenly she jerked upright, a hunted expression on her face, her eyes searching the forest all round them.

There was no sign of movement to disturb the strict geometry of the tree trunks. They set off again. Soon – though in fact they'd been going for not much more than a quarter of an hour – the forest thinned out and the ground became mossy. High up above the trees a pearly light spread out from an oily sky. He was pushing the chair and walking along as he'd done in the old days, yoked to someone who was very dear to him. And as he advanced towards the negation of any itinerary, of any will to keep on walking, he was endowed with superhuman strength. He felt as though he'd been living closed in on himself for months on end, and only the act of pushing could make him complete and allow him to escape. What he was experiencing today confirmed something he'd never really accepted, though he conceded that it was manifestly true, and had found it to be a constant throughout the years he'd spent with Fra Cosimo: the

98

only thing he was fit for was pushing a wheelchair. He couldn't see any higher mission for him on earth. When he was pushing, all his other skills and talents – he had a good few of them, including geology and writing, on which he'd pinned so many hopes – faded from his mental horizon like misty vapours over the plain. Nothing else was more real than that, and while he was pushing Olga Grekova-Leber towards the radiant edge of the forest, he mused on the fact that the truth of this woman, who had spent so many years, and with such immense talent, playing the part of a dethroned queen, was to be pushed, to submit to this total subordination to someone else's will. And, he thought, however much she tried to escape this preordained role by deluding herself, all that endless business of going over and over what her late husband had said and done, the Leber Foundation and its vast wealth, the fact that she was waiting for war, the contempt and hatred she felt for the human race – all that merely formed a pathetic mental background, and was of no more significance than an eyelash floating on the surface of the sea, compared to what she was going through now in this wheelchair.

Then they reached the edge of the forest and remained suspended in mid-air, spellbound. Earth ended there, on that platform of close-cropped grass, and spread out before them was the whole of space, with its snowy pyramids in the far distance, its cloud castles and its airy balconies. Instinctively he stepped back, drawing the chair towards him.

'Push me to the edge, where you can see those three stones,' she insisted.

He could see now that the precipice didn't start as close to the forest as he'd imagined, that the narrow meadow formed a series of terraces. The place she wanted to go to was on the farthest of these terraces. By lifting the front wheels off the ground, and simultaneously pushing the chair and holding it back, he managed to reach this last overhanging shelf. Beyond it the mountainside had caved in on itself into the valley – a clean break, as though it had been sliced off by a giant wielding the cutting edge of a shovel. He wedged the brake on tightly, took off his belt and strapped her firmly to the back of the chair, then pushed it to the edge.

'Nothing's changed,' she observed. 'I always have the same feeling when I get to this spot. You're turning your back on the world, you can feel it behind you, pushing you. You try to forget it and, even when you're quite alone, it pushes you to the utmost limit.'

He turned round, glancing quickly at the edge of the forest. There wasn't a breath of wind, yet the heavy branches of the fir trees were bobbing down limply. The shadows beneath the trees seemed to be rising from the earth like vapour, and something stirred among the lines of tree trunks.

'The last time I came here was with Samuel,' she went on. 'We were standing on this same spot, near the three stones, and I told him I'd decided to go back down to the plain and start acting again. I'd been living at the fortress for just over two years when I suddenly said to myself: "If you don't go now, you'll never get away, you'll become part of these mountains and forests for ever." It was a rebellious outburst – my last. Samuel grabbed me by the shoulders and I could see from his expression that he was going to fling me over the edge. But then his arms dropped to his sides and he merely said: "As you wish."'

Ahead of them, as far as they could see, apart from the futuristic pylons carrying high-voltage power lines, there was no sign of human habitation, nothing to make you think that man had systematically settled here. She lit a cigarette. A whiff of light tobacco wafted through the air, an indoor smell that briefly made nature seem utterly intangible.

'You've got nothing to fear from me,' he said. 'The one and only thing I want is your well-being.'

He went back to the edge. Man is the only thing that counts, he reflected. Pain and sweat, filth and barbarity, disability and human strength – everything else is illusory and we might just as well jump over the edge this very minute.

'You must leave. Pack your bags this evening, get away from here before it's too late,' she said, half under her breath.

100

Again he peered intently at the forest, and this time he distinctly saw a shape slipping into the shadowy undergrowth.

'I think Tanguy's been spying on us for some time.'

She shrugged her shoulders, then closed her eyes. He walked over to one of the stones and sat down. A kite rose up from the abyss and hovered over them, so close it seemed to be keeping them under observation. When he walked back over to her he found she was asleep, her head on one side. He took off his jacket and put it round her shoulders. Then, reluctant to take the gun, he started walking slowly along the edge of the precipice. He turned round every now and then to keep an eye on her, asleep on the edge of the world. Soon she was out of sight. He'd climbed up towards the forest by now and realised he found it hard being alone, yet near her. As he retraced his steps he spotted an oddly shaped object at the foot of a fir tree, half buried under lichen and tree bark. It turned out to be a trap, an antiquated type of mantrap, hastily camouflaged. The air was getting cooler, the sky was clearing, and the close-cropped grass was sparkling in the light as if there'd just been a heavy shower. In the forest no birds sang. As he came up to her he thought she was still asleep, but then saw that her eyes were open.

'We don't need to go back just yet. I'd like you to take me somewhere else not far from here,' she said. 'You won't need to push me, we can get there in the jeep.'

They went back to the jeep. On the way back through the forest her fears suddenly returned, but she did her best not to show it. As they drove towards the cross ride, the sun appeared above the fir trees, behind a curtain of mist, looking huge and with a halo round it. And while he was strapping her into her seat, he again had a feeling that they were being watched.

They drove along the main ride in the other direction. A short way along she pointed to an opening in the trees, a service path once used by woodcutters but now overgrown. He drove the jeep straight at a clump of ferns. Immediately beyond it he was forced to drive at a walking pace beneath a tunnel of low branches, letting the windscreen push them aside. Here and there blueish rings of light shone down through the trees on to carpets of moss. Then the forest opened out, like a broad shadowy doorway leading into the hushed, contemplative atmosphere of a clearing. Half-hidden beneath the vegetation were piles of logs chopped many years ago – whoever had once had the right to chop firewood there must have forgotten about them. But one whole section of this area of cleared forest was out of reach, behind a double row of openwork fencing running right through the middle of it and plunging deep into the forest.

'The Great Wall,' she said tersely. 'Samuel invented the name. They forced him to put it up so that our land would be completely fenced in. It runs for over fifty miles altogether. As you can see, there's a track running beside it, but it's so overgrown it would take you a couple of days to drive right round it.'

He parked the jeep near the fence and they sat there silently for a moment or two. She was shaking her head as though she found it hard to believe this incongruous obstacle really existed.

'What's it for?' he asked eventually.

She looked at him as though he'd just said something not quite nice.

'To stop the animals getting out, of course.'

'What animals?'

'Oh yes, of course, I was forgetting. Tanguy didn't explain about . . .' Her voice tailed off. 'Samuel was a great animal lover – by which I mean he loved wild animals. Every time he went off on one of his trips he'd come back with a male and female of some species capable of adapting to our climate and producing offspring – various species of wolf, bears and lynxes. The experiment was a great success, so much so that before he had the Great Wall built the animals would get all over the place, terrifying the local farmers and woodcutters out of their wits. The local council insisted he must either put a fence right round the estate or slaughter all the animals.

102

He decided to spend a fortune putting up the Great Wall and laying out the track.'

The light was waning. She shivered as she sat there strapped to her seat. She wound up her window and let out a groan. They could see their breath in a pale vapour. He started up the engine and switched the heating on.

'Would you like to drive along beside the fence for a little way?' he suggested.

She shook her head. 'My legs are hurting. I wanted to see the Great Wall again in the thick of the forest – it's somehow a part of me. Samuel thought the earth was going to be laid waste, so he planned his estate as a Noah's Ark. He used to say that nowadays men are in control of their destiny, and for the first time in human history there won't be any emissary to intercede between them and death, because they've destroyed all the emissaries – they've destroyed God, they've destroyed philosophy, and they're so pig-headedly determined to show themselves no mercy that they've destroyed anything that could save them. And now that they're naked in the face of the total destruction to come, their destructive instinct can finally win the day. At the end of his life he thought we should pat ourselves on the back for having arrived at that supreme moment when evil is going to destroy evil, when evil is going to vanish from the face of the earth along with man. When he wasn't closeted in his studio or listening to the owls, he used to walk back and forth on the bastion for hours on end. I'd keep him company sometimes as he ruminated, and we'd walk side by side, with me thinking: You're wrong, you know, everything's already been destroyed. No one's realized it because objects and living creatures still look the same, but inside, there's already nothing left but death. We're living on a dead man's planet, we're dead too, fated to wither, not to be consumed by fire.'

There was silence all round them. Shapes were growing blurred and only the double row of fencing still had its crisp outline, its straight lines and angles like prison bars in the motionless twilight. Gathering in the shadows beneath the

103

black branches, a whole host of creatures lay in wait. As the earth slumbered, the confined space of the clearing swarmed with the shadowy creatures conjured up by its dreams. The engine was running in slow motion. Suffocatingly hot, greasy air was wafting out of the heating vents, dulling their senses.

'We should get back before it's completely dark,' he suggested. She was mechanically rubbing her aching thighs as she looked straight ahead, unseeing.

'D'you know what I sometimes think – particularly now?' she asked. 'I think that nature invariably makes mistakes, that nature itself is a mistake. Forests, mountains, seas, this endless twilight, and sight, human sight – it's all a trick. We're all there is to existence. What Samuel never grasped was that I was more alive when I was acting than when I lived at the fortress. I'm going to let you in on a terrible secret – Samuel was afraid of death, he was quaking with fear at the thought of his own death. He wasn't interested in what was going to happen to other people. His life's work, the whole of his career reveal his helplessness in the face of common-or-garden death. He wasn't waiting for war, he was waiting for his own death. War was merely a pretext, and he would have been quite happy to cover the whole planet with shelters just to protect himself and no one else. It took me years to admit this, but actually I realized it right from the start. He knew that I knew, that I'd delved down into the depths of his being, deeper than he could himself go by that stage. He knew that every day, every night, I would place him on a pedestal, only to knock him off again – continually raising him up and then bringing him down again, several times an hour, in the space of a few minutes. But, though he didn't realize it, he did have a means of defence against my perspicacity – Hecuba. He hated the character of Hecuba, and gradually, although we never talked about it, as he couldn't dissociate her from me, he started hating me.'

He had turned the jeep round and was driving back the way they'd come. A crescent moon was shining on to the treetops, icy and pure. While he was driving along the bottom of a gorge luxuriant with vegetation, everything fell totally silent. He couldn't hear the throbbing of the engine and the jeep seemed to be driving itself, gliding smoothly into a legendary night, while the forest closed over them as in a dream. Then something happened that made everything seem totally unreal.

A shape loomed up out of the woods a few yards ahead of the bonnet, followed immediately by another, then another. The three silhouettes froze in the middle of the path, hypnotized by the headlights. He braked. At the same moment he saw her unhook the gun, take aim. The windscreen shattered. The air shook with the explosion, then there was a leaden silence. One of the three shapes was lying on the ground in the beam of the headlights, the other two had vanished. A plaintive howl rose up somewhere in the forest, very close to them. She turned towards him.

'Wolves,' she said. 'They're not usually all that dangerous, they've got enough to eat. During the winter Tanguy gives all the animals regular feeds, but sometimes he slacks off a bit.'

She raised the gun again. The moon was shining through a gap in the trees on to their laps, its starry light picking out the splinters of glass. He opened the door and climbed out of the jeep. 'You must be mad,' he said softly. On the path ahead of him the wounded creature was trying to crawl out of the beam of the headlights.

'We weren't in any danger, there was no point in shooting it,' he said, walking over to the wolf.

Another shot rang out. The wolf shuddered, then, after a few convulsive jerks, lay rigid in death. Now there was howling all round them, drawing closer, then moving away, magnified by the echo. But he could still hear quite distinctly the clicking sound of the gun breech and the two cartridge cases dropping on to the floor of the jeep. He started walking over to the body, but was pulled up by short by a peremptory voice: 'Don't be idiotic. Come back. There are a lot of them and their blood's up now. They might easily attack us and I haven't got any more cartridges.'

They returned to the ride, the vast expanse of sky and the

105

crescent moon. They didn't exchange a word as they drove to the fortress. Félicité was waiting for them at the top of the steps, puffing frantically on her pipe. He'd never seen her in such a state of anxiety. She rushed forward to meet them and suddenly, once she was sure they were still in the land of the living, her usual impassively placid demeanour returned. When he opened the rear door to take the wheelchair out, she pointed the stem of her pipe at him and gave him a cryptic wink. He felt someone looking at them, turned round and caught a glimpse of Tanguy slipping out of sight behind the building. He lifted Olga Grekova-Leber out of the jeep. When she was in his arms she flashed a bold-as-brass look at him and said: 'Thank you for taking me out. We must do it again some time.'

12

While the weather held he returned to the quarry to prospect virtually every day. But then his enthusiasm dwindled when rain, snow and cold set in.

He had dinner with her every evening now. The winter and the nights drawing in brought them together and often, at the end of the evening, he would walk back with her to her bedroom. He would push her through the main hall, then along the short stretch of corridor, walking slowly to make the short journey last as long as possible. Sometimes he would bend secretly over her to breathe in the fragrance of her hair. With every step he took, he experienced to the full the weight and the scent of this broken body, drowsy with the wine that had stripped it of its usual reserve. They rarely spoke, but there was an unspoken understanding between them. Her physical presence became so overwhelming on these occasions that it completely enveloped him, leaving him desiring nothing in the world except to continue pushing her like this right through the night, all over the fortress, in a state of exaltation such as he'd no longer been able to imagine.

Since he'd stopped prospecting, he'd transferred his field of inquiry to this woman in her wheelchair. He was uncovering a deposit buried deep within her, difficult to get at, since it was hidden beneath several strata of extremely hard rock. He was taking his time. As the years went by, he was increasingly discovering that he possessed a capacity for being rapt in wonder, as though his present life would be followed by another and then another, and so on until both time and desire were exhausted. But desire was growing and time was inexhaustible. I'm close to death, he told himself. Merely thinking this increased his zest for life, and banished death to the realms of improbability. And this woman was there, as though he had never known any other woman, as though he was rediscovering the existence of woman on earth. He didn't expect anything specific of her, so was spared the feeling of melancholy that arises from the gulf between a mental image and reality. At this stage they were making no demands on one another, but in the most demanding of all contexts – respect for one another's existence. Sometimes, as he leaned over her to breathe in her fragrance, he felt a sudden urge to cover her breasts with his hands, seize her by the chin to turn her face towards him and kiss her on the mouth. A door was open, but there was no urgency about stepping through it.

Very early one morning, before daybreak, there was a knock on his door. She was outside. For the first time since the accident she'd consented to use the lift and leave the ground floor.

'I've come to see if you're comfortable,' she said, as if he'd only arrived at the fortress the night before.

He didn't know what to say. There was a smell of insomnia in the air and Samuel Leber's manuscripts were scattered all over the table. She looked round, clearly flabbergasted. The bareness of the room seemed to have made her aware for the first time of the presence of a man who had up to then been invisible, on the verge of not existing at all.

'You don't ask for much,' she remarked, sounding subdued.

'I spent eleven years in a cell barely sixty feet square, with no furniture except for a bed, table and chair.'

After that first outing, her attitude towards him had changed in a way he couldn't quite put his finger on. It was as though with each day that went by, she undid another lace in the strict mental corset she'd forced herself to wear for so many years. The hard light in her eyes, once ever-present, had virtually vanished, with only the occasional faint glitter to remind him of it.

'Please forgive me for not having looked after you better, but I really couldn't,' she said. 'You've been an invaluable help over these last few months – in every way.'

'But I haven't done anything!' Indeed he felt now that he hadn't performed his secretarial duties at all, but had spent all his time walking and prospecting for his own purposes. He raised his arm and, in a gesture of helplessness, let it drop back on to the table. 'I haven't put together enough material yet for even the first volume of your husband's complete works – which is what you took me on to do – and there are going to be at least a dozen of them. No, I haven't done anything . . .' He tailed off.

She steered the wheelchair over to the table, glanced briefly at the sheets of paper black with Samuel Leber's handwriting and picked one up, running her eye idly over it. 'There's no urgency about it. You aren't planning to leave tomorrow, are you? Speaking for myself, the whole project doesn't seem anywhere near as important now.'

A shrug of the shoulders emphasized her lack of interest as she turned her back on the table, banishing the architect's *oeuvre* to a distant room in her past, now under lock and key, that she would never go into again.

On the evening of Christmas Eve something in the secretary that had long been slumbering started stirring, something both violent and gentle that was suddenly coming back to life. Tanguy had cut down a fir tree in the forest, as he did every year, a superb specimen that Olga Grekova-Leber had had put up at the foot of the twin staircases in the main hall and then decorated herself with the help of Félicité and Virama. All the people connected with the fortress were there,

108

apart from Varlaam and two of the Tamils, who'd stayed with Sarachchandra. A starry cluster of candles lit a gathering of giant shadows, flickering against the tall white walls. She was sitting in the circle cast by the tree, her eyes huge and sparkling. She was wearing a low-cut off-the-shoulder dress and a few silvery spangles glittered on her bare skin. The vertical light cast by the flames made her sparkling skin seem wondrously soft. Sitting slightly away from the tree, he watched her intently, unable to tear his gaze away from that softness, from that naked flesh. Tanguy was staring at her too, and as he stood there in the shadow cast by the Chinese chest, he would sneak the occasional furtive glance at the secretary.

The Tamils were talking loudly and drinking beer, their incomprehensible conversations peppered with Sarachchandra's name, recurring again and again like an incantation. Even on this festive occasion they still looked stern and preoccupied. The chrome fittings on the wheelchair were gleaming, as she sat there with her hands on the rubber part of the wheels. He noticed some specks of dried mud on the wheel rims and on the bottom of the chair back. Flesh, earth, earth flesh – he saw the fact that the chair hadn't been cleaned as an unmistakable sign. He walked towards the tree, but stopped a few paces away from her. As he moved he set the flames flickering and they cast a tall shadow on the wall, like a leaning tower. She turned round slightly in her chair, then went back to gazing at the tree. Outside, the dogs had been disturbed by a fox or a wild boar and started barking – it was an appalling sound and the whole hall froze. The Tamils, petrified, stopped talking, clutching their beer glasses, and even the candle flames became as still as glass. I should never ever have come here, he thought. She's wrong, I shall leave tomorrow.

The next day, Christmas Day, came and he didn't leave. He set out early, in a drizzle hard enough to soak him through. He felt the need to walk, to give the inside of his head a good airing. Dragging his insomnia and his unsatisfied desires along after him, he walked in the direction of the kennels and the falcon house, without any particular aim in view. As he strode along the path he found himself walking in the fresh tyre tracks of the jeep. Then, cutting across country, he climbed up towards the forest, walked through a young fir plantation, and soon heard Tanguy's singsong voice.

Making no attempt to keep out of sight, he had a good look at what he was up to. He was wearing tall boots and walking backwards and forwards between a trailer attached to the back of the jeep and a series of prehistoric-looking granite feeding troughs scattered round the clearing. On each of these journeys he would lug a shiny black plastic bag humped on his back and tip its contents into the troughs, then break off for a moment or two and let out a wild grunting sound that reverberated right to the edge of the forest, where there was much toing and froing, a blur of startled animals milling around in the dank half-light. The wild boars would emerge warily from the woods and make for the troughs, their snouts raised to sniff the air. They would grunt too, but apprehensively, almost like an entreaty. Then one of them would recover its self-assurance, stir its ungainly grey body and lumber forward, followed by the others, all of them staring intently at Tanguy with their little eyes. The troughs were filled to overflowing with a yellowish swill, which he was busy stirring with a branch. When he returned to the trailer, the animals made a determined surge forward. One elderly boar got as far as the nearest trough and stopped the others getting to it. At one point Tanguy turned round suddenly when he was on his way back to the jeep and made as if to charge them, letting out a piercing yell. They panicked, barging into one another, and streamed back in disarray into the shadows – all except the old boar, which merely raised its head and went on guzzling away, its hideous little tail waving about. Tanguy burst out laughing and one of the hounds in the kennels started barking, a mournful sound, oddly filled with desperation, that turned into a wail. As he was heaving the last of the bags on to his shoulders the secretary moved out from beneath his fir tree, walked past

110

the falcon house and the kennels – a pair of rough wooden huts with corrugated iron roofs, their planks gaping apart – and went over to him.

He had no idea what he was going to say, though he had the feeling he wouldn't take kindly to being caught in the act of feeding the wild boar. Olga Grekova-Leber had told him that this wasn't now part of his job, but something he did off his own bat, and that none of the people living at the fortress – except Samuel Leber in the old days – would have dared disturb him while he was attending to the animals. He had some sort of secret and very close relationship with them that played a key part in his life, but no one knew exactly what it was. When the secretary left the woods to enter the forbidden territory of the clearing, he didn't ask himself what he was up to, but simply strode ahead, carried along by the conviction that this had to happen, that it was essential at this point that he should force an entry into Tanguy's secret world.

As he passed the jeep he glanced inside it. The rifle was lying on the front seat. He watched as Tanguy trudged with his heavy load towards the last of the troughs, emptied the bag's contents into it, then straightened up, gasping for breath. It was only then that he spotted the secretary. He didn't move, simply stood there waiting, blinking, his hair plastered to his skull by the drizzle.

'Come to give me a hand, have you, your eminence?' he said eventually.

'You're too late. I've finished now. But seeing as we're both of us here, I can offer you a return match.'

The secretary walked up to him as though he was going to shake his hand. The revolting brew overflowing from the troughs gave off a foul stench of offal and rotten vegetables. It started raining heavily. The wild boar were clustered together now, eating greedily. Their young were getting in their way, slipping in between their legs, but they took no notice of the two men.

'What sort of a return match, Tanguy?'

Tanguy hitched up his trousers, tightening the piece of string

111

he was using as a belt. His face remained expressionless, but this lack of expression hid a confused mixture of feelings, one of which quite clearly predominated – a sort of lust.

'I've been wanting to touch you for a long time now, your eminence. To grab hold of you with these hands of mine, covered in shit.'

Actually, as he held out his hands the secretary thought they looked amazingly clean, considering the work they'd just been doing, clean and tiny too, compared to the thickness of his arms. The palms were pink and plump, as if they belonged to an over-indulged child.

'Why not?' he said.

A surge of impatience suddenly shot through him, as though he was getting ready to break down the door leading into a bedroom where a man and woman were frantically copulating. Tanguy clenched his fists and let his arms drop to his sides.

'You see that drinking trough in front of the kennels? I suggest we have a little bout of wrestling, your eminence. The winner will be whichever of us manages to throw the other into the trough.'

The 'trough' was a hollowed-out tree trunk overflowing with gallons of blackish water and turning the ground all round it into a sea of mud. He didn't wait for a reply – it was a foregone conclusion – and they headed for the kennels. Tanguy remained serious, concentrating hard, just as he had during their first contest. When they got close to the trough, all five German pointers started yapping away, and kept it up throughout the fight.

It was soon over. Tanguy set the rules -- no fists or feet. Standing up to their ankles in mud, the two men sized each other up for a moment, then hurled themselves on each other. Tanguy uttered the same grunting sound as he had to the wild boar, then the rest of the fight took place to the accompaniment of the dogs' heart-rending howls, without either of the men making a sound. They grappled with one another, rolling over in the mud. The secretary forced Tanguy to topple over so that he was beneath him, but, showing greater strength and

112

energy than the secretary had expected, he managed to turn over, got up to a kneeling position and grabbed his opponent by the scruff of the neck, shoved his head under his arm and tightened his hold. But this turned out to be a miscalculation. The secretary got to his feet almost effortlessly, with Tanguy clinging to his neck, tossed him over his shoulder and hurled him to the ground. He lay there for a few moments, stunned, face down in the mud. The secretary made no attempt to grab hold of him, and during those interminable seconds there was no sound but the dogs barking and the fitful gurgling of the water trickling into the trough. Tanguy rolled on to his side and clung tightly to the secretary's legs, but couldn't manage to throw him off balance. The mud had even got into their mouths by this time.

'You're pretty strong, Tanguy, but I'm stronger than you, and what I'm going to do now is fling you into the trough.' With that he grabbed hold of him by his shirt and the seat of his trousers and lifted him up till he was holding him virtually at arm's length.

At one point during this manoeuvre Tanguy's flushed face was thrust up against his own. Tanguy drew back his head and in a last convulsive movement that could have sent the secretary crashing to the ground as well, he summoned up his last reserves of strength and butted it against his opponent's. But the secretary didn't let go and took a step towards the trough. Tanguy's shirt tore, the top half of his body toppled slowly forwards and he plunged in head first, his arms spreadeagled across the sides of the trough, which took him into its embrace like a coffin.

The secretary walked away without turning round and set off for the fortress, pursued by the pointers' frantic barking. He felt no satisfaction whatsoever at having defeated Tanguy. But as he was climbing back up towards the woods, leaving the wild boar clustered round the feeding troughs, one thought kept on turning over and over in his head: I promised myself I'd let Tanguy get the better of me, but I didn't. This thought and the way his heart was beating aroused considerable misgivings, but

113

excited him greatly too. His mouth was gritty with mud. He spat some of it out, but he didn't find its acrid taste repellent. With every step he took through the clearing he expected to feel a bullet in his back. The wound on his forehead was bleeding and the blood was getting mixed up with the mud. Shoot! Go on, shoot, will you! We're at war now, he said to himself.

He went back the way he'd come, and was soon standing under the same tree, but the man who'd paused here a little while ago was somehow different now. Before heading into the fir plantation he glanced back over his shoulder. Tanguy was standing in the water trough, stark naked except for his boots, sluicing himself down.

That evening, before the dinner to which everyone at the fortress had been invited, Olga Grekova-Leber joined her secretary in the library. She was wearing the same outfit as on Christmas Eve, an ankle-length black sheath dress that made you forget all about her disability. But he noticed that it showed signs of wear and he was touched by these visible marks of the passing of time. They didn't detract from her beauty, it was more that by making her seem vulnerable, they gave her an extra radiance. He had the feeling that she hadn't been to bed. Embarrassed, he fingered the gash on his forehead, but she didn't seem to notice it. Sitting on her lap was a gaily wrapped package. She held it out to him, without saying anything.

There were three books inside. He walked round the desk and sank into the chair, folding his arms and looking at her. Now he simply had to talk to her, but the words wouldn't come.

'They were in the library,' she said.

He shook his head, picked the three books up one by one, fanned them out on the desk.

'I know.'

'Don't think I'm being nosy,' she said in a rush. 'It's just that from now on I'd like everything to be completely clear between us.'

114

'Yes, of course . . .'

He broke off, breathing hard and still staring down at the covers of the three books. He was starting to feel oddly light-hearted, but he didn't let it show. He too yearned for total clarity, but he was even more attracted by the subtlety of chiaroscuro.

'I knew you hadn't given me your real name right from the start,' she said. 'But it doesn't matter in the least, your name . . .'

He interrupted her. 'No! It's true that I wrote these books. I wrote them a long, long time ago. I was mistaken at the time. I thought I'd put them behind me for good, but they're still there. I don't disown them – they're my corpses.'

She murmured a name, his name. He walked over to her and put his hands on her bare shoulders, both his thumbs pressing hard against her neck as though he wanted to strangle her. She lifted her face towards him. Her eyes were wide open and showed no trace of fear as he bent over her and plunged his whole being into their depths.

PART TWO

Flesh

1

Once a week Varlaam brought up a bundle of material from the press agency. Olga Grekova-Leber and the secretary went through the papers, then filed the cuttings in the metal cupboards. This took up two or three hours every day. They'd caught up with the backlog and the archive room now had a relatively well-ordered look about it, and you could get round it without difficulty. Its order was made up of the incurable lack of order in the world below as it got bogged down in contradictions and ineffectualness in every possible sphere. Their hands black with printing ink, they would plunge silently into these bloodstained swamps, and little by little the facts would take precedence over the words, reality would gain the upper hand over abstract theory. And so, slowly, what Samuel Leber had prophesied was coming to pass – the world was becoming totally figurative. Through working in the archives, as the 'natural history of evil' grew fatter and developed its own sinister set of themes, the secretary became aware that he too was waiting, that he was becoming part of the wait, and that the wait was becoming part of him. In the evening, when he was washing the earth's impurities off his hands, he would reflect that the role of printing was geared less to transmitting positive knowledge than to making men unrelentingly aware, as the centuries rolled by, of the wretchedness of the human condition, and of their helplessness when they tried to drag themselves out of the mire. Then he would push her out of the archive room into the snowy courtyard and both of them would drink in great gulps of ice-cold air.

The temperature dropped to minus 1 Fahrenheit. He would open both of the windows in his room and stand there stark naked in the purifying cold for as long as possible. He would think of the man trapped in the glacier, covered over by now with tons of snow, and after a few minutes he would cut himself off inside the cold as if he were in a blazing furnace. When he closed the window again, so numb he could hardly move, he would feel like a blade heated till it was white hot, then plunged into a bucket of water. Often, once the cold had got right into his bones, he would let out a long-drawn-out cry that would reverberate in the ravine and up to the crystalline sky, shooting out beyond his body like a licking tongue of flame. While he was standing there in front of the open window he would concentrate on a rocky spur festooned with icicles as long as swords, or on a lone larch clinging to the rock face, covered in frost. He would project himself into them so completely that he would lose his own identity until the scalding sensation of the cold became unendurable.

One morning, well before dawn, at that nebulous moment when night has absorbed all matter and anyone still awake is the very embodiment of solitude, his insomnia was broken by a sudden urge to see her. He went down into the darkened fortress and stood motionless outside the door to her rooms. He watched his hand reach for the handle and pull it down in slow motion. He wasn't thinking of anything at all. He longed to melt into the darkness, and the only physical signs of his continued existence were a dull throbbing in his groin where the artery was beating, and a hardening of his penis. The door wasn't locked and he went in, feeling his way through the hall to reach the bedroom. He could hear the hissing sound of her breathing now. Was she really asleep? He doubted it, but stayed on guard beside the bed, leaning back against the wall, watching over this recumbent effigy whose beloved profile was silhouetted against the pillow, like a snow-white mask. When a grey light started seeping through the curtains, he withdrew. Before leaving the room he turned round. She had just stirred in her sleep and though her eyelids were closed, he had the feeling she was watching him.

He let a few nights go by before repeating his experiment.

120

Once again he found the door open. After that he would come back at regular intervals. Often there would be every indication that she wasn't asleep. On one occasion she even opened her eyes, looking calmly at him through a veil of dreams before slipping wordlessly away, shutting the door of sleep behind her. His solitary wakefulness was over. He was watching over someone, and his insomnia was vindicated. One night something happened that he could never have foreseen: day followed on from night without the transitional phase of dawn, and he suddenly found himself standing in a slanting ray of white light at her bedside. He realized that he'd fallen asleep on his feet.

Some time after this she took him off to the suite of rooms where Samuel Leber had lived – they'd been left unused and locked up since his death – and showed him a brand-new set of cross-country skiing equipment. That afternoon he took a gun, strapped on a pair of skis for the first time for twenty years and, well wrapped up against the cold in the lynx coat, glided off across country, the powdery snow crunching beneath his skis.

After that first time he would set out every day for a few hours' skiing and became so proficient that he could tackle the roughest terrain. When there was no snow during the night he would return to the same tracks as the previous day and venture even further afield, so much so that often he wouldn't return to the fortress until long after dark. He'd use a torch strapped to his forehead to light his path, but his eyes would take very little time to get used to the darkness, which was never pitch black, and some animal instinct would prove to be a near-infallible guide. A little daylight would be trapped in the snow crystals, and even on the darkest nights phosphorence would radiate from the ground as he glided over its milky surface. Sometimes a lone wolf would break cover, racing away ahead of him, its ears laid flat against its head. With a bound it would head for the forest and slip between the trees like a shadow.

She said she'd like to see him skiing. One bitterly cold afternoon, when the sunshine was icily bright, he pushed

121

the wheelchair along the path that was regularly cleared by Tanguy, then tamped down with the Caterpillar. He left her at the top of a strip of pasture that plunged down in a single sweep to the cliff overlooking the ravine. Apart from a few boulders sticking up here and there, it was an expanse of newly fallen virgin snow. He launched himself on to the slope at an angle, aiming for the first bend in the path and crossing it in a single leap, then braked to a halt lower down, in a shower of powdery snow. She followed his progress with a pair of binoculars, muffled up in furs from head to foot. She signalled to him and he shot off head first down a slope that became steeper. Then as the snow was getting deep, he thrust the weight of his body backwards, glided between a pair of rocks and scoured out a few wide loops, with the cold sun full in his face. Just then, overlaid by the rasping sound of the skis and the whistling of the wind, he heard a voice calling his name, a voice from his childhood. He picked up speed, swooping straight at a boulder forming a natural ski jump ahead of him. He couldn't see anything beyond it but the sheer drop of the ravine, a blue gash where he was going to soar like an eagle. The voice was calling to him, the jump was getting closer and he couldn't see the far end of the pasture, which broke like a wave against the edge of the cliff. But it didn't bother him now. His feet were no longer touching the ground as the snow rushed away beneath his skis. He bent his knees, preparing, as he straightened up, to fling himself skywards – then all of a sudden a vision flashed through his mind. He saw the three books on the desk in the library and remembered what Fra Cosimo he said: 'You'll soon understand that though your pride makes you disown these books, because you consider them less than perfect, they're your only true reality.' He straightened up too abruptly, just missed the rock, toppled over on to his side and rolled over in the deep snow.

When he came to, he felt as if he'd gone on falling for hours. He pulled on the straps of his bindings, heaved the skis towards him – both of them had been yanked off on impact – got to his feet, then turned to face the top of the slope. She was watching him through the binoculars. He took a step forward and sank into the snow up to his hip. He supported himself on his other leg, but that sank in too. He stretched out on his side, took ages to get his skis on and thought that up there in her wheelchair she must be getting bored. When he eventually managed to get to his feet, he realized he was only a few yards from the edge of the cliff. He returned to the path and set off between twin banks of snow.

'I was terribly afraid for you,' she said when he got back to her. But her face didn't betray any sign of anxiety, and the though flashed through his mind that she would have been quite capable of looking on dispassionately as he flung himself over the edge of the ravine. She was smoking – and had clearly smoked a great deal, judging by the number of cigarette ends strewn about on the snow round the wheelchair – but this heavy smoking didn't necessarily mean that she'd been worried. He undid his skis, stuck them into a bank of snow and sat down beside her to get his breath back.

'Did you call out to me while I was skiing down?' he asked.

She gave him an odd look, bit her lips and didn't answer straight away.

'When I saw you were getting dangerously close to the edge of the cliff, I called out to you inside my head. Anyway, you were too far away, you wouldn't have heard.'

Neither of them said anything for a moment or two. The snow on his hair was melting and trickling down the back of his neck. The sun was going down now and they were already in the shade. His chest was covered in ice-cold sweat and felt as if it had a damp cloth wrapped round it. It had been stupid of him to make a huge effort to do something he hadn't yet had enough practice at. She placed a gloved hand on his shoulder.

'I think you had that fall because of me,' she said. 'I'd like to see you go down again.'

He thought he must have misheard, but stood up all the

123

same. She was looking straight at him, smiling innocently. 'Only I don't want to see you fall this time.'

He took a deep breath.

'You'll get cold waiting for me.'

'Oh, no! I'm not a bit cold,' she insisted. The innocent smile was still there.

He felt a muscle spasm in his chest and had difficulty swallowing. The shadow of death was swarming into the ravine and creeping up the mountainside. He grabbed hold of the skis and strapped them on. He had a good look at the expanse of snow so that he could pick a different route down – the idea of skiing in his own tracks suddenly seemed repellent. Then, without saying a word, he shot off down the blue slope. It was growing harder as it froze over and crunched beneath his skis. She settled herself comfortably in the wheelchair, adjusted her fur hat and picked up the binoculars.

Tanguy drove along the path to the heliport three times in both directions to tamp down the snow, and when he brought the Caterpillar to a stop he'd made a passageway that was as wide as an avenue. Not a speck of ground in the near vicinity of the fortress had escaped his skilful ministrations. The Caterpillar was brand new and a garish yellow. It was on the go all day, and he was no doubt planning to tamp down the whole estate. Once a week he would set off to feed the animals on the edge of the land attached to the fortress. He would stow the large plastic bags in the back of the driver's cab and disappear for a couple of days. As he did every year when a shoot was in the offing, he was giving them double rations, to fatten them up and make them slow on their feet. The Caterpillar went into service again to mark out the main beats for anyone taking part in the shoot who didn't fancy venturing into the thick of the forest. Since their most recent trial of strength Tanguy's attitude to the secretary had been one of obsequious servility – which he found a great deal more alarming than open hostility. They met on the path to the heliport, the secretary on skis, Tanguy at the wheel of the Caterpillar.

'Have a good run, your eminence, God speed!' he bellowed when they passed one another. 'The cop'll be here tomorrow. Your humble servant!' With that he spat into the snow.

That same evening she told him about the man Tanguy had called 'the cop' – public prosecutor Alexis Muller, a close friend of Samuel Leber. But when he wanted to know why he was coming to the fortress, she was unforthcoming.

'Alexis comes to see me once or twice a year, in memory of Samuel. He was a great help after the accident.'

From her tone of voice when she spoke that last sentence, he realized that it meant exactly the opposite. It was quite clear that Muller hadn't helped her – he'd tormented her. And as so often happens, there comes a time when you can't do without the people who torment you.

The next day, as Tanguy wasn't there, she asked him to push her to the heliport to welcome Muller. She rejected the idea of using the jeep, but gave no explanation. It was a bright day and their breath created powerful jets of steam. The path Tanguy had tamped down was frozen over and he had no trouble pushing the wheelchair along it, jolting over the corrugated patterns created by the Caterpillar tyres. Above them, the fir branches bobbed down beneath their snowy burden, and every so often a shower of powdery snow would come cascading down. The helicopter landed shortly after they got there. She bent her head and pressed her hands against her ears. She stayed like that till the engine stopped running, her face puckered like a withered apple.

The short, gaunt figure who appeared when Varlaam opened the door must have been about sixty. The fur hat he was wearing made his head seem disproportionately large for his slight body, so that they didn't seem to fit together. Although he was wearing thick-lensed glasses, the secretary's attention was immediately caught by his eyes – they were grey, slightly protuberant and had an intent look about them. As soon as Muller had climbed out of the helicopter he turned them first on Olga Grekova-Leber, and then, more searchingly, on him. Although Muller was some way away, he spotted something

125

odd in his gaze – the left eye was full of life, while the right seemed dead.

A rapid comment came from the wheelchair: 'I'll have lunch with him. Afterwards he's bound to want to meet you.'

Muller came over to them, moving rather stiffly. Varlaam pulled a suitcase out of the hold, large enough for a stay of several weeks. There was something official about this arrival of a public prosecutor: the atmosphere was somewhat strained and both guest and hostess seemed embarrassed. When he bowed to her, he held himself stiffly. Yet it was quite obvious that they knew one another well, very well in fact.

'So we're back together again, Mrs Leber. Thank you for having me to stay.' His voice was piercing and he spoke with unusual warmth. It was obvious from the way Varlaam picked up the case that in spite of its size it was virtually empty. She pretended to brush away an insect.

'I call you Alexis, do stop calling me Mrs Leber. We've known one another for ten years now.'

'Yes, but you're a star, and I'm nothing but a humble lawyer.'

There wasn't a hint of irony in his reply and he seemed to be a genuine admirer of hers, though this didn't mean she was immune from criticism.

'I'm nothing at all nowadays. But I presume – I've always presumed – that you insist on being formal so that you can keep enough distance between us to be able to exercise your judgement freely.'

She suddenly seemed to remember that she had a secretary and introduced him. Muller studied him gravely, with the same intent look as before, bending his head slightly to peer over his glasses. But behind the seriousness, the secretary was intrigued to catch a glimpse of friendliness and fellow-feeling.

'I knew Mrs Leber had taken someone on – I'm glad it's you.'

The allusion underlying this comment mystified him and the thought that Muller knew who he was left him feeling distinctly uneasy and worried. But perhaps he'd got him mixed up with

126

someone else? They set off for the fortress. Muller kept on pulling up his scarf, which made him seem like one of those elderly bachelors perpetually worrying about draughts. He was taking cautious little steps on the slippery snow, without moving his shoulders and arms, as though the whole of his middle was tightly encased in a corset.

Then Olga Grekova-Leber suddenly leapt in with a blunt: 'So you haven't given up? You're going on with your investigation – if you can can call it an investigation?'

He dug his hands thoughtfully into the pockets of his overcoat. His forehead crinkled into a thousand fine wrinkles and the whole of his very expressive face took on a gloomily introspective look.

'Indeed I am,' he said after a while. 'What would I do with myself if there were no more truths to be revealed?' He suddenly shot her such a sharp look that even his dead eye lit up. 'You don't need me to tell you that the situation's going from bad to worse – most countries have taken emergency measures and I'm afraid it won't be long now before Samuel's prophecies are fulfilled. The war may not happen exactly as he predicted, though – fate still has a few tricks up its sleeve . . .'

'That's just it!' she cut in. 'What's the significance of the truth you're looking for here, compared with the catastrophe that's about to overtake us? How on earth can you waste your time on these trifling matters at such a fateful time?'

A tolerant smile hovered over Muller's face, giving it a mistily mellow look. The bottom half of his lenses misted over.

'What do you think?' The question was addressed to the secretary, though he wasn't looking at him. 'Can truth be measured? Do we judge its worth by the repercussions it has, or does it represent an absolute? Is a major truth truer than a minor truth?'

The figure in the wheelchair grew tense, banging her fist on the arm.

'You're playing tricks, Alexis. Some things are important

127

and others are less so, and that's all there is to it. It makes sense to deal with the important ones. You've been coming up to the fortress four or five times a year for the last seven years now and you don't do anything when you get here. You used up all the questions you could possibly put to me long ago. We just chatter on about nothing in particular now, and you spend a couple of days roaming round the house and then go back down. I've never refused to have you staying here and I've stopped asking why you want to come. Let's just say that I find it entertaining to watch you trying to find out the truth about a lifebelt that's gone missing on board a sinking ship. But I'm getting tired of it. Why have you come here today?'

He drew his scarf more tightly round his neck and clasped his hands sanctimoniously together. He seemed well pleased and sure of himself. A lump of snow large enough to send him sprawling to the ground fell right in front of him, but he took no notice.

'For the usual reason. Though there is a little something extra this time. There's a lot of talk about this refugee from Sri Lanka. There's even a rumour going round that he's dead, that you've got rid of him.'

She quivered with indignation. They went through the postern gate. Félicité had been scattering breadcrumbs round the courtyard and there were jackdaws busy pecking at them, perched on the snow like typographic symbols on a blank page.

'It's all lies. The man's perfectly well,' she said, speaking as calmly as she could manage. Then, turning to the secretary: 'You tell him.'

The wheelchair swerved slightly, hitting Muller in the thigh, and he very nearly fell. The snow was melting on the flagstones and although she weighed so little, the wheels were sinking in.

'I haven't seen Mr Sarachchandra for several weeks, but we do know that he's in excellent health. His compatriots have taken charge of getting food and other supplies to him.

128

Apparently they've built a hut at the entrance to the cave he's decided to live in. He's a brahmin and he's quite simply withdrawn from the world to live the life of a hermit. He spends his time praying and meditating, as all those who renounce the world do.'

Muller kept on shaking his head, but he wasn't listening – he was following his own train of thought. He suddenly stopped dead in the middle of the courtyard, as though he'd just remembered some crucial detail.

'Come on now, Alexis, don't worry about Sarachchandra,' she said. 'If you feel like it, Varlaam will take you to White Cow Hole tomorrow.'

The sky was getting progressively darker. It was still only halfway through the morning and the light was already like twilight, dull and lifeless. The fortress was starting to stick up like an old stump of tooth from its snowy gums and the oppressive atmosphere of Sunday afternoon in winter hung over the forest.

Eventually Muller asked: 'Where's Tanguy? We haven't seen him yet – it's usually him who pushes you.'

His dead eye seemed deader than ever and the other eye roved fruitlessly over the courtyard and the façades of the buildings, as though Tanguy might be hiding there. She bit back a smile.

'He's left,' she lied.

Muller was racked by a fit of coughing. His glasses fell into the snow and he picked them up with a shaking hand, putting them back on without dusting the snow off. Then he pulled himself together, starting to look distinctly weary.

'Where's he gone?'

'I was joking. But I can see you'd be very put out if he did leave.'

Muller must have been relieved, but no trace of it showed on his face. It wasn't so much a case of self-control as that he was delving deep within himself, into the dark waters of his anxieties.

'I probably should,' he admitted, smiling. 'Tanguy's a key

129

aspect of the truth.' Then he turned to the secretary and gave him an amazingly friendly look through his snow-spattered glasses. 'Do forgive me – it's very ill-mannered of us to talk in riddles in front of you, about things you clearly know nothing about.'

'Quite right too! Let's go in, I'm starting to feel cold,' she said. 'You know full well, my dear Alexis, that my legs could freeze without my being aware of it. Then gangrene would set in and they'd have to cut them off, and that really would be pretty upsetting, I can tell you.'

When they got near the front steps the jackdaws flew off and perched on the chimneys. The grey light took on a yellowish tinge. Long icicles were dangling from the gutters – they were yellow too – and the rough-rendering on the fake façades had cracked in the frost, allowing glimpses beneath it of the fortress as it really was – the prestressed concrete invented by Samuel Leber. The secretary pushed the wheelchair as far as the dining room, feeling as if he was pushing Muller along too, since he seemed to be so bowed down beneath the weight of his immense responsibilities.

As he was going into the kitchen he passed Tanguy slipping furtively away, clutching under his arm a newspaper bundle containing his lunch.

'So you saw the cop, did you?' he sniggered. 'He's out to get me, but I'll make sure he doesn't! I bow before you, your eminence!'

He walked over to sit in front of the hearth, where there was a roaring fire. While Félicité was getting his meal ready he watched the flames, which were burning so fiercely, licking upwards so frantically that they illustrated another facet of immobility. As he ate he watched Félicité polishing her kitchen range, her pipe clenched in the side of her mouth. Above the fireplace were the fossils he'd dug out of the quarry, arranged in a row on the joist of the canopy. Every day now she would perform what was virtually a religious rite, climbing up on a pair of steps, dusting the fossils one at a time, then gazing at

130

them, bewildered but beaming with delight. If he happened to come in when she was in the middle of this ritual, picking up a fossil between thumb and index finger, removing the pipe from her mouth for once, then blowing gingerly on it, he would think of that well-known geologist whose guiding principle was that in all the predicates when we *see* a fossil, in fact it's the fossil that's seeing us. Félicité was holding up a sphenopteris dating back to the Devonian era to get a better look at it, and the whole of the vegetable kingdom from its earliest beginnings was gazing at Félicité.

He was just finishing his lunch when Muller appeared, asked for a glass of wine and sat down opposite him. He was acting like a regular visitor to the fortress, and a somewhat melancholy benevolence shone out of his every gesture and his every look, as though he was returning to the place where, in his unhappy past, his life had become bogged down in failure.

'I see you like having your meals in the kitchen, just as Samuel Leber used to during those last months of his life. Did you know that Félicité isn't her real name? Samuel gave it to her. Her real name is Esmeralda Capron. But it doesn't matter, does it? And yet . . . and yet, if you keep on not calling things and people by their real names, you end up not knowing where you live and you sink back into chaos. You can see what's happening all round us now.'

'I haven't been out of the fortress for seven months now. I've no wish to do so, and I can do something useful here.'

Muller wasn't asking him any questions, but there was something inquisitorial in the very reticence of this man who liked expressing himself in a series of hints and allusions.

'I understand. Take as much care of Mrs Leber as you did of Fra Cosimo at La Verna. Except that maybe you shouldn't be quite so conscientious. I know things were a bit awkward for you after his death. You were accused of . . .' – he paused – 'of negligence.'

He looked the prosecutor straight in his good eye. But although it was very sharp, he couldn't detect any hostility in it. Alexis Muller was hunting for the truth, and as he pursued this unlikely quest, he was taking all the lies of the world on his shoulders.

'You're very well informed.'

'Oh, dear me, yes! Throughout my career I've been very well informed, as you put it, and yet I've never once felt I'd got close to the truth. Being informed isn't the same thing as knowing, and factual reality isn't the same thing as the truth. You're a scientist by training, so you know that an object being observed changes according to the observer. In your case, I've made a stab at getting hold of some information. Your past is not my concern, but you're living at the fortress, in close contact with Mrs Leber, and that's what counts. Nowadays my whole attention is focused on the fortress, my field of inquiry is restricted to this microcosm full of dark corners. Since I can't accede to a wider sphere and deal comfortably in generalities, I have as it were taken the fortress as my specialist field. This does of course mean that I've admitted how powerless I am, but I haven't got many years left to me, and I'd like to feel that this last phase of my life will be illuminated by a ray of light, or even a tiny speck of light in the whole vast universe.'

He was bundled up in an anorak and sitting with his back to the fire, but he didn't seem to find the heat trying. He spoke with modesty, his hands spread out flat on the table in front of him, and his words were rooted in a past full of unfulfilled ambitions, but one that had been spared feelings of bitterness. He gave the impression of being a man who had his obsessions under control, who was possessed of indomitable stubbornness and an unusual degree of patience.

'But what are you trying to find out?' asked the secretary.

He didn't seem to hear the question. Lost in thought, he polished the lenses of his glasses on his scarf, glanced at Félicité, who was sitting quite close to them, as hieratic and stately as a mother goddess, then asked insistently: 'I'm going for a walk – would you like to come with me?'

It wasn't snowing properly, just a few scattered flakes floating about in a sky that was nearly blue. They walked across the

132

courtyard to the keep – Muller seemed to know the fortress inside out. They went out of the guardroom via the door leading to the parapet walk. It was covered with snow and as they walked along it they would sometimes find themselves sinking in to halfway up their thighs. Muller went first, leaning forward against the wind, and the secretary followed silently behind. He realized now where he was being taken. Between the crenellations, deep drifts were forming as the snow was driven by the wind against the inner wall of the parapet walk. The heaped-up snow was frozen and crunched beneath their feet. When they reached the foot of the tower, Muller stopped beside a machicolation to get his breath back, brushed the snow off it and peered down into the ravine.

'This Tamil business is a nuisance,' he said, as if to himself. 'With this very cold weather, if anything happened to that man the Sri Lankan government would be told about it right away. They might accuse us of not honouring our agreements to grant their people asylum and that would create difficulties on the diplomatic front. On the other hand we can't force him to come back to the fortress. He's responsible for his own actions. What do you think?'

His expression was so detached that it was very hard to believe he was seriously concerned about 'this Tamil business'. He bent down to have a good look at some small scratches in the snow, tracks of birds' claws, a few brief distinguishing marks fallen out of the sky, and some droppings that had already frozen hard.

'Are you concerned about what happens to Sarachchandra for diplomatic or humanitarian reasons?'

Muller started banging his hands together again. He pulled first one leg then the other out of their snowy mould so that he could reach the outer wall of the rampart, where the snowdrift sloped down.

'I know what you're thinking,' he said. 'What does the fate of one individual signify in a world teetering on the brink? Well, to my limited way of thinking, the individual has priority because I'm not in a position to be concerned with mankind as a whole. I'm interested in this man first and foremost because he lives at the fortress, so he's one ingredient in the mystery, in the same way as you are.'

'Is there a mystery?'

Muller screwed up his eyes mischievously behind his glasses and pulled up the hood of his anorak.

'There's always a mystery, anywhere, in anything. And getting at it doesn't mean destroying it by revealing it, but doing it justice. I'd like to walk on a bit further. Would you mind following me?'

They started struggling through the snow again, continuing along the parapet walk as far as the main bastion. In some places the snow was deep enough to reach up to the top of the crenellations, forming a broad shelf, and as they looked at it their gaze slid straight on uninterrupted towards the sheer drop of the ravine. Tanguy had dug a trench running from Olga Grekova–Leber's rooms to the watchtower housing the cable car, and some of the snow lying beside the main living quarters had been cleared, leaving a passageway that had already been half filled in with snow. Muller tried to open the watchtower door, but it was locked. Anyway, what might he have found on the other side that he didn't already know about? The bucket covered with ice, the cable car platform buried beneath a crust of fluffed-up snow, the cables iced up, and the apparatus left to its own devices in its concrete cage since the onset of winter. But he still went on standing outside the door for some time, without saying a word, and then, as though he was declaiming some sort of 'Open, sesame!' he absent-mindedly said the same three words over and over again: 'The decelerating mechanism, the decelerating mechanism . . .', finally turning to the secretary and looking him up and down from the depths of his hood. Shaking his head, he said once again: 'The decelerating mechanism – that's the key to it all.' He banged on the door several times with the palm of his hand, stooped down to have a look at some recent footprints in the snow – Tanguy's probably – and straightened up, suddenly looking utterly despondent, as though all the strength had drained out

134

of him. His head only came a few inches above the walls of snow on either side of the trench. He flung back his hood and stood on tiptoe to catch a glimpse of Olga Grekova-Leber's windows. Then a gleam returned to his good eye.

'After Samuel's death,' he said, 'the insurance company asked for an inquiry. They'd had to pay out a huge sum – his life was worth millions. The police were convinced the accident was caused by the decelerating mechanism failing. I came up here with a technician and he checked the cable car over with a fine toothcomb. It was working normally. Either someone had repaired it since the accident, or else . . .'

He raised his arms to heaven, then let them drop again and, drawing his scarf tightly round his neck, wrapped himself in silence. They retraced their steps. Muller was trying to walk in his own footprints, and at the same time, with each step he took he seemed to sink down into himself. When they got back to the keep, which was filled with the icy chill of a mortuary, the secretary said, shaking the snow off his boots: 'Tanguy was operating the cable car. D'you think . . . ?'

Muller looked up at him through his misted-up glasses and shook his head for some minutes:

'Not Tanguy, no, it's not as easy as that,' he said in a low voice. 'Nowhere near as easy . . .'

The helicopter slipped over on to its side in the icy air, stirring up clouds of snow above the fir trees, and Varlaam went on flying at low altitude, just above the treetops. Then the forest gave way to the plateau, a bleak and lifeless place dotted with scrub and bushes white with frost. Varlaam leaned over to look at the ground. The helicopter followed suit, dropped sharply down as though it was caught in an air pocket, then righted itself. Below them a pack of wolves were racing off in terror, searching without success for somewhere to hide. Varlaam let out a yell of triumph, flew down lower, chased them for a moment or two, then climbed up again. Further on they saw a lone she-bear lumbering along, her cub following along behind and capering about in the snow. Muller showed

135

no interest in what was happening down on the ground. He sat hunched in his seat, terrified, his glasses pushed up on his forehead so that he couldn't see. When they came within sight of White Cow Hole, the first thing they noticed was Tanguy's Caterpillar, the only splash of colour in a grey world. Varlaam brought the helicopter down beside it, on the landing area he'd tamped down.

The plateau looked like the steppe and for a few seconds they just sat there in the freezing cold that was seeping through the cockpit, stupefied by a sense of loneliness. To the secretary, who was surreptiously watching him, Muller now seemed the very picture of doubt and anxiety, so much so that he wondered how on earth his lungs were still managing to breathe in air and pump it out again. Then they roused themselves from their momentary stupor, clambered out of the helicopter and made for the swallow hole. The edge of the hole was crisscrossed with a maze of Caterpillar tracks and a wide white avenue stretched away over the plateau, dug so deep into the snow that odd bits of earth and rock were visible. But the Tamils had used shovels to clear a way through to the confused jumble of rocks and boulders round the swallow hole, right up to the entrance to the cave. Muller hesitated before setting off along the steep path dropping sharply down from the ridge to the first sugarloaf hillocks, then decided he had no choice but to follow the others. The complete silence was broken only by the dull echo of their footsteps crunching on the snow and the breathing of all three men. They were walking inside a cathedral fashioned from ice, its sharply etched decorative details festooning the vaulted roofs of the caves, and every now and then ringing down an openwork grille reaching right down to the ground, its bars translucent and milky white. As they climbed down the air became less cold and a gust of almost mild air rose up from the depths. Sarachchandra had selected one of the caves with a very high roof and it was probably one of the deepest too, so although the hut the Tamils had built was a respectable size, it looked no bigger than if it had been put together from children's building blocks. When they reached

136

it, Tanguy came out with Ramanuja, and stepped forward to meet them.

'This is a pretty impressive delegation, your eminence, I must say, but you're wasting your time – he doesn't want to see anyone. And especially not you, Mr Prosecutor.'

Muller shrugged. He pulled his glasses down on to the bridge of his nose so that he could have a good look at him over the top of them.

'You look in fine fettle, Tanguy. I see you're still as hefty as ever – and as friendly.'

A raw gust of wind careered down the sloping sides of the swallow hole. Instinctively the three men hunched their shoulders and bent over forwards. Inside the cave were sacks of potatoes and crates of frozen vegetables, half hidden beneath a tarpaulin. Tanguy turned on his heels and strode energetically up the slope. Then Ramanuja, who had meanwhile gone back into the hut, came over to them and told the secretary that his brother had agreed to a brief meeting with him.

As soon as he'd stepped into the hut and the door had shut behind him, the stifling, overheated atmosphere grabbed him by the throat. The hut was divided into two small rooms, the floor and walls of both of them covered with rugs. The heat given off by a wood stove created a Turkish bath atmosphere. Incense was burning on a charcoal pan and the air was so smoky he felt he could scarcely breathe. Ramanuja helped him take off his coat, his movements as gentle as a woman's, and with considerable ceremony invited him into the second room.

Sarachchandra was sitting with his legs crossed on a rug on the floor, surrounded by cushions. He tilted his head to indicate that his visitor should sit down beside him and they sat there for some time in silence. By now the secretary was better able to take in the fact that he had nothing specific to say to him, except to express his approval of what he was doing. He gradually started to breathe more easily, the heat began to seem bearable and he experienced a mild feeling of well-being. He thought that he'd be very happy to stay there, in silent communion with this man whose serene composure filled the

137

little house with benign vibrations. Eventually Sarachchandra started speaking in his impeccable French, his voice gentle and well modulated: 'I know you've travelled a great deal and that you've made several visits to my country. I shall never see it again, so I'd like to hear you talk about it.'

He hadn't been expecting this and didn't remember having told anyone about the travelling he'd done, except possibly Olga Grekova-Leber. He was momentarily taken aback, then summoned up what he could remember of his most recent trip to Sri Lanka, and started talking about it rather clumsily. It had been fifteen odd years ago and his memory of it was somewhat hazy. But gradually, as one digression led to another, the past rose up from oblivion; he recreated it as he told his tale, but it was as if he was talking about someone else's experiences. Sarachchandra didn't say anything, merely listening with a look of quiet contentment, swaying his head slowly from left to right as though he was nodding in time to some inner music, then, still swaying, he shut his eyes and kept them closed. He was smiling, his hands resting palm upwards on his bare calves. Ramanuja came up to the secretary and whispered in his ear, speaking in pidgin English:

'He will never see his country again and all of us also not, sir.'

The interview was over. Ramanuja was very attentive, helping their visitor to his feet. Before he left the room the secretary turned to look at Sarachchandra, who was still nodding his head and seemed very far away now. When he walked out of the hut, feeling slightly giddy, a blizzard was sweeping into the swallow hole, making a noise like a roaring furnace. Varlaam and Muller were stamping their feet outside the cave, trying to keep warm, and said pointedly that he'd stayed nearly an hour with the brahmin.

They went straight back to the fortress, though Varlaam had hoped to stop on the edge of the forest. He'd put some traps down and wanted to recover any game caught in them. (So it isn't Tanguy who uses that method, thought the secretary, very surprised.) But the wind was blowing too hard and he gave up the idea of landing there. Muller, looking peevish and annoyed, didn't say a word during the flight back. Varlaam landed in the courtyard and before they'd had a chance to clamber down Olga Grekova-Leber appeared at the top of the steps.

'Well then – is he alive or isn't he?' she called out to Muller as soon as he'd set foot in the courtyard. It was starting to snow and the flakes were rolling over their clothes like miniature marbles, close-textured and crystalline. The little figure stepping forward cautiously on the icy snow stopped suddenly, looking anxiously up at the sky.

'He's alive and well for the time being,' he said very quietly, drawing his scarf tighter.

2

Shortly after Alexis Muller's visit Varlaam flew up Morel, the engineer responsible for checking over the equipment below ground level. As he needed a good two days of methodical work to carry out routine checks and make sure the machines pulsing filtered air into the huge shelter were working properly, he would stop for a rest on the spot whenever he could find the time. Olga Grekova-Leber recommended that the secretary should go down with him. Morel had been Samuel Leber's trusted mentor and had acted as his technical advisor throughout the period when the shelter was being built. He didn't seem overjoyed at the prospect of taking someone with him, since it was bound to slow him down, but he agreed out of friendship for Leber's widow. The idea of at last being able to go down into this buried city appealed to the secretary – he had become so used to walking on top of it day after day that he often forgot it was there. But at the same time he found the thought of it off-putting. He eventually made up his mind to go after hearing the metaphor Morel used to describe Samuel Leber's design:

'Try to imagine that beneath our feet there are three ocean liners built inside the mountain, one of top of the other and each of them as big as the *Titanic*,' he said curtly, not sounding as if he felt any particular admiration for this great architectural feat, the only one of its kind in the world. 'Mr Leber's scheme was an extraordinary humanitarian act, but to my mind, apart from the technological feats it presupposes, it isn't up to much compared to the Gothic cathedrals.' His expression was surly and cagey. 'I mentioned ocean liners. If you prefer a more spiritual image, think of something fifteen times the size of the interior of Amiens Cathedral.'

The main entrance to the shelter was outside the fortress, in the forest. But Samuel Leber had arranged for it to be accessible from inside the fortress too, and they used this separate entrance – a huge metal-clad door hidden behind a tapestry in the library. It was operated electronically and opened on to a lock chamber equipped with another door of the same type. When they'd gone through it and it had swung to silently behind them the secretary momentarily panicked – he had no idea how to open the two doors, and if anything happened to Morel, he'd find himself locked in. Morel could see how uneasy he was and took him through the system for opening the doors from the inside. It was both sophisticated and straightforward, in that it enabled you to use a locking device to prevent anyone ever getting in from the outside if the fortress was under enemy attack. On the far side of the second door was a goods lift that took them down to the shelter's first storey.

'We've got light up to here,' said Morel. 'But I can't switch on at the mains for such a short visit, so we'll have to do our tour in the dark.'

He took a powerful torch out of a small attaché case. The lift came smoothly to a halt and the two men stepped out into a corridor plunging deep into the darkness and looking like an ordinary corridor in any modern hotel. There were rows of doors on either side of it, fronting ominously silent rooms, and when Morel ran the beam of his torch over a one-bedroomed flat equipped exactly like a run-of-the-mill council flat, the secretary had a presentiment that the disaster had already

140

happened, that everything up above had been burnt to a cinder, and the ashes were already cold. He felt like a child shut up in the cellar while the house is burning down. Instinctively he looked up at the low ceiling, which made the whole place feel oppressive – and saw Varlaam's helicopter climbing up one last time into the bright blue vault of the sky. Morel then launched into a long-winded explanation, but he didn't listen to it because his ears had vanished: all he had was eyes glued to the beam of the torch, which was now drawing them like a magnet along the corridor. At any moment he expected to see the blind cohorts of those who are about to die, coming forward to meet them.

He wasn't listening, but the key data did still get through to him: nearly two miles of corridors on each storey; 150 dwelling units for up to five people and one-room flats for single people; each section had its own generator powered by solar energy captured at ground level, and its own storeroom containing five years' worth of food rations; and so on. The words were plopping into the silence like bullets into sacks of sawdust and before long they were standing in front of double doors leading into Samuel Leber's private flat. Here, once the shelter was finished, his widow had consigned the priceless items from her late husband's collection to perpetual darkness. Morel fiddled about with the dozens of locks on this safe within a safe. When the door swung open, the secretary thought of the old cemetery down in the town where Leber's remains should never have been laid to rest – they belonged here, among the Renoirs, the Degas and the Klees, the Khmer statuettes, the Chinese bronzes and the T'ang horses. These wonders were fleetingly disinterred by the torch, then promptly flung back into the darkness.

By now Morel had retreated behind a stubborn silence that boded ill for the rest of their tour. As he trained the torch on the hygrometer to check the humidity level, the secretary was suddenly convinced – even though he never slept – that he was dreaming, and he drew back into the shadows so that he could immerse himself more thoroughly in the numbing

141

strangeness of his dream. And yet it was all very real – Morel's angular profile, the ritual vases from the Chou dynasty, and the paintings, their gilt frames occasionally throwing off reflections as the torch focused briefly on them, providing the sole flash of light against the dense blackness of the walls. It was all true, from the beginning of a man's life to its end, true in a way that Alexis Muller couldn't even dream of: the soul of man and its blurred facets, lit by an invisible source of light – imposture, cowardice, lies, displayed for all to see in the brilliance of a diamond. As the shadows became denser, so the truth of a soul shone more brilliantly in its dazzling imperfection, in its mud, right down to the deepest tunnel in the mine. God was so far away!

'It's essential that the humidity content in this room should never vary – we are in a museum after all,' Morel pointed out. The secretary drew back even further, stood still in the doorway and could feel the corridor behind him, like a river whose sluggish waters were as black as night. But Morel pinned him savagely to the wall with the beam of his torch and said in his surly tone: 'You deserve a medal for looking after Mrs Leber.'

They threaded their way along the corridor in the opposite direction, plunging head first into the hazy glimmer of the torch. The secretary turned round several times to peer into the bottomless night, checking that he was being followed. Yes, the unchanging presence buried beneath so much peat and grey wadding was moving forward behind him, quickening its pace to catch up with him, to become one with him in a loathsome embrace, just as a jellyfish, tossed by the breakers, is eventually stranded on the shore, a lifeless and viscous heap. Morel was walking ahead of him, taking no interest in anything that wasn't connected with his work and following a marked itinerary where even the obscure and gloomy depths of man were catalogued according to the physical laws of the universe. 'There's no question of deserving a medal. I've always looked after disabled people – starting with my mother,' he said, as though this subterranean trek had inspired him to summon up

142

memories of the dead. Morel turned round in surprise, but the torch beam was still trained on the ground and further on, far away in time and space, the wan light of the goods lift indicated the way out of the tomb – though it was sheer illusion to think you could ever get out.

'Oh, I see, your mother was disabled,' said Morel, though his tone suggested something quite different was preoccupying him. The secretary took a deep breath. So you could still breathe down here, with all this complex apparatus pulsing air into every last nook and cranny of this subterranean city, keeping it up without a pause, like pumping oxygen into a body long engulfed in the deadly sleep of coma.

'I was thirteen when she went down with polio. She couldn't breathe without an iron lung.' Their voices had a muffled ring because of the concrete, which smothered them as soon as they'd spoken, so that for a moment you weren't sure whether any words had actually been said. Morel was gazing down absently at the torch beam, looking shattered at a stroke of fate that was no real concern of his. 'How very sad,' he said, or words to that effect, then set off again. But the secretary grabbed him by the shoulder, moved up very close to him, so close he must have felt his breath on his cheek. 'That's not all,' he said in a whisper. 'One day she asked me to switch off the machine when she was asleep. I did as she asked.' As he spoke he was thinking: It's always been the same, I've always had death clinging on to my arm as I trudged along through life, savouring its heady female scent. We're so far from God down here. We aren't anywhere, not even enduring ordeal by suffering. We can say anything, knowing it won't have any repercussions, yet still nothing eases the pain.

This time Morel trained the torch on his face and gave him a suspicious look. 'You've got a peculiar idea of a joke, I must say. This place must be getting you down. Come on, I'm going to show you the food store for this section. There's a whole herd of animals in the freezer.'

They went on like this, inspecting several of the floors in systematic fashion. They all looked much the same. With every

143

hour that went by the secretary felt that a series of physical collapses was occurring, rather than time flowing by, slack and fluid, but he wouldn't allow himself to look at his watch. Every time they spent a few moments beneath the overhead light in the lift, the two men would surreptitiously study one another. Each decided that the other was inadequate, and unpredictable. It would have been hard to pinpoint whether this impression was caused by the enigmatic quality of any individual, or by their being cooped up together in the darkness. Yet as they plunged deeper into the mountain, they seemed to grow further and further apart, whereas you would have expected the opposite to happen in these circumstances.

'It's the first time anyone else has come with me on my tour of inspection,' Morel admitted. 'I think it's better if I'm on my own.' When they came to one of the dwelling units on one of the endless series of floors, they decided to take a few moments' break. They sat down at the kitchen table, which was covered with a sprinkling of fine concrete dust, keeping silent amidst the earsplitting hubbub of absolute silence. Eventually Morel asked, clearly embarrassed: 'Was it true what you said back there, about your mother?' The torch was lying on the table. Its oblique light shone up on them from below, turning their features into death masks.

'Absolutely true.'

There was a protracted silence, and all of a sudden the flat door swung on its hinges, making a creaking sound. Morel gave a start, trained the torch on it with an unsteady hand, then, with a sigh, put it back on the table.

'I know what you're thinking,' said the secretary calmly. 'You think I'm off my head, and you may be right. Just think that if some sort of accident were to prevent us from getting out of here, if we had to stay here, just the two of us, in this vast empty city of the dead, overflowing with everything we need to ensure our survival, it would only be a very short while before we'd start thinking about killing each other. Just picture it. After weeks of being alone, we'd be lying in wait round every bend in the corridors, clutching any improvised weapon we could lay our hands on, to bash each other's skull in. Yes, I'd quite definitely kill you and then kill myself. Or vice versa. It would be a fight in the dark, in total silence, a fight to the death inside a tomb.' He let a moment go by before continuing. Morel coughed and pushed back his chair, knocking the table. The torch fell off and went out. He got up and started fumbling around for it. The secretary could hear him combing the floor with his hand and cursing under his breath.

'When Samuel Leber built this shelter, he didn't think of everything, or perhaps he thought too highly of the human race,' he went on, speaking into total darkness. 'He didn't picture what would happen if thousands of people took refuge in here and were forced to live here for years on end – the same old scenarios would recur, the old warlike instinct would surface again, rival factions would be set up, with opposing ideologies; the various parties would split up into splinter groups, and in this circumscribed world, hatred would flourish like the green bay tree; with everyone at such close quarters, aggression would rapidly build up and violence would spread like wildfire . . .' He tailed off.

Morel had found the torch but couldn't get it to work. He banged into the corner of the table again and let out a groan of pain. 'I find your pessimism insufferable, and quite without foundation,' he protested, searching for his case, where he presumably carried a spare torch. The secretary made no attempt to help him. He was having trouble stifling an uncontrollable urge to laugh.

'Can't you see how ludicrous it is for you to be fumbling about trying to find a torch in this hi-tech place designed to save the human race?' he asked. He was looking straight ahead of him in the dark, at a concentric ring of light growing bigger all the time. This translucent disc, its edges fringed with blue and red, was slowly revolving on its own axis. He opened his eyes wide, aware that this spectrum of light wasn't in front of him but behind him, at the back of his eye sockets, set in a matrix of blood. The disc reminded him of a star, but also of the mouth of a well, and suddenly a feeling of immense relief flooded through him, a quiet elation such as can never be produced by any concrete phenomenon. Morel was maintaining a dignified silence as he bustled about. His dignity filled the darkness – but didn't give off any light. Then he knocked into the case and shouted out in relief. A few minutes later the light was back.

'We must get out of here,' he ordered. 'We've wasted too much time already.' And then they were back in the corridor.

The shelter's internal structure was like a ship's. The engine room was at the bottom, in the hold of the mountain, and when the lift came to a standstill after a journey down that seemed to go on for ever, the secretary tried to work out how far down the ravine they were now. He could hear a continuous humming sound, but wasn't sure if it was produced by the silence itself, by the various machines, or by the blood pumping through his veins. Then beneath the humming he could suddenly make out the sound of water, tenuous but insistent, like a fountain trickling away behind a padded door. Morel, apparently once again preoccupied chiefly by the job in hand, operated various cut-out switches and after the long trek through the darkness, a dazzlingly bright light beat down on a tangle of pipes, dials, turbines, huge ventilating pipes and other bits of equipment whose function was utterly mysterious to the uninitiated. A vista made up of gigantic load-bearing piers stretched out into the distance among the machinery, and in a recess near the goods lift, between two pipes small enough around to allow a tallish man to walk through without ducking, the secretary came across a pathetic-looking camp bed, a candle stuck in a bottle and a few boxes of matches.

Morel caught him looking at them and launched into a series of grumpy explanations, all about such matters as the size of the engine room, the number of engineers who'd spent four years working on it, the colossal cost of the whole operation, and so on. Then, as he clearly wasn't a man to bear grudges, or perhaps forgetting he'd already said it, he repeated his

146

remark about the shelter not of course being anything to write home about compared to the great Gothic cathedrals. Then they took a look at the control room, a huge raised cage equipped with dozens of screens. Many of them were used to check that the machines were working properly, and to keep an eye on the key points on the twelve floors of living accommodation. But some of them, the largest ones, had a very different function. Morel asked the secretary to sit in front of one of them and, with a cryptic smile, switched off the strip lighting. He fiddled with potentiometers on a console, and soon a picture appeared in the bright snowstorm on the screen. It was such an extraordinary picture that he didn't realize what it was at first. A rabbit. A small wild rabbit hopping about in the snow. Further away, a blackened tree trunk – an uprooted fir tree, half buried. Then the rabbit slipped out of range and the landscape changed. What now appeared on the screen, a very clear picture seen in close up, was scree made up of snow-topped rocks, and higher up, an embankment and a line where you could just make out a path. Then the whole ravine suddenly loomed up on the next screen, viewed from the same angle as when you were looking down into it from the ramparts, the forest on the shady side with its coating of frost and, seen through the opening of the gorge and its blocks of ice carved into fantastic shapes, the town and the plain.

Morel explained that Samuel Leber had felt it was important to be able to see what was going on in the world outside. Video cameras had been placed one above the other running the whole height of the cliff. The direction they were pointing in could be adjusted from the control room, and nothing could happen in the ravine without those watching from inside being aware of it. Morel brought the rabbit back on screen and followed it as it made a faltering attempt to find something to eat. Although it was so small and so vulnerable, it was displaying amazing energy, its vitality, seen at one remove, seeming commendable, yet at the same time of very little consequence. As the secretary watched, enthralled, nature

147

revealed the infinite subtleties of its tiniest details, its fleeting metamorphoses, its movement – fir tree branches bobbing down gently in the breeze blowing up from the ravine, and whipping up the occasional flurry of snow. But in the present circumstances, and in the case of the people doomed to live on down here, it was and always would be nothing more than a peepshow. At the press of a switch Morel wiped out these images from another world, then said, with sudden self-assurance: 'Now I'm going to show you the little door.'

They made their way to the far end of the engine room, passing between the pipes for the fans, the air-conditioning equipment, and the bulky, shapeless pieces of apparatus that act as anti-radiation filters. The 'little door' was there, between two colossal pillars. It was an iron door painted yellow, but you scarcely noticed it because it blended into the concrete and because it was so small it seemed to have been designed for dwarfs. Morel pulled a lever slowly down. There was a clicking sound but the door didn't open.

'Everything's as it should be,' he said, with a disarming smile. 'Can you hear it? Listen . . .'

The secretary now felt as if he was inside one of the piers of a bridge. Again he could hear the sound of running water, but this time it was as if a mountain stream was rushing down somewhere very close to them, behind a row of willows. An automatic time switch leapt into action and the door opened by itself. Behind it was yawning darkness. Two very different worlds met here. Their nostrils were filled with the acrid smell of the waters from the beginning of time that flow from one layer of the subsoil to another, endlessly being converted from water vapour into a liquid state and vice versa, and with the exhalations of the limestone, simultaneously moist and dry, being formed in perpetuity. Ticking away against the background noise of the subterranean river they could hear the clock of geological time, the drops that, dripping down over the millennia, fashion the endless variety of shapes within the matrix of the earth, where the world goes on being reborn day after day, outside human time. The vast cavity beyond it, lit

148

by floodlights, was filled with a light that was both misty and glaring. You could sense that the darkness, filled with the rushing sound of water, stretched well beyond the floodlight beams. Stalactites and stalagmites, palely bulging, glimmered like exposed human organs. The river, so transparent that it was invisible, was flowing over a chute of smooth stone between banks of calcareous concretions worn smooth by water dripping from the vault of the roof, sometimes bone white, sometimes flesh pink. The sound it made continued far away into the darkness of the gulley. They walked forward on wobbly planks, to a rock in the shape of a truncated geode overhanging the underground river and some stone madrepores.

'This river is derived from the one running through White Cow Hole,' said Morel, shivering. 'We don't know where it ends up – Mr Leber didn't want to send anyone off to search for it. We installed pumps upstream and they provide part of the shelter's water supply.' He told the story of how the cave had been discovered when the shelter was being dug out, how some of the engineers had wanted to use it and why Leber had been against the idea. Then they walked back along the slippery planks. The cold wasn't coming from the air – the temperature in the cave was higher than in the shelter. It was caused by the damp, and by the vast amount of time sealed up in here. When they were halfway through the return journey the secretary asked: 'What happens if the door shuts?'

He considered the question for a moment, as though such a possibility had never crossed his mind.

'It can't shut, there's a blocking mechanism. Don't worry, there's no danger whatsoever of our getting shut in the cave.' There was a touch of contempt in his tone.

'But just supposing it did?'

Morel stared at him haughtily, clearly irritated. 'There's no danger of that. I worked on the safety device on the locking mechanism myself.'

Once they were back on the right side of it, the little yellow door clanged shut behind them. Morel was now going to get

149

down to work properly in the engine room, snatching a few hours' sleep on that wretched little camp bed, then continuing his tour of inspection for what might be the last time – before the secretary stepped into the goods lift to go back up to ground level, he admitted that if there was a catastrophe, he wouldn't take refuge there himself, he'd go out and die in the open.

When the shelter was being built Samuel Leber had put him in charge of the technical side of the project – it had been an overwhelming assignment, which he'd carried out day after day, living permanently on site, spending virtually all his time underground, he told the secretary, the words suddenly tumbling out.

'For over ten years, a hundred and twenty-six months, to be precise, I hardly ever set foot outside here. I didn't think about anything except my work and its future repercussions. Mr Leber was constantly reminding me that the success of the whole enterprise rested largely on my shoulders, that he hadn't just entrusted me with responsibility for the whole project, but with the survival of several thousands of people. Even my dreams were full of mathematical formulae.'

When the secretary was back in the fortress it was almost dark. A few stars were already flickering in a turquoise sky and an arctic light was shining on the snow. He went out on to the bastion and gazed at the forest. The hours below ground had left his mind feeling drained. He still had the dry taste of the concrete in his mouth and his heart was filled with utter loathing of himself and of everything. He had no wish to meet Olga Grekova-Leber, so he went down to the kitchen, opened a bottle of wine and settled down in front of the fire. Later on, when he'd drunk a second bottle, he felt an urge to get some fresh air and went to fetch a gun, strapped on his skis and glided away from the fortress into the frozen night. He decided to pause for a while in a clearing, stretched out full-length in the snow and looked up at the Milky Way. A deep breath dilated the vault of heaven. He felt at home here,

150

there was always a place for him, at any time, in the freedom of unalloyed solitude.

3

Barks and the occasional shot rang out in the forest, not far from where the Caterpillar was driving along a ride. It was barely light and it had started snowing again.

'What fools they are, they've already started shooting!' she said. 'They'll go on like that all day, shooting at anything that moves.'

The previous day the Tamil beaters and Tanguy had spotted three stags and some roe deer. The men taking part in the shoot were sticking to a relatively limited area – walking with special snowshoes turned out to be exhausting, and often quite impossible because the snow was so thick. None of the people on the Leber Foundation board was a genuine sportsman, none of them showed any enthusiasm for the shoot or enjoyed trudging around for hours in the snow and the cold. 'They're always gloomy until some blood's been let,' she said. 'But once they've shot their first quarry, their adrenalin starts flowing. The ones who haven't killed anything don't want to get left behind – in the end their greed will out, one way or another.'

As the secretary had turned down the idea of taking part in the beat, she'd asked him to take her to the shooting lodge, a ramshackle mock-Gothic building that was left abandoned the rest of the year. Tanguy had taught him to handle the Caterpillar in his own inimitable fashion, by taking him out for hours on end over the most bumpy terrain, without once opening his mouth or deigning so much as to glance at him. On several occasions the contraption very nearly overturned, but Tanguy handled it with extraordinary dexterity. When they got back, he drew up outside the dovecote he'd converted into quarters for himself and disappeared into his lair without uttering a word. 'He's livid that you're not joining in the shoot,' she told him over dinner. 'And he's jealous at the thought of your spending the day with me while he's paddling around in the snow with their lordships.'

'Their lordships' had arrived at the fortress the night before – eleven businessmen, who were no doubt very different types of people, but they merged together by virtue of their single function, crouched over their financial speculations. Varlaam had deposited them in the courtyard in two batches. The bitter cold had driven them across the icy snow to the entrance steps, where the mistress of the house received them like an empress receiving her vassals, polite but condescending. The secretary watched the twin arrivals from his window – the same absurd ceremonial, the same clumsy gestures, beneath a sky with low cloud cover but holding back its snow. This sudden visitation from the world below seemed to him like a skit. It was already dark and the courtyard, so brightly lit it seemed to be daytime, looked like a skating rink where a virtuoso ice-skating exhibition was about to take place. When the second group disembarked from the helicopter and the men set off for the steps one at a time, thrown off balance by the cold, he was overwhelmed by a feeling of deadly boredom, and all he wanted to do was shut himself up in his room and not stir from there. Before they came she'd begged him to attend the sessions. 'You're under no obligation, but it would be a great relief to me if you did. Don't say anything, just watch and listen. I'll feel calmer if you're there.'

The following day the Leber Foundation's annual board meeting lasted for twelve hours or so, with hardly a break. The agenda was impressive. He sat there in silence, listening. The higher the stakes, the more difficult it was to see why they were so high – it all seemed to sink to the level of a tedious charade. And when one of 'their lordships' allowed himself to be carried away by passion, anger or indignation, you simply couldn't believe his emotion was genuine. There were several outbursts of this type, though. During one of them, she leaned towards him and said in a whisper: 'If he doesn't manage to persuade us to invest in this venture, he'll lose a few million in commission.' After sitting through the meeting, there was one

152

obvious fact that stuck in his mind: as the sense of insecurity and the threat of war grew, so the Leber Foundation's earning capacity increased. There was nothing particularly unexpected about this, and no one seemed surprised. If the catastrophe they were all expecting did actually occur, the Foundation would earn even more money, because the shelters it was designing and building all over the world were bound to spawn an increasing number of requirements – they would need to be maintained, extended, made more complex, and during the survival period, however long it lasted, the number of practical needs would go on increasing, as they had in the past. Thus after a day of bitter debate, it became clear that from now on the Leber Foundation's chief objective would be 'survival management'. Shortly after the meeting had ended, when they'd all retired to their rooms, Olga Grekova-Leber joined her secretary in the library. She was clearly exhausted. 'I'm not interested in it any more,' she confessed. 'There wasn't a single moment during the proceedings when I felt really interested. I think there's only one thing I want to do now – our expeditions together.'

Although you couldn't really call them expeditions at the moment, they could think of them in those terms as they sat squashed up close in the narrow cabin of the Caterpillar. He turned into a narrower path. The mist thinned a bit, a few tangible shapes appeared and soon they could see the shooting lodge, in what had been a clearing but was now overgrown. It looked pretty gloomy with its swollen mounds of snow collapsing off the roof and forming great heaps that came right up to the windows. Although there were a few signs of life – a couple of shovels, a pair of skis stuck into the snow just outside the door, a trench dug right round the building – they didn't take away from the impression it gave off of being no longer in use. She pulled a face as she looked at it. 'Ghastly, isn't it? It isn't so bad inside. There's a big fireplace and a stove that gives out plenty of heat.' He left her in the Caterpillar and went inside, into a room adorned with endless rows of animals' heads – threadbare boars' heads covered with

153

cobwebs, stags, brockets with their first horns, roe deer with a greenish tinge in their eyes, their muzzles covered with dust and mildew. Beside the most impressive of these beasts were brass plates, blackened with age and engraved with the names of their executioners, dead too now, these many decades. The fireplace was so tall and went back so far that several men could fit easily inside it, and on the canopy above it a pair of eagles were poised to swoop on their prey, their crops torn, allowing tufts of old straw to spill out. Arranged in a horseshoe in front of them were leather sofas stained with mildew. In the middle of the room a rustic table that had clearly seen off quite a few generations seemed to be waiting for some ogres' banquet. On either side of the fireplace were piles of logs and kindling reaching right up to the ceiling. He also discovered a pantry with a stone sink – judging by the blackish lumps still sticking to it, it was used for the last rites of cutting up the bag from the shoot – a butcher's block covered with a sheet of oilcloth, and cases of wine and spirits for the evening. He lit a big fire, filled the stove with logs and went to fetch her.

'Tanguy hasn't aired it,' she observed as soon as they were through the door. He put her down on one of the sofas, as close to the fire as possible, slipped a cushion under her feet and put another log on the fire. It didn't take long before the walls were covered with patches of damp and the windows had steamed up. A stale smell of mildew and bird droppings hung in the air as it warmed up. It was still early. The others wouldn't leave the shoot for a bite to eat till midday. They might not come at all if they hadn't managed to shoot anything, and he wondered why she'd been in such a hurry to get here. The chimney was cold and wasn't drawing properly. He had to prop the door half open, but soon the smell of the fire gained the upper hand and in spite of the smoke, they now felt they could breathe.

She took off her fur hat, leaned her head against the leather back of the sofa and stared into space. He had the feeling she was expecting him to do something. More shots rang out, quite close to the lodge, and the pointers' excited barking started up again.

154

'We've never had it so cold or had so much snow during a shoot,' she said. 'They've only got what they deserve, though. They're wild beasts themselves.' There was a short silence, punctuated by the crackling of the logs. He walked over and sat beside her, but she didn't seem to notice. 'Yes, they're wild beasts,' she went on, 'every single one of them has betrayed Samuel's ideal by setting up various fiddles and rackets to line their own pockets. In fact they're all terrifyingly good shots, but only when they can operate on terrain undercover, in a murky half-light. Just once a year I want them to stalk out in the open, to kill in full daylight and reveal just how clumsy they are. This shoot is a way of humiliating them – I put a gun in their hands and humiliate them.

'Samuel was someone who couldn't see further than the end of his nose when it came to judging people, and he let himself be swindled and exploited by them. He'd invite them on a shoot, convinced he was doing them a favour, but in fact they've always loathed the shoot. I realized that right away, which is why I've kept up the tradition. They're rotten shots. They've been coming here for a shoot in the forest for the last twelve years and they're still rotten shots. They don't understand the first thing about this type of quarry. The shoot will go on for a couple of days. Over those two days they'll walk and stalk their quarry in the cold and the snow, and tomorrow night, since I don't want them under my roof, they'll sleep here, huddled up together on these clapped-out sofas, after drinking themselves into a stupor to keep the cold out. They're men, they've each got a wife and various mistresses – even the oldest of them has got a string of mistresses. Tanguy'll keep an eye on them . . .' She broke off and turned to face him, smiling, her eyes shining, then suddenly became less communicative. 'I've got something I must ask you, but I'm too much of a coward . . . Pour me a glass of vodka. You'll find everything in the room next door.'

He brought her her drink and helped her take off her coat. The chimney had warmed up now, the fireplace had stopped smoking and the stove was giving off a life-giving heat that

155

warmed their backs. Although she still said nothing, he could guess now what it was she was expecting of him, and it fitted in with his own most burning desires. She quickly drained her glass. He came back to sit beside her and had a drink himself, looking at her. She let herself be looked at, turning so that he could gaze at her profile. Its sharp line slackened below the chin, becoming touchingly soft and flabby. Then she turned to face him, and it was her turn to scrutinize him, running her eyes in amazement over his forehead and lips, like a blind person's fingers.

'I'd like you to kneel down in front of me,' she said, speaking very clearly. He took off the lynx coat and did as she asked. 'Now lift up my skirt. I want to know if my legs repel you.' Nothing about you repels me, he thought, but he remained silent. He pushed her thick wool skirt up to her knees, uncovering her wasted legs. 'Higher!' It was a command. As he was hesitating, she suddenly jerked it up as far as the waist herself. He laid his hands on her thighs, let them slide as far as the groin. His loins were on fire, urging him to move in closer, till the top half of his body was half lying on her legs. First his hands touched her, then his lips. He breathed into the fragrant wool of her tights, his nostrils filling with her female smell. Nuzzling his head between thighs that felt as hard as wood, he seized her beneath the buttocks, then moved up to her waist. He was very aware of every movement he made, and amazed that after such a long period of chastity, the gestures still came so easily. When he slid his fingers between her tights and her skin, his mouth still clamped to her, she said in a whisper, so quietly he wasn't sure he'd heard properly: 'So I can still feel.' But straight after that she pushed him away, and when he was back on his knees, she took his face between her hands. For just a second, the disabled woman he knew and the woman he was discovering appeared as two quite distinct entities and he toppled backwards in astonishment. The pressure of her cold palms on his cheeks grew more insistent. Olga Grekova-Leber drew her secretary's face towards her. 'I've got another favour to ask,' she said. 'I'd like you to wipe the table. Yes, that big table.'

The snow was heaped up on the window frames. The sun, shining out of a dazzlingly bright sky, seemed very close. He found a cloth in the pantry. It was stiff with dirt, but he managed to wipe off the dust and bits of fallen plaster from the ceiling. It was a huge, solid table, probably once used for cutting up carcasses, judging by the knife marks on the top. She poured herself another drink. He could hear the neck of the bottle clinking against the glass, which she once again downed in a single gulp. A fleecy light flooded the dark wooden surface of the table. Every object in the room seemed to be waiting for some event that was slow in coming. He wiped the condensation off one of the window panes so he could look out. But he couldn't see anything except the shadow of the Caterpillar, looking oddly far away, and the skis thrusting up like twin blades into the insubstantial texture of the daylight. He filled the stove right to the top with small bits of wood and returned to the fireplace. The dogs were barking furiously and he even thought he could hear shouts. Then he picked her up, carried her to the table and laid her down on it.

Her eyes huge, she stared up at the ceiling, breathing heavily. When he lifted the lower half of her body so that he could take off her tights, she raised herself up on her elbows and looked down incredulously at her bare thighs, the dark tuft of pubic hair and her emaciated legs lying disjointedly on the wooden surface like a pair of amputated limbs. 'What are you doing?' she asked. 'You're crazy . . .' But she did nothing to stop him. He pulled her towards him until the lower part of her back was right on the edge of the table, caught hold of her legs below the knees, opened them like a pair of nutcrackers and flung them over his shoulders. Because of his height, he had to hold up her pelvis at arm's length, so that only her shoulders were still touching the table. She let out a shriek when he entered her, then started moaning softly. Standing there facing the misted-up window, dazzled by the bright light shining through it, he watched himself going in and out of

157

her, feeling woefully inadequate. Still moaning, she pulled her skirt up higher, her hand slid down her belly and she started masturbating frantically, furiously. 'Say something, talk to me, talk to me . . .' she implored. Her eyes closed. He couldn't say anything. He couldn't have spoken the words she wanted from him because his thoughts were in turmoil, flying off at a tangent all over the place. His mind was wandering far away from her, then came back, bemused by this gaping flesh, by this body he was floating above without ever really touching it, even though he was inside it. Her hand grabbed hold of the root of his penis and squeezed it violently. He accelerated his thrusts, driving harder and harder into her, but he was only trying to cover up the fact that his heart wasn't in it and his vigour was already ebbing away. She squeezed harder and pulled him inside her as though she wanted to pull him up by the roots.

They say that in the split second before you die, you see your whole life flashing past. That's what happened to him now: his life was rushing past and taking him away from the present. 'Come! Please come!' she screamed, clutching on to his shoulders, pulling him towards her, forcing him to stay close to her. He let her legs slip off his shoulders, pushed her back towards the far end of the table and lay full length on top of her, his face buried in her neck, overcome with remorse because his thoughts were still elsewhere, and every now and then he could see himself lying on top of this woman who meant everything to him – yet he couldn't make real contact with her. She shuddered, he felt her back arch beneath him several times, in a series of amazingly vigorous spasms that lifted him up. Then she stayed there for a few seconds with her back arched, as if her orgasm had left her suspended in mid-air, and lay still. But he had played no part in it. He pulled himself gently away from her, drew her skirt down over her legs. Then the shot rang out.

The window pane behind him shattered, a shower of buckshot sprayed into the ceiling above his head, between a couple of beams, and the plaster fell in on them. He stood there for a moment, dazed, then rushed out. Outside the window where the shot had been fired, he found an empty cartridge case lying in the snow, which had been trodden down by a pair of snowshoes. The tracks led off towards the forest, but there was no sign of any movement. He scanned the garlands of frost festooning the undergrowth, walked a short way towards the forest, then gave up. Whoever had fired the shot could easily be lying in wait behind a tree, holding him in his sights. He walked over to the Caterpillar to fetch his own gun and went back in. As he went to shut the door he heard shouting coming from the forest – this time there was no mistaking it – and individual cries as well as the general hubbub.

She was lying curled up on the table. He dashed over to her and carried her to the sofa. Her face was wet with tears, but she wasn't crying.

'He'll kill us,' she said wearily, not seeming to care much. 'But first he'll play with us, like a cat with a mouse.'

He poked the fire, then sank on to the sofa beside her and poured them another glass of vodka each.

'That wasn't a great success,' he muttered. 'I'm sorry.'

She laid a hand on his arm.

'It doesn't matter in the least. If Tanguy lets us alone for long enough, we'll do better next time.'

Just then yells and shouts erupted outside, in front of the shooting lodge. The sky was getting steadily darker, but there was no snow. A pall was hanging over the forest. He walked cautiously over to the window. Two of the people on the shoot were just emerging from the forest, walking awkwardly in their snowshoes, their legs wide apart, looking worn out. Then three pointers came into view behind them, yelping and leaping about in the deep snow. He made up his mind to go out.

'There's been an accident, a dreadful accident,' one of them stammered, getting his breath back. 'The others are just coming.'

They unfastened their snowshoes, then went inside – it didn't even occur to them to take off their coats – and collapsed on to

159

the sofas. A few seconds later other members of the shooting party and three Tamil beaters turned up, preceded by Tanguy. None of them was saying anything, but they were carrying a man's body rolled up in a blanket. All that could be seen was a few tufts of hair, covered in blood and stiff with frost. Tanguy was staring straight ahead, his mouth twisted into a grimace. When he saw the secretary standing in the doorway he didn't bat an eyelid, but he looked even more sullen.

'This moron was trying to show off – he disturbed a she-bear in her lair,' he mumbled. He looked the secretary straight in the eye, then, speaking to the men carrying the body, issued an order: 'Lay him down on the table – that's where corpses and halfwits go.' Then he shot straight into the pantry, came back with a bottle of vodka and drank half of it down without stopping to draw breath. The Tamils laid the body down and timidly withdrew. Then Tanguy walked over to the table and whipped off the blanket: 'Look, your eminence, have a good look at this!'

The man had been hideously mutilated. The bear had torn off half his face, and one eye, still whole, was dangling from a pulpy mass of bleeding flesh. But the worst part, the most shocking part, was that thing laid along his chest, like a detachable component – his arm, wrenched from his body.

'Did he die straight away?' asked the secretary.

'While they were carrying him here,' said Tanguy. 'I killed the bear. She was an old friend – I was upset at having to do it.'

Then they were pulled up short by a macabre laugh.

'So you were upset, were you?' she said. 'And where were you, may I ask, while this man was getting himself killed?'

Tanguy's arrogant manner crumbled and he hung his head. 'In the forest.'

'In the forest! The forest's huge! I'll tell you where you were – outside that window. Your orders were not to leave the shoot for a second. You're responsible for that man's death. Now, come and fetch me, I want to see him.'

The hounds, scenting death, were circling round the lodge, howling and whining. The door had been left open and the cold was sweeping into the room, while the wind blew the snow inside.

'It would probably be better if you didn't,' said the secretary.

There was a subtle change in the light. A shadow passed across the window and crept along the body lying on the table. It suddenly came to life, making a languid movement, as though the man's chest were heaving with a sigh of pleasure. The arm lying on top of him rolled off and fell to the ground with a dull thud, but no blood spilled out. Tanguy and the secretary, horror-struck, didn't move.

'Come on now,' she called out. 'Am I going to have to crawl over?'

'We could show you his arm for a start,' muttered Tanguy. 'If his eminence isn't afraid to pick it up.' He started walking over to the sofa.

'Oh, no! Not you! Now listen, Tanguy, you're never going to carry me anywhere again, you're never going to lay so much as a finger on me. Now clear off! Get out of here!'

Meanwhile other members of the shooting party had arrived, covered in snow, and were standing sheepishly round the table, knocking their frozen feet against one another. One of them unwittingly kicked the arm under the table. The dogs charged into the room and came over to sniff at it, yelping. The secretary carried her over to the mutilated body. She looked at it for a long time, not with repugnance or morbid curiosity, more with the professional interest of a forensic expert, and as though she were already weighing up the consequences of this death. Then, in a few short sentences, she made her decision known, reminding everyone that she was the boss – Madam President, as she insisted the board should call her.

'We can't take him back to the fortress in the Caterpillar. Clear a landing strip in front of the lodge and we'll go and fetch Varlaam. No one is to leave until the helicopter gets here. The shoot's over, gentlemen.'

A brace of roe deer, a few hares and a wild boar were lying

161

in the snow, stiff with both rigor mortis and the cold, their muzzles covered with blood. The men who'd shot them kept on glancing resentfully at them, going into the lodge only to walk straight out again, irresistibly drawn by this evidence of their proficiency, dividing their time between the dead man and the dead animals, two different facets of the day's bag. Tanguy was sitting on one of the window sills, cleaning his gun, taking no more interest in what was going on. The men found some axes and using them plus their hunting knives, set to without enthusiasm to clear the undergrowth. The secretary strapped her into the Caterpillar and let in the clutch. He was driving very fast, not worrying about jolting her, looking straight ahead. It wasn't long before he noticed she was crying, without making a sound. Then she recovered her composure and started talking.

'It's awful, awful. D'you remember that first time you came to the fortress? You hardly said a thing, you were just replying to my questions. We women like people to be enigmatic. But we have the foible of being prepared to go to any lengths to get to the bottom of the enigma, rather than letting it go on as it is. Anything that can be proved isn't really crucial. We don't know what we want, or what we want is so petty! I loved you as soon as I saw you standing there. I longed for you to touch what was left of life in my body. I realized straight away what a bully you could be – that's why I took you on. You despise me, I know. You won't allow yourself to, because I'm disabled, and because you're basically a moral person, but you do still despise me. You've no idea how contemptuous your composure and your silences are! You came here to make me suffer – no! let me say my piece, even if I've got it wrong! – to make me suffer and to humiliate me, because you humiliate yourself every single day, every single second. You haven't got a drop of self-esteem, but you can't bear being the only one to suffer and be humiliated, you've got to drag others in too. That's what you were trying to tell me back there.'

They were within sight of the fortress now. She started sobbing again, fierce sobs that shook her whole body.

'You're dearer to me than anyone else in the world,' he said, drawing up outside the postern gate.

Instead of soothing her, this declaration prostrated her even further. He undid the straps, lifted her out and held her close.

'Don't think I'm weeping for that man who died, or for anyone else. I'm weeping for myself, just for myself.'

4

A column of dirty smoke was spiralling up into the overcast sky and blazing torches made of paper were streaming high above the bonfire, burning themselves out and then fluttering back down into the snow. He drifted from the edge of the woods towards the two Tamils who were bustling about round the fire. The old newspapers were glowing but hadn't really caught properly. They were having to use a pitchfork to lift up the layers of paper to let air get in underneath, and when the blaze was dying down, empty whole drums of petrol on to it. He unstrapped his skis and watched them at work. All round the bonfire and as far as the fortifications, the snow was strewn with bits of charred paper on which you could still read fragments of printed text, like death announcements with their black borders. The Tamils would placidly stir up the fire, then move back to get a good look and watch with no sign of emotion as ordinary everyday history went up in smoke. He walked over to them, feeling rather embarrassed with his gun slung across him, but they paid little attention to him, merely greeting him politely and remaining rather aloof. Before they flung the papers on to the fire they would cut the string on the bundles, chatting a bit among themselves, and sometimes bursting out laughing.

Another Tamil appeared, carrying a bundle of papers in each hand. He put them down and then, to the secretary's surprise, walked straight over to him, whereas his compatriots were still showing no interest in him, though their attitude was deferential.

'Why don't you leave this place, sir?' he asked in strongly accented pidgin English, shaking his head disapprovingly. 'It is not a good place for you.'

He thought at first he was in their way, standing near the fire, and that they didn't like people watching them working. But that wasn't what the man meant. He turned to face the fortress and nodded towards it.

'Oh, I see. You mean the fortress?'

'Yes, why do you stay? My fellows and myself we will leave very soon.'

Looking at the fortress through the charred newspapers raining down made him think of citadels set on fire after a long siege, and suddenly he felt that the man's question was apposite.

'I'm staying for Mrs Leber,' he said.

A broad smile lit up the Tamil's face. He bent his index fingers and knocked them together several times, nodding mischievously: 'I know, Mrs Leber and you, like that!' Then he burst out laughing and joined the other two by the bonfire.

The secretary hoisted his skis on to his shoulder. They felt very heavy. His shoulder blade was bruised from wearing the gun slung across his back and his knees hurt. He was cruelly aware of his whole body. 'Like that . . .' he said to himself. Then just as he was coming up to the postern gate the air started vibrating, and he felt the slipstream caused by the blades chopping at the air before he heard the din of the helicopter itself. It loomed above the roofs, spiralled round, and hovered on a level with the main buildings. Then it came slowly down and landed in the courtyard, surrounded by a tornado of puffed-up snow.

It wasn't Varlaam's machine but one belonging to the state police force. Ever since that death during the shoot, the world below had been sending up official representatives, and as each day came round the secretary expected a visit from Alexis Muller. But he failed to put in an appearance – in this case there was no truth to be established, since death is in itself a truth that can't be established. The man in charge

164

of the inquiry, a young police inspector, said he regretted to have to inform Mrs Leber that from now on the local council would not allow shoots to be held on the land attached to the fortress except during the official shooting season.

'All this fuss will die down,' she kept on and on saying, when she came across a news item about the tragedy and photos of the fortress in the papers she was sorting through for material for her archive. She was going backwards and forwards in her wheelchair, propelling it vigorously up and down the corridors, and when she had, at least to outward appearances, managed to calm herself down, she would announce, banging on the arm of the chair to convince herself: 'Anyway, the whole story's a sham. They've all got it wrong. That man who died wasn't really a man in real life, he was playing at being a member of the Leber Foundation board, just as we all are, because the Leber Foundation is nothing more than a game now, the shoot's only a game, that creature . . . that she-bear was only one of the props in the game and no one will ever be able to prove otherwise.'

Three people got out of the helicopter. Two were uniformed policemen, the other a man who looked like an official of some sort and was looking about him uncertainly, as though he'd turned up there by mistake. The pilot had left the engine running and the blades were turning about as fast as an antiquated ceiling fan. The secretary was just walking out to the top of the steps when Olga Grekova-Leber came out.

'What do you want?' she shouted out to the three men as they were on their way across the courtyard. 'I'm not seeing anyone. Get out, and take that filthy heap of scrap metal with you!'

The official was clutching a fat briefcase to his chest, with the two policemen a few yards behind him. He stopped at the foot of the steps and his deep-blue eyes clouded over.

'I've come from the regional authority, Mrs Leber. I telephoned yesterday and you agreed to see me today.'

165

She pretended to think it over for a moment, then asked him in. She insisted that the policemen were to stay outside and didn't ask the official into her rooms, but saw him in her private hall. Although it was suffocatingly hot in there, he was too timid to take off his coat. He perched right on the edge of his chair and promptly started sweating. He seemed dreadfully shy and overawed. She propelled the wheelchair over to the window and looked out at the parapet walk with its covering of snow.

'You may speak in front of my secretary,' she said, not to him but to her own reflection in the window pane.

He put his briefcase on the ground at his feet and took out an envelope covered with sealing wax, but then suddenly didn't know what to do with it. She was too far away for him to hand it to her, and anyway she had her back to him. The secretary realized how flummoxed he was and took the envelope, but just as he was about to give it to her, the man cleared his throat noisily and went scarlet in the face. By now the sweat was running down from his temples on to his cheeks.

'I feel I must tell you, Mrs . . . er,' he began, trying to sound self-assured, but his voice went out of control straight away. '. . . I must tell you how very moved I am to be with you here today. I've seen you on stage several times in various different places.'

She turned to face him at last, raised her eyebrows and studied him closely. She relaxed and her expression became almost friendly.

'In various different places, did you say?'

'Yes. In Paris, when I was a student, then in Geneva, and . . .'

'Ah, in Geneva,' she interrupted, 'then it must have been in *Phèdre*. I only ever played Phèdre there. Yes, well, I'm glad, I do hope you weren't disappointed.'

There was a little something of playing to the gallery in her tone. She glanced at the secretary out of the corner of her eye and lit a cigarette. The official was looking more

166

self-confident, but he was sweating even more profusely than before. Then he noticed the envelope in the secretary's hand and remembered he was there on official business, not to talk about the theatre.

'Would you like me to . . . er . . . to tell you what this official ruling says, or would you rather read it yourself?'

She waved her hand impatiently. 'You tell me.'

His shoulders drooped and he looked as if he was about to burst into tears, but he pulled himself together and started speaking very fast, staring down at his shoes. The regional authority had issued a ruling that all the dangerous animals on the whole of the Leber estate were to be destroyed, and their pelts were to be retained so that a forestry inspector could ascertain that the order had been duly carried out. 'By all the dangerous animals we mean the bears, wolves and lynxes,' he added. 'All those animals your husband tried to acclimatize here, only too successfully. Despite the . . . er . . . the fence Mr Leber had built, the local people have never been at all happy about having those wild animals living nearby. The local council have had a large number of complaints, which is why they decided to refer the matter to the regional authority. You'll find all the details set out in the order. These dangerous animals are to be destroyed by next July at the latest, in other words the order is to be carried out next spring, since the current climatic conditions make it difficult to do it now. But as soon as the weather improves, you'll have to take the necessary steps. The police are willing to put a dozen men at your disposal, all of them good shots, to carry out this . . . er . . . work for you.'

She was paying close attention to what he said and for some time now had been smiling a hard little smile. There was an unpleasant glint in her eye.

'Now isn't that quite absurd?' she said, turning to the secretary. 'The international situation has deteriorated to such an extent that the various nations are expecting the worst to happen before many more weeks go by, tens of millions of people are liable to be burnt to a cinder over the next few months, and the gentlemen at the regional authority are frightened of bears!'

Now that he'd done his painful duty her visitor at last plucked up courage to wipe the sweat off his face. He seemed to be utterly distraught at having to play the part of spokesman and would no doubt have preferred to declare his undying admiration for La Grekova all over again, instead of having to undergo this torture.

'Fear is a fundamental truth too, you know,' she told him. 'These days it could perhaps be said to be *the* key truth. I shall carry out the regional authority's orders within the time limit – personally, I've never been a passionate animal lover. But as for the offer of police assistance, it's quite out of the question. I shan't allow a single one of them to set foot on my land ever again.'

She went out of the hall and they heard her asking one of the Tamils to fetch Tanguy. Then she came back and manoeuvred the chair till she was facing the official, close enough to bring him out in a lather all over again. 'As you've seen me as Phèdre, and perhaps as Hecuba in *The Women of Troy* too, and as you seem to be a theatre lover, which is unusual for a civil servant, I feel I can ask you a rather personal question. Have you got someone in your life you love more than yourself?'

Completely taken aback, he rose from his chair, then sat straight down again. He was frowning in concentration, but couldn't think of a suitable reply. Then Tanguy came to his rescue. The door to the main hall slammed, unsteady footsteps pounded across the flagstones and he appeared in the doorway, looking distinctly unkempt, his face puffy, fairly drunk but still capable of standing upright. He didn't come any further into the room, didn't give anyone the time of day, looked them all up and down one at a time, then hiccoughed loudly.

'This gentleman has brought us some bad news, Tanguy,' she said, making no attempt to hide her satisfaction. 'We're going

168

to have to destroy all the dangerous animals, all the animals. The regional authority's issued an order. I thought you could see to it. You're familiar with their habits, you know where to find them and you're the best shot I know.'

He staggered as though someone had struck him a violent blow from behind.

'You can't mean it!' he stammered. 'Why?' Then he just stood there looking punch-drunk, completely stunned by the news.

'If you don't feel up to doing the job yourself, the police will attend to it,' she said with a sarcastic smile.

He took a step towards the wheelchair. By now his face was dark with a mixture of hatred and incredulity and he looked as if he was about to pounce on her. Sensing this, she backed the chair away, banging into the official, who had another coughing fit. When he was able to speak again, he announced in his most official voice, though with the greatest reluctance: 'You can destroy the wild boar too. There are too many of them and they ruin the crops. Since September the local council has deemed them to be harmful.'

It looked for a moment as if Tanguy's anger was going to be vented on the official but, as he was sometimes capable of doing even when he was in a furious rage, he managed to retain his self-control.

'The wild boar living on this estate can't get out because of the Great Wall. It's not them that's ruining the crops and I shan't destroy a single one of them. Anyone who gets it into his head to lay a finger on my wild boar is a dead man.'

He turned on his heel. The official closed his briefcase and stood up.

'A man with character, I see,' he said in a low voice.

'Yes. And if you ever come back here – which I hope you don't – I'd advise you to stick with your bodyguards.'

A storm was getting up. A howling wind was sweeping into the courtyard and small stinging snowflakes were flying about, hard enough to scratch your face. The official was halfway

169

down the front steps when he remembered something and climbed back up again.

'I couldn't answer that question you asked me just now. I'm a loner. I'm not married and I haven't got many friends. But I have got someone in my life I love more than myself – my dog.'

He bowed to her, and looked doubtfully up at the sky. Then he did something they'd never have expected him to – he plonked his briefcase on his head as if it were a hat and made a dash for the helicopter, with the two policemen, who were blue with cold by this time, hot on his heels.

She started laughing. Then she looked at the secretary, who was lost in thought.

'What are you thinking about?'

'About your husband. If you agree, I'd like to go back to working on his manuscripts.'

The helicopter engine was now at full throttle and neither of them could hear what the other said. They stayed at the top of the steps in the shelter of the porch until it had melted into the gusting wind.

Once the hubbub had subsided, she said: 'Apparently when the slightest thing goes wrong, they drop like stones.'

After this remark they listened hard, but nothing happened, and within a very short time they could hear nothing but the howling of the wind, a flex whipping against the bricks on one of the chimneys and the postern gate squealing on its hinges. She shivered. 'His dog . . . He loves his dog more than himself,' she said faintly. He pulled the chair inside and asked where she'd like him to push her. 'Nowhere. I'm going to take myself off to my bedroom until lunchtime, then eat with you by the fire in the kitchen. About Samuel's manuscripts – do whatever you think's best. You're completely free now. Don't feel you still need to account to me for how you spend your time.'

She moved away, pushing forcefully on the wheels, sitting very upright in the wheelchair, as proud and haughty as if she bore an illustrious and indestructible destiny. Deep down

170

inside himself he was thinking: She may have granted me my freedom, but it's only another form of slavery.

5

During the last few weeks of winter, she would summon him again and again to take her out all over the estate. They'd spend the morning working on the archives, have their lunch in the kitchen, then, no matter what the weather, set off into the snow-covered landscape, venturing as far as the Caterpillar's petrol tank would take them. She would lay down the route they were to follow. Securely strapped into her seat, she would suggest the most risky of itineraries. Once the danger was over she would burst out in a fit of hysterical laughter, then sit hunched in her seat and announce: 'You see, we're safe and sound.' One day she found she'd misjudged her staying power and asked him to help her relieve herself. She didn't show any sign of embarrassment about asking this, which he found disconcerting. 'I don't want to wet myself, you know. You'll have to carry me, it's the only answer.' He undid the straps and carried her to a spot beneath a fir tree. His arms could barely feel her weight, but he was sweating profusely. She gave him detailed instructions and he held her like a little girl, clutching her under the knees, with her skirt pulled up and her back propped up against him. She wasn't wearing her fur hat and as he was leaning forwards, her hair was tickling his chin. He inhaled deep draughts of its plant-like fragrance, keeping his eyes half shut, while the jet of steaming urine gushed out into the snow with its sprinkling of dry pine needles and cones. The sun was filtering between the branches and they were bathed in a stripey light. Minute shavings of ice sparkled in the blue of the sky like silver filings. Then he lifted her up higher, holding her round the waist so she could adjust her clothes herself, and straightened up, laying her across his arms. 'Thank you,' she said, with a complete lack of affection.

The thaw set in before the end of March. It took less than a day for the whole of nature to liquefy. The foehn sent its sour

171

breath throbbing through the valleys and deep down beneath its surface crust the snow collapsed. His skis sank into it as though it were a waffle, feeling as hard and heavy as cast iron. The boulders rose up out of the meadows, as black and glossy as reefs at low tide, and the dazzling whiteness of the snowfields grew tarnished. While the wind continued to blow, the sky had a creamy look about it, and a wan sun shed light the colour of rancid butter. He couldn't get out on his skis, or take her out in the Caterpillar, so they were confined to the fortress, listening to the icicles clattering down from the gutters, great chunks of snow sliding down the roofs and crashing into the courtyard, and the haunting sound of water streaming down the drainpipes.

The thaw seemed to pose a threat to anything solid. The jagged outlines of the mountains were growing rounder, the very peaks seemed to be filling out, and the most precipitous summits were sticking their rocks out like bits of a shattered framework. But it was the forest that offered the most desolate sight. After spending months paralysed beneath their burden, the branches had at last shaken off their covering of snow, but instead of springing back, drooped down beside the trunks like dead wings. The fir trees looked like old paintbrushes left to soak. Beneath the milky vault of the sky the mountain was peeling. Its flesh was rolling down into the coombs with muffled snarls, and inside the glaciers the noise of the ice cracking reverberated, sounding muted, as though guns were being fired underground. Then one night the wind suddenly dropped and a wave of cold broke over the land, vitrifying everything.

The next day the sun rose in a sparkling sky over a landscape sealed beneath a film of ice, and sailed over the mountain ridge, lighting up one by one the facets of a giant mirror. Everything was gleaming like wet marble. The secretary strapped on his skis so that he could venture out on one last cross-country run. He was surprised to see how thick the ice was. When he was only just outside the fortress he realized he wouldn't be able to travel even a hundred yards on it and went back to fetch

172

the skins. Then he set off along the main path, experiencing the greatest difficulty in driving the sharp end of his ski sticks into the ice. Soon, cutting across country, he climbed up towards the forest, until he was pulled up short by a loud report. It was such a shock in the frozen, motionless silence of early morning that he could feel it banging in his chest. A second shot exploded, a sharp, dry sound, then another and another. They were reverberating from over by the kennels, and although he hadn't taken a gun with him, he turned off in the direction of the shots without stopping to think.

On the edge of the fir plantation he came across crampon marks. So Tanguy had come on foot, and not to feed the animals, but for some quite different reason. He took off his skis, cut through the closely planted rows of trunks and stopped on the edge of the forest. The sun was fingering the tops of the fir trees but the clearing, filled with subtly shaded light, curved round in mauve shadow. A bright cold light brushed the kennels and the falcon house. Tanguy was standing near the water trough, his legs firmly planted on the ground, taking aim with a squat rifle with a scope and a short barrel. He had put some boxes of ammunition on the frozen surface of the trough and every five seconds or so, keeping his eye glued to the scope, would squeeze the trigger, aiming at a target somewhere down below the clearing. The secretary couldn't at first make out what it was. With each shot he fired he moved the barrel a fraction of an inch, and with his filthy leather jacket, his felt boots and his forage cap pulled right down as far as his eyebrows, he made you think of some primitive war machine.

The secretary glanced round the clearing and eventually spotted his targets. They were suddenly lit up when the sun rose above the forest and its first rays struck the depths of the shadows. Down there, not far from the edge of the forest, the narrow rim of the feeding troughs emerged with a sparkling of mica, on a level with the snow, tracing black runic characters beneath a thin film of ice. On each of the characters, arranged in alternate rows, Tanguy had lined up

173

dozens of empty bottles, belly to belly. When the powerful bullet hit them they would explode, and all that was left on the snow was tiny fragments of glass no bigger than a fingernail. He never missed. Soon the whole scene was bathed in a serenely transparent light. His eye still glued to the scope, imprisoned in his solitary concentration, he had cut himself off from the outside world. When the magazine was empty, he would fill it with breathtaking dexterity, not looking at what he was doing, then calmly take aim again. Every now and then as the rifle kicked back it would make the top half of his body judder very slightly, but that was all, and over 150 yards away the bottle would explode without touching its neighbour.

When he was out of ammunition Tanguy went back into the falcon hut and closed the door behind him. The secretary waited under the tree for a moment, but he didn't reappear. Several of the bottles were still standing on the troughs. They were in full sunlight now and floating above a dazzling carpet of glass. Yellow smoke rose from the flue sticking up out of the hut and a stale smell of grilled bacon hung over the clearing. He turned back, plunged into the shadowy light and the close-packed silence of the fir plantation, collected his skis and continued on his way through the frozen landscape.

The wave of cold broke against the mountains and fell back again. It started raining. It rained for virtually the whole of April, the mist hanging down from the sky in greasy tatters that clung to the fir trees, dawdled up the ravine and eventually vanished into the low-lying clouds that had produced it in the first place. The curtains of rain drew back and swung to again, driven by the winds, and at the altitude where the fortress was the snow melted in a few days, leaving nothing but a few scattered patches on the meadows, and drifts so deep they wouldn't melt until the summer sun shone on them.

During that month Varlaam was taken ill and he paid only a couple of quick visits to the fortress. He brought the papers from the agency, virtually all of which, in a sudden outburst of ludicrous optimism, were now telling their readers that there wasn't going to be a war. 'After forty-two years of peace and progress, the general consensus is that a war between the developed industrial nations in the West and the other nations couldn't happen except by accident.' Every now and then, the press, acting with the agreement of politicians, would decide that it would be a good idea to reassure the nation. Olga Grekova-Leber and the secretary spent two whole days and nights sifting through the eighty-odd daily papers and fifty-odd weeklies. They would cut the articles out and sort them into categories by date and by geographical area. The secretary had somehow managed to work out how to use the microfilm equipment and would film the cuttings, develop the films and file all the material in the metal filing cupboards. 'The destructive capability of modern weapons, the interdependence of the capitalist economies and a growing awareness among individuals of the value of human life mean that military confrontations are now an anachronism. Even the generals have realized this, and so have the politicians, and not a single one of them, anywhere in the world, is currently in favour of war . . .'

Entering into the spirit of her project, and finding it somehow fascinating, he would read this drivel – ninety per cent of the 'Archive of Evil' consisted of journalists' drivel – and think back to a contribution from Fra Cosimo during a meeting held long ago by the chapter at the monastery in connection with the prayer for peace in the world: 'We'll have to pray for viruses to be destroyed too, dear brothers. In a single year, 1918, just after the armistice, Spanish 'flu killed thirty million people throughout the world.' The lamps in the archive room burned day and night, casting a pitiless high-noon light in which the shadows were reduced to nothing and every object sat there in its inner certainty, stripped down to its essential truth.

At the end of the second day, when they'd cleared the backlog, she slumped into a lethargic stupor before her map. His back aching from hours of sitting on an uncomfortable chair without moving, he stood up and gazed out at the waterlogged courtyard. Torrential rain was flinging up cascades of spray above the flagstones. His memories of many a rain-soaked spring in the trying climate of La Verna merged with the present. Praying, chanting the responses, pushing Fra Cosimo, reading St Augustine and Meister Eckhart by candlelight for the umpteenth time, practising daily at overcoming his will by going at it hammer and tongs, like Tanguy hammering away at the bottles, his trips to Asia, people now dead, books he'd written, women taken for the sake of it, and then praying again, in a world lived in as though no god had ever been invented – all this flashed through his tired brain in just a few seconds. He looked at his fingers, which were black from handling newsprint. The worst war of all is declared on us by stupidity, he told himself, and superficiality lies at the heart of the most rigorous thinking. For everything we think is superficial; the important thing is to sign a peace treaty with superficiality that we're not ashamed of. He decided to leave the archive room, but just as he was about to go, his eyes met hers.

'I know what you're thinking,' she said. 'But don't go yet. I've just come to a decision. I'm going to cancel my subscription to the press agency and I shan't have a single newspaper or magazine in the fortress. We'll live in complete ignorance of what's going on down below, taking an interest only in the present moment. We'll lock up the cupboards and close the bolts on this room for ever, and as soon as the sun comes out again we'll set off. You'll take me miles away into the mountains, we'll go through the Great Wall, leaving the gate open, and we'll go on to the glaciers, as we did in my dream.'

He went straight to the kitchen. He wasn't hungry, but thirsty, thirsty for a glass or two of wine, for a fire, for so many things. Thiru and Virama, the two Tamils who helped Félicité, were sweeping the floor with bone-weary gestures, as though each of their brooms weighed a ton. They seemed preoccupied. He sat down right in the fireplace, very close to the fire, and became totally engrossed in staring at the flames. But soon he felt a hand on his shoulder. He looked up and met Virama's gaze. He was looking nervously at the ground, the whites of his eyes tinged with a liverish yellow.

'Sorry, sir, but I have to talk to you,' he said in his broken English, 'because you have to know that Sarachchandra stopped to take any food for three days.'

His first reaction was to wonder what the man wanted from him, but it was obvious that he was only trying to let him know about it. It crossed his mind that the brahmin might be trying to draw attention to himself for political reasons.

'Is he on hunger strike?' he asked. And immediately saw how absurd the question was.

'No strike, sir, just fasting.'

He apparently had nothing else to say. He went back over to the other Tamil and started sweeping again. The secretary suddenly felt intense admiration for Sarachchandra, and a twinge of jealousy too. Although he was well aware that nothing would make him change his mind, he called Virama over.

'I'd like to see him,' he said. 'As soon as possible.'

Virama leant on his broom. He didn't seem surprised and his expression was one of placid indifference. At that point the secretary noticed that the floor they were sweeping was spotlessly clean.

'As you like, sir. I shall transmit your request,' said Virama as he went back to his work.

6

'Push at your own pace. I'm not frightened any more, I trust you. Never mind about me being jolted – I quite like it actually.'

He was holding the wheelchair so that it was tilted up on to its back wheels. It was a new power-driven model with balloon tyres designed for rough terrain and at the moment he was holding it back rather than pushing it, since the stony path dropped sharply down the side of the col catching the full force of the morning sun. In the far depths of a pale sky a cloud front was advancing at a leisurely pace to meet them.

At long intervals a volley of shots would ring out, though it was hard to tell how far away it was because the mountains were bouncing back the echo. The sound rolled through the azure sky and the advancing clouds suddenly seemed to speed up. Each time a shot rang out she would give a start. Neither of them made any comment, but they were both thinking of Tanguy. The shots were very widely spaced, and what made them particularly alarming was that they burst out at irregular intervals, and always just when they weren't expecting them. Remembering what Varlaam had said about Tanguy – 'He only ever shoots when he's sure of hitting his target' – he would picture, in the confusion of the moment, what species of animal had just been brought down, wondering if it had been killed outright or was waiting in its death throes for Tanguy to put it out of its misery.

They'd set out intending to be back in time for lunch. It was their third outing since the beginning of May and the secretary had been allowed to decide on the itinerary. It would perhaps turn out to be a bit more more difficult than the two earlier ones, but it did still come into the preliminary category, getting them into training for future expeditions. As long as they kept to the sunny side of the ravine the ground was dry and firm, but when they reached the bottom of the col and abandoned the track leading to the town to continue along the north face, which never saw the sun, the path became virtually impassable. The wheelchair would sink into the muddy puddles filling the potholes up to halfway up the wheels and she would move the top half of her body in an automatic reflex action, as if to lift up her paralysed legs. But the footrests would completely disappear beneath the mud, drenching her boots up to calf height and spattering her skirt. She didn't seem to resent this. 'Come on! Push! Don't worry, what does a bit of mud matter!' she would say with a laugh. Just as when he used to take Fra Cosimo out, it would be brought home to him that he was nothing but a tiny piece of the whole, but one that was crucial to its overall harmony, as well as to his own.

When they reached the foot of the patch of scree they

encountered an obstacle that cast serious doubts on the feasibility of the whole enterprise. Rain and melting ice and snow had filled a dip in the ground and it was impossible to tell how deep the resulting pond of stagnant water went. Fifty yards or so further on the path re-emerged from the water. Although it wouldn't be easy on this rocky terrain covered with brushwood he decided to go round the pond, but she was against this.

'Let's try to go through it, it'll be fun. Cut me a stick, then you can push me and I'll poke down with it to see how deep it is.'

He did as she asked, after warning her that the new wheelchair might be damaged if it was treated like that. He pushed it into the pond a bit too fast. She leaned as far forward as she could with the straps and plunged her stick into the water with a patriarchal gesture that had something majestic about it, determinedly lifting it out then lowering it again, as though she was conducting a military march. For the first few yards the pond turned out to be very shallow, but suddenly the path running out of sight below the surface dropped down, the wheelchair sank in further, then the ground level rose again. Her legs were ploughing through the water like the stern of a ship and twin ripples were crinkling on the surface, fanning out slowly and peacefully. With every step he took he was afraid of getting stuck, but the wheels went on turning over even and pebbly ground and he wasn't finding it too difficult to push her in the very mild sunlight, under the watchful eye of battalions of clouds. As in the old days with Fra Cosimo, every detail round him was uncannily sharp and clear. And the details of every object his eye alighted on, linked together like a chain in the same way as words build up a sentence, told him the story of all these objects, told him what they were like. A heap of twigs, a spider's web spun tautly across the crozier of a fern, a chip in a piece of stone – they all said something to him, painting a clear word picture of the history of forms and matter since their earliest beginnings. By fixing his gaze on just one small pebble he could find out all there was to know about the mountain, and in the muddy water he was

179

now breasting he could read how the remotest glacier was fashioned. Through his observation of these details, the lines of an overall intelligibility were gradually being sketched in, and these lines, thousands of them, like the warp of a piece of cloth, were weaving round him the cocoon that held him at the heart of the universe. But this sense of oneness, this revelation of the god hidden in these little details, this feeling of happiness at being part of the world – he only experienced them as fully as this when he was pushing a disabled person in a wheelchair.

'I'll keep the stick,' she said, when they were back on dry land. 'It'll come in useful on the way back.'

'We shan't be coming back this way. There's another path that runs along the sunny side of Maupas Valley. You can get to it a bit further on by cutting across country.'

She looked at him over her shoulder. 'You're amazingly knowledgeable about the area. But I'll keep the stick all the same.'

A gust of wind ruffled the surface of the pond. The sun went in, then immediately reappeared. He took off her boots, then pulled off her socks, wringing them out, but she preferred to remain barefoot inside her boots. He was moved by the pearly whiteness of her legs and by how tiny her curled-up toes seemed. Just as they were about to set off-again another shot rang out, but very muffled this time, a bit like the memory of an unpleasant sound that has already started to fade.

'He's shooting with the Smith & Wesson automatic – a nasty weapon,' she said with a shudder.

Before long they abandoned the path and set off across grazing land. For getting on for an hour he struggled over spongy ground to reach a path lower down on the north side of the valley, the one that led to the col via the other side of the mountain. The wheelchair's electric motor had stopped working after the pond episode and if it hadn't been for the balloon tyres there wouldn't have been any point in using such a heavy and cumbersome contraption. They were zigzagging among molehills, clumps of gentians and the bone-like stones

180

scattered about on the meadow, which didn't seem to present a major obstacle but were in fact very dangerous. He would find a rhythm suitable for the type of terrain: pushing the chair over a grassy surface where the earth was uniformly loose required a very different technique from when he was negotiating grazing land, where the springy ground would suddenly become as squelchy as a thick carpet saturated with water. He could only hit on the right rhythm gradually. When the terrain and its dips and bumps were starting to make themselves felt right up into the wheelchair handles, when the exertion of his muscles seemed to carry on inside the metal tubing, then the ground, the wheelchair, its occupant and the person pushing it would merge together in a highly subtle way. But he was still a long way from achieving the state of grace he'd managed without difficulty when he was pushing Fra Cosimo. He felt full of strength and energy, but clumsy – the chair would slip out of his control as if it had a life of its own, over which he exercised little authority. On several occasions over this short stretch he couldn't stop the wheels sinking in and the chair tilting right over. She would let out a shriek of fright, then when the chair was upright again and came to a standstill would conceal her fright by calling out: 'It doesn't matter a bit, let's go on. Push!'

When they got back to the forest he realized he'd misjudged. The ground hadn't dried off there either and there was a smell of mud and wet bark wafting through a coppice of fir trees with nothing much in the way of branches, their bare trunks shooting up out of the ground like the masts of a flotilla of ships becalmed beneath the mossy floor of the forest. To get back to the path, stretches of which were still covered in snow, he'd have to clamber down a fairly tall bank covered with a tangle of ferns and brambles. He tilted the wheelchair back on to its rear wheels and took it slowly down. A shot rang out and he very nearly let go of the handles. The wheels got stuck on a branch caught up in a tangle of brambles and jammed completely. Hanging tens of feet above a path she couldn't see, she suddenly said, sounding completely calm, her steady

181

voice quite inappropriate: 'I don't understand why you gave up first geology and then writing to become a sort of social worker. I really don't understand . . .'

He eventually set the wheelchair down safely on the path and jumped down to the foot of the bank. It was starting to rain.

'Do you really think people have to be able to justify every single one of their actions, every single one of their thoughts, and that there's a rational explanation for everything?' he asked as he was getting his breath back.

She hunted about in the canvas bag hanging over the arm of the wheelchair and took out a cigarette. Her offhand manner, the fact that she was oblivious of the huge effort he'd put in, totally infuriated him.

'It wasn't a question. I was simply pointing out how puzzling I find it,' she said. Then she started smoking, taking a sensual pleasure in every puff.

The sky was growing progressively darker. The light was fading and in the cloistered silence a cuckoo sent out its monotonous and uninspired call. Soon the firs gave way to larches and the rain became harder. After a stiff but short uphill stretch the path emerged from the forest on to a narrow plateau, then climbed up to the col in a series of wide zigzags. Curtains of rain were sweeping down on to the larch branches and the delicate green of their young leaves.

'We're slightly sheltered here, but once we're out of the woods the path is liable to turn into a sea of mud,' he said, manoeuvring the wheels on to a patch of snow that, much to his surprise, proved able to take the weight of both the wheelchair and its occupant.

Ever since he'd got them down the bank tiredness had been seeping into him like a warm and pleasantly painless balm, acting as an anaesthetic. He didn't ache at all, but his muscles were growing stiff and his body was sinking into a hazy sleep in which the commands issued by his will were getting through only in a series of intermittent flickers, like a sea-mark glimmering through the fog. Another shot blazed out, the

182

protracted sound unfurling slowly before being swallowed up by the sputtering of the rain on the branches. She gave a start.

'Alexis Muller's given me some information about you,' she said suddenly, while the echo of the explosion was still reverberating. 'It wasn't too difficult finding it out, as he'd already read one of your books. Thanks to him, I even know that you lived in Africa for a time, in Namibia, where you had a job as a geologist in a copper mine . . .'

'A uranium mine,' he cut in.

He grabbed hold of the wheelchair and in an attempt to put an end to this conversation dashed off energetically out of the woods, making sure he kept the wheels out of the deep ruts in which he was squelching about himself. In a few minutes they were soaked to the skin. As he concentrated all his energies on a determined effort that was beginning to outstrip his capabilities, he could see the path climbing up more and more steeply above her head – she was sitting there silently now – and when he worked out the distance he still had to cover before they reached the top of the col, he admitted stoically that he wouldn't be able to make it. Looking at the hermetically stoppered horizon he could picture the heavens going on discharging their water to the end of time, maintaining the same vertical and unending flow. The rain was beating down silently now in the motionless air, yet the atmosphere was filled with turmoil, a turbulent stillness like the eye of a storm. He brought the chair to a halt, dispassionately contemplating his palms, which were lacerated by several burst blisters. The path climbed steadily up to a ruined building on a piece of mountain pasture, then veered off at an angle higher up following the line of the mountainside and ran along the gently sloping shoulder before the stiff climb up to the col, which seemed to go on for ever.

'We'll stop for a few minutes' rest in the sheepfold,' he said, while through the closely woven curtain of rain he could see another path, a sun-drenched one this time, rising up towards heaven like Jacob's ladder – the narrow road to

183

Bibiena where he'd pushed Fra Cosimo twice a week for ten years.

'You can have a rest. I'm not tired – I'm sitting down,' she pointed out sarcastically, wiping her face, which was dripping wet.

He looked at the path, following it up the steep mountain-side, the embankment of light-coloured stones tracing a shaky line in the grass on the pastureland, which was starting to spring up again. But he was thinking of that sunny hillside rearing up like a rocket launcher towards the dazzling blue of the Tuscan summer and how he used to give up as he stood at its foot, while the old monk would shake his head, saying in his booming voice – the words never varied – 'One day, *piccolo*, by the grace of God, you'll get over that hurdle, pushing me with one hand tied behind your back!'

In front of the sheep-cote a metal drinking trough was over-flowing with water. The building was in ruins and the roof had fallen in, but they discovered a windowless hut with dry-stone walls. It was a type of pigsty, the ground inside covered with mouldy straw and the entrance too narrow for the wheelchair. He undid her straps and carried her inside. But as they couldn't both get through the entrance together, either facing forwards or sideways on, he laid her down on the ground, went into the sty, got hold of her beneath the armpits and dragged her towards him through the mud. She didn't object, but she was looking up at him from the depths of her helplessness with a startled expression, her eyes seeming huge, and when she was propped up in the darkness, soaked to the skin and covered in mud, she started shivering.

'The wheels on the chair have seized up. I'm going to try dipping it into the drinking trough to get it clean,' he said, going out again. He was just starting to straighten up in the driving rain when he heard her calling out. He stuck his head through the opening and saw that she'd rolled over on to her side and was starting to crawl.

'Don't leave me alone in here,' she pleaded.

As he backed in he tripped over a stone buried under the straw and finished up on all fours beside her. He stayed there for a moment, dazed, then began laughing, laughing as you can only do when things have become quite desperate, when what you should be doing is hanging yourself from the nearest tree. He rolled over to lie face up and all of a sudden, amid the musty smell compounded of mouldy straw, long-dead fires and animal dung, he breathed in her smell. Lying there resigned to her fate, her expression very confused, she seemed to be waiting for something and looked like a drowning woman who's been dragged out of the river and is just clinging on to life. Her lips were trembling. He thought she must be cold and wanted to warm her up. But a sudden wave of affection mixed with savagery swept over him and flung him against her. He saw a hand raised towards him as if to caress him and felt a stinging sensation on his cheek. Then an arm went round him and her nails dug into the back of his neck. He wrenched himself free from her embrace. The rainwater trickling down from his hair on to his face and down inside his collar was mixed with a warm liquid and as it ran into his mouth he gulped it down greedily. As she lay there beneath him she was holding her face up towards him, its nakedness unutterably lewd.

Then she started murmuring a sort of litany: 'Kill me, tear me apart . . .' and his hand rummaged about feverishly in a tangle of soaking wet garments, clumsily pulled up her sodden skirt, undid his flies, extricated himself and plumped heavily down on top of her. She let out a gasp and went on reciting her incantation. He wrenched himself out of her and thrust frenziedly back in lower down. Her body jerked so convulsively he thought he could feel her legs coming back to life. He plunged in as far as he could go, got to his knees, grabbed hold of her legs under the thighs, again feeling a momentary flicker of life, and set up a frantic rhythm. He could hear the rain lashing the mud just outside the entrance to the sty and the water flowing out of the tap into the trough. But oblivious of everything except the act he was peforming, he was staring

185

intently at his genitals and hers. Even if lightning had rained down on the sheep-cote he wouldn't have been deflected for a single second from his primal task. His thrusting movements were those of his remotest ancestors before a first glimmer of light illuminated their savage darkness.

He was poised between her legs, his pelvis resting on the ground and absorbing the momentum of his thrusts via his spine. And before long, subjugated by this rhythm that united all men in a common instinct, he was attacked by a blinding pain in his lower back and could feel his spine boring down into the ground. He wrenched himself up, emerged from her anus and plunged into her vagina, which she was holding wide open for him. When he had penetrated her completely she jerked convulsively and flung her head back. There was a faint cracking sound but he paid no heed to it. Both pain and rapture were now conveyed through silence. As he lay full length on top of her he could feel her disjointed legs splayed out in some way he couldn't quite fathom beneath the bulk of his own body, like the legs of a celluloid doll. He raised himself up slightly to catch a glimpse of her face, which was on a level with his solar plexus, and saw that it was completely relaxed and smooth, with a blissful expression. So he stepped up his rhythm. The lower part of his abdomen was smarting where the buttons on his flies were lashing against it and his belt buckle was whipping against her pubis. Then he laid his cheek against the damp straw and all his remaining strength was spent in a series of short spurts.

A muffled groan rose up from beneath him. He rolled over on to his back and stayed stretched out there, sunk in gloom, his mind and limbs drained. Then a spring was released and he experienced a sudden urge to launch into action, to shake off this deadly sense of resignation and get away from the stench of this abandoned pigsty. He crouched, lost his balance as he was adjusting his trousers and sat down with a jolt. She was looking at him, an insistent look that weighed him down, like a broad hand pinning him to the ground, and he knew he would never be able to shake off its weight, wouldn't even be tempted to shake it off. 'You made me come all right,' she said from the bottom of a well she couldn't manage to climb out of. 'I can't feel anything, but I think you've broken my leg.'

It was raining as hard as before outside, if not harder. She rolled her skirt up higher over her stomach, then raised herself up on her elbows and, smiling somewhat apologetically, examined that part of her anatomy that was no longer entirely hers. He was so appalled it took him a while to recover. He leaned over her and realized straight away that there was a slight dislocation in her shin. He ran his fingers gently along the bone – her skin was no thicker than parchment paper – and fingered the break with the same sensitivity of touch he used when he was running his hand lightly over the leaf-like image etched on a fossil.

'It's broken,' he said, running his hand caressingly down the leg from the knee to the ankle. 'It's definitely broken. How did I manage to do it?'

'When you lay down on top of me. My legs are as brittle as matchsticks. It doesn't matter, honestly, I'm not in any pain. The only thing is, I shan't be able to walk.'

At the time he was too appalled to pick up on this odd slip of the tongue but later on, when he was climbing up the steep path, it came back to him and he started having doubts. But now he didn't know what else to do but stroke the broken leg – the blood was spreading in the tissues torn by the bone.

'We'll leave the wheelchair here and I'll carry you to the fortress,' he said. 'I'll never forgive myself, never.'

Still smiling, she brushed her hand against his cheek.

'But I forgive you.'

They had to leave the sheep-cote in torrential rain and once again he had to bring himself to drag her along the ground to get her through the doorway. To stop both her legs swinging about and make sure they stayed parallel, he bound them together, with the good leg acting as a splint. In the depths of the seething mass of clouds, between twin mountains wreathed

187

in mist, a round window was opening up to reveal a determinedly clear sky from which a slanting ray of light was shining
straight on to a tiny patch of brilliantly green forest. This brief
appearance by the sun put heart into him and he slipped his
arms beneath her back and her thighs, lifting her as gently
as he possibly could. Wherever I go something catastrophic
happens and I feel it's my fault, he thought as he set off. I
only have to appear and those who love one another start
hating instead, those in good health fall sick, once-flourishing
institutions go downhill, people stop trusting others and rows
break out.

He was looking at the steep climb ahead of him, with the
rainwater hurtling down it as if it was an irrigation canal, and
doing his best not to jolt her too badly. Every now and then
he'd give a sideways glace at her broken leg and ask: 'Are
you all right?' She'd nod to say that she was, keeping her eyes
closed. When he'd covered a hundred yards or so he realized
he wouldn't be able to put her down before he reached the
top of the col. On one side of them the bank formed an
earth wall taller than he was, on the other the edge of the
path had collapsed and fell away towards the pasture like a
sheet of scree. She had put one of her arms round his neck to
hold on to him and as he moved forward she clasped him in
an ever-tighter embrace. There wasn't a trace of anxiety on
her face, but every now and then she'd open her eyes and
he could see that her gaze concealed everything and revealed
everything at the same time. He turned round to see how far
they'd come. The abandoned wheelchair beside the drinking
trough shone with a dull gleam.

The window boring through the clouds on the horizon
formed by the mountains was turning into a substantial patch
of clear sky. The rain was still falling where they were, but the
other side of the valley was brilliantly sunny. He felt as if he'd
shrunk since he started walking. He'd reached the limit of his
strength, yet this limit was constantly receding, while the top
of the col was getting nearer. As he walked he was taking
deep breaths, concentrating chiefly on keeping his breathing

188

regular and even. Her body was gradually seeming like a minor appendage, an organ whose painful growth he was resigned to carrying with him, as though the rib that had turned into Eve was still attached to Adam's body. One minute it was raining, the next the rain had stopped. He didn't take this in at first and when the sun came out he noticed she was dozing in his arms.

She woke up when he stopped beside a flat rock on one of the bends in the path and stretched her out on it. She looked round her in wonder while he examined her injured leg. From her foot right up to her badly swollen knee, twice its normal size by now, it was a greenish yellow.

'Help me get undressed,' she said. A strong high-altitude wind was sweeping across the sky and in a few minutes the clouds had been driven towards the mountains. As he hadn't moved she said again: 'Undress me.'

He helped her take off her rain-sodden clothes and pulled himself up on to the rock beside her. The sun was now reaching its highest point and shedding an infinitely gentle warmth. Misty vapour was rising from the fields. The landscape, glazed over with light and as brightly coloured as an illuminated manuscript that had just been painted, seemed to have sprung newly minted from the mind of the Creator. He was overcome with exhaustion but numbed by an animal sense of well-being. She was resting with her arms and legs slightly apart, her pubis jutting up. The muscles of her thorax were noticeably well developed due to the effort needed to manoeuvre the wheelchair, and her soaking wet hair was spread out round her face. Seeing her like that, delivered up body and soul to the sun, he felt that neither fire nor sword, nor a total ransacking of the planet, could disturb her ritual stillness.

Her leg didn't seem to be getting any worse, but in full daylight he could clearly see the fracture in her shin, a little way above the ankle. Anyone else but her would have been in terrible pain. He stretched himself out too, letting the sky flood into his eyes.

For years I went on stubbornly working, he told himself,

189

as though my reserves of energy would never give out. Then one day the thoughts stopped coming. I stood and stood in front of the window in the daylight, smoking, and nothing would come. I would see the deserted streets and a stream of ideas would be flowing along them like blood in the draining channel in a slaughterhouse, as though an insipid liquid were pouring out of all the minds still asleep, with a few choice morsels floating on the surface. I would find my thoughts again among this stagnant flood, those harrowing thoughts that for year after year had bloomed in front of my window in the hopeful morning, though they must later fade.

Several shots rang out. It was impossible to tell how far away they were, but they were certainly closer than any of the previous ones. She opened her eyes at the first detonation. She remained motionless except for her eyelids. 'It sounds like an axe striking the trunk of a beech tree,' she said half under her breath. 'They use chainsaws now, but in the old days, when I was a child, you used to hear axe blows ringing through the forest, setting up an echo in your heart. After a moment they would become less frequent because the woodcutter was getting tired, then they'd speed up again. At that point you'd hear the untouched part of the trunk make a cracking sound and the tree would come crashing down like breakers on the shore.'

It didn't take them as long as they'd thought to reach the fortress because someone came to meet them.

Once they were over the col he cut through the forest to avoid the endless twists and turns on the path. She was shivering and feverish and starting to be in pain. It wasn't her injured leg that hurt – she still had no feeling there – but the back of her neck. She said that the tiniest jolt meant that a spike stabbed into her and out again. When she started groaning he would look for a dry spot where he could lay her down and wait till she was feeling better. During one of these enforced pauses they heard the jeep climbing slowly up the path, so close they could have caught sight of it through the foliage. Before long it stopped, as though the driver had had some inkling that they were somewhere near here among the trees. A door slammed. The engine had been throttled down but went on running and its purring sound merged with the buzzing of the insects, the birdsong and the gentle throbbing of the raindrops forming strings of beads on the branches. They didn't move.

'If it's Tanguy, let's keep out of sight,' she whispered.

Then down below them on the path they heard someone whistling a popular song. The driver was clearly waiting for them to show themselves, and though neither of them said anything, they were both asking themselves the same question: What does he want from us? He stood up. The whistling stopped and Tanguy's voice rang out.

'Make up your mind, your eminence. I shan't wait much longer.'

At first he didn't move. Then, abandoning any sense of self-respect, he called out to Tanguy, lifted her up and returned to the path.

When they emerged from the woods Tanguy opened the door on the passenger side and lifted up the rear door, then went to sit behind the wheel without asking any questions. He'd stopped whistling. There wasn't the remotest trace of sarcasm on his face, but an almost unendurable inner tension. While the secretary was strapping her into her seat, then climbing in himself and settling down in the back, he sat with his hands firmly on the wheel, staring straight ahead. His cheeks were hidden beneath several days' growth of beard, he was giving off a strong smell compounded of alcohol, animals and smoke, and his clothes were revoltingly dirty.

'How did you find us?' she asked, her voice sounding amazingly firm and steady.

'Félicité . . .' he mumbled, without further explanation, jerking the jeep round to go back the way he'd come. The secretary was sitting on the metal floor of the jeep, clinging on tight to stop himself being shot from one side to the other. The Smith & Wesson with the scope was lying

191

within reach on a rug. Checking first that Tanguy couldn't see him in the rear mirror, he took hold of the barrel. It was still warm and there was grease running down the breech, which was spattered with gunpowder. She asked Tanguy a question but he either didn't hear or didn't want to hear. Shouting this time to make herself heard above the sound of the racing engine, she commented: 'You've done a lot of shooting today.'

He still didn't reply. He sat there with his jaw clenched, as though the words had turned to stone in his mouth and couldn't get out, so were rattling against his teeth. 'How many animals did you make it at the last count?' she persisted. The secretary wondered how on earth, in the state she was in, she could take an interest in such a topic. Tanguy darted a glance at her that was full of resentment and submissiveness.

'Don't worry about that now,' he said grumpily.

Her broken leg was banging against the door with every bump in the path but still she went on asking. Eventually he blurted out: 'Three pairs of bears with eight cubs, about twenty wolves and twelve lynxes. The lynxes have bred, so there must be twice that now.'

Now that she'd dragged an answer out of him, she smiled, a smile made bitter by exhaustion.

'Judging by the number of shots you've fired over the last few days you must have destroyed quite a lot of them,' she remarked, while the fortress, looking improbably large, loomed up as they turned out of the woods.

Varlaam's helicopter was parked in the courtyard and seemed to be waiting to take off. Tanguy drew the jeep up at the foot of the front steps and Varlaam rushed over. Félicité was standing on the bottom step, upright and with a stern expression, sketching out her silence in the smoke of her pipe. While Varlaam was frantically undoing the straps and lifting her out, she gave Tanguy a cryptic look and said quietly: 'We left the new wheelchair behind in the sheepfold. Go and fetch it, Tanguy.'

7

Our inner battles are almost always continued in external and universal battles whose rules and consequences we generally fail to master, but on which we sometimes recognize, to our alarm, our own personal stamp [Samuel Leber had noted in one of his exercise books]. Every war is our war, even if – especially if – we are its victims, and the echoes of our own violence hover over the remotest battlefields. For we are never innocent and I know that in the coming destruction, blended in with an endless number of destructive passions, there will appear something of that wordless anger that Olga and I feel for each other . . .

The rest of the text was illegible. The lines that came after that had disappeared beneath crossings out in different coloured inks, probably added at some later date. He ran the magnifying glass along them, but it was no use – apart from the odd letter showing through he couldn't make anything out. He wondered whether Samuel Leber had crossed out virtually a whole page after reading it through again, or whether someone else had done it after his death, his wife for instance. But in that case, why not simply throw away the whole exercise book? He went over to the window and leant on the sill. The countless voices of the torrent filled the darkness and a gentle breeze was wafting up from the depths of the ravine scents redolent of moss and daffodils. As he leaned out he caught sight of the shadow of the watchtower to his right. He thought he could make out the cable and remembered Muller's words: 'The decelerating mechanism, that's the key . . .' Then he heard a stealthy sound behind him and when he turned round he saw that someone had slipped a note under his door.

'My brother agrees to meet you,' it read. 'Be there tomorrow afternoon.'

He'd been waiting for this reply for the last two weeks and it seemed to him now that something of Sarachchandra's soul was there beside him, somewhere in the starry hush of this spring night.

He set out in mid-morning as he wanted to get to work with his hammer in the swallow hole before his meeting with Sarachchandra. It would take him about fifty minutes in the jeep to get to the middle of the plateau and he drove at a leisurely pace through a translucently clear day, the light seeming to penetrate right through into the very heart of things. Somewhere on the estate, more on the north side of the valley, where the forest had been left to itself and was turning into an impenetrable jungle of brushwood and thick bramble bushes, shots rang out again and again, though at infrequent intervals, revealing Tanguy's whereabouts. He'd set out on foot with three of the dogs several days ago and was scouring the woods, not going back to the fortress at all.

When he got near the opening to the swallow hole he was surprised to find a meadow scattered with tall buttercups, their huge golden-yellow heads sticky. This was the first time he'd come here over land and he wasn't sure he'd reached the right spot until he drew up on a ledge overhanging the swallow hole and the tentative line of the track, covered with grass that was already tall enough to tickle the chassis of the jeep, disappeared among the jumble of broken stones. For a moment or two he contemplated this luxuriant and quivering growth, this miracle of fertility on what he had known only as arid and desolate terrain, then went over to study the rocky cirque of the swallow hole with a practised eye. It didn't take him long to discover that there was little there to interest the geologist and he abandoned the idea of taking his prospecting equipment. He sat down and focused his attention instead on the caves. They were spread irregularly over three levels, many of them linked by a ghost of a path cut into the rock face, filed down by wind and weather until it was no more than a line, a stave on the musical score of the rocks. And yet for hundreds of years a whole cave-dwelling population had tramped up and down these paths, and the silence of the swallow hole still bore witness to their passage on earth.

194

It wasn't even midday yet but impatience dragged him out of his reverie and he set off along the path leading to the hut. What was he expecting from this man who hadn't swallowed any food at all for the last two weeks, his survival depending on the occasional sip of sugared water? What right did he have to interrupt for a single second the meditation that was enabling him to proceed on his way towards the absolute? The great figures of history who have cut themselves off, the anchorites, those who lived in the wilderness, had always held a great fascination for him – their mixture of determination and self-denial, of inordinate pride and blind faith, made them very nearly inhuman, and thus endorsed the view that the true greatness of humanity lies in the strength of withdrawing from the world.

When he was within sight of the hut he found that it had taken on the same colour as the rock, its wooden planks bleached by rain and snow. There was a tall pile of logs next to it, very neatly arranged in layers rising up one above the other beneath the arching vault of the cave. Then, as he was approaching the cave entrance, surprised at how immaculate it all looked – there wasn't a sign of refuse – a couple of Tamils appeared. They were still in their teens and their expression was one of quiet contemplation. He didn't recognize them – they weren't on the staff of the fortress and had no doubt been recruited from among the local Sri Lankan community. They didn't say anything but took him to the little room he'd been into before. Sarachchandra was lying on a bed of rush matting in the half-dark. He held out his arm in a gesture of welcome that was still full of energy. His hair and beard were longer but his fast didn't seem to have affected him physically, though he stayed lying down.

'Welcome! Come and sit beside me.'

The timbre of his voice hadn't changed either. It rang out softly but firmly and those few words were enough to reveal the inner harmony of this hermit for whom language had now gone beyond a simple statement. He sat down beside him with his legs crossed, on a folded rug in front of an improvised altar

195

made from an upturned crate covered with a cloth. On it an oil lamp and some sticks of incense were burning, in front of three naive pictures of Vishnu, Shiva and Ganesh, the elephant god who is the patron saint of educated men and women. It was as hot as it had been on his earlier visit and he was surprised to see that the stove was still burning, even though the temperature outside was almost summery.

'Please don't think I've come to persuade you to give up your fast. No, I've come to . . .' – only a moment earlier he hadn't known what he was going to say, then suddenly it all seemed blindingly obvious – '. . . to talk about myself.'

Sarachchandra, sensing how awkward he felt, stilled his fears with a wave of the hand.

'I'm told you've written several books and lived in a monastery. Is that right?'

'Yes, it is. I spent ten years looking after an elderly monk at the charterhouse of La Verna in Italy. But how did you know?'

Sarachchandra gave him a mischievous wink, then rolled over on to his side and threw him a look that was totally without curiosity, yet encouraged him to confide in him.

'Nothing remains hidden,' he said, speaking so softly the secretary had to strain to catch his words. 'I spent many years at the fortress, working first for Mr Leber, then for Mrs Leber. I learnt a great deal, a great deal. I know virtually everything there is to know, we all do. The only people who don't know are those who don't want to know, or who don't know that they know. But what became of that elderly monk?'

On the ground a dark, shifting line was running over the patterns on the carpet from one wall of the room to the other. Before answering he focused his attention on this moving line, as though the vigour or otherwise of his thoughts depended on it. He was saying to himself: I'm going to talk, just as he might have said: I'm going to make a landfall after a long sea voyage. But at the same time that sea voyage now seemed remarkably unadventurous. And so he talked, staring down as he did so at the column of ants going backwards and forwards without once deviating from their trajectory.

'He's dead. According to what the doctors said when I arrived at La Verna, Fra Cosimo – that was his name – ought to have died several years earlier. He was suffering from cancer of the oesophagus. But I must start by telling you about our first meeting. I was coming up from Arezzo by motorbike. About a mile before you get to the charterhouse the road climbs up the side of a small valley, then goes down again, as straight and steep as a playground slide. At the bottom of the hill I could see two silhouettes in the middle of the road, one sitting, the other standing. They were both monks. I was going very slowly because the road was full of potholes and they watched me coming downhill, looking absolutely petrified, as though I'd just landed from another planet. I slowed down as I passed them and called out a greeting. The monk pulled the wheelchair on to the side of the road. Neither of them returned my greeting but the disabled monk held out his arms towards me and I just had time to see an expression of pure terror mixed with ecstacy in his eyes. The next day the monk who was pushing him told me that when he saw me appear at the top of the hill, Fra Cosimo had cried out: "At last, *figlio*, the Devil has come for me!" Later on I often used to come back to that same spot, but then I was doing the pushing. I'd have to stop there, abandoning any idea of pushing the wheelchair up such a steep hill. And every time Fra Cosimo would say the same thing: "One day you'll get over that hurdle, pushing me with one hand tied behind your back!" In spite of my age, Fra Cosimo always called me *piccolo*, "little one". I never once heard him use my name, and I was delighted, because I didn't want to hear it ever again, or any other name.

'Every morning I would take him from his cell to the chapel, lift him out of his wheelchair and sit him in the last stall. He was very heavy, but this little ritual meant a great deal to him. I'd leave him in the chapel for most of the day. He'd spend hours muttering a jumble of curses taken from the endless literature of the *contemptus mundi*. Visitors who came into the chapel

197

when he was there would be alarmed by the way he sat there without moving, staring at them with his red eyes. At such times his whole body expressed anathema and an unremitting apocalypse. He would let off steam in that way because God refused to grant the only prayer he ever offered up to him – that he should be recalled to his Maker. Throughout the ten years I spent looking after Fra Cosimo he didn't let a single day, a single hour go by without making his wish to die abundantly plain. It took him some time to accept that I wasn't the Devil come to take him – in fact he never really accepted it – and he would ask me to kill him over and over again. As the months and years went by his wish to die increased, and so did my attachment to him. He hated me because I wouldn't put him out of his misery, and meanwhile I wanted one thing and one thing only – for him to find life bearable, to find a little peace. At first he disgusted me. I thought he was loathsome, cantankerous, temperamental, spiteful – and a liar. Then something happened that turned that old man into the person who was dearer to me than anyone else in the whole world.

'I'd been living at La Verna for a bit over six months – life in a monastery didn't suit me any better than any other type of life – when one day I went into his cell without knocking. He was standing in front of the wheelchair, quite still, but standing on his own two feet. He didn't seem surprised by my bursting in on him and was smiling unpleasantly. "You've elected to push my wheelchair, *piccolo*. Your road to God requires you to make that effort. If you stopped pushing me your life would lose its meaning." I wasn't prepared to confront this cynical outlook and yet after spending the night thinking it over, I decided to forget the episode and go on pushing him as if nothing had happened.'

Someone came in, as silent as a shadow, put a glass of water down beside Sarachchandra and promptly vanished. He opened and shut his heavy eyelids several times but didn't say anything. In this tiny hut built inside a cave, which was itself inside the open mouth of a swallow hole, the world outside

198

filtered through to them merely by means of a little patch of silvery light staining the motionless water in the glass. He was afraid for a moment that he might have tired the brahmin, but he indicated by a movement of his head that he wanted him to carry on with his story.

'After Fra Cosimo's death a charge of manslaughter through negligence was brought against me. I was put on trial but acquitted through lack of evidence. Fra Cosimo had an old revolver he claimed to have stolen from a German officer during the war. I can't tell you how many times he asked me to take him into the forest and put a bullet in the back of his neck. When he used to take the revolver out from under his habit during our walks and lay it across his lap I'd pretend not to show any interest, or else make a joke of it. But it wasn't easy. One day he said; "If you kill me you'll go to prison. But you're in prison anyway, so what's the difference?" "Do it yourself," I replied. "I can't commit a crime like that." "Because you aren't brave enough." He gave me a look, clearly disappointed. "It's not that. You're the one who isn't brave enough. You've got a mission to carry out on earth, so go ahead and do it." Then one day he tried my patience to breaking point and I decided to try a little experiment. I was convinced he was really a coward. I took the revolver when he held it out to me, checked the contents of the magazine, slid a bullet into the breech, all of this with great seriousness, using deliberate movements, and in full view of him so he could see what I was doing. Then I went to stand behind the wheelchair and pressed the barrel against the back of his neck. He was holding his breath, sitting quite still, not saying anything, waiting. We were in a chestnut grove and I could hear the breeze among the leaves and birds singing. He was right: I was the one who wasn't brave enough. When I lowered the revolver he sighed and held out his hand for me to give it back to him. "There you are, I was pretty sure you hadn't got it in you. Let's go on with our walk."

He didn't know if Sarachchandra was still listening or if he'd dozed off. He wasn't showing any sign of life and for a moment

199

he was afraid he might have died. But there was a vein throbbing on his temple. During the silence that followed he glanced round the tiny room and again saw the column of ants. He had the feeling they'd stopped moving, their laborious toing and froing halted by some paralysing ray. His own hand lying on his knee seemed lifeless, and although smoke was rising from the sticks of incense they weren't burning down. Then he turned his head towards Sarachchandra and this very slight movement made him feel as if he'd already passed over to the other side and his movements and thoughts were happening only in his memory. When he took up his tale again this strange sensation was still there, making him feel giddy.

'I used to take Fra Cosimo out all year round, unless there was snow on the ground, using one or other of three paths where I could push the wheelchair. One autumn afternoon he asked me to push him as far as possible into the woods. He never took any notice of how tired I was, never worried about what I was thinking and never asked me anything about my life before I came to La Verna. Trees, tall trees, especially beeches, exerted a powerful attraction for him. He could sit there for hours gazing at them because, he used to say, he could sense divinity in them more than anywhere else. What he meant by divinity only he knew. On that particular walk he was pulled up short by an exceptionally impressive-looking beech and asked me to give him time to meditate there for a bit. After that I often had to push him back to the same spot, because he wanted to see the tree at different times of year. Yet it was a very old tree, and diseased, just as he was, only he didn't realize this. In the late spring we spotted a mark on the trunk in red paint. Some of the other trees bore the same mark. Both of us knew what this meant, but when I spelled it out for the first time he flew into a terrible rage. "That's absurd. You're absurd. You may have great generosity of heart and charitable instincts and devotion to duty, but you don't use any of them to serve God, they're there to serve yourself, so that you can save your own soul through your lack of worldliness. The vow of poverty you took when you bequeathed all your money to the monastery was quite pointless. You didn't need to come here to play at being an oblate – the whole wide world is a monastery for anyone who wants to withdraw from the world into himself . . ."

'The woodcutters responsible for that part of the forest set to work during the summer. When their day's work was over they used to return via La Verna and the bursar would give them a glass of wine. As the days went by I would question them discreetly about how their work was progressing. The beech was the largest tree to be included in this light thinning operation and would be one of the last to be felled. The day before the sacred tree was due to be cut down I warned Fra Cosimo and asked if he wanted to be there. He nodded and I remember the exact words he used after that, because they were the last words he spoke to me: "Failure is what excites you most, *piccolo*. You have a horror of success. If you make a mess of your life you'll have been a success. But making a mess of your life in the full knowledge of what you're doing is rather unusual."

'The next day I pushed him to the edge of the area being thinned. The tree rose up in the middle of the felled trees, solitary and majestic, and God was caressing its boughs and foliage for the last time. I stopped the wheelchair among the brushwood. The woodcutters hadn't seen us – there were three of them – although we were very near the beech. When one of them walked over to it with his chainsaw Fra Cosimo signalled to me to move away. The terrible racket burst out behind me. I turned round and saw that the woodcutter was sawing away at the tree on the wrong side. Fra Cosimo was leaning forward, leaning on the armrests, staring at him intently and at the tree. He'd forgotten all about me . . .'

Sarachchandra's chest was rising and falling in a barely perceptible movement. He'd been asleep for some time now and at this point as he lay there resting his slumber was so fragile that it was as though life was beating away beneath a film of ice. One of the young Tamils was waiting respectfully in the doorway and when the secretary stopped talking he let a

201

little time go by, then came in, knelt before the altar, lit some more sticks of incense in front of the portraits of the three gods and turned towards him, his face full of a stolid gentleness.

'You must let him sleep now, sir,' he said, picking up the glass of water, which Sarachchandra hadn't touched.

But then the hermit turned over suddenly in his sleep and his arm knocked against the altar crate, which toppled over on to the column of ants. This movement in his sleep was extraordinarily violent, expressing a categorical refusal. The secretary stood up with a creaking of joints, staggering. He felt uneasy, as though this unconscious gesture from Sarachchandra meant that he was rejecting what he'd just confided to him.

During his climb back up the swallow hole he sat down when he'd got some way away so that he could have a good look at the hut he'd just left. Or had he left it? Wasn't he still sleeping on a bed of matting surrounded by incense fumes, weakened by fasting and watched over by Ganesh? He stayed sitting there for a long time, waiting for something to happen, though he didn't know what. He couldn't tear himself away from this place where a man was calmly letting himself die. He'd never envied anybody except those very rare beings who are capable of ending their lives, not out of passion, not out of morbid despair, but as the result of a rational decision.

When he got back to the fortress he found Olga Grekova-Leber and Félicité sitting at the top of the front steps. One was reading and the other, sitting very upright on her chair, was grinding coffee, holding an antiquated coffee mill wedged between her thighs. The two women made an odd-looking pair, yet a feeling of peace and serenity emanated from them. The courtyard was divided into two halves by the shadow and behind a flimsy curtain of light he heard a child's laughter burst out inside the building.

It was so unexpected that he stood stock still. A little girl appeared in the doorway and poked her laughing face between the two women. Then a man tightly buttoned into a spotless light-coloured suit joined her. He recognized Olga

Grekova-Leber's doctor, come to have a look at her broken leg and change the plaster. She ran her hand through the child's hair, and he felt that this one little gesture told him more about her than all the speeches she'd spouted at him over the months. It was obvious that the little girl felt quite at home. She wasn't intimidated by the place or the people and the oddity of her carefree presence here rooted him to the spot.

Nobody had noticed him coming into the courtyard. The doctor put his bag down beside the wheelchair and tapped the plaster, which was supported on a metal strut resting on the footplate of the wheelchair. It was still wet and shone dazzlingly white in the sunshine. The little girl slipped away and ran down the steps. She was holding a skipping rope with bright red handles. The doctor was talking to Olga Grekova-Leber.

'I'll come back in ten days' time. The bone will mend very quickly because you aren't using your leg. I imagine Varlaam's at the heliport, isn't he?' He said goodbye to the two women and caught up with the little girl, who was looking at the secretary in alarm, and patted her on the bottom. 'We're off now, Sabine. In a few minutes we'll be up in the sky.'

When they reached the secretary, who hadn't moved, the child looked suddenly awkward and turned away. The doctor laughed and pushed her forward. 'My grand-daughter,' he said. 'Don't worry about Mrs Leber. I'll take the plaster off a month from now. She isn't in any pain – she can't feel anything from the hips down.'

He hadn't been expecting this detail.

'Do mean she can't . . . er . . . that she can't feel anything in her pelvis either?' he asked. The little girl walked off and started skipping. He had a feeling the doctor knew exactly what he was thinking.

'I can't give you any precise information. Only she knows what her body feels. But a medullary traumatism of this severity affects the nervous system over a very large area. However, the nerves may still be intact in some parts of the body.'

As he watched the doctor and the little girl walk away and go through the postern gate he could hear her moaning in the sheep-cote. She can't feel anything from the hips down, he repeated to himself.

She didn't ask him about his visit to Sarachchandra and appeared to be preoccupied with something else entirely. He felt quite unable to summon one of the Tamil servants and went in himself to fetch a bottle of white wine and a small round table. They sat there drinking in silence until the sun disappeared behind the roof.

'Has Varlaam spoken to you?' she asked suddenly, shutting her book and moving the wheelchair so she was facing him.

'What about?'

'Oh, I see, he hasn't told you? He's going into the air force next month. He's been called up and we've lost our pilot.'

He didn't know what to say. He was looking through his glass and feeling completely ground down. We're puny creatures, he was thinking, and even though we're in this fortress, we're totally vulnerable. We're surrounded by dreadful people and we haven't any inkling that there are such huge numbers of them. They see the worst of our perversions as mere childish follies. We could act out the theatre of cruelty for a thousand centuries and they would still see us as mischievous children playing with a pop gun. He felt Olga Grekova-Leber staring intently at him, her expression clouded by some sort of avid desire. He raised his glass as if he was proposing a toast, lifted it to his lips but didn't drink from it.

'I've never talked to you about it, but Morel told me what you said to him about your mother,' she said, moving the wheelchair until she was sitting beside him. 'He didn't believe you, of course.'

'He was quite right not to!'

The retort had just slipped out. He glanced at Félicité as though he was afraid she might be able to hear this conversation. With her brick-coloured skin she reminded him of those ancient statuettes of pre-Colombian female deities moulded in red clay. Saliva was gurgling in the stem of her pipe. She

204

wasn't doing anything else apart from smoking now, but this activity was far from superficial and went way beyond its own significance. All of a sudden Olga Grekova-Leber moved so close she could touch him and with a quick movement snatched up his hand and lifted it fervently, feverishly to her lips. He experienced an uncontrollable twinge of disquiet, but didn't dare pull it away.

'Well, let me tell you I'm quite sure you told him the truth and you really did do the deed,' she whispered, leaning over him.

8

They had reached the highest point on the estate, a bare, rounded peak topped by a belvedere built in the same style as the shooting lodge. Its wooden staircase was still there, its steps rotten but still in place, climbing up towards a cloudless sky. The sun was beating down as if it was high summer and to get there he had just spent over three hours pushing the wheelchair along a never-ending path rising gently but inexorably. As in the old days with Fra Cosimo he wasn't talking as he pushed, but endlessly humming and sometimes even singing the opening bars of Bach's *Musical Offering* at the top of his voice, or the beginning of Mendelssohn's violin concerto. When he had to give of his utmost to get over a particularly difficult stretch she would suddenly seem to be as tensed up as he was, urging him on with: 'Come on! We're getting there! Push, push!' She would say these few words over and over again, in the same tone as when she was saying imploringly: 'Kill me, tear me apart!' when he was entering her, and then he would start singing, bawling out *The Musical Offering* or the Mendelssohn concerto, always one of those two, and life seemed possible again. When they got to the top, carrying the midday sun on their sweating brows, she turned round several times to encircle the panorama with her pitiless glance and eventually announced:

'I don't love nature. What I love is being here with you. I

love it when you push me. I love your hands on the handles of the wheelchair, your panting when you're toiling away, the muscles in your arms, in your thighs. I love every single jolt you inflict on me, every pebble on the path. But not nature! And please don't assume for one minute that it's easier to be pushed than to push. Don't give yourself the leading part in the drama. When it comes to the evening I'm as exhausted and as aching all over as you are, because though you may not realize it, I'm pushing at the same time as you are, and it's you I'm pushing – and you're much heavier than I am.'

He shrugged off his rucksack and flopped down on the warm grass, which crackled underfoot. These days, out of sheer habit, though he knew it was ridiculous now that he'd given up prospecting, didn't even think of doing so, he would take his tools with him every time they set out, in the same way as he might have lugged along any other reminder of a period in his life that, though perhaps not happy, had at least been satisfactory. But he felt a bit ashamed of this: he knew it was more a case of his complying with that melancholy desire to conform that prompts man to glorify his past than with any genuine motive, since his life was beginning again with each new day and all the days that preceded it stayed in his memory no longer than footprints on the sea shore. He had cast aside his worldly wealth and subsequently his personal life by turning his back on an existence lived among other beings. Yet he hadn't really cast aside anything, hadn't renounced anything at all. Apart from his body, this demanding piece of machinery that enabled him to push the wheelchair and, after a fashion, become one with this woman, he had never possessed, had never coveted anything concrete. And the only reality that impinged on his consciousness at this moment, while his gaze roamed unseeingly over the gigantic alpine chaos and its countless hostile peaks, all of them requiring of anyone attempting to scale them a ludicrous amount of perseverance, physical strength and courage combined, the only tangible phenomenon whose unstoppable progress over his will he could calculate with any precision, was the erection

206

that had been lifting up the crotch of his cotton trousers for the last few moments and was proving increasingly awkward.

He took the picnic ingredients out of the rucksack and laid them out. But it made no difference and he suddenly noticed that she was giving him an odd look. He filled a tumbler to the brim with a light red wine and took it over to her. When she took it from him, her shining eyes plunging deep into his, the desire he hadn't even felt a minute earlier was like a wave breaking over him. She drank down the wine in a single gulp, her eyes never leaving him for a second, then tossed the beaker into the grass. Licking her lips, she laid her hand firmly over the bulge in his trousers. 'Get it out,' she said hoarsely. But he had been distracted by a butterfly serenely fluttering round them – a little glimpse of paradise – and, still licking her lips, she unhurriedly unbuttoned his flies, with obvious relish, as though she was opening the door of a larder. Now everything's going to happen as planned, with the inevitable outcome, he thought, remaining passive, allowing her to get on with it. He was looking at the skeleton of the belvedere and its dark wooden staircase that had been vainly resisting wind and weather for decades. When his penis shot out into the open he seized hold of it himself and popped it between her lips, like bread going into an oven. Her mouth was hot, as hot as a vulva. A hand slipped inside his trousers, which were down round his hips by now, and closed over his testicles, squeezing them gently, rhythmically. He grabbed her by the hair and guided her. When he thrust too far down her throat she would gag, coughing, but keep him in her mouth and continue her toing and froing, gulping him down still more greedily. She would occasionally stop to catch her breath, but very quickly, and for a few seconds the hand would stop squeezing his testicles and hold them flat on its palm like a piece of fruit lying on a dish. Then before wolfing him down again she would briefly contemplate his penis with its coating of saliva as though she was trying to decide which bit she was going to tackle next as she ate her way through the banquet.

He felt it coming slowly but surely in his arched loins. Gradually the rigidity of his penis spread to the rest of his body, a spasm hardened his groin and, keeping his eyes fixed on the same spot – her dusty plaster and the purple and swollen toes poking out of it – he was wondering: Where's Tanguy at this moment? Maybe he's watching us through his binoculars. Maybe he's getting ready to put a bullet through our shoulder blades. Mightn't that be just what she wants? But the serenity of this place suggested otherwise. Nature, which she claimed to dislike yet was savouring with such relish, was turning out to view with lordly lack of concern anything connected with human savagery. At the exact moment when a vision of Tanguy raising his rifle to his shoulder and taking aim at them loomed up among the images peopling his imagination, he grabbed hold of her head on either side as if he was snatching up a pitcher by its handles, slapped it against his belly and, in a series of spasms, ejaculated into her mouth.

After that they had their picnic. She ate and drank greedily, but his mind was elsewhere. He was amazed to be still alive, amazed at everything, like someone who's woken to find he's been dragged out of the ruins of a town after a bombing raid, and transported here, to the radiant stillness of the mountains. He noticed that her cheek wore a scar of dried sperm, poured some water on to his handkerchief and wiped it off. She looked at him, languidly, gratefully, finished off her sandwich, tapped a hard-boiled egg against the armrest of the wheelchair, shelled it and held it up, moist and shiny, against the light.

'You're one of the pure in heart,' she said. 'But you're constantly preoccupied by the idea of purity, which makes you deeply ambiguous.'

She gobbled the egg up in a couple of mouthfuls then, having eaten her fill, turned the wheelchair to face the sun and closed her eyes. After a few moments her head drooped on to her shoulder. He thought she'd dozed off, but as he started to walk towards the belvedere she called him back. 'Don't leave me! Don't ever leave me again! I need you. I'd been asleep for years and you woke me up, you wanted me.

I didn't disgust you. I shall always be grateful to you for that, whatever happens. But you must swear you won't abandon me. Go on, swear!' He swore. Then she really did fall asleep and her brow, serene and inscrutable, was gently stroked by a lock of hair floating in the warm breeze.

They left the belvedere in mid-afternoon. When they were halfway back he decided on a much quicker route that would take them straight to the shooting lodge. He was familiar with the difficulties it involved, and knew they weren't insurmountable. They left the original path and set off into the rustling forest, accompanied by the chattering of a solitary jay. Birches and holm oaks mingled in with the fir trees, the forest grew thicker, and as they proceeded noisily through the undergrowth they would sometimes start a woodpecker, which would shoot skywards with a mocking laugh. On one occasion when they'd stopped for a rest she told him that no forestry work had been done on the estate for the last fifteen years, because her husband couldn't bear the idea of felling a tree.

'He didn't like woodcutters,' she said. 'He thought of them as murderers. I think one of the reasons why he took on Tanguy was so that there'd be one woodcutter less in the area.'

Between the dense thickets there flourished an impenetrable tangle of bramble bushes and patches of ferns dating back to the Quaternary era that were as tall as a man. It took a long time to go round them, but he was pushing in the anteroom of eternity now and his innate sense of direction made the concept of a goal to be attained seem one of the least important of his preoccupations. He was pushing for the sake of pushing, his hands welded to the wheelchair handles – they'd gone back to the familiar old chair, which was light and easy to manoeuvre – pushing in order to discover, in performing this backbreaking act, this act that went beyond devotion to duty and self-sacrifice, beyond the idea that she was entirely dependent on him too, the mere possibility of persevering with the act of being.

When he was getting them across a gulley he would arch his

back and lift up the wheelchair plus its occupant, as though he was lifting their twin destinies so that he could snatch them up out of the unfathomable depths of irrationality and put them down, safe and sound, on terra firma. At such times he didn't give her any warning. Strapped firmly to the wheelchair, she would wave her arms about frantically, and when its wheels were back on the ground would burst out as a matter of form with: 'You might have warned me!', or else praise his skill, always using the same words: 'Bravo! Well played! Push, go on, push!' And he would push. She trusted him completely now. She would leave him to prevail over the laws of nature, and the thought that he might fail would never enter her head. Feeling that this trust was a vindication of his life, perhaps even a sign of love, he would proceed slowly on his way through the trees, experiencing the fundamental sensation of a communion between them that grew ever closer as time went by.

He'd been pushing for over an hour when the forest thinned out and the ground sloped less sharply. The odd empty cartridge case lying on the ground showed that Tanguy had been that way recently. When the mossy roof of the shooting lodge appeared among the range of bright greens of the foliage, he suddenly had a feeling that something was amiss and stopped pushing.

'Does it strike you that there's a peculiar smell here?' she asked. Ahead of them the undergrowth was filled with the humming sound of a power station. He sniffed the air and listened, keeping an eye on the shooting lodge, bits of which were visible through the gently swaying branches, and experienced that apprehensive, highly threatening feeling that hits you just before you return to civilization after a long period in the wilderness.

'I don't know why, but I've got a feeling Tanguy's here somewhere,' she said, lowering her voice. Then she held her handkerchief to her nose. 'Good God, what a stink! And we forgot to take the gun too.'

It was certainly the first time they'd left the fortress without taking a gun with them, but as things had turned out, what use would a gun have been against a smell?

'Would you like us to go round the lodge?' he asked. 'I think we should go and see what's going on, though.'

She hesitated. She looked anxiously round again, then made up her mind.

'Come on, push! The smell's quite appalling, but I want to know what's causing it.'

They found the lodge door wide open. All the window panes except one had been broken; a couple of window frames had been wrenched away from the brick wall and were dangling down against the front of the building, which was pitted with bullet holes. It looked as though the place had been repeatedly captured after an enemy assault. One of the sofas was standing outside in front of the door, its innards hanging out, and beside it, its surface black with dried blood, was the big table, with a venison knife with a long tapering blade stuck into it. Empty bottles were lying all round the table. And a little way away there was a peculiar-looking stack of something – a pyramid of bloodstained animal pelts, snouts, half-open mouths, their teeth shining through streaks of bloody spittle, ready to bite, a tangle of antlers, tusks, ears, dozens of severed heads piled up and overlapping in a way that suggested some attempt had been made to arrange them in a symmetrical and balanced pattern – a foul heap of putrefying hunting trophies.

The decapitated bodies, black with flies, were strewn round the clearing. Some of them still seemed to be stirring beneath the bunches of insects swarming in and out of their entrails and eye sockets. Many of these remains had clearly been rotting there for weeks, and had been half eaten by other creatures, who had then themselves been slaughtered and eaten up. Harmless creatures – does, stags, roedeer, hares, wild rabbits – easily outnumbered the genuine predators in this charnel house. Beneath the clumps of flies he spotted a few wild boar carcasses, some half-starved lynxes no bigger than cats, three wolves and just one bear. To notch up such an impressive bag Tanguy had clearly shot at anything that

211

came within range, and had no doubt done hours of stalking simply to bag a squirrel, a fox or a badger. He couldn't see a single bird. How on earth had Tanguy managed to bring all his prey here, after presumably killing them all over the estate, he wondered. Even when it's mortally wounded, an animal doesn't always fall to the ground where it was shot. You have to track it down by looking for clues: hoof prints, blood, hairs, bones, bits of internal organs (frothy, bright red blood means lungs; dark red blood means the liver; if it's mixed with yellow and green, intestines).

His mind was seething with questions, but he couldn't put any of them into words because everything repelled him now, including language, for that too was dead, a rotting carcase among rotting carcases. He didn't dare look at her. He felt guilty, as though he was personally responsible for this massacre, and always had been. But he sensed that she was thinking along the same lines, that they were both experiencing the same feeling of utter dismay – they wouldn't have been any more shattered if they'd come across a pile of rotting human corpses. And both of them saw this carnage as presaging an epidemic of all-embracing horror, and saw Tanguy's insane butchery as heralding a bout of collective insanity.

He pulled the wheelchair under the trees. Beneath the low branches, the stench plus the buzzing of the flies took on the consistency of organic matter. She retched and started vomiting over the side of the armrest. He wasn't feeling too good either, but he held her head and for some strange reason, while she was vomiting he felt his own nausea subside and the smell didn't make him feel ill any more. She flung herself abruptly back in her straps, gasping for breath, her eyes swimming. He didn't say anything, simply grabbed hold of the wheelchair and set off into the forest as fast as he could.

As he pushed he was asking himself: Why did Tanguy spare the birds? Why on earth? He was walking very fast for this type of uneven terrain, but he felt calm and well in control. It felt as if the wheelchair wasn't touching the ground, his exhaustion had vanished, and for the first time since he'd started pushing

212

her, he had the feeling that he'd got his touch back, those virtuoso skills he'd once possessed and Fra Cosimo used to describe as divine grace. He would have pushed like that if bombs had been raining down on them, aware of the danger but invulnerable. He didn't stop until they reached the fortress. Just before they went through the postern gate he caught sight of Tanguy rushing into the dovecot. That fleeting vision provided an answer to his question. The aviary, he thought suddenly. He didn't kill the birds because of the aviary.

He spent the night watching over her as she slept. She was feverish and spoke a great deal in her nightmares. Most of what she said was unintelligible, though a handful of quite distinct words amid the rambling gave him food for thought for some time. 'The bucket, Tanguy, the bucket, promise me . . .' That was as much as he could make out – after that she went on with her disjointed rambling, delivered in a mumble. She would wake up at frequent intervals but remain only semi-conscious; and she didn't recognize him even though he was leaning over her. On one occasion she mistook him for Samuel Leber. He intercepted such a look of horror on her face that he had to shake her until she was fully awake, and as he gazed at this face that for a few seconds had been so distorted by mental anguish that it was unrecognizable, he felt thoroughly frightened too and thought to himself that terror in the soul is no less real than terror in the barrel of a gun. When she had at last taken in who he was she drew him towards her. 'You don't wish me any harm, do you?' she stammered. 'Stay with me, get into bed with me, please do, please.' He lay down fully dressed, took her in his arms and hugged her tight like a terrified child. Eventually she grew calm and fell asleep, and he was alone, basking in the warmth of this living mystery. He didn't remember switching off the light and lost track of time. He probably slept too, for all of a sudden a new day had dawned.

Although she was still feeling the effects of her ordeal, in the late afternoon she decided to send for Tanguy. All her anxieties

213

promptly came flooding back and she asked the secretary to stay with her. 'I'll ring the police tomorrow morning,' she said, 'I'll have him locked up. But meanwhile I want to see him. I've got to see him.'

The interview didn't last long. Tanguy turned up in a loose white shirt and a clean pair of trousers, close shaven, his hair and beard neatly trimmed, apparently sober. She saw him in her private hall, which was where she'd ordered him to kill the animals, with the official looking on. He arrived full of overweening arrogance, walking with his somewhat swaying gait and completely ignoring the secretary. She kept her hands clenched on the wheels of her chair, her face very pale, her manner icy.

'We were over at the shooting lodge,' was all she said. A dazzling smile lit up his face.

'Then you must have seen how hard I've been working.'

'Indeed we did. And you'll be carrying on with it in the madhouse.'

He took a couple of paces towards her. His mouth was still smiling, but his grey eyes were glazed and staring.

'I'll be going back into the forest tomorrow. They wanted me to kill the animals and I'm killing them. As your husband would have said, Mrs Leber, I'm a perfectionist. I shan't stop shooting until there isn't a single animal left alive on this lousy estate. I'll kill them all, down to the last rabbit. All of them, I tell you.'

The secretary had never heard him speak at such length. He thought. I'm going to give him another thrashing. But he didn't move. He felt perfectly capable of grabbing hold of him, lifting him up and flinging him into the ravine if need be, but he didn't move, because he didn't feel any hatred for him.

'Why aren't you killing the birds, Tanguy?' he asked.

To begin with his expression froze, but then his features crumpled. Yet he didn't so much as glance at the secretary – it seemed as though nothing could make him avert his eyes from the void he was staring into.

'Don't try anything on with me, Mrs Leber,' he said after

a while, his voice low but determined. 'If you make the least bit of trouble for me, you know what'll happen.'

He turned on his heels and left the room. She let out a long-drawn-out wail, hid her face in her hands and burst out sobbing.

9

Sarachchandra died on 21 June, the summer solstice, after sixty-eight days of fasting – an exceptionally long period. Ramanuja brought the news to Olga Grekova-Leber. He told her that his brother's last wish had been to be cremated according to the rites of his religion on the spot where he'd died and that a few hours before his death he'd expressed the wish that all those living at the fortress should take part in the funeral. That was when she realized how very awkward her situation was.

Sarachchandra was one of a group of political refugees who'd held both a residence permit and a work permit for several years. He was officially a member of the local population and there was a file on him at the local records office. His death needed first to be certified by a doctor, then his mortal remains would undergo the same fate, give or take a few minor variations, as those of any other citizen. Although the problem of his death was more complicated and much more awkward than that, those were the points she tried, without success, to explain to Ramanuja, who refused gently but firmly to yield to reason. Both he and his compatriots were determined, he said, to stop anyone coming near the body, and were prepared if necessary to use force to prevent anyone getting into the swallow hole. Throughout this conversation his refusal to cooperate was voiced quite calmly and he never once tried to argue. It didn't take her long to realize that this apparent gentleness and calm was digging a swamp big enough to swallow up a whole civilization and its rational arguments. Sarachchandra was to be cremated not the next day but the day after that, at sunset.

That same evening she telephoned the doctor who was treating her leg and early the following morning Varlaam deposited him at the heliport.

'I'm perfectly happy to issue a death certificate, but it won't really help,' he said, realizing the problem straight away. 'If everything's to be legal, the police would have to be there. You know that it's strictly forbidden for anyone at all to be buried in the open countryside, still less to be cremated, unless there's a special permit – the sort of thing that's issued in exceptional circumstances a couple of times a century. Anyway, you're liable to be accused of manslaughter through negligence for letting him die on your estate.'

A little while later Varlaam, the doctor and the secretary were taking off for White Cow Hole.

Varlaam deliberately didn't fly over it, but landed the helicopter some way away, switched off the engine and waited until the blades had come to a complete stop. Flocks of cumulus clouds were racing past, driven by a high-altitude wind and casting their pot-bellied shadows over the barren wasteland. The three men sat there in silence, all of them feeling awkward. As he was the only non-Tamil who'd been allowed close to Sarachchandra during his fast, the secretary decided to go down first. He'd given up any hope whatsoever of persuading the Tamils, but didn't say so to the others. He felt as if a hiatus had just cut into the fragile fabric of the natural order and those clouds whirling round above their heads, when there wasn't a breath of wind at ground level, added greatly to this impression. The doctor was wearing a crumpled suit of an old-fashioned cut, in cream-coloured linen, and a panama hat with a black ribbon round it. With his somewhat stiff and starchy manner he had a colonial look about him. He was clearly worried and trying very hard to feign indifference. They went over to the edge of the swallow hole. Varlaam and the doctor sat down on a couple of boulders and watched the secretary disappearing behind the ridge.

No sooner had he gone past the first hills than he stopped dead. He couldn't believe his eyes. Many of the caves were taken up with makeshift camps, in each of which a large number of Tamils, both men and women, were busy with domestic tasks. There were fires burning all over the place inside the swallow hole and it looked as if some prehistoric tribe had just risen from the dead and taken possession once again of its primeval home. Nobody was paying any attention to him. He went a bit further down and looked for the hut, but couldn't see it. He soon realized that it had gone for good. It had been taken apart and the planks had been used to make the pyre even bigger – it was large enough now to stretch for several yards, filling the entrance to the cave, and preventing his seeing into its depths, where white silhouettes were bustling about in the half-dark. Sarachchandra's body was no doubt at rest behind the pile of wood. The following day it would be hoisted up on to it, sprinkled with scents and covered with petals. Beside the pyre were bunches of wild flowers stuck into tin cans filled with water, and there were more of them in each of the caves with people in them. He spotted another detail: each camp had its own improvised altar with sticks of incense burning on it and wafting fragrances of opium and jasmine all over the swallow hole. Then three men armed with sticks appeared and barred his way.

He didn't recognize them – they came from outside the fortress too. As far as he could tell, large numbers of Tamils had headed here from the four corners of the land to attend the funeral ceremony, taking no notice of the fence running round the estate. Having slipped silently on to the land belonging to the fortress and walked as far as the swallow hole without anyone having any idea they were there, they would no doubt leave again just as discreetly, as long as they were left alone. He felt very much on their side and was reluctant to retrace his steps without making some attempt to help.

The two men weren't displaying any real animosity towards him – it was more that they were being obstinate. They didn't ask any questions, simply stopped him going any further. He asked to see Ramanuja. They conferred together in whispers, then one of them walked off in the direction of the pyre. While

217

they were waiting he had a better look round at the caves. The harder he looked, he felt that the number of Tamils was increasing all the time. They were probably over a hundred of them, perhaps a third of the whole refugee community. There weren't many women, no children at all, and only a handful of teenagers as far as he could tell from that distance. However he was too far away to be able to grasp what exactly they were so busy doing in the caves. The whole place was silent. He couldn't hear anyone calling out: they were all toiling away without talking, poring over some mysterious task. Men with serious faces were moving about between the various camps, carrying luxuriant bunches of flowers, buckets and all sorts of items specially transported to the swallow hole, as they were essential if the dead man's soul was to travel beyond his body. Then Ramanuja came over and explained what was happening.

They were preparing the offerings and the funeral feast. Each family was contributing something and the many unmarried people would join in with them to do honour to Sarachchandra, who had become a saint by renouncing life on earth. When the secretary wanted to know how all these people had managed to get there without attracting attention, Ramanuja scowled and didn't answer.

'You know that this type of meeting isn't allowed in this country,' the secretary pointed out. 'Mrs Leber has been put in a very awkward situation legally.'

The man's face darkened and he gazed at the secretary with a hostile expression.

'Why did you come here today, sir?' he asked.

The secretary calmed him down, explained why he'd come and asked him to let the doctor certify that Sarachchandra was dead.

'No, sir, it's impossible. Please don't insist,' he said, though his tone was more conciliatory now.

He didn't want to put any more pressure on him. In fact he felt relieved and looked round the swallow hole for a moment or two. The natural order wasn't cracking after all.

It was simply that a new type of order was setting in.

'I understand. We'll be here tomorrow for the ceremony. All of us except Tanguy, I'm afraid.'

Ramanuja's smile returned. His face even took on a somewhat mocking expression, and when he insisted that Tanguy would be there too, this confirmed the secretary's suspicions about the part Tanguy had played in the whole episode. Ramanuja bowed and went back down towards the caves, followed by the two men with sticks – they were playing with them now, laughing like children.

The secretary went slowly back up the swallow hole, stopping several times to have a good look at this population of silently meditating figures thousands of miles from home, perpetuating a ritual that hadn't changed for centuries. All of a sudden he was struck by how incongruous the whole situation was and started laughing. He found Varlaam stretched out full-length in the grass with his arms wide apart, sucking a blade of grass, while the doctor was pacing up and down impatiently, his panama hat askew, his tie undone. He waited for a moment before letting them know he was back. This reality – with two particularly disturbing features in the shape of the helicopter and the doctor's bag lying in the grass – didn't seem any less incongruous than the reality he'd just left, except that this time he didn't feel inclined to laugh.

The doctor, irritated at having been dragged out on a wild goose chase, didn't say a word on the way back. When they were within sight of the fortress Varlaam took off his headphones and turned to the secretary.

'Has Mrs Leber said anything about me?'

'Yes.'

'I'll be sad to leave you.'

'You won't be far away. We'll often see each other.'

He shrugged his shoulders, then concentrated on his controls, starting on a long side slip to the heliport. The forest raced towards them, so fast that its contours were flattened out. For a moment the ground seemed to rear up vertically like a dark-green wall and it looked as if they were going to

219

smash into it. The doctor heaved a querulous sigh. Varlaam gave the secretary a wink, straightened up the helicopter and took it slowly down towards the concrete landing strip.

We struggle for years on end to acquire a disciplined method of working. We have a picture in our minds of what we are accomplishing, and we believe that we are fulfilling ourselves with sincerity and humility; but all of this is erroneous from the outset, because that discipline we acquire, and that fulfilment, are many miles away from the true focus of our attention. Not only are we unable to cope with the difficulties we experience in finding with each new day that we're spiritually 'on the top of our form', i.e. at peace with our conscience even in so far as the turmoil of our inner life is concerned, but we are also misled by the fiendish independence of the tool we use to achieve this – our intelligence – in that we think we have it under control, yet more often than not it conditions our thinking and inveigles us, thanks to its own magnetic attraction, into pursuing goals that are very different from the goals we had set ourselves. Thus I believed that I was in control of architecture, whereas in fact architecture had always been in control of me.

He held the exercise book out to her, but she wouldn't take it. It was the second time she'd come to see him in his room. The warm night air was coming through the open window. The muddy smell of the gorge was wafting up the ravine and a lone nightingale perched on the side of the cliff modulated its song in the darkness.

'I don't want to know anything else about Samuel,' she said. 'He's dead and we're still alive. I don't know why I listened to you – we've got other fish to fry now.'

They had had dinner together in the kitchen beside the fire-place, though the fire had gone out, and had drunk and talked

220

a great deal. Then they'd gone their separate ways without finding a solution to the problem caused by Sarachchandra's death. Later on she hadn't been able to get to sleep and had woken Félicité, then joined him in his room when he was in the middle of deciphering the minute letters Samuel Leber had used for writing his last notes.

'Why do you think your husband used a writing method that's virtually illegible? Definitely not to prevent anyone reading it – there's more to it than that.'

She shrugged her shoulders in annoyance and with an edgy movement propelled the wheelchair towards the window. She'd removed her make-up and her face was shiny with cream, her features drooping with exhaustion and anxiety.

'How do you expect me to know? Because he'd gone mad, I suppose. Do you really think Tanguy's been talking and the whole town's aware of what's been going on in the swallow hole?'

'He may not have. But I wouldn't trust the doctor if I were you.'

'The doctor won't talk. I've paid him to keep his mouth shut and he isn't a man to break his word. But I'm afraid my money can't help me beyond that – I'd have to buy off every single official in the whole of the province.'

'You can afford to.'

She pushed back an imaginary veil dangling over her forehead and looked out. He suddenly experienced the full physical force of the dark drop into the ravine. She was sitting on the edge of it and it seemed to him that no wall could protect her now. He had come into the world robbed of any destiny and here he was now, experiencing a feeling of being present – a voyeur powerless to intervene – at one of those unpredictable and trivial incidents that suddenly alter the course of a person's fate and upset what appears to be its sequence. The incident hadn't yet happened, yet there seemed to be no way of preventing it.

She lit a cigarette but let it burn down without smoking it. The blue curls of smoke were spiralling up in the darkness, ethereal in this oppressive atmosphere. Now at last he could put into words an idea he'd been turning over in his mind ever since he got back from the swallow hole.

'Maybe you should get in touch with Alexis Muller.'

He could tell from her edgy smile that this possible course of action had been constantly on her mind, but that it went very much against the grain to ask Muller for advice, particularly since in this case he was probably the only person whose advice carried any real weight.

'Muller's a public official. He'd be duty bound to report to the powers-that-be, and within twenty-four hours the swallow hole would be crawling with policemen, plus a retinue of journalists and every conceivable type of muckraker and nosey parker. I don't want anyone here – I couldn't stand it.'

He remembered his conversation with Muller and how determined he was to unlock her secret. He could see the little man with his grey eyes saying with steely conviction: 'I haven't got many years left to me, and I'd like to feel that this last phase of my life will be illuminated by a ray of light, or even a tiny speck of light in the whole vast universe.'

'Muller's got a lot of influence and he knows how stoical the Tamils are. If you explain the situation to him, he'll realize that if the police intervene they'll offer strong resistance, and it's not in a public prosecutor's interest to instigate a massacre, or make the police a laughing stock.'

For a moment she was clearly put out by the logic of this argument, but she didn't answer. Then her attitude changed completely. She peered at her cigarette. It had burnt right down to the filter but the ash hadn't dropped off and she lifted it up very carefully until it was at eye level.

'By this time tomorrow Sarachchandra will be like this cigarette,' she mused. She blew on the ash, flung the cigarette end out of the window, then propelled the wheelchair over to the bed and turned seductively towards him. 'I'm exhausted. I think I'll spend the night here. You'll wash me and put me to bed, won't you?'

222

10

The following morning she telephoned Muller and a couple of hours later Varlaam was landing at the heliport with him. The little man was wearing a woollen suit that was much too thick for the time of year. Everything about him made you feel that wherever he went it was always winter: he was constantly seeking warmth and a place of refuge that was in fact unattainable, yet he never gave up. The secretary noticed that he looked just the same. He was undeniably pleased to see him, as though over and above the usual feelings there was some sort of tacit understanding between them. Yet almost simultaneously he began to feel that Muller posed a serious threat, and that his presence at the fortress flowed from a preordained and ineluctable process that was slowly being played out. When he saw him coming over to meet him, putting his metal-rimmed glasses straight as he did so, he intercepted the smugly undaunted look of a chess player who's just set up a series of moves that's bound to defeat his opponent. And yet the old gentleness was still there, lurking in the depths of his good eye.

He felt it would be tactful not to sit in on the conversation between Olga Grekova-Leber and Muller, even though he'd been invited to do so. But later on she admitted, sounding both calmer and preoccupied: 'You were quite right. He won't say anything, for the time being at any rate. Not just for the reasons you referred to . . .' She broke off after this cryptic admission, then added: 'We're still in an awful fix though.'

After lunch Muller drew him aside and again they found themselves on the parapet walk, as they had five months earlier. This time Muller didn't make any reference to the cable car.

'I love this view,' he said, sitting between two of the crenellations. 'I'll never grow tired of it – it's quite different from anywhere else.' Then he moved straight on to another topic:

'We haven't seen Tanguy yet. I hear he's been put in charge of . . . er . . . getting rid of the dangerous animals on the estate. Has he been performing that sinister task?'

'He's been living out in the forest for several weeks now, shooting at anything that moves.'

He told Muller about how they'd discovered the charnel house. 'Mrs Leber's convinced he's gone mad, but I think he's doing it out of despair. And I'm responsible for his despair, through no wish of mine.'

The little figure stared at him intently over his glasses, as though he wanted to put across some crucial revelation without having recourse to words.

'Tanguy's always been in despair. In claiming responsibility you're narrowing his despair down quite remarkably. Forgive me for speaking frankly, but I have a feeling you've failed to appreciate a large number of factors, and since you arrived at the fortress you've been as it were living in a country whose customs you haven't fully understood. Silence speaks louder than words here. As I was saying to Mrs Leber a few moments ago, a large number of relatively unimportant facts nibble away at the foundations of things that seem to be very sturdily built and eventually they collapse, even though we thought they were as steady as a rock. The death of . . . er . . . of this Tamil is a relatively unimportant fact, we're all agreed on that, but its repercussions could have highly undesirable consequences for Olga.'

The secretary found this sudden use of her first name and the implied familiarity disturbing. He had a feeling that it indicated that her relationship with Muller was more complicated than he'd thought.

'What do you intend trying to do to prevent such consequences?'

'Oh well, anything in my power, which means not very much. It's more difficult to bring about a man's administrative death than physically to kill him. If Mrs Leber isn't to be pestered over this business, the Tamil would have had to vanish without trace. It seems reasonable to suppose that if his disappearance

224

isn't reported no one will check the files. Needless to say, if the story were to leak out, that would be enough to bring us back to square one.'

An odd coincidence occurred at that point. The two men sized each other up for a second or two in silence, as though each were reading the other's thoughts. Ever since Muller's use of her first name the secretary had been wondering: Was he her lover before the accident? And suddenly, though nothing happened except that they exchanged glances, he had his answer. At exactly the same moment he could read the same question in Muller's eyes, and he realized that unwittingly he too had just given him his answer.

'It wouldn't suit your purposes for the story to leak out, would it?'

'Indeed it wouldn't. Mrs Leber is well aware of that. I wouldn't want life at the fortress to be disrupted before I've had a chance to find what I'm looking for. And if it were disrupted by some external factor, any form of search would become impossible.'

'What happens afterwards?'

'After what?'

'After you've found what you're looking for.'

Muller gave him a friendly dig in the ribs, then promptly resumed his serious expression.

'Afterwards we'll all be dead,' he said. 'Olga suggested I should come with you to the swallow hole. What do you think?'

The door to the keep slammed and Varlaam appeared. He'd been looking for them for some time, as Olga Grekova-Leber was refusing to get into the helicopter, so they'd have to drive to the swallow hole in the jeep and would need to leave shortly if they were to get there in time for the ceremony. He referred to 'the ceremony' as naturally and casually as if it were some run-of-the-mill village fête. The secretary went up close to Muller and whispered, sounding suddenly very earnest: 'It's too late to back out now. Do come with us.'

They reached the swallow hole at the end of the afternoon. Not a word had been spoken during the journey, as the tone had been set at the outset by Félicité's wordless grief. Her admiration for Sarachchandra was almost mystical and she sat throughout the drive sunk in a mournful meditation that nothing could have dragged her out of, conducting an inner monologue that seemed to be taking place inside the thick walls of an Aztec pyramid. Muller watched her covertly all the time, clearly fascinated, as though for the first time in his life he had come face to face with a hermetically sealed truth that, as he well knew, he would never be able to fathom.

Ramanuja was waiting for them, along with all the Tamils from the fortress. They were wearing white beneath the stormy sky and seemed drenched in light as they sat on the dark grass. They stood up all in one go and swarmed round the jeep. One of them opened the door on Olga Grekova-Leber's side, but left the secretary to carry her over to the wheelchair. He pushed her as far as possible along the path to the swallow hole and when the uneven ground made it impossible to continue, a couple of the Tamils took it upon themselves to pick up both the chair and its occupant. She protested weakly while they were lifting her and starting off down the first spur leading to the caves nearest them. They put the chair down several times so that they could get their breath back but refused to let anyone else take over. There was an infinite gentleness in their spirited and determined attitude, which was very different from grief – they weren't mourning the death of a loved one but rejoicing at the blessed transmigration of a soul. She didn't say a word until the path ran beside a ledge offering a sweeping view, and she took in at a single glance the whole of the swallow hole and its population.

The secretary was walking behind her bearers and saw her shudder. Since his last visit there were many more Tamils gathered there and all the caves within easy reach were now occupied. Most of the cave dwellers were crowding round the cave that Sarachchandra had chosen as his hermitage. He was lying on his pyre surrounded by flowers and offerings as if he was ensconced on a pedestal, apparently waiting for the fire to be lit. Wherever the terrain made it practicable for people to clamber up there were figures perched on any available spot not too far from the funeral pyre. Some of them were in the most precarious positions and they too seemed to be waiting, without really waiting. Here and there dogs and children who had recently arrived were rushing about from one cave to the next. Several men were standing guard in a lackadaisical fashion on the flat area round the pyre. It was swarming with people, but no one was pushing and shoving and the overall mood was apathetic, though every now and then a nervous shudder would sweep through the crowd, threatening violence, then die down straight away.

She ordered her bearers to put her down. For a few minutes she was quite unable to find words to express her dismay, then she looked round frantically for Muller.

'Do you realize what this means – these people here on the Leber estate, less than two hours' walk from the fortress?' she asked, raising her voice. 'It means that next time ten thousand, a hundred thousand people could invade my land without my knowing anything about it, while I'm quietly lying in bed inside this impregnable citadel that can withstand a hundred-megaton bomb, yet could be invaded by a handful of gangsters armed with sticks in two seconds flat.' Muller had stepped forward right to the far end of the ledge and appeared not to hear what she was saying. He was staring down in fascination at the broken tiers of the swallow hole rising one above the other. 'It's you I'm talking to, Mr Prosecutor!' she called out. 'What am I to do now?'

He wrenched himself reluctantly away from the scene before him, shrugged his shoulders wearily, but didn't reply straight away. Her angry dismay, Félicité's hieratic and wordless grief, the Tamils' silence – he seemed to be utterly enthralled by it all, yet not really affected by it.

'Would you have preferred me to send in a squad of police?' he asked eventually. 'Of course you wouldn't. By tomorrow your servants will be back at the fortress and all these good

227

people will be on their way back down to the plain. As for those gangsters you referred to – don't worry, you'll soon be properly protected.'

She didn't have time to ask him what he meant. A tremendous thunderclap shook the air. The sound was trapped in the swallow hole for a moment or two, heads were raised and a tremor ran through the crowd. Ramanuja asked them to follow him. He had arranged for a sort of alcove to be made ready for them so that they would be under cover if it rained. Flares were already being lit in the area round the pyre, where there was some sort of commotion going on. The sky was rent by a flash of lightning, thunder rumbled beneath the clouds and every now and then shouts would ring out. The secretary peered closely at the uneven ground inside the swallow hole, looking for Tanguy. He couldn't see him anywhere, but remained convinced that he was hiding somewhere lower down, among the careful jumble of rocks, and that sooner or later he would put in an appearance.

A chorus of voices rose up from Sarachchandra's cave. They were calling Ramanuja. The light was rapidly fading as a black sky streaked with purple closed in over the swallow hole. Their alcove was above the largest of the caves, quite a long way from the pyre. The Tamils put the wheelchair down on a carpet of mown grass strewn over the sandy soil, then slipped away. Félicité took a bottle and a glass out of her bag. She filled the glass and handed it to Olga Grekova-Leber. She took it with an unsteady hand and drained it at a gulp, took a deep breath, then slumped back against the back of the chair and undid the straps. She was struggling so hard to regain her self-control that her temples were throbbing. She opened and shut her eyes several times, then smiled.

'Well, Alexis, what did you mean by my being properly protected?' she asked calmly. The doctor had removed her plaster and as her trousers were too short a bandaged ankle no thicker than a child's wrist was visible.

'It's no longer a secret that the commanders of the mountain infantry have decided that the fortress and its surroundings

228

form a key strategic site. You'll be hearing from them before long now.'

To begin with she didn't react in any way. She was still smiling cryptically.

'I hate soldiers,' she said quietly.

'You hate the whole world. You'd be quite capable of putting yourself at risk to get rid of someone you consider undesirable . . .'

This remark wiped the smile from her face. She raised her eyebrows, then seemed to be turning over in her mind what were clearly painful thoughts. The secretary was now feeling very uneasy, almost unbearably so. Varlaam, who had been looking at Sarachchandra's cave through his binoculars for some time, now created a diversion.

'They're setting light to the pyre,' he said, holding out the binoculars to her, but she shook her head. The secretary took them and hung on to them throughout the ceremony. He trained them on the cave where the crowd was squeezing in.

An elderly man with a beard like a *sadhu* was thrusting his resin torch between the branches, then pulling it out and raising it above his head with a flourish. He proceeded slowly right round the pyre, kicking out distractedly at the dogs following him round. But there was no sign of a flame licking up. The planks from the hut formed a sort of raft at the top of the pile of wood. The dead man was stretched out on it, his arms by his sides and his eyes wide open, watching the flies flitting round his face. The secretary could see everything quite clearly, probably better than if he'd been close to the pyre. Then thick yellow smoke rose up from the smouldering fire and for a moment the cave disappeared from view. He could hear shouts and coughs and the crowd started to surge beneath the vaulting roof of the cave as people began to pour towards the sides of the flat area round the pyre for fear of being asphyxiated, slipping as best they could into the empty space to avoid suffocating. Then a flare shot up like a phoenix's quill feather on the side of the pyre, dancing gaily and poking its slender blue barbules out through the lattice of branches. The *sadhu* started laughing. He crouched down beside the flame, blew on it mockingly, stuck out his tongue in defiance. But suddenly he had to step back because with a rush of air a whole lot of flaming tongues licked out a few inches away from his beard, and almost immediately the whole of the pyre re-emerged from its swaddling bands of smoke.

Sarachandra's features were clearly visible through the binoculars and appeared much as before, except that there was some subtle difference, as though a mask of himself as a young man had been superimposed on his face in death. Something was moving near his left eye – a butterfly flapping its wings. It flew off. The fire still had a long way to go.

'Why did I agree to come?' Olga Grekova-Leber was thinking aloud.

'Out of curiosity and because you're nicely brought up,' said Muller, sitting down beside Félicité. She had taken a large piece of leather out of her bag and had started on some sewing whose purpose was unclear. She would put the skin on a little board and, using an awl set into a wooden handle, hit it with a series of short, sharp blows. But her mind wasn't fully on this mysterious task, and every now and then she would glance towards Sarachchandra's cave, as though she was moving from one unreal situation to another.

An atmosphere of quiet contemplation now prevailed throughout the swallow hole, so much so that they could hear the fire smouldering in the depths of the funeral pyre. The secretary trained the binoculars on the various caves in turn, trying to spot Tanguy, but couldn't see any sign of him. He then concentrated on Sarachchandra. For a good while there was no real indication that the fire had caught, except for some bangs and crackles lasting a few seconds, the occasional scattering of sparks and columns of smoke wreathing up to the roof of the cave, where they hung like banks of mist drifting about. Part of the bottom of the pyre caved in, causing the top to topple slowly over. An anxious muttering rose up from the crowd. Sarachchandra's body half sat up as the planks on which he was lying suddenly tilted. He turned to face the

230

swallow hole but didn't slide off. As he perched there with his blankly staring eyes open he seemed to be waiting for someone out there among the crowd of people watching him to point out the way he must go to find supreme peace.

Even the dogs dashing energetically round the pyre froze as if terror-struck. Where the branches had given way in the incandescent heat, the flames at last spurted up into the open air, licking at the saint's feet and ankles, timidly at first, then becoming gradually bolder. He suddenly looked so alive that they expected him to react in some way to the pain. Olga Grekova-Leber retched and turned away. As the secretary looked through the binoculars Sarachchandra seemed so very much there, so close, that he could feel his own flesh burning from the plumes of flames enveloping the dead man's legs. As an invisible flame fingered his shirt, it caught fire and fell away in a scattering of ashes, revealing a peculiar-looking corset wound round his chest, like an outsize cartridge belt. Then a veil of smoke drifted along his body up to his chin, like a sheet being modestly pulled up to cover his nakedness.

Suddenly, with appalling violence and accompanied by a furious hissing sound, something shot out of Sarachchandra's chest, flashed through the half-light of the swallow hole and exploded high up in the sky, dropping to earth in a shower of light. It was over in just a few seconds. During the stunned silence that followed, frantic applause and the sound of Tanguy laughing reverberated as far as the most distant caves.

'The rockets . . . That's why they asked me to buy some rockets!' exclaimed Varlaam.

Over on the pyre Sarachchandra's eyes had burst. The bones in his legs were visible beneath the charred flesh, looking amazingly white, and the air was filled with a suffocating smell of human barbecue.

'Where's Tanguy? Can't you see him?' asked Olga Grekova-Leber.

Muller and the secretary peered at the hillocks and over-hanging rocks where the Tamils who hadn't been able to get any closer were crowding together, but couldn't spot Tanguy

231

anywhere. A bloated sky streaked with flaming torches was hanging motionless above the swallow hole. Darkness was settling into the undulating folds of the mountainside and short-lived gusts of wind wafted along with them a smell of rain that drove out the smell of grilled flesh. Muller borrowed the binoculars and trained them on the pyre, which was now well and truly ablaze and seemed to be rising up with the flames. But an air cushion swelling up beneath the planks Sarachchandra was lying on was delaying the moment of combustion, so instead of bursting into flames the corpse was blistering and exploding one limb at a time. A black mass was pouring out of the open belly in a slow stream, like an umbilical cord linking the body to the blazing furnace.

'Until those planks start burning he'll grill like a sausage on a grid,' Muller remarked laconically, lowering the binoculars.

Sarachchandra's cave was now virtually filled with smoke and the last of its occupants were pouring out of it, clustered in little groups. They were laughing and joking, calmly carrying on with their conversations, showing no more interest in the saint now that his salvation was assured and his soul had taken wing. The dogs were barking frantically at the fire, snarling as they moved in close to the pyre, then backed away, their ears laid back, waiting impatiently for the moment when they would be thrown their share of the quarry. Sarachchandra's ribs had burst through the flesh on his chest and were sticking up out of him, but he still looked like a man seen through a fiery screen.

'Take me back up. I don't want to stay here another minute!'

Muller leaned over Olga Grekova-Leber, his expression a mixture of affability and cruelty, and laid the binoculars across her thighs.

'Don't act the sensitive little woman, Mrs Leber,' he said softly. 'Look, it's only a man burning. We'll stay until the cremation's over. It generally takes three hours for a human body to be burned right up on this type of pyre, and your servant wasn't exactly plump when he died.'

232

She took up his challenge, picked up the binoculars and looked him up and down contemptuously.

'I wonder which of us is most frightened of death,' she remarked, training the binoculars not on the pyre but on the sky, which was filling with a muffled and unbroken rumbling sound. And the first drops started falling, warm and heavy.

Shouting broke out in the swallow hole, then laughter. The Tamils who'd started to move away towards the caves sat down wherever they happened to be and waited for the sky to burst open, just as the saint's belly had. For a few minutes the swallow hole was engulfed in almost total darkness, then an explosion blew off a whole expanse of sky and it cascaded to the ground in a waterfall, exposing in the far distance a patch of unsullied evening azure set ablaze by the setting sun, like a pyre of light suspended in mid air among the thunder clouds. They all looked up towards this apparition and in the twinkling of an eye all of them were soaked through. But instead of putting out the blaze, the rain breathed new life into it. The flames rose higher, churning up the shadows and flinging them against the vaulted roof of the cave, and Sarachchandra's hair, which by some miracle was still unscathed, now flared up in a single puff of air, placing a flaming helmet over his face, which melted like a wax mask. Then at last the charred planks collapsed into the incandescent embers and the body was engulfed.

She laid the binoculars across her lap. 'It's raining again. It never stops,' she sighed.

They were in the dry, their alcove sealed off by a curtain of rain. Varlaam, deathly pale, was wiping the icy sweat from his brow. Félicité folded up her piece of leather and put it away in her bag. Lightning was lighting up the swallow hole in a series of quick flashes and Muller pointed out a silhouette striding up the path, his rifle slung across his chest. Tanguy was walking with his head down, oblivious of the rain whipping against him, looking huge in the flashing light of the storm. Varlaam uncoiled his giant archangel's frame, and before anyone could stop him bounded after Tanguy like a wild beast.

'I'll fix it somehow so that the regional authority doesn't

233

poke its nose into his affairs,' Muller said to Olga Grekova-Leber, with a return to his previous friendly tone. 'I promise you won't be bothered by anybody over that business with the animals.'

She shrugged, flung the secretary a highly meaningful glance that he failed to understand, then, without saying a word, again trained the binoculars on Sarachchandra's cave. The growling noises coming from the wet embers were drowning out the sound of the rain, which was driving down more and more heavily on to the shapeless heap of charred branches with little flames licking energetically along them.

'It isn't over yet,' she said half under her breath. 'The bones haven't burned.' And as her legs were dangling against the wheelchair, the secretary kneeled down in front of her and put her feet back on the footrests. Over in the cave the dogs had been driven away by the fire but were now moving back towards the funeral pyre.

PART THREE

War

1

The arrival of the Tamils, the fact that large numbers of them had been able to slip on to the estate without being detected, meant that a hole had been blasted in its impregnable defences. Olga Grekova-Leber was aware that from now on the outside world – 'the world below', as she called it – could encroach on the fortress, and that there was nothing they could do to prevent it, since there would always be an accomplice on the inside.

A few days after the cremation, she sent Varlaam to the swallow hole to see what sort of state it was in. He was clearly very uneasy when he came back, saying – and there was no question of suspecting he might not be telling the truth – that there was nothing left to indicate that the ceremony had ever taken place, not so much as a heap of ashes, and nothing to show that the caves round about had been recently occupied. He said it was a bit as if they'd flung themselves down into the swallow hole with their refuse. At first she refused to believe him, but in her heart of hearts she knew he was telling the truth, and that this was one of those truths that you might come across at the fortress.

She shut herself up in her rooms and refused to see anyone except Félicité. Even when she was lying down she could feel the real world crumbling round her. For two whole days and nights, she subsequently explained to the secretary, her bed was perched on top of a tall clay hill, its sides wearing away so fast that she soon found she was marooned like a stylite on top of a pillar of powdery earth, listening to the stones slithering away beneath her. Yet she didn't call out, and she refused to let Félicité carry her to her wheelchair, because the chair was in a much more precarious situation than the bed, and she would never be able to keep it under control. Once the two days and nights were over, she asked Félicité to bring her the Leber Foundation files. During this spell of dizziness it suddenly occurred to her that the dividends that were still swelling the foundation's coffers and her own were the ultimate reality on which she could find a firm foothold. The money on which she had built her church was still as steady as a rock, but the church was empty. Gigantic sums were going on multiplying, for political and financial reasons described in detail by the acting chairman of the board in a long series of despatches, though she rarely opened them these days. She could use her money to buy all the things she didn't need. But she couldn't buy a new life, only the useless things that any life metes out in generous quantities. She couldn't buy a new pair of legs.

'After Samuel's death, I milked all the illicit operations spawned by the Leber Foundation in its five years of existence for all they were worth. I amassed as much money as I could, kept an eye on every source of income to make sure I got my percentage,' she'd admitted to the secretary a few days after they'd come across Tanguy's charnel house. 'I was trying to get better, to forget. It didn't take long for the riff-raff surrounding me to assume I was cast in the same mould. They were right – I'm riff-raff too, but not the same type of riff-raff as they are. Money interested me solely because I knew it was the cause of all the world's disasters, because I could see it was an endless source of misfortune and the main reason behind the apocalypse. Anything pleasurable that money can buy bores me. The arts bore me stiff, travel, yachts, sandy beaches, blue sky, the tropics – they all bore me. Seas and plains, lakes and mountains make me yawn. Money! I haven't set foot in town for the last seven years. I never stir from here, and I can go for a couple of weeks without changing my clothes . . .'

Later on, tormented by another idea that obsessed her, she'd asked his advice: 'How should I set about scuttling the Leber Foundation and its unofficial companies? Should I expose

238

the various misappropriations of funds and fraudulent and extortionate operations perpetrated by the board members? Or set up a bogus holding company, sell the majority of my shares to it, then put in some cunning devil to run it for me, with a brief to ruin us? Ruin us, did I say? Even if I were to behave in the most totally outlandish fashion for several decades, I still wouldn't use up even a tiny fraction of the capital!'

She didn't want to get rid of her money to satisfy some moral ideal, or because the futility of wealth – however relative – was becoming a burden to her, but because she felt an urge to experience the heady delights of losing, without launching into a new game. As she was too proud to accept the idea of someone else benefiting from this loss – 'one of those loathsome crooks like the specimens you saw here' – and sufficiently well up in financial matters to know that a fortune like hers can't simply be scattered on the waves from a ship's deck, like an urn full of ashes, she was getting caught up in an increasing number of speculative ventures from which she derived less and less enjoyment.

'Just my luck,' she would say. 'Just when people's fortunes are constantly in danger of crumbling, mine's getting bigger. I could leave it to the State. But I loathe the State, and it would only be used to buy war planes. Starting in my teens, and right up to when I lost the use of my legs, I used to be endlessly obsessed by the idea of suicide. For years I managed to survive only because every single day I would recite Hecuba's lament. But as soon as I finished up in this wheelchair, the urge to die completely vanished. And now that you're here with me, and I've grown fond of you, I feel that death is a less attractive proposition than life, and always will be.'

Every now and then, when he was secretly watching her, he would detect, in its raw state, something of that monstrous quality that was normally hidden behind her outward characteristics, but would rear its head even when she was asleep. He thought about her all the time. Her presence blotted out all the other presences he might have thought of, consigning the past to a shadowy background where even the memory of Fra Cosimo dwindled and grew dim. When they met anywhere, when he was pushing the wheelchair, carrying her to the bed, lying on top of her, he would go on thinking about her, contemplating her life inside his head. And soon her physical presence would become something of an obstacle, until eventually she was completely swallowed up by the thoughts she aroused. When that happened, the pure idea of love would be borne in upon him, quite indescribable, with the devastating force of a tornado.

'If I were to sell my majority holding in the Foundation to a company wealthy enough to buy it, my fellow-directors wouldn't waste a second – they'd hire someone to kill me,' she'd told him a little while before the ceremony in the swallow hole. 'I'd give certain instructions to my banks and before the various operations had been set in motion, they'd put a bullet through my head. They watch me like a hawk, because they're afraid of me, and in particular they know that with a mere five telephone calls I could ruin several of them, and have a few of the others locked up! We've been at war for a long time now.' She repeated it several times: 'Five telephone calls . . .', then after thinking it over, corrected herself: 'Three would do it.'

2

During those two days when she stayed locked up in her bedroom, he made no attempt to force his way in. One evening he was walking back to the heliport with Varlaam when Tanguy barged into them as he rushed through the postern gate. He was spending all his time in the forest now, day and night, putting in an appearance at the fortress only when he'd run out of ammunition. His rifle was balanced across his shoulder and he was holding it by the barrel. He seemed terribly het up. 'Won't be long now, your eminence!' he mumbled as he dashed past them. They watched him race up the front steps. Late that night, when the secretary had turned all the lights out and was stretched out on his bed, he thought he could hear voices outside on the bastion. He got up without making a sound and went over to the window. The starry sky sucked him up in a dizzy whirl, everything turned upside-down and he had to cling on to the stone window ledge for a moment – Olga Grekova-Leber and Tanguy were outside the watchtower, beneath a slender crescent moon.

Tanguy had put the key in the lock, but was having trouble opening it, and even at that distance he could hear him swearing. He stepped back and suddenly the door opened, slowly, as though someone was pushing it from inside. No one appeared, though. For a moment neither of them moved, then she said something and swivelled the chair round so she could have a good look at the sky. The secretary, crouching in one corner of the window, let his gaze wander through the vault of heaven too, and when he looked down again, they'd disappeared into the watchtower. He leaned out further. The ravine seemed to be a bottomless pit and the rushing sound of the torrent seemed to come from far away, yet so filled the air that he could hear nothing else. Then suddenly, while he was staring intently at the pale outline of the little building clinging to the edge above the sheer drop, the futility of his own existence hit him with the force of a punch landing squarely in the middle of his face, and the summer night shrank and closed in to form a torture chamber. He went on feeling dazed until a slight humming sound took his mind off his anguish, and he realized that Tanguy had just started up the cable car engine.

The darkness hid the cables, but he was so familiar with the flowing, curving line they cast across the sheer drop of the ravine that he could see them as clearly as if it were full daylight. During the few interminable seconds after the electric engine had been switched on, those twin cables assumed such significance that there was nothing else in the world. A metallic sound rang out, like a gong being struck. He heard what sounded like a laugh, quickly stifled, and, no longer worried about them seeing him, sat down on the window ledge. Whispering floated up to him through the open door of the watchtower, but judging by the few words

241

he could hear, he had the impression that only one voice was speaking, a third voice he didn't recognize. Another clanging sound reverberated. This time there was no mistaking it – it was made by the bucket banging against the platform railing as it swung. The humming sound of the engine grew louder. Tanguy stuck his head round the door, looked first to the right then to the left, and finally up to the tower window. His glance lasted only a fraction of a second. The secretary clung on to the window frame but made no attempt to keep out of sight. He was well aware that he ought to intervene – this awareness was looming larger and larger – but he went on sitting there, somehow feeling that by not moving he was punishing himself for a sin committed so long ago he couldn't now remember what it was he'd done.

The space in front of the watchtower vibrated, the darkness stretching tautly across it like a sheet. At that point the dark shape of the iron bucket appeared, then slid soundlessly forward for a few yards, came to a standstill, swaying very slightly, and remained suspended in mid-air. The cables had vanished and it was floating in a state of weightlessness, temporarily held up by nothingness, no longer linked in any way to terra firma. The way Tanguy had settled her into it, she looked as if she was sitting in a boat that had been anchored for the night. She was sitting quite still, allowing herself to be gently rocked by the pitching bucket. He could only see her shoulders and her hair, since she was facing into the ravine, but could just make out the back of the wheelchair, secured firmly to the bucket. Then she raised her arm and signalled in the direction of the watchtower. The engine started humming again. The bucket swooped on down and he felt it was plunging into the black body of the mountain, whose bulk was rooted on the edge of the darkness as it sketched its flawlessly jagged silhouette beneath a star-studded sky.

Again it came to a standstill, but it was only just visible now. All he could see of her was a pale ghost that faded as he strained to make it out. And before long the bucket continued on its downward swoop and vanished from sight altogether. He stayed there a moment, peering into the yawning darkness that had just swallowed up a human form, leaving not so much as the memory of it behind. Then eventually he recovered the use of his limbs, left his room and went down to the keep.

His mind was made up now. He waited for a moment, leaning back against the cold stone in the pitch black, breathing heavily. They've really taken me for a ride this time, he was thinking, though with no feeling of hatred or anger. He was picturing how he was going to fling Tanguy into the ravine, but however hard he tried, he couldn't manage to feel the slightest twinge of hatred. He felt his way across the guard room like a blind person and groped for the door leading on to the ramparts. I'm going to kill Tanguy, he was saying himself. He didn't really believe it, but felt convinced by now that the deed couldn't be put off any longer. Yet both Tanguy and the idea of death seemed equally absurd. When he came out on the parapet walk, the bucket was just coming up to the watchtower.

After the chilly, dry feeling of the stone, the warm night wrapped itself round him like a cloak. Her voice rang out. He realized she was calling Tanguy names from inside the bucket, but couldn't catch a single word of what she was saying. Suddenly, as he walked forward along the parapet walk, a long-drawn-out cry spurted out of Tanguy's throat, like a rutting stag troating, and something large and shiny flew out of the watchtower. The wheelchair hurtled down into the ravine, bouncing off the rocks, and he could hear the noise of shattered metal, bringing showers of gravelly marl down with it as it fell, and gradually growing fainter. Then everything was silent again, an oppressive silence, as though all the air had drained out of the valley.

He knew she wasn't in the chair, but for a second or two he began to wonder, because the silence dragged on, and it was a long time before the rumbling of the torrent again made itself heard. Then her voice rose up again. It was only very slightly muffled by the walls, and this time he could make out every word: 'That's what you wanted, isn't it? Why did

243

you bring me up so quickly? And now take me back to my bedroom.'

He didn't move when Tanguy kicked open the door and hurried across the bastion, almost running, with Olga Grekova-Leber clutched tightly to his chest. He went on standing there after they'd disappeared into the main building, as if he'd taken root in the parapet walk, not knowing what to do with himself. Instead of going back to his tower, he left the fortress. He felt an urge to walk, to walk until he dropped, then lie on the ground. Once he'd gone through the postern gate his eye was caught by the outline of the dovecot and he went over towards it. The door was ajar and he could see into Tanguy's lair. It was lit by a pair of paraffin lamps, so most of the huge inner space was in the half-darkness, its walls covered with snares, rat traps, guns, and a collection of ropes hanging down in thick plaits from wooden stakes. The dim light coated this cluttered decor with an unearthly, motionless aura, as though all these things were dozing in its halo. On the table, along with the lamps, were several sheets of paper covered with wild-looking handwriting, a piece of cheese spiked on the blade of a dagger, a stuffed owl, some old copies of the *National Geographic*, a full bottle of wine and several spotted dog-eared photographs of La Grekova playing her various parts. He was intrigued by the sheets of paper. It had never occurred to him that Tanguy could read and write, yet he felt quite certain that it was his writing. Apprehension got the better of his curiosity and stopped him going in. He left the dovecote and set off towards the col.

As he was walking he couldn't wrench his thoughts away from Tanguy – only minutes earlier he'd been planning to kill him. Then gradually his inability to feel any hatred for the man, which had so paralysed him that it had in the end prevented him from doing the deed, however much he wanted to, was superseded by a feeling that the two of them were somehow complementary, that they were one and the same, unthinkable as that idea was. And he remembered what she'd said about Tanguy a few days after he'd arrived at the fortress:

244

'You'll start off by thinking he's mad. You'll see him as very brutal, but then you'll find out that there are some disturbing parallels between his madness, his brutality and yourself.'

He stopped at the top of the col, sat down on a boulder and contemplated the distant shadow of the fortress outlined against the fading sky, like one of those cut-out landscapes on black paper, and after a few moments he started seeing it as a sleeping ship taking in water via a tiny hole in its hull.

3

He continued along the lateral moraine as far as he could, then when the ground became completely impassable brought the jeep to a halt less than a hundred yards from the glacier face. A cold, dry breath was wafting out of a forest of seracs dirtied by alluvial deposits. From there he could just make out a path climbing up in a series of zigzags through scree made up of micaceous boulders sparkling like gold nuggets. Perched on a shady spur overhanging the glacier, well above the flow and invisible at first glance because it was built of the same stone, the mountain hut seemed like a supernatural extension of the rock, and it was a long time before it started looking like something man-made. He took the big leather bag and the canvas bag out of the back of the jeep, then went to see to her.

Although he was by now fairly experienced at it, he still had to think about how to get her into the bag properly before lifting her on to his back. The basic system was quite straightforward. She'd designed a sort of leather pouch to fit herself, with four openings for her arms and legs and a framework made up of aluminium tubes and straps similar to an ordinary rucksack. 'It means you'll be able to carry me, but your arms will still be free and my weight will be evenly distributed across your back,' she'd explained when she first showed him the peculiar-looking harness Félicité had made. The most difficult part was getting the bag over her without making her feel humiliated. First of all he had to spread it out on the ground, leaving it gaping open, then lay her down on it, push her legs into the holes – she could see to her arms herself – and hoist her up and fasten her in. The bag was big enough not to restrict her movements completely, and to prevent her being squashed up against his back.

Their usual outings round the estate weren't enough to keep her happy now. She longed to go further away, yearning for inaccessible mountain tops, and feeling a need for purification through cold and solitude. Every day now she'd talk about that wonderful scene she'd dreamt of a few months earlier, when she'd been in her wheelchair in the midst of a snowy waste, experiencing a feeling of infinite freedom and bliss. This craving for wide open spaces and for a state of being completely abandoned, far from God, this ecstasy at the idea of becoming estranged from herself – which may have been nothing more nor less than an insatiable aspiration towards assimilating the universe totally into oneself by means of the intellect – furthered his own secret aspirations.

Once he'd got used to the idea of the bag, he could see that it did have a considerable number of advantages. Quite apart from the fact that it meant they could now tackle a wide variety of outings, it did away with that tiny but nagging distance that the wheelchair put between them. He wanted to think only of the practical aspect, but the sensation of munificent power aroused by feeling her body so close to his, the way her paralysed legs dangled against his thighs as he walked, very slightly bent beneath these few pounds of human life, her arms flung round his neck and her hands laid flat against his shoulder blades so that she could pull herself slightly away from him, her breath on the back of his neck when she let her head droop against his – after the cable car episode, which he never referred to, the fact that she was abandoning herself to him in all these various ways brought him almost total relief.

'This method might seem humiliating, for you as well as for me,' she said the first time he hoisted her on to his back. 'But I know we're beyond feeling humiliated.'

After only a week of walking in the area round the fortress, she wanted to embark on a long hike. She would refer again and again to the mountain hut on the Bear's Tooth, and he would keep postponing it. The weather went on being hot and sultry. There was still a clear sky, but behind the mountain tops, unmoving and well in the background, cumulus clouds drenched in light formed layer upon layer of gigantic puffing cheeks. He went into training until the beginning of August. They would leave very early in the morning, before sunrise, and be back in time for lunch. By the end of the first session, when he'd been walking for three hours, he realized that the lower part of his back was bleeding where the leather and the frame had rubbed it. But when he was carrying the bag he didn't feel any pain and it didn't take him long to incorporate her weight into his own. To begin with, because of his lack of stamina for that type of physical exercise, he was forced to put the bag down every quarter of an hour. Then the intervals between these breathing spaces got longer and soon he was capable of walking without a break for fifty minutes.

She wasn't exactly uncomfortable in her bag, but her legs hurt because they were dangling down without any support and the pain would become unendurable long before he had run out of steam. When that happened he would keep on walking, but would grab hold of her legs, wedge them on his hips and massage them gently, from the groin to the ankle. He could feel her gradually becoming less tense as he tenderly clasped the lifeless limbs round his waist. Whenever he started massaging more slowly before the pain had completely disappeared, she would put her arms round his neck, prop her chin up on his shoulder and whisper into his ear: 'Go on, go on . . .', and the joy he felt at this prayer would stay with him until he was overcome by exhaustion.

He found out exactly how much stamina he had one day when he was climbing up the col with the sun beating straight down on them. He'd been walking for over an hour without a break and just as he was coming to the flat rock he'd laid her down on a few months earlier with her broken leg, the veins in his temples started pounding. A blinding light exploded beneath his eyelids, as if the sun was surging into his blood, and he thought he was going blind. When he recovered his sight and heard her thumping his shoulder with her fists to order him to stop, he suddenly realized he'd reached the limits of his endurance.

He covered the few yards to the rock, wondering whether he'd be able to summon up enough strength to take the bag off his back. He sank back against the rock, pulled down the straps and went on standing there between her parted thighs, his face drenched in sweat, smiling foolishly. That was the moment Fra Cosimo chose to loom up ahead of him in his wheelchair, in the overflowing summer light. He sat there with an inquiring look on his face, clearly in a state of ecstasy, his chest split from top to bottom by the branch of the beech tree, and without opening his mouth asked a question that sang in the secretary's ears like a shout: 'What is this gentleness that can sometimes affect me, seizing hold of me so violently and so sweetly that I no longer recognize myself, and know not where I'm transported?' Then he faded from sight.

The secretary turned towards her. Sitting there stuck in the bag, she was looking at him with concern. 'Right,' he said, mopping his brow. 'The training period's over. We'll go to the hut on the Bear's Tooth whenever it suits you.'

With the bag firmly strapped to his back, he embarked on the stiff climb up through the scree. The stones were slithering about beneath the soles of his shoes and the weight of the bag was dragging him backwards, so that with each step he took he was on the verge of losing his balance. To begin with she kept her arms nervously clasped round his neck, then as they climbed higher she gradually relaxed her embrace. He was moving forwards at the regular rhythmic pace of the mountain dweller, breathing noisily. He would set himself a specific number of zigzags to be achieved before he stopped for a breather, and to calculate how much ground they'd covered. Before long the jeep came into view at the foot of

248

the scree, looking tiny, and the path continued horizontally across the side of a mountain the colour of malachite, way up above the glacier, whose crinkled surface was glistening like a skate's belly. He reckoned it would take him three or four hours to climb up to the hut and he'd decided to husband his strength. She was carrying a heavy bag full of food slung across her, a pair of crampons to get them across the glacier, and a couple of sleeping bags. The haversack was digging into her shoulder and she couldn't endure its weight for long at a time. He would put her down whenever the type of terrain made this practicable, and they would sit there for a few moments side by side, stunned by the sight of the vast and motionless expanse of the mountains.

During one of these pauses she made a confession: 'The business with Sarachchandra has somehow leaked out. The regional authorities have told the police and they want to appoint a board of inquiry. They've asked Muller to chair it. He'll do what he can to slow the proceedings down. What do you think?'

She didn't seem particularly bothered, or rather something else was bothering her.

'I think you can rely on Muller. Up to a point.'

She gave him a sidelong glance, sitting there on top of the open bag with her back propped against a rock. She'd lost weight. Her leather trousers were too big for her and hung loosely round her hips.

'Yes, up to a point, I suppose.'

For over two hours the hut remained out of sight. Then it suddenly appeared on the overhang of an escarpment, facing them but on the other side of a narrow pass covered with snow that they would have to get across. In the pure mountain air it seemed both very near and yet still very far away, as the deep gorge made up of dark boulders seemed so hostile and depressing. The path continued along a granite ridge facing due south, then made its way across a shady and forbidding slope as far as the névé. On the north face, which probably never saw the sun, they could just make it out as it slunk furtively away

249

into the marl, but the virgin snow at the bottom of the pass showed no sign of footsteps. She assured him that no one ever used the hut now, not since a spring avalanche had swept away the terrace, plus the five climbers who happened to be having a rest there. As the crow flies, they weren't much more than a couple of hundred yards from the windowless wall facing them, its undressed stone perched on top of a cliff. The building was as it were turning its back on them. Its outline silhouetted against the ultramarine sky formed a patch of shadow that looked as forbidding and sturdy as the peaks jutting up all round it. He set off again. They plunged into the cold shade in the pass and an hour later, after a break on the edge of the frozen névé, were directly underneath the hut.

The path went round the spur on the south side and in a few minutes they were back in full sunlight. It wasn't possible to reach the hut via the pass, so they had to embark on a long detour and get back to the glacier flow, which split into twin avenues of snow, each of them rooted in the blue slope of a mountain mass. After the gloomy shadow they'd left behind, the virgin expanse of snow stretching as far as the eye could see over the glistening series of domes prompted them to stop again. He wasn't really tired, and although he could feel a burning sensation in his chest whenever he breathed in, he felt happy. He was still in some pain from a few sores at the bottom of his back that hadn't yet healed. But although the concept of performing a feat was quite foreign to his nature, his determination to hold out against the pain pushed back the limits of his physical and mental endurance quite remarkably, making him feel that in the dense shadowy areas of his body a door was opening on to the uncharted territory of the spirit. He put her down, settled her comfortably facing the glacier and took a few dried apricots out of his pocket. Just then there was a burst of laughter from up by the hut.

They looked at each other in silence. More laughter could be heard, then everything went quiet. He decided to go and see on his own. He walked for a few minutes, went round an escarpment and realized that the building was much closer than he'd thought, at the top of a steep and rocky path that represented one final test of his endurance. A group of men were walking about on the terrace that was supposed to have been destroyed. Several of them had stripped to the waist and were soaking up the sun. They seemed to be in very good spirits. Regulation army shirts and underwear were hanging up on a line to dry, and from where he was standing he could see neatly piled rifles lining the terrace from the door of the hut to the far end. He watched the men for a moment, keeping out of sight, and tried to count them – he reckoned there must be about thirty of them. Then he went back to where he'd left her.

He had trouble persuading her. It was much too late for them to go back down and he didn't feel up to carrying her any further. But she didn't want to see anyone, and particularly not soldiers.

'We've come up here to enjoy the solitude, not to spend the night with a whole gang of young males. Leave me here with a sleeping bag and go and join them if you feel like it.'

He realized she was ashamed to show herself and switched to a new tactic.

'Don't you remember telling me a little while ago that we're beyond humiliation? It's too cold at night for you to sleep out in the open.'

She looked distressed, then after a silence filled with intense irritation, she pulled the two halves of the bag towards her and slid her arms into the holes.

'Let's get going,' she said. He leaned over her, fastened the frame and lifted her up as though she weighed nothing at all, then set off again.

4

When he was in the middle of climbing up the steep path, she pressed her hands against his back to pull herself away from him, pushed her dark glasses up on to her forehead and surveyed the hut and its terrace, where twenty or so recruits were clustered against the railing and following their progress in stunned silence. She ran her eyes calmly over their solemn young faces – none of them seemed to be making fun of her. 'They're children!' she said. Then three of them came racing down the path to meet them. The one in front, an officer, was still straightening his tunic and buttoning up his collar, while the other two, who were carrying a stretcher, were displaying their bare brown chests.

'They think you've been injured,' he said, keeping on climbing. Now that he'd recovered some show of soldierly dignity, the officer slowed down to say something, but stared speechlessly at the odd-looking pair they made. The secretary had been walking with his eyes glued to the path, but now he looked up, smiled at the officer and asked him to let him go on climbing at his own pace. By this time the officer was looking them up and down in disbelief. Eventually he recovered his powers of speech and stammered: 'Has there been an accident?'

'You could say that,' she said sharply. 'An accident that happened seven years ago.'

The stretcher bearers had come to a halt and moved on to the side of the path. When the secretary walked past them, one of them whispered: 'It's Mrs Leber.' She didn't hear, but the officer stiffened to attention for a split second. He wasn't more than thirty and there was a book sticking out of his tunic pocket.

Several of the soldiers hurried over when they reached the terrace, but the secretary got rid of them in the nicest possible way and put the bag down on the bench himself. The officer ordered the men to bring out the only comfortable chair in the hut, a folding chair with arms, then stood there for a moment or two, not knowing what attitude to adopt. Once she'd been settled into the chair with a rug over her legs – though she promptly flung it off, as the sun was so hot at that altitude – he introduced himself. His name was Captain Rollus, of the first mountain infantry division and, he added, blushing beneath his tan, when out of uniform he was doing literary research. He hid his embarrassment by waving his arm in a sweeping gesture that took in all the men on the terrace.

'This is one platoon of my company. The other men are based at the hut on the Maupas. Our brief is to comb the area and set up observation posts.' He hesitated a moment, then turned towards her with a bow, as though he was about to kiss her hand. 'After that, Mrs Leber, we're going to re-form on your land. I imagine you've been warned about that by the general staff.'

He didn't seem to be unduly thrown off his stride by the coincidence of their having turned up at the hut just when he'd received the directive from the army high command. You had the feeling that this man, who was shy one minute and very self-possessed the next, would never be thrown off his stride, however unusual the situation – perhaps because of his love of literature. The secretary shot a scathing glance at her – she hadn't warned him about any of this – went over to the railing and leaned on it.

'Why are you combing the area?' he heard himself ask. 'What's the point of all these observation posts?'

Rollus walked over to him and when he saw a slender hand placed beside his on the railing, a hand that bore no blemishes from handling firearms or scaling mountains, he recovered his composure. He turned to face the glacier, and the staggering, sterile beauty of the place took his breath away.

'I expect you mean who are we observing? From the purely strategic point of view, we're as it were up on the country's ramparts on the lookout for a remote-controlled enemy attack by air. We're in touch with our ground-to-air missile bases round the clock, and in theory the radar stations that have been set up all the way along the border should enable us to . . .' He broke off and suddenly started laughing. The secretary looked at him in amazement, then glanced at Olga Grekova-Leber. She was dozing, her face turned towards the sun, taking no interest now in all the things that had been preoccupying her only a moment or two earlier.

'Strategically, in theory . . .,' he went on, still laughing

253

like a little boy. 'We – my men and I, that is – have spent several months up in the mountains and we like it here. I'm in command of this company and I carry out the general staff's orders without asking pointless questions – for the simple reason that there aren't any questions to ask.' As he swivelled round to lean against the railing the book fell out of his tunic pocket.

'Have you read Sterne?' he asked, picking it up. 'I keep on rereading *Tristram Shandy*. I'm reading virtually nothing else at the moment. Before I was called up I was working on a thesis on humour in eighteenth-century European literature. I'm doing a bit of work on it here – we haven't got much to do. To be honest, we've got nothing else to keep us busy other than what we invent for ourselves. That keeps us going for two or three hours a day, it depends, and after that we sunbathe on the terrace, or play cards, and sometimes we have a go at shooting moufflon. In the early days I thought it wouldn't take long before we got tired of living like this, and the men would start getting impatient about going back down. But it hasn't happened. I'm not in the least ashamed to say that as each new day comes round we dread being ordered to return to our unit. We feel safe here, and although none of us ever mentions it, I know we're all thinking the same thing: the people on the plain will get it in the neck and we'll be spared. Who on earth would think of bombing these mountains? Afterwards, of course, we'll have to cope with surviving, but for the moment we're well provided for – they send us up supplies by helicopter once a week.'

He was tapping the book against his palm and looking thoughtful. It was starting to get chilly. The soldiers casually pulled on their shirts and tunics. Two of the recruits were being very attentive to Olga Grekova-Leber, bringing her bread, salami, cheese and wine, and putting it down on the pine table – the colour had been bleached out of the wood by the snow. These very fit-looking young men with their suntans, energetic and idle, active and lazy by turns, gave off an aura of instant happiness, of sheer joy at being alive

254

– the secretary had never noticed this to the same extent in anyone else. Some of them were gazing dreamily at the glacier and the mountain peaks as they enjoyed a smoke. A crystalline gleam in their dreamy eyes showed that they were fleetingly being touched by the beauty of the world in all its dazzling perfection, and that without realizing it they were catching a glimpse, in the fading light of this snowy wilderness, of the eternal presence of Isaiah's hidden god. With every day they spent up here they experienced the incomparable feeling of living, without any specific aim in view, well hidden beneath the steel petticoats of their War-mother, so much so that their blithe lack of concern seemed like a fundamental virtue.

'Don't think I'm a born optimist – rather the opposite in fact,' Captain Rollus went on. 'Even if we manage to avoid war this time, that's no reason for rejoicing. What I like about Sterne is that his hero is virtually non-existent. You ought to reread it. I expect you remember the business with the clock, don't you?'

He was interrupted by one of the soldiers coming over for his orders. The secretary rummaged about in his memory, staring unseeingly in the direction of the glacier, which was throwing off a dark light.

'Yes, I think I remember. When his parents are in the process of conceiving Tristram, the wife asks her husband: "Pray, my dear, have you not forgot to wind up the clock?" That's it, isn't it?'

Rollus burst out laughing, a ringing laugh that made the soldiers on the terrace turn towards them, while Olga Grekova-Leber looked at them in amazement.

'Well done! It's ages since I've met someone who's read Sterne.' He roared with laughter, his brown face taking on a slightly crimson tinge. 'Poor Tristram! What a start in life – not as important as a clock!' He put the book back in his pocket and buttoned his tunic up to his neck. The sun was slipping behind the mountain closest to them, which seemed totally to dominate the scene as it gradually laid its brown shadow over the hut. Soon it had disappeared from view,

255

but the glacier and the peaks facing the two men were still ablaze. The abrupt way this split the alp up into two distinct zones seemed to dampen the captain's delighted enthusiasm somewhat. Speaking to no one in particular, but loud enough for them all to hear, he ordered: 'Everyone's to take his gun and clean it. Tomorrow we'll do some target practice on the – glacier.'

The secretary looked up at the sky and stared thoughtfully at the flag, hanging limply in the motionless air. Every now and then a marmot's shrill whistle would flare up. An answering call would come and the two sounds, distorted by the echo as it flung them to the most distant coombs, fleetingly made the space seem depressingly huge.

'Do you really stick to the colour ceremony?' he asked in surprise.

'We run the flag up every morning and lower it again every evening.'

Olga Grekova-Leber remarked that she was hungry and thirsty. Rollus, apparently suddenly remembering the food on the table, hurried over to her. He went on standing near them while they ate, and the secretary could tell he was dying to ask something. He didn't help him out but suggested he should join them in a glass of wine. He refused, becoming suddenly withdrawn and shy. At that time of day the mountains were so awesome that a cold and sepulchral silence brooded over everything – a silence that, if you weren't careful, became completely overwhelming. A blue glow lit the men's faces as they took their Bren guns from the pile, moving at a leisurely pace but with determined expressions, and lumbered into the hut with them. The captain cleared his throat and at long last emerged from his silence.

'I hope you don't mind my asking, but . . . er . . . do you often use that method for getting about?'

She raised her eyebrows and pretended not to understand the question.

'What method? Oh, I see, I expect you mean the bag. Yes, fairly often. Needless to say, I couldn't agree to it with anyone

256

except the man I love.' She was looking him squarely in the eye now and he didn't dare look away. 'That bag is a token of love such as you'll rarely have the privilege of seeing, young man.'

Rollus shook his head and laid his hand on the book, as though he expected Tristram Shandy to rescue him. But in the end he escaped simply by using the excuse of having to give some orders and disappeared into the hut. As he went in his shoulder just grazed a row of crampons hanging by their straps from the front of the buildings and they were alone on the terrace in the fading light, with the tinkling sound of the metal crampons clinking against each other. She sat there with the rug over her lap, sipping with obvious enjoyment at a mediocre wine, just as if it was an excellent vintage. She seemed to be making the best of the situation now.

'We knew from what Muller said that the army would put troops in at the fortress one day, so why didn't you tell me the general staff had contacted you?' he asked.

'Because I want to forget about it.'

'What's going to happen?'

'I don't know exactly. I had a letter from a colonel something – I don't remember his name – telling me that at some point between now and the end of the month a division will move into position on the estate.'

'A division? But that means hundreds of men!'

'I don't know anything about the army. I may have got it wrong.'

'And you agreed?'

'I didn't have any choice. If war does come, they want reception centres set up for the civilian population who will be coming up here to take refuge in the shelter. But I don't want to talk about that now. Don't go on at me about it.'

The leather bag was still sitting on one of the benches. He took off the frame, folded it very carefully and put it down on the table in front of her. The cold was rising up from the darkened glacier. The last of the peaks not yet in darkness were bathed in a light that made you think of the sea. They

257

were anchored to the earth by thousands of millions of tons of rock, yet somehow ethereal, as though they were held aloft by the limpid light. An irrational sadness now swept over him, so poignant that he went back over to the railing and leant on it, so that she wouldn't guess what he was feeling. Captain Rollus reappeared, surrounded by a few of the men. They were carrying kitbags and started larking about on the few flat shelves of ground round the hut.

'I've had the top dormitory cleaned out. The men who've been using it will sleep under canvas tonight, and tomorrow night too, if you decide to stay on. Don't worry about them, they love it. They're very excited about Mrs Leber being here and I think they'll have a request to put to her this evening.'

They watched in silence as the tents were pitched. The men weren't talking much among themselves, just what was needed to deal with the practical details. Their movements seemed to have grown more sluggish as the night drew in, yet they were getting the job done quickly, with deft gestures that spoke of long practice. They were clearly as happy as small children at the prospect of spending the night in a tent and weren't deterred by the cold – it was really biting now, as it seeped into the shadows. The secretary was suddenly struck by the absurdity of it all and burst out laughing. Rollus looked at him askance, failing to understand.

'May I ask what's so funny?' he inquired, half in jest. But he had already grown serious again and his face suddenly took on a gloomy expression, which the captain found even more disconcerting.

'It doesn't matter. I was thinking of that business about the clock they may have forgotten to wind up . . . Tell me honestly, what's the point of all this play acting?'

Rollus didn't at first understand what he meant by play acting. When he suspected what he was getting at, he frowned and walked up and down for a moment or two, as though he was thinking it over. Then with an abrupt about-turn he plonked himself down in front of the secretary and his face took on a mocking expression.

258

'A mountain in labour . . . brought forth a mouse,' he quoted in a prophetic tone, raising his index finger. Then he turned to face the tents and called out, in a mock-domineering voice: 'Hurry up, for God's sake! How the hell did I get landed with these slowcoaches! We'll lower the flag in ten minutes.' And he whispered to the secretary: 'That bloody flag!'

'You know there won't be a war. Everybody knows it. It'll all happen differently – and be much more deadly.'

He could see her over the captain's shoulder, talking to one of the soldiers. Silvery lights were flickering in her dark hair, and her tired face, as white as the moon, was dazzlingly beautiful. He'd never seen her as radiant, as coaxing, as she was with this young recruit who was sitting back on his heels in front of her, speaking to her in an undertone.

'I hope you're right,' said Rollus, moving away from him to bawl out an order – they were all to fall in on the terrace.

Within a few seconds the platoon was drawn up in front of the flagpole, standing to attention. The flag jerked down, limp and frayed, the rope creaking hideously on its pulley. One of the soldiers unhooked it, tossed it over his shoulder with a distinct lack of deference and took it into the hut. 'Stand at . . . ease! Dis . . . miss!' ordered the captain, already sounding detached, as though all this – this play acting – was no longer any concern of his. The day was officially over.

She complained of being cold and one of the men took off his tunic and put it round her shoulders. Then a little group formed round her – it was all very spontaneous, their attitude a mixture of deferential and good-natured. Yet still no one was brave enough to speak. A couple of acetylene lamps had been lit and the terrace was drifting on the twilight like a raft, while below them the glacier looked like an elongated sandbank. Inside the hut the men were now drinking and playing cards. Although nothing happened, except for the odd glance here and there, she seemed as much at ease among these young men as if she'd been surrounded by her own brood of children. As no one could pluck up enough courage to speak to her, Captain Rollus came to the rescue of his fellow-soldiers, not taking

259

the lead as one of the privileges due to him as an officer, but returning to his old role of literature specialist.

'Almost all of us are too young to have seen you on stage, Mrs Grekova, but we know all about you. You're referred to in school textbooks and any teacher remotely interested in the theatre refers to you as the greatest of contemporary tragic actresses. Please don't think that your . . . er . . . accident has eclipsed your reputation – it hasn't, and I'm sure there are still people all over the world talking about you every single day. Having you here with us is . . . er . . . utterly amazing, fantastic, and . . . er . . . we'd be delighted if you'd agree to recite some passages from *Phèdre* or *The Women of Troy* for us this evening.'

Anyone who didn't know her well could easily have thought her cold and haughty now. The captain's request seemed to have made her tense up completely, but the secretary knew that in fact this tension showed how difficult she was finding it not to let them see how moved she felt.

'Very well, I'm touched,' she said crisply. 'But now I must rest.' She turned to the secretary, her eyes looking misty and somewhat moist. 'I'd like to lie down for a moment.'

The soldiers moved aside and he took her in his arms. He was struck by how limp she felt suddenly. The silence of the mountains was once again taking hold of the men, and mixed in with it was something resembling a primitive fear. Rollus went on ahead. There was an open fire in the main room, which was cluttered up with tables, paliasses and skiing gear. When they came in the men interrupted their card games and stopped talking. In that confined space there was a stale smell of rifle grease, cooking and cigars. They climbed up to the upper floor, a square room furnished with bedsteads and paliasses, while Rollus went back down, his boots clattering on the granite steps.

He sat down beside her and she drew him towards her, guiding his mouth towards hers. They kissed. They kissed as they'd never kissed before, pausing only to draw breath, fill their lungs with the fleecy smell of the army blankets,

260

then drink in one another's breath once again. All the time they were kissing they kept their eyes open, gazing hungrily into one another's eyes, seeing nothing else, but their bodies remained chaste. Sounds of merrymaking drifted up through the floor, its roughly cut boards letting some light through the cracks between them, plus the occasional whiff of cigar smoke. 'Hold me tight, be gentle, affectionate, just for once . . .,' she whispered. Why such dreadful anguish? he thought with a dry sob, burying his face in her breasts. So much love, pent up for so long in the brimming fountain of his heart, suddenly overflowing and choking him. She was stroking his hair with a rocking motion of her body, lulling him like a baby. 'I'd like to stay here all winter,' she whispered. 'Everything would be covered with snow, and we'd go into hibernation like bears. But we must go back down to our battlefields . . .'

The noise downstairs came to an abrupt halt. A nasal voice spluttered on the radio. Rollus reported on the day's activities and received his orders; then there was a shrill sound like a grasshopper calling, followed by crackling. 'Over and out!' came Rollus's voice. And immediately the hubbub started up again. The secretary straightened up awkwardly – all his limbs were numb – then rolled over on his side, his face puffy, and the sudden movement triggered a loud crash that jerked him upright on the paliasse. A Bren gun propped up against the bedstead had toppled over. She let out a gurgling laugh and again drew him towards her. 'A bit later on I'll make those boys happy,' she said.

His eye was caught by a very detailed map of the region. The tiniest fold in the terrain was recorded on it and he tried to spot the fortress, taking some time to work out where it was. In fact all he needed to do was follow a series of red arrows, no doubt marking the planned troop movements and all converging on the fortress.

'I shouldn't really let you look at that – you may be a spy,' said Rollus mischievously, pointing to two places on the map. 'My company's here and here. In about ten days' time the two platoons will advance on Big Hat glacier, taking the route marked by the arrows. When we get to this junction point here three other companies will meet up with us, then we'll all march off to Mrs Leber's estate. The plan of campaign says we're supposed to get there on the twenty-eighth of August, but other instructions may be issued between now and then, and we're already fairly behind with the general staff's schedule.'

The fire was sputtering. In the glare of the acetylene lamps the magazines and breeches of the automatic weapons hanging on the walls were shiny with grease and the row of black helmets on one of the benches made him think of the empty shells of some species of giant beetle. One of the recruits came over to them, with something glittering in his hand. He held it out to the secretary.

'I'm a friend of Varlaam's,' he said. 'I think you must be the geologist he's told me about. I found this the other day on the moraine when we were doing some firing practice on the glacier.'

The secretary turned the little mineral over and over in his hand, puzzled, then walked over to get a better look at it in the lamplight. He scratched at it with his nail, bit it, then signalled to the soldier to come and join him by the fire.

'It's gold,' he said. 'Gold with quartz underneath. I thought at first it was copper pyrite, commonly known as fool's gold, but it's gold all right.'

He held out his palm in the firelight, rolled the little nugget along it, then handed it back. The soldier looked at it in disbelief.

'Gold . . . are you sure?'

'Absolutely. It won't make you rich, but in a few years' time, if you're still alive, you'll be able to tell your children you struck gold on Bear's Tooth Glacier.'

The soldier looked at him, totally bewildered, as though he'd just been told that someone had put a curse on him. He went back over to his fellow-recruits playing cards and said gloomily, tossing the nugget of gold on to the table: 'I've

262

struck gold! It's bound to be a bad sign – you'll see, we'll get given an order to go back down.' And as he slumped on to one of the benches, the first female voice these young men had heard for weeks rang out with such authority that they all stopped talking straight away.

She was speaking *mezzo voce*, with a somewhat harsh intonation. Sitting on her folding chair by the fireside, she let her gaze hover above the heads of the soldiers sitting round her on the floor. And those who were only mildly interested in this display of virtuosity put down the little glasses of spirits they'd been downing in rapid succession and, out of sheer curiosity, sat there quietly and listened.

'I'm going to recite a passage from Euripides' *The Women of Troy*. Talthybius, a captain in the Greek army, orders his men to set fire to Troy. Then Hecuba speaks to the other women.'

Captain Rollus was standing beside the map with his arms folded, leaning back against the wall. He was staring intently at her, his eyes shining, and suddenly he looked like a child.

> My hour has come. The gods have pity on me! This is
> My last ordeal, to sail away and see Troy fall
> In flames.

Keeping well in the background, the secretary withdrew into the shadows, among the helmets and the guns. A few steps away from him the door was still ajar, revealing the starry night. He could feel the sharp tang in the air round his ankles. She seemed to be looking at him as she spun out her despairing soliloquy, but he was wrong – her face, half hidden in the firelight, was turned elsewhere as she twisted and untwisted her long fingers, and while her whole face was moving in the flickering light of the flames, her mouth seemed to remain motionless. He moved still further back, banging into a table. A glass of spirits fell off and rolled along the ground. The soldier was so spellbound he made no movement to stop it, didn't move a muscle even when it shattered. The secretary felt out of it now, like a nought

263

on the abacus of mankind. A peculiar thought came to him: 'Thou hast raised me for a moment into thy light, then, having deemed me unworthy, hast cast me out into darkness . . .'

With each word she spoke she was slipping away from him, plunging energetically into the labyrinthine corridors of the lines, her royal progress not that of a dethroned queen, but full of pride and disdain, even when she was voicing utter despair. That's what these young men find so fascinating, he thought – the way she seems so fiery in the midst of nothingness, so pugnacious in the midst of despair. Yet he had never seen her looking so tiny and frail, so totally concentrated, so alone, so much so that he couldn't bear to go on looking at her.

> Up, aged feet; if you can climb so far,
> I will stand here and bid farewell to my poor city . . .

She was wearing herself out with grief. He could do nothing for her – for good or ill – and this sense of his own uselessness was suffocating him. He crept stealthily outside. The cold seized him by the throat. He gulped down a big mouthful of air as he looked up at the pole star and this brought him solace. No one had noticed him. He was gliding through time like a night-time swimmer in the glimmering waters of the open sea, hearing voices somewhere in the darkness, on the deck of some invisible ship. But he was used to that – lone crossings, with no shore in sight, ever, and the sky with all its stars reaching down to the sea.

> Listen, temples of gods, beloved city,
> Ravaged with flame, flowing with guiltless blood! . . .
> Dust mingled with smoke spreads wings to the sky,
> I can see nothing, the world is blotted out!
> Earth and her name are nothing;
> All has vanished . . .

Scraps of lines were drifting out to him. He walked across the terrace, went down steps that seemed to plunge down into the mountain, then proceeded through the tents in the black marl, walking towards the pyramid looming up ahead of him, and inside him. In the cold light of the stars the snow-clad peaks appeared before him – mausoleums, row upon heartbreakingly endless row of them, forming a city of the dead as vast as the universe. 'Pray, my dear, have you not forgot to wind up the clock?' he said aloud. Then as he gazed at the Plough he rediscovered thoughts from long ago, thoughts now worth little yet once his whole life. He realized with a jolt that the hut was now in complete silence and turned back. The clapping and cries of 'Bravo!' made him jump. As he stepped up on to the terrace he thought that, like the late lamented Samuel Leber before him, he loathed *The Women of Troy*, loathed Hecuba, loathed the whole tragic repertoire.

The following morning she woke up late and so totally drained that there was no question of their leaving the hut. She made no attempt to overcome her exhaustion but simply gave in to it, as though now that she'd achieved the goal she'd set herself, she was abandoning any other inclination she might have harboured, however slight. He helped her to get washed, carried her on to the terrace and made some coffee. They sat in silence watching the curtain slowly rise over the glacier and the coombs. The scenery was enveloped in banks of slumbering mist. Patches of it, gently nudged by air currents, were drawing back in slow motion, gradually allowing the scenery to emerge into the full light of day, as though the mountains were being newly fashioned as they watched. The soldiers had already left. He found a message from Captain Rollus pinned to the door of the hut: 'Please spend today resting too. Enjoy the sun and the peace and quiet. As I don't want you to be disturbed, I've given up the idea of firing practice on the glacier. But you'll have to go tomorrow: if it gets out that I've been harbouring civilians, I'll find myself being courtmartialled. There's plenty to eat and drink – help yourselves to whatever you feel like.'

They stayed on the terrace all day. Sitting there with her face smothered in sun cream, she was joining in the boundless stillness along with the landscape – it was completely motionless

265

except for an illusory quivering in the air. He came across the captain's copy of *The Life and Opinions of Tristram Shandy* – no doubt he'd left it there deliberately. He sat down at the table and read it. In the early afternoon he fried some eggs and bacon and opened a bottle of red wine, and they had their lunch, with her sitting on the folding chair while he ate standing up by the railing. Later on, when he was surveying the mountain tops through the binoculars in the hope of spotting chamois or ibexes, or any other living creature, she gave him a piece of news that didn't really come as a surprise, and couldn't cast a serious cloud over the peripheral peace of that day, even though it heralded difficulties to come.

'Ramanuja's told me he wants to leave the fortress at the end of the month. The others will be leaving with him. Another Tamil is opening a large Indian restaurant down in the town and he's giving them all jobs. Tiresome, isn't it?'

He merely nodded in agreement and went on peering through the binoculars. But he couldn't see any sign of an animal, nothing but stone, ice and snow. The sun was still high in the sky when the platoon got back. The men climbed up the path in single file in their white camouflage overalls, their guns and ice axes slung across them, worn out from hours of walking in the mountains. The captain was as exhausted as they were. He ordered them to stand at ease and once they'd taken off their overalls they flopped down all over the terrace and inside the hut.

'You've been reading Sterne,' said Rollus, beaming delight-edly, when he found the book open on the table. Then he went in to have a lie-down. The flag was lowered with unceremonial haste. The men polished their boots, cleaned their guns and had an early supper. Despite their exhaustion they exuded a quiet, animal-like contentment.

When the meal was over Olga Grekova-Leber and the secretary went back out on to the terrace and stayed there until the sky was studded all over with stars.

'What did those boys get up to all day in the mountains?' she asked.

266

'They were walking,' he replied absent-mindedly. Then he realized that this reply – like most replies – was unsatisfactory, and that he hadn't taken her curiosity seriously enough. But he couldn't give her any more details and she didn't press him. From now on everyone could engage in whatever idiotic activity they fancied and it wouldn't make any difference. Anything that is nothingness must be taken away, and so carefully hidden that you don't even have to think about it, he told himself as the cold started to seep into him. We mustn't know anything about nothingness – must have nothing to do with nothingness, and yet all living things are pure nothingness.

At first light next morning she woke him out of a deep sleep. She wanted to leave while the men were still asleep. She wanted them to remember her as Hecuba, not as a disabled woman being lugged around in a bag. They went downstairs in silence, past the sleeping soldiers. But they found Rollus doing his exercises on the terrace in T-shirt and underpants. He didn't seem surprised at seeing them up and about so early and showed them a different route so that they could get to the bottom of the glacier by walking beside the lateral moraine.

'I've been told you've got a superb library at the fortress, Mrs Leber,' he said shyly. 'Would you allow me to use it?'

Once he'd put her down on the folding chair, the secretary unfolded the bag on the table and got their things together. Everything was tinged with mauve and the mountain tops were edged with a border of daylight the colour of limpid water.

'The library was designed to be used at a time when there wouldn't be a single book left on the face of the earth. But meanwhile I can't see any objection to its being put to good use. But now I'd like you to leave us, captain.'

He gave a farewell bow and went back into the hut. The secretary laid her out on the table and strapped her into the bag. He found it very easy and was surprised at his own dexterity. He slipped his arms through the straps, then lay back and straightened up with the bag on his back.

'By the time the sun comes up, we'll have got almost as far

267

as the glacier,' he said as he went down the steps. Then he glanced at her over his shoulder and smiled.

5

'Please go and fetch the binoculars and push me on to the bastion,' she said. 'I'd like to check something.'

He pushed her as far as the parapet walk and parked the wheelchair in between two of the crenellations, so that she had a bird's eye view of the whole of the ravine. A night of storms had left the air clear and pure and everything seemed very close, standing out with surreal sharpness. He sat on the ramparts and unobtrusively leaned over so that he too could check on something lying in the green depths of the ravine. She kept the binoculars trained on the little town. Even without them the church steeple and the roofs of the Old Town stood out clearly, along with the plate-glass windows of the tower blocks, which were set ablaze then grew dark again by turns as the clouds raced across a chaotic sky.

'They've done a lot of building in a short space of time,' she said. 'The suburbs are spreading further and further out – it won't be long now before the industrial estate runs right into the suburbs round the capital. Samuel used to claim that we can only build ruins nowadays, that modern towns and cities and modern buildings in old towns are nothing but ruins. The way he saw the modern world meant that he believed that architects' minds were only capable of producing embryo ruins, and that there was nothing for time to do, since the effects wrought by the passing of time were constantly being planned for in advance. He used to say: "Time must be disappointed at how little we give it to get its teeth into – it deserves better."' She'd gone on looking through the binoculars while she was speaking and their weight was making her hands shake. Then she turned towards him and asked a question. The way she looked at him suggested she was expecting him to do the impossible, though she didn't know what this implied: 'Are you still reading through my husband's manuscripts?'

He thought he could hear the sound of a car engine and had a good look at the forest on the other side of the ravine. He could make out the track here and there between the tree trunks, but there was no sign of any vehicle.

'Yes. I've been doing some reading and editing whenever you leave me enough time to get on with it. I've been coming across some unexpected passages.'

She gave him a surprised and disapproving look. She tried to smile, but he sensed that she was still turning something over in her mind, as she had been for the last three days, ever since they got back from the hut on the Bear's Tooth. The sound of a car engine became more distinct. He wondered if she'd asked him to come out on to the ramparts with her simply because she wanted to see how far the town had expanded and to talk about Samuel Leber, or because she was expecting someone and couldn't contain her impatience.

'In that case you no doubt know what Samuel thought: there's no point nowadays in any architect worth his salt putting up buildings for letting – that side of the business has been taken over by mass-production developers and by financiers – it's got nothing to do with art. He used to insist that there's no one, anywhere in the world, with the remotest idea of what human beings really need in the way of accommodation. He felt that the reason behind second-rate housing wasn't just that it was depressingly uninspired and that there was a lack of proper funding, but the sterility and futility of a civilization with no philosophy and no god. He was convinced that the signs of the coming destruction were already there for all to see in everything man undertakes, even in his loftiest ventures, that they're visible in the tiniest stroke of the architect's pencil, in the minutest electronic connector inside a computer, because man is no longer capable of producing anything but death. I don't know if he wrote that – I don't give a damn if he did or didn't – but during the last few months of his life, when the Leber Foundation had already been perverted, he went on saying day after day, like a litany, that there were virtually no human beings left, that spiritually and intellectually the

269

human race had as it were already become extinct. And day after day I would wonder how I could stop him . . .'

He took the binoculars from her and put them down on the ramparts. The clouds were racing past above their heads, making them feel that the natural movement had gone into reverse, as if the earth was turning the wrong way beneath a motionless sky.

'I thought you'd stopped worrying about Mr Leber. I'm not much use to you then.'

'Don't say that! You're doing an enormous amount for me, but you can't help me with everything. What I'd like to know is whether . . . er . . . whether the unexpected passages you've been reading ever include any references to me.'

Leber had mentioned his wife just once, on the page that had been almost completely crossed out. But instinctively he lied.

'No, none at all. He only talks about general topics.'

Her expression was a mixture of irritation and relief.

'About general topics – and about himself, I imagine,' she sighed.

Just then he spotted the car driving quickly up the track to the fortress. It was a large grey Range Rover and as it went through the gaps in the forest reflections flashed off the metal. Before long it was out in the open and he could get a good look at the driver through the binoculars. He knew he'd seen him somewhere before, but his memory of him was dark and shadowy, like someone seen in a dream, and it took him a while to put him back into the context of his own life. Morel, the shelter's engineer, was now sitting there clinging to the steering wheel, but in his mind's eye he could still see him opening the little yellow door leading down into the bowels of the earth and fumbling about in the dark for his torch.

'What's he coming up here for? Is he going to do another round of inspection?' he asked.

She averted her eyes and with a smooth, flowing movement backed the chair away from him.

'I asked him to come to see to some practical details before

270

the soldiers get here,' she said, rushing over her words. 'I can't tell you any more than that.'

He still couldn't understand how a woman of her temperament could suddenly give in so easily, acting in a way that was so alien to her true character.

'Why don't you write to the colonel saying you don't agree to their intruding on your privacy? It's your home, the army can't get away with trespassing on someone's land in peacetime,' he said crossly.

'Yes they can. When the work on the fortress had been completed, Samuel signed a rider giving permission for the army to occupy the estate if there was some compelling strategic reason. It was also stipulated that any buildings apart from the private living quarters can be requisitioned for billeting officers. I'm going to go and make Mr Morel welcome now. He'll be having lunch at the fortress – do join us if you'd like to.'

She didn't ask him to push her but spun round and propelled the chair vigorously across the bastion, its wheels churning heavily through the gravel. Just as she was coming to the door to her rooms, a sudden impulse made him call after her, without stopping to think:

'Wait! Can you tell me what your new wheelchair's doing at the bottom of the ravine?'

Her hands clenched on the wheels and she brought the chair to an abrupt halt. She didn't turn round, so he couldn't see her face, but he knew the question he'd just asked had hit home and that she'd make him pay for it. After a moment she said in a lacklustre voice:

'Tanguy threw it down there.'

'He could have done the same with you.'

'He could have. But he didn't.'

When he was back in his room he watched from his window as Morel drove into the courtyard. He parked the Range Rover at the foot of the steps – she was waiting at the top – and climbed heavily out, like someone crippled with rheumatism. But it was obvious from his grey, drawn face

271

that the rheumatism was in his head. He was carrying the tool case and the secretary decided that she must have been lying, that he was indeed here to do an extra tour of inspection inside the shelter. Then another thought flashed through his mind, but he dismissed it straight away. He watched Morel walk slowly up the steps, looking distinctly uncommunicative, and realized he'd been reluctant to come. Two of the Tamils were sitting on the ground in the shade cast by the building, playing dice. They took no notice of Morel and when she called out to them to come in and serve lunch they got to their feet like automata, smiling and unconcerned. He moved away from the window and thought that under the age-old pressure of this lack of concern, our world could easily split open like a walnut shell.

The message had been slipped under his door and he recognized the handwriting at once: 'TOMORROW MORNING AT THE KENNELS. WELCOME TO YOU, YOUR EMINENCE!'

He set off without a gun and without telling her where he was going. When he left the fortress after an exhaustingly sleepless night, a new day was dawning slowly and laboriously, wreathed in hazy mist. As soon as he was out in the fresh air his strength returned and his mind cleared. He could tell from the smells, from a feeling of sluggishness in the earth, that autumn was worming its way stealthily into the last days of summer, and this infinitesimal change, which had occurred only in the last few hours gave him a highly sensual thrill. When he turned off in the direction of the kennels, taking his time and swinging along cheerfully, it occurred to him that after months and months of walking dangerously, he was at last striking out towards a specific goal. The darkness was still lingering in the fir tree plantation. As he walked through it he remembered a precept from one of Meister Eckhart's sermons, one that Fra Cosimo had liked quoting: 'Those who seek nothing, neither usefulness, nor the inner gift of self, nor holiness, nor reward, nor the Kingdom of Heaven, but have renounced everything, even that which is theirs, in such men is God honoured.' He

272

reached the clearing shortly after six and looked round for Tanguy, but couldn't see him anywhere.

There was no sign of life round the kennels and the falcon hut. Usually the dogs scented anyone or anything that came near, but they made no sound. He lingered for a moment, having a good look round, wondering if Tanguy hadn't been playing some trick on him. Nature was silent – there was no birdsong to be heard and the only sound was the intermittent spluttering of the trough. The door to the falcon house was ajar and swung to occasionally with a creaking sound, as though someone was keeping watch from the shadows. He strode off purposefully towards the huts, surprised that his footsteps didn't set the dogs barking. When he'd almost reached the kennels he saw them stretched out on the muddy ground.

The wire netting door was open and the five German pointers were lying there in a pool of their own blood, their throats slit from ear to ear. The hunting knife was lying in the dust a bit further on. 'Tanguy!' he shouted. His shout set up a weak echo but there was no reply. He rushed over to the falcon house, which was empty. As he was coming back out he heard the sound of wings flapping above his head. One of the falcons shot out of the foliage and rose up high in the sky, then started gliding round the clearing in a circle. He searched about in the woods for the other birds. Everything was transfixed – even the falcon seemed to have turned to stone in mid-air, though it did give the occasional lazy flap of its wings to keep flying at that height. He went back to the kennels. The blood was still wet, so the pointers had only just been killed – there was still a flicker of life in the wide-open eyes of one of them. He laid his hand on its side, which was still warm, then straightened up in a fury and yelled out Tanguy's name.

He was standing a few paces behind him, the rifle with its scope casually pointing in his direction, his left index finger on his lips.

'Not so loud, your eminence, you'll wake them up,' he whispered.

When the secretary bore down on him he put both hands on the rifle and stepped back a few paces.

'What made you kill the dogs, Tanguy?' he asked stupidly, walking past him to get out of the kennels. The sun was coming up above the tops of the trees now and half the clearing was already full of light, the granite feeding troughs sparkling in the pink grass. He suddenly felt as if he had his back to the wall, a wall made up of unfathomable and totally meaningless reality.

'You're an intelligent man, your eminence, or so they say, but there's a lot you don't understand. Your intelligence is like a torch beam – it lights up what's just ahead of you and everything else is in darkness. And you're going to die with all that darkness round you. Where's your gun?'

Still keeping an eye on the secretary, he glanced furtively from the kennels to the falcon house, then his gaze slid over the drinking trough and on to the edge of the forest.

'Don't bother to look – I've come unarmed.'

For a moment Tanguy seemed taken aback. The rifle barrel drooped down and the secretary might just have had time to pounce on him – he thought of it anyway, but with a total lack of determination.

'Like a lamb to the slaughter . . . What a shame, your eminence! You see those two stakes?' He jerked his chin in the direction of a couple of posts stuck in the ground facing each other, about a hundred yards apart. 'They're the spot I picked for the two of us. I hammered them in just now, before I dealt with the dogs, and now, seeing as you haven't got a gun, I'm going to have to deal with you the same way.'

He blinked hard, dazzled. The secretary sensed that his resolve was weakening and thought: Everything's going to be all right. The air was warming up. Thousands of insects were flying about in the sunshine. Again he could feel autumn in the drowsiness of the foliage and the delicate blue of the sky.

'What do you want revenge for?' he asked. Tanguy had steadied the rifle and had stopped shaking.

'Don't want revenge, your eminence. I don't like you, right

274

enough. You've robbed me, but I don't give a damn for that old bitch, and that's not why I'm going to kill you. I'm going to kill you because you're an animal too, you're vermin, and things have gone far enough.'

What Tanguy was saying seemed both nonsensical rambling and at the same time completely accurate. A question flashed through the secretary's mind, a question he felt was of such moment that it would no doubt mean he could take charge of the situation once again.

'What happened with the decelerating mechanism, Tanguy? Do at least tell me that before you kill me.'

He didn't seem at all put out. His face darkened and took on an expression of such concentration, looking so mournful and haggard that for just a second, before he took in what was really happening, the secretary felt sorry for him. The rifle barrel rose up until it was on a level with his head. He saw Tanguy's finger stiffen on the trigger and it was then he realized he was going to fire, either now or later, but there was no escaping it. Tanguy's expression clouded over. He went over to the water trough, moving sideways, and sat down on the edge of it, his eyes never leaving his victim.

'I did a lot of walking during the night, my feet hurt,' he grumbled to himself. He kicked off his boots, keeping his hands on the rifle, and turned round slightly to dip one foot into the water. A blissful smile lit up his face.

'Don't worry, your eminence, you won't feel a thing, I'm using split bullets – your head'll burst like a pumpkin.'

He was still smiling, but this time there was nothing joyous about it. An expression of gentleness crept into his face, like a nostalgic memory. Flies were starting to buzz round the pointers' bodies. He must play for time – a few seconds, perhaps a whole minute. Somewhat oddly, he wasn't afraid. He was experiencing a numbing sensation of time growing thicker and flowing very slowly round inside him. Keeping his finger on the trigger, Tanguy pulled a cigar out of his shirt pocket, lit it with an old tinder lighter hanging from his belt and inhaled with a sigh of sensual pleasure.

275

'That's good, that is, your eminence,' he said. 'But you wouldn't know anything about that.'

I'll walk quickly away, he thought. He won't dare shoot me in the back. But he wasn't sure that there were enough scruples left in this world of ours to stop anyone shooting someone in the back. Tanguy wasn't a free agent any more. It wasn't just that he'd been overtaken by his own cruelty and his own madness. His cruelty and madness were no longer his. In the blindness of the collective conscience they were the expression of a universal human cruelty and madness – and those were quite capable of killing anybody, by any method. I'm going to try something, he thought. But he realized he couldn't move any more. And then at last the fear broke over him like a wave, his head became boiling hot, his gut knotted up. He felt an urge to defecate and thought he was going to collapse. He stared intently at the blueish bore of the rifle and sought some justification for the death that was about to mow him down, but couldn't find one. Then, like a confession addressed only to himself, but one on which his last hope of absolution depended, he realized what he'd been refusing to admit for some time – his faith in life wasn't strong enough to sustain him. He didn't believe in anything any more, except the terror he was feeling at this moment.

'Fire, Tanguy,' he said.

The falcon, no doubt recognizing its master, was flying lower and lower, describing concentric circles above the water trough.

'Just a moment more, your eminence . . .'

He shut his eyes. When he opened them again he saw Tanguy popping the rifle barrel into his mouth. His big toe, dripping with water, barely fumbled for the highly sensitive trigger and the rifle went off. A geyser of blood and bone spewed up towards the sky, towards the falcon, and Tanguy's body toppled over into the trough in slow motion.

For a long time he didn't react in any way, just stood there staring at the scarlet water in the trough and Tanguy's half-submerged body. The explosion seemed to have torn a hole in an air cushion – he could hear the birds singing again and the water peacefully gurgling into the trough. And suddenly it was as if the exhaustion of all those sleepless nights was sweeping over him and he swayed on his feet. I mustn't stay here, he kept on telling himself. I must get away. I'm alive. Feeling light-headed, he staggered to the edge of the forest. He would have liked to vomit, to shit. He stopped several times to lean against a tree trunk but nothing would come out. He walked across the fir plantation, continued a little way across country, then flopped down on to the grass and fell fast asleep.

When the police helicopter landed at the heliport he felt quite incapable of getting out of the jeep. He went on sitting behind the wheel while the six men – a couple of firemen and two policemen, a police inspector and a forensic pathologist – leapt out with a stretcher, oxygen cylinders and a whole lot of first-aid paraphernalia that made him smile when he thought of Tanguy's head bursting open. 'Like a pumpkin,' he said to the gaping inspector when he asked him for more details. Then he clammed up completely and they couldn't get another word out of him.

They drove him back to the clearing, where he took no further interest in the proceedings. The firemen pulled Tanguy out of the trough and when they saw the bloody pulp dangling from his shoulders they left him to the pathologist, who examined him gingerly and unfolded a tarpaulin. One of the policemen leaned against the kennels and vomited.

'Did he do that?' asked the inspector, pointing at the dogs. The secretary nodded. The whole operation took some time, as they had to measure out the piece of ground and take fingerprints from the rifle and also from the knife they'd found in the kennels. Then the inspector asked him if he'd got a shovel and insisted that the men were to bury the pointers. While they took it in turns to dig, he came over to stand beside the secretary and launched into a monologue, casting doubtful glances at him from time to time.

'There's certainly no shortage of tragic happenings at Mrs Leber's. First of all there was that man who got himself killed by a bear, then Tanguy . . .' He broke off, then went on: 'Mind you, it was bound to happen one day. I'd known him for ages – he wasn't quite right in the head. Mrs Leber shouldn't have kept him on after that business with the cable car. It's odd all the same that you just happened to be passing by this morning, so early too. Oh yes, of course, you were out walking and you heard the shot. I expect you're often out walking, aren't you?'

He watched the men digging hurriedly, an expression of disgust on their faces, and when they'd finished they dragged the dogs into the trench and covered them over. The firemen heaved Tanguy on to the stretcher but the back of the jeep turned out not to be long enough, so two of the men had to stay in the back to hang on to it during the return drive.

'We're going to put the body in the helicopter and then go and see Mrs Leber,' said the policeman.

The interview was soon over. She saw the inspector and the pathologist in her private hall, together with one of the policemen who was to take down her statement. She'd asked for the shutters to be pulled across and it was very dark in there. The policeman perched right on the edge of his chair, a tiny typewriter balanced on his lap.

'Let's have a little light in here, if you please, so that my colleague can take down your statement.' The inspector's request was made with that familiarly jovial manner people always use when they're trying to lighten the atmosphere in moments of drama. Olga Grekova-Leber had a horror of familiarity. She refused to open the shutters or switch on one of the lamps, which increased the tension considerably.

'Now look, Mrs Leber. I could force you to come with me to the station. I've been advised not to because of your disability and your . . . er . . . Your standing in this part of the world means that you enjoy substantial privileges, but they won't last for ever, you know.'

The secretary hadn't told her about what had happened in

the clearing until he'd recovered some semblance of mental equilibrium. At first she'd seemed unmoved by Tanguy's suicide, merely commenting: 'It's just as well.' But less than an hour later she was in a state of feverish excitement – he'd never seen her like that – and couldn't sit still. She charged frantically about all over the fortress in her wheelchair and propelled herself backwards and forwards across the courtyard, talking to herself out loud and occasionally taking her hands off the wheels to fling her arms about like a madwoman. He realized what was happening and made no attempt to calm her down. The inspector's last sentence made her burst out into scathing laughter.

'You won't last for ever either, inspector! And you can rest assured that my privileges will last longer than you will if you go on harrying me like this. As for the rest, I shall discuss it with Mr Muller and with him alone.'

The inspector didn't let this put him off his stroke. Instead he withdrew behind a screen of hypocritical humility.

'Very well, madam. The matter has already been referred to Mr Muller in any case and he'll be calling on you very shortly. I'm going to have a talk with your secretary now. After all, he is the key witness.'

That evening they had an early dinner in the chapel, just the two of them. The last rays of the setting sun were shining down through the pointed Gothic windows straight on to the altar-cum-sideboard and the holy spirit in the cut-glass decanters poured its faceted light on to the flagstones with a generous hand. She was quite calm now, almost languid. She was drinking large quantities of a ruby-coloured wine, going into raptures over it. When she held it up so that it caught the sunlight the colour grew deeper and it left an oily tinge on the glass. The Tamil servant kept the decanter in his hand and as soon as her glass was empty would glide up behind her on his bare feet and fill it so nimbly that they never spotted him doing it.

'Tanguy was the illegitimate son of the woman Samuel bought the fortress from, the Countess of Ott,' she told him during dinner. 'She got rid of him as soon as he was born by handing him over to a charcoal burner and his wife and paying them an allowance to look after him. After that she didn't want to know anything about him – she simply forgot him. When he was twenty-two – he'd been a woodcutter for years by then – he got drunk one evening and raped a girl who turned out to be Ott's daughter, and therefore his half-sister. They locked him up and it was when he was in prison that he discovered who he really was. When his sentence still had a year to run Samuel got him released with Muller's help and in return for substantial bail. I never knew why he did it. I wonder if he knew himself.'

It was on the tip of his tongue to ask her something – the same nagging question. But perhaps he wasn't really all that keen to find out the truth, or perhaps he suspected that the truth was coming out a bit too fast. Tanguy hadn't made any revelations before he died – he'd killed himself so as not to make any.

But he did ask her one thing: 'Did Tanguy have good reasons for killing himself?'

She smiled at him over her glass, holding it up towards him as though she was about to propose a toast.

'To us, to our love. Anyone always has perfectly good reasons for killing himself if he delves down a bit.'

'When you delve down you can come across reasons for living too.'

'I wouldn't know. But why is everyone always so keen to think that life and reason go hand in hand?'

He sensed that the time had come to talk to her about a crucial matter than had been preoccupying him for several weeks, since Sarachchandra's death in fact. He'd been turning it over and over in his mind, and now with Tanguy's suicide it had assumed even greater urgency.

'We must get away from here just as soon as we can,' he said. 'Get a few things together that you really need and then let's go away, taking Félicité with us.'

She put her glass down and stared at him, her expression

280

a mixture of stunned amazement and incredulity. But in this incredulity there was an element of hopeless detachment and he could see that she had reached a point of no return in which she was resigned to her fate. Such determined resignation was tantamount to open revolt.

'Would you really go away with me?' she said, speaking very quietly.

'You've got a place in Mexico. Send instructions that the house is to be got ready for us and then let's leave.'

He was amazed at his own determination now, at how businesslike he was being. What he was saying voiced what he was thinking, but not everything he was thinking.

'I've only been to the house once, eleven or so years ago. It's infested with scorpions.'

'Well, we'll drive them out then!'

Her face clouded over.

'I'm afraid we can't do that.'

'Why not?'

'Because you can't drive out scorpions.'

6

A few days before the end of August Captain Rollus and his men reluctantly left the mountain hut on the Bear's Tooth and set off for the rallying point at the foot of Big Hat Glacier. The route marked on the map the secretary had been studying went through an area without any name at all. The topographical survey had resulted in nothing more than a blank space – the surveyors had apparently deemed it unworthy of their attentions. It was in this wilderness in the heart of a wilderness that the captain decided to bivouac, drawing a red circle round an abstract piece of terrain about halfway between the hut and the rallying point. The men marched for six hours over very uneven terrain, loaded down with cumbersome radio equipment, plus all their mountaineering gear, their own weapons and a couple of heavy machine guns. Roped together they went over deep coombs covered in ice and crossed two unnamed glaciers before eventually climbing back down into a lateral valley filled with a forest of sky-blue seracs. When they finally reached a grassy plateau level enough for them to pitch a dozen tents the light was fading. Rollus let the platoon have a short rest, then ordered them to lay out the camp. They were surprised to find traces of oil on the grass and clear signs that a helicopter had landed there not long before. But they were so exhausted that they merely put forward a few wild theories before eating their supper and crawling into their tents.

The next morning the cook was going down the moraine to fetch some water from one of the countless rivulets trickling out of the glacier when he spotted something in one of the seracs nearest to him, but couldn't quite make out what it was. He went as close as he could and was suddenly panic-stricken. He did manage to pluck up enough courage to have a better look and it was soon quite obvious that there was a man in there, lying askew in his gangue of ice, like an angel turned into stone in mid-flight. He raced back up to the plateau and found Captain Rollus sitting on a boulder, deep in *Tristram Shandy*. A few minutes later the whole platoon, shocked into silence, was gazing at the amazing discovery.

The captain's behaviour at that point was so peculiar that it was etched on the soldiers' memories ever after. He stepped forward on to the moraine, facing towards the serac, and stiffened into a perfect salute. He came back over to his men, badly shaken but quite calm and clear-headed, and ordered the radio operator to get through to HQ and report the discovery. 'This is pure fiction, I've never seen anything so much like fiction in the mountains,' he remarked several times, while the radio operator ran up to the camp. The recruits were rooted to the spot and when he ordered five of them to go and fetch ropes, ice axes and pitons it took them a moment to respond to the order. Most of these young men had never seen a dead person before, let alone a dead person looking so alive you couldn't believe he was dead.

'Personally, I think we should leave him where he is. He's

got used to it and he looks as if he's reasonably comfortable there,' said the captain, sounding very serious. 'But we'll obey orders.'

The men set off at the double to fetch the equipment and headed towards the serac with their captain. Seen from below and close to, the deep-frozen mountaineer really did seem to be flying, or launching into a comic dive into eternity. 'His hat's on crooked,' one of the men remarked. Another pointed out the gash on his forehead, above his eyebrows. They were talking quietly, as though they were afraid he might hear. Rollus was studying the wall of the serac looking for a suitable spot for climbing up – the man wasn't more than about twenty feet above them, but up a sheer cliff. Then he came across steps cut into the ice, with holes on either side where pitons had once been hammered in. 'Curiouser and curiouser . . .,' he said, trying to imagine what had been going on. 'Someone's been to call on him, or perhaps he cut these steps himself so he could go off for the occasional stroll,' he said as the radio operator arrived, out of breath, to report what HQ had said: they were to get the man out of the glacier and bring him along to the rallying point.

Rollus stood there dumbfounded. 'That's ridiculous,' he muttered to himself. 'We might manage to get him out, though I don't quite see how, but as for transporting him anywhere – it simply can't be done.'

His men knew that he never lost his temper or became irritable, but would sink into a puzzled reverie for a few seconds, then eventually adjust to what was happening, holding himself sarcastically aloof. 'Ask them to send us a helicopter with pneumatic drills and something to put the . . . er . . . him in,' he said to the radio operator, gesturing discreetly towards the mountaineer. Although his eyes were shut, and despite his deceptively dozy attitude, with his face squashed up against the natural window with its row of air bubbles, he seemed to be taking considerable interest in what they were saying. The men started driving in pitons and fastening ropes to them. But when it came to putting in the last of them, on a level with the dead man, none of them was brave enough to do it. So it was Captain Rollus who made the first face-to-face contact. He stayed on the last step for some time, clinging on to both ropes, until the soldiers standing in a huddle at the bottom of the serac started feeling worried at how long their tête-à-tête was taking.

'He's been there a long time,' he said to reassure them. He realized that sweat was pouring off him, as the sun was high in the sky by this time and beating straight down on to the glacier. He was still hanging on to the ropes when the radio operator came back and told him there weren't any helicopters available, so they'd have to manage as best they could. A brief wave of anger surged through him, then he came back down and studied the serac, thinking hard. 'What we'll do is drive pitons in right round him and we'll work on a doubled rope, with ice axes.'

He gave the necessary orders to his lieutenant and climbed back up to the camp to make radio contact with HQ himself. He managed to get through to the divisional commander – the same colonel who'd told Olga Grekova-Leber that the fortress would soon be occupied by his troops – and told him of his doubts about making a success of the operation without adequate equipment. But the old soldier was adamant. He promised to send him a helicopter as soon as one became available, but for some reason Rollus had a feeling that this promise would never be kept. 'Take as long as you need and bring that chap down,' ordered the colonel. Then they were cut off.

As he came out of the tent he saw that about ten of the men were busy at the foot of the serac and another three were already hanging from the ropes at different heights. He stood there for a moment contemplating the scene, and gradually his anxiety turned into curiosity. In the silence of the coomb he could hear the axes chipping away at the ice, plus calls and shouts from the men, who now seemed, like him, to be viewing this unusual situation with stoicism. Three of them had hoisted themselves up to the top of the serac and were hammering pitons in there. One of them slid down the ice wall on doubled rope, exactly on a line with the mountaineer, and when he was just above him started cutting into the ice in a straight line. Soon there were a good ten men clinging on to the serac and wielding axes.

How long has he been there? wondered the young captain. Since the beginning of this century probably, judging by his get-up. Between nineteen hundred and nineteen-ten, at any rate before the First World War, he calculated out loud, suddenly musing on all the historic events that this 'messenger from the past', as he was now calling him, had avoided, and on the number of potential deaths his fall into the glacier had shielded him from. He was aware that this line of reasoning was quite absurd, but it made him feel somehow dizzy, arousing an invigorating mental rapture.

'Do you realize that millions of people were ripping one another's guts out with bayonets, sleeping in the trenches on a heap of corpses, puncturing their gassed lungs, while that chap who ought to have been at the front was quietly taking it easy in the ice?' he said to the radio operator, who gaped at him in amazement. A long string of names, dates and figures, all jumbled up, crowded in on him – names that had a fine ring to them because they were still sufficiently fresh in his memory to stir his emotions, but were none the less abstract, like time, and like death. Over on that ice sepulchre the soldiers were slaving away at a dangerous job, forgetting as the hours went by what a macabre business it was. By the end of the day, spurred on by their captain's eager impatience – he had joined them on the serac and was busy tapping away – they weren't so much obeying orders as responding to a childlike curiosity and a vague longing to prise a secret from the world beyond.

Only a few of them managed to get any sleep that night. They were obsessed by that other man keeping watch in the glacier as he had for decades, and those who did get to sleep dreamed of a being who was looking at them and summoning them over to him. A lot of them sat round the fire speculating about him until the last embers went out, and they went on whispering inside the tents, while his presence crept in among them, life and death blended together in a single being. 'How old is he?' they were wondering, not: 'How old was he?' 'What nationality is he?' – there was something about his clothes that suggested he came from abroad, Britain perhaps, or America – 'What town does he live in?', 'What's his family like?' and so on.

Captain Rollus's rank entitled him to have a tent to himself. He'd put *The Life and Opinions of Tristram Shandy* back in his kitbag and taken out Lewis Carroll instead. He felt that *Through the Looking Glass* was well able to adapt to the situation, somewhat aesthetically perhaps, but after the day he'd just had, his conscious mind was as much in need of reassurance as of being filled with wonder. He was exhausted and soon dozed off over his book like Tweedledum, to dream not of Alice but of Tweedledee, who was asking him, pointing to the man in the glacier: 'He's dreaming about you. And if he stopped dreaming about you, where d'you think you'd be?' 'In this tent, of course,' he answered in his dream. Then he woke up with a start, dripping with sweat, sat on his sleeping bag and for a tiny fraction of a second, still half caught up in his dream, he thought: No, I wouldn't be anywhere, because I'm nothing but a kind of idea in that man's dream.

Next morning the real technical problems started. Although they'd been working away with their axes for a whole day, they'd only managed to cut into a very thin layer of ice. The mountaineer was much deeper than they'd thought – it had been an optical illusion that he was right at the surface. And even supposing they did get through to him, there was always the danger that one of the picks would injure him, and none of the men felt sufficiently confident – or thought he had enough patience – to cut round the body with a knife, as a sculptor would if instead of carving a shape out of a block of material, he was freeing a character already inside it. Also, once the body had been removed from its protective shell it would rapidly decompose, and then there would be no question of taking it away. The most sensible method – indeed the only one that would work – would be to cut out a block of ice with him inside it. But they hadn't got any sophisticated equipment, so how on earth could they get the block out of the serac and then lower it to the ground without breaking it?

The lieutenant suggested a solution that wasn't foolproof, and was certainly unorthodox, but did have a number of advantages. They would set up a heavy machine gun facing the serac, standing it on something to raise it up, and then the gunner would fire backwards and forwards in a sawing motion, following the lines of the smallest possible right-angled parallelepiped. He would keep on firing until the impact of the bullets had gone deep enough for them to be able to complete the process with their ice axes and the cutting edge of their shovels.

Rollus was sceptical, but ordered some of the men to fetch the machine guns. There was something about the scheme he found rather distasteful: it reminded him of those circus acts where a knife thrower tosses his daggers round the body of a beautiful young woman. However often he told himself that the man was dead, he still couldn't quite believe it, and was tormented by the thought of the stray bullets that are virtually inevitable when a machine gun is blazing away. To make things easier, the parallelepiped needed to be no more than about six feet high by five feet wide, which meant really precision firing was needed. He listened out and kept on peering up at the sky, still hoping a helicopter might turn up before they embarked on this risky venture. But the sky remained empty and the coomb went on being lulled by the peaceful hissing sound of the water running over the pebbles on the terminal moraine.

They set up the machine guns on a stony mound about thirty yards from the serac. This was very close for weapons of that firing power and the gunner wouldn't be completely protected from ricocheting bullets, but they had to take that risk if his firing was to be effective. Then Rollus, not feeling very happy about it, ordered a dummy run on the next serac along. The cartridge belt in the breech of the gun sparkled like a gold necklace in the sunshine. The appalling din made the air in

287

the coomb quiver. The soldiers glanced anxiously round, as though they were afraid the mountain might split open and roll over them. But the result was satisfactory. The bullets made holes about the size of tennis balls and penetrated well over a foot and a half into the ice. 'All right then, let's get going,' said the captain to the gunner, who was known for his unerring accuracy. 'But do make sure not to damage him.'

The gunner took off his tunic and shirt and put on his helmet, as though he was going to confront a whole enemy regiment single-handed, in desperate circumstances. The other men moved away. The anxiously solemn mood that prevails before a battle had now taken hold of the whole platoon. Rollus squatted down beside the gunner. The first volley of fire went off, the barrel slowly moved and over on the serac the ice exploded with deadly accuracy, a mere inch or so from the mountaineer's body. Rollus was holding the cartridge belt, which was unwinding at lightning speed. Soon the gun had to be reloaded. Then after the horizontal firing came the vertical firing, which was more tricky. But again the gunner proved to be remarkably accurate – the line of bullet holes was virtually straight all the way up. As the captain remarked, not a single enemy soldier would have been able to get through his line of fire. Two boxes of ammunition had been used up and there was only one left. 'We'll have used virtually all our ammunition in this first battle – and we won't even have won a victory,' Rollus remarked to the gunner. When the dust from the ice had settled and they had a clear view of the serac, the soldiers looking that way shuddered. The mountaineer had opened one of his eyes – it was colourless and completely opaque – and was staring at them through it.

After lunch they went back up on to the serac to clean out the gashes made by the machine gun and make them deeper. There wasn't much more digging to do, and soon they'd cut the ice away all round the block. Then came the problem of how to get it out. The artificer had the answer. While he was making up tiny charges of nitroglycerine, which were to be placed in the grooves in the four corners of the rectangle,

288

the men tautened a rope net after attaching it firmly to the ice to prevent the block toppling forwards when the charges exploded.

Sitting there on a rock, Captain Rollus felt vaguely frustrated. While the mountaineer was trapped in his block of ice they wouldn't find out who he was – if he had identification papers on him they wouldn't be able to get at them until the ice had melted. He watched with half an eye as the soldiers threw the rope net over the serac. They were stripped to the waist, the top half of their bodies shiny with grease, like Africans with their brown skins, and wearing snow goggles with dark rounded lenses that made them look like a team of welders fitting the various bits of the mountain together. Then an idea struck him, an idea that wasn't exactly dishonest, but was against regulations, an idea that was in a manner of speaking pure fiction. When the men had fastened down the rope net and put the charges of nitroglycerine in place, there was nothing left to do but activate the detonator. If it turned out that the artificer had miscalculated, the whole thing would blow up.

Once they'd made all the final preparations the men got well away from the serac. When the charges blew up the serac gave a convulsive judder and they thought for a moment that the whole thing was going to collapse. But the block of ice they'd cut out tilted forward on its own, with the man inside it, and was held back by the ropes. The soldiers burst out clapping – it really was a considerable feat of human ingenuity. They lowered the block cautiously to the ground – it must have weighed many hundreds of pounds. Once it was down, none of them dared go over to it. They stood some way away, gazing thoughtfully at it, and suddenly one of them glanced up at the serac and shouted: 'The ice axe!' Near the hole where the block had been, the ice axe the mountaineer had dropped as he fell was floating in the ice, looking as if it would go on falling for ever. Rollus sent one of the recruits to fetch a tarpaulin and instead of asking someone else to do it, used it to cover the block of ice and the man inside it himself, like a shroud.

Then, to everyone's amazement, he proclaimed: 'Tomorrow you can stand at ease all day. We'll set off again at dawn the following day.'

'Take as long as you need,' the colonel had insisted. During their rest day the men carried out just two tasks: they hoisted the block of ice up to the camp and used a couple of pairs of skis, the protective plates from the machine guns and some ropes to put together a cross between a sledge and a stretcher that could be pulled over the snow and carried where the ground was uneven. The weather was still fine and warm and beneath its canvas wrapping the ice was slowly melting. Rollus was sitting outside his tent reading Lewis Carroll and glancing over every now and then to see how the melting process was coming along. In the early evening he issued an order that the block was to be attached to the stretcher. They had to remove the tarpaulin, which was sopping wet by now, and wring it out, and one of the men who was dealing with this – with a mild look of disgust on his face – remarked that if it was just as hot the next day, the ice would have melted by the evening. Which was exactly what Rollus wanted to happen.

The four men in charge of the stretcher went down as far as possible, hugging the névés. On three separate occasions the man trapped in his little bit of glacier slipped out of their grasp and slithered at breakneck speed down the mountainside, finishing up against a rock with a loud crushing sound. The third time the tarpaulin was torn off and the block of ice cracked. Captain Rollus's heart cracked too, and when the deep-frozen mountaineer smashed against the rock he felt pains all over his body. The men's tempers were beginning to fray. They were growing tired of this forced march with a corpse for company and for the very first time in three months of communal living the captain had to issue threats to force them to obey. After the third fall there were no volunteers to rescue the block of ice and the men he picked to do the job eventually obeyed, with many a grumble, only when he reminded them that the order to bring the body back had come from none other than the colonel. The block had cracked diagonally across and sticking up out of a broad split were a tuft of greying hair and a piece of great coat in some neutral colour. The body was still completely trapped in the ice, but the man's face was now only a few inches from the open air. When they'd patched up the stretcher they set off again, and in the late afternoon reached a building on an abandoned stretch of pasture.

The next day, when they were getting ready to strike camp, a sinister cracking sound rang out and the swollen tarpaulin wrapped round the block of ice lifted up in two places, exactly as if the man had just broken open his mould and was getting ready to make an appearance. No one moved. They all stood there staring intently at the huge, sodden bundle, picturing in horror what was happening inside. Another few convulsive spasms shook the tarpaulin, then it subsided even further and eventually remained motionless. They heard a light hissing sound, like a sigh. 'Private Ducrey and Private Luc, go and see what's going on in there,' the captain ordered. The two recruits didn't seem to have heard. 'It's the ice that's . . .' said one of them, without specifying what he thought. Then young Rollus's self-control snapped. 'Lieutenant, pass on my orders to these men,' he said very quietly between his teeth. The lieutenant, a tall thin man with a baby face, hung his head and held his tongue. The captain took a deep breath, a very deep breath. He concentrated hard, thinking of that terribly funny scene in *Alice*, the 'Lobster Quadrille' episode, when the mock turtle sings in a melancholy drawl: '. . . would not, could not, could not, would not, could not join the dance . . . Then he walked straight over to the stretcher, stood stock still in front of the block of ice for a moment, and calmly started pulling the ropes tight. When he'd finished he grabbed hold of his own pack and without so much as looking at the platoon ordered: 'Forward . . . march!'

Halfway through the morning the four soldiers carrying the stretcher caught a whiff of something. They exchanged disgusted looks and kept on marching. They were following the gentle slope of a wide-mouthed valley with a stream running

291

through it and soon the first trees appeared, a few scattered arolla pines and some larches. They hadn't seen any vegetation for weeks and were childishly delighted at the sight of the trees. The sun was beating down and as they climbed down lower the air became progressively warmer. They could virtually see the ice inside the tarpaulin melting. Every hundred yards or so the men carrying the block would put it down and have a rest. After an hour another four of the men would take over from them, but their burden was getting lighter and lighter and the block of ice was now only a third the size it had been when they set off.

The smell was becoming more pronounced – a sweetish, sickly smell – and then it turned into a truly awful stench and the men put the stretcher down. Captain Rollus was marching at the head of his platoon. He came back and realized at once what was going on. The little jingle was going round and round in his head: 'Will you, won't you, will you, won't you, will you join the dance?' And at the same time he was thinking: We're going down, we're going back to civilization, we're going to war. Then he turned to the corporal and ordered him to tell two of the men to undo the ropes and take the tarpaulin off. 'Now at last we'll find out who he is,' he said. But the corporal didn't detail anyone. The recruits had flopped on to the grass, well away from the stretcher, and were smoking. Nothing and no one could have got them to move.

'I think it would be better if we left that . . . er . . . that thing here and went to join our unit, sir,' said one of the officers in a respectful tone. Rollus didn't hear. He walked over to the stretcher, apparently not bothered by the smell. So there it is, once again I'm going to do the job myself, he told himself. All of a sudden the tall thin lieutenant with the baby face loomed up between him and what was left of the block of ice. 'You shan't touch that, sir . . .'

Once again Rollus filled his lungs with air and held his breath. Things were happening too quickly, and insubordination was going too far for him to be able to keep them under control, and in any case he had no wish to do so. Instinctively, without his knowledge, so to speak, he felt on his hip for the holster of his service pistol. Without knowing how it had got there, he could feel in his hand the butt of the pistol – which, according to army regulations, shouldn't have been loaded. The report and the impact of the recoil that made it jerk in his hand became confused for a moment in his harassed brain and, his eyes wide with surprise, he saw the lieutenant double up, lurch backwards a few paces, turn round, then, in slow motion, collapse head first against the stretcher. None of them had really taken in what had happened when a helicopter loomed up from the mountainside above them, circled a few times over their heads, then flew down to make a landing.

Right at the beginning of September the divisional staff set up their quarters in an uninhabited wing of the fortress. The various regiments gradually converged there and were billeted in the surrounding area. These manoeuvres were carried out in highly disciplined fashion and much more quietly than they would have expected. On the major-general's orders the armoured unit was expressly forbidden to come anywhere near the fortress and the tanks set off for the plateau with the swallow hole, which was to become a firing range.

One morning Varlaam landed a Super-Puma at the heliport and hurried over to the fortress to see Olga Grekova-Leber and the secretary.

'Here I am back again!' he said, clearly delighted. Then he drew the secretary aside and pulled a piece of paper out of his pocket. 'D'you remember that man in the glacier? They've found him – a company that happened to go that way. They managed to get him out of the serac and take him quite a long way down, but he disintegrated en route. The captain went mad and killed one of the other officers. They found some documents on him. Look, read this.' It was a photocopy of a memo from the Czech Embassy to the Interior Ministry. 'Joseph Mrozek was born in Brno in 1873 and disappeared at the beginning of August 1914,' it said. 'Shortly before he disappeared he had been called up to fight alongside the Allies. He was considered to be one of the three leading writers in Czechoslovakia.'

'D'you know what I think?' asked Varlaam, standing there impeccably turned out in his tight-fitting airforce uniform, his hair cut very short at the back. 'I think he ran away from the war and deliberately went up there to die.'

7

A few days after Tanguy's suicide Alexis Muller had himself driven up to the fortress. It took him a long time to get there as the track was blocked by an endless stream of army vehicles and earlier on it had been broken up by the tanks on their way up to White Cow Hole. A little way beyond the Great Wall, which was being guarded after a fashion by an infantry regiment, he found the secretary waiting for him as agreed. The two men went over to the edge of the forest and sat down on a tree trunk. Muller took several sheets of paper out of a folder and the secretary immediately recognized Tanguy's handwriting.

'Before we go any further, I must warn you there's nothing I can do to help her. I'm not the only person who's got this confession,' Muller told him. Behind his lenses his face was expressionless and when he held out the sheets of paper a shudder ran through him. 'Of course she can always deny it. Tanguy's mental state these last few weeks will be used as evidence in her defence, but I know that by now a summons to appear in court is being posted to her and it will be followed by a warrant for her arrest, on a charge of murder.'

Among a whole lot of rambling passages in which he tried to tell the story of his life, how he'd constantly had to repress his passion for Olga Grekova-Leber, how he felt undying gratitude to Samuel Leber, Tanguy recounted in meticulous and coherent detail how seven years earlier, at her behest, he'd damaged the cable car's decelerating mechanism; how day after day for weeks on end she'd persuaded him that his mission on earth was to put an end to her and her husband's sufferings by flinging them over the edge and then killing himself. While he was reading this, the secretary glanced up inquiringly at Muller several times, but his face was as obstinately blank as a brick wall.

'Don't you find all this utterly improbable?' he asked.

Muller took off his glasses and started polishing them frantically with a little piece of shammy leather.

'No. In fact I'm convinced it's absolutely true. I knew it all along, but I didn't have all the details.'

'What would you have done if Tanguy hadn't sent this confession to anyone else?'

Muller had been expecting the question and gave a bitter smile.

'He didn't, so what's the point of asking?' Then suddenly he stopped meticulously cleaning his glasses and turned towards him. For the first time since the beginning of their conversation he detected a glimmer of humanity in Muller's good eye.

'And yet . . . er . . . I should be shocked at your asking such a question of a sworn magistrate of my standing, but in fact . . . er . . . I'm rather pleased. Let's say that you're temporarily relieving me of my responsibilities. I was looking for the truth and now I've found it – or rather it's found me. The worst fear a man or woman can have is that nothing else will happen, that everything has already been written. Now in my case everything's been written, the story's over and I know that in the years left to me no other story will ever really be able to get started. Mrs Leber is an obnoxious woman but also a remarkable woman – I've often wondered how she manages to be so good at making people love her.'

It was starting to rain and they both retreated beneath the branches of the trees. Muller shivered again, as if winter had already seeped into his bones, and pulled up the collar of his jacket. The chauffeur had been pacing up and down but now got back into the car. Soldiers in battledress walked past, glancing inside and making no attempt to conceal their curiosity. In his present exceptionally lucid state the secretary didn't miss a single detail of what was happening. He felt as if he had multifaceted eyes and exceptional powers of hearing. The ravine was abuzz with the endless noise of the lorries, yet he could hear the jackdaws cawing as they wheeled round the fortress, drops of water falling in the depths of the woods, and the silence, like a wall of shadow behind their backs. Muller took a folding umbrella out of his briefcase but didn't open it, making do with clutching it to his chest like a sceptre.

'I thought it odd that you wanted to see me before Mrs Leber,' said the secretary.

'I'm paying her an official visit, and I've got a court official with me, so there are some things I shan't be able to say to her. In particular that I'm going to try to delay the summons for another few days, a week let's say, and she should take advantage of this to make herself scarce. If there's a trial she'll be acquitted, but it will be very long drawn out and she'll find it intolerable. Samuel Leber used to own an enormous *hacienda* near Guadalajara – you should advise her to take refuge there.'

At this point the secretary was thinking of Colonel B, a huge, easy-going man almost as tall as he was and half as broad again. He'd come in person to the library to tell him that Muller wished him to meet him on the track leading to the fortress. And he felt compassionate towards Muller: with his devious and convoluted emotions he'd been forced to play a double game for such a long time.

'I've already suggested it to her,' he said. 'But she won't agree.'

'Why?'

'Because of the scorpions.'

He gave a caustic laugh, then in a flash his sarcasm vanished and he looked completely dejected.

'Scorpions . . . Yes, that's quite right, the whole area's overrun with scorpions. There've been a lot of articles about it in the natural history journals. Olga didn't want to go there again because of them. Apparently they've tried everything to drive them out of the houses, but to no avail. It doesn't bother the locals, but foreigners can't stand them. They can't

296

stand the idea that they might die every time they get into bed at night or pick up their towel. Samuel was fascinated by scorpions, for all sorts of reasons, but he was ashamed to admit to this fascination, goodness knows why. He confided in me one day and I suspect that his sole reason for buying a ranch in that god-forsaken place was because of the scorpions. The wretched creatures appeared on earth about five hundred million years ago and they've more or less failed to evolve. Nothing's ever been able to destroy them, not even geological upheavals or ice ages. And some species of scorpions are so good at withstanding atomic radiation that within a few hours of an explosion the French army found some that were still alive on the thermonuclear site at Reggane in the Sahara. Yes, most of them are two or three hundred times more resistant to radiation than man – that must have given Samuel food for thought. As Olga is disabled, she's twice as vulnerable. And the scorpions in the area round Guadalajara are so poisonous they can despatch you to the next world in a couple of minutes. But after all no one's forcing her to go there – she's wealthy enough to be able to buy herself a luxury house anywhere in the world.'

Then seizing hold of the secretary's arm in an unexpectedly strong grip, he whispered: 'Take her away! Get away from here, make a quick getaway!' Then he snatched up his briefcase and without even thinking of putting up his umbrella left the shelter of the trees and dashed off across country in the icy rain – it was raining heavily by now. The secretary caught up with him in a couple of strides and forced him to stop.

'You can't really call it murder – she was supposed to die too.'

The little figure hugged himself, bent his head and hunched up his shoulders as though he was trying to protect himself from some danger from above.

'Yes, but she knew about it. Samuel didn't.'

Another battalion went past quite close to them, with the hoods of their greatcoats pulled up. They glanced in amusement at these two civilians, one so tall and the other so short, looking as if they were about to come to blows out there in the meadow, in a zone earmarked for more serious fighting. The secretary was thinking of that exact moment, etched for ever on his brain, when he'd jammed the wheelchair brake on and walked away from Fra Cosimo, while the circular saws made their terrible racket as they attacked the base of the beech tree.

'What makes you so sure? They may have come to some agreement.'

Muller pulled himself together and jerked himself free.

'Be careful – you're getting your own story mixed up with theirs!'

8

Olga Grekova-Leber and the secretary were watching from the top of the steps as the Tamils struggled to pile their luggage on top of an army jeep. They hadn't been allowed a lorry and were managing as best they could, leaving behind many of the large number of things they'd accumulated over almost eight years at the fortress. However Ramanuja refused to leave behind anything whatsoever that had belonged to Sarachchandra, so the dead man's luggage took up more room than the bags of the living. They seemed to find it entertaining to have the soldiers there, but their attitude to all that was going on at the fortress was, as usual, one of unobtrusive detachment. This detachment didn't mean they were insensitive or ungrateful. It expressed their natural ability merely to pass by, here or elsewhere – anywhere where, in the end, you need only gloss over that ephemeral state that afflicts all earthly creatures.

'I've never understood them and I never shall,' she admitted, with tears in her eyes. When they'd finished loading the jeep, they came up the steps one at a time to say their farewells and kiss her hand. They did so with great warmth, but with impatience too – you could see their thoughts drifting into their big brown eyes, and a fathomless melancholy came gently down over their faces, like a gossamer veil of shadow.

Ramanuja handed each of them a visiting card bearing the words:

Vassanti Restaurant
Indian & Pakistani Food

The two older Tamils got into the jeep, which then moved off, while the other two set out for the town on foot, walking at a leisurely pace. They turned round several times to wave and when they'd disappeared through the postern gate she grabbed hold of his hand.

'I know what you're thinking,' she said. 'You think we should follow their example, don't you?'

'Yes, I do. But I've asked you to leave so often over the last couple of days that I shan't say anything now.'

She squeezed his hand more tightly.

'Now that you know everything, or almost everything, what are your feelings for me?'

'They haven't changed – you know they haven't.'

'So you love me and you're not afraid of me? Would you be prepared to go on living as you have since you first arrived here?'

'Absolutely.'

The anxiety completely left her face.

'I've made a decision and I shan't change my mind now. I *am* going to go, but I'm not going to leave the fortress.'

He'd been expecting it, he'd prepared himself for it in his head, but hearing her say it with such detachment felt like a betrayal and left him badly shaken. A tiny glimmer of hope always keeps on flickering, somewhere, to break down even the strongest defences. She pulled an envelope out of her little bag and handed it to him. 'Read this. It's the last trick I shall play on poor old Alexis.'

It was a sort of pact, in Samuel Leber's handwriting and signed by both him and his wife:

My wife and I have decided by common consent to leave this world that we now find so hateful. Everything that

299

happens brings us further proof that it is ludicrous to put any trust in the human race. I personally have lost any desire to save it from the annihilation that has been its lot from the outset and my career has been a failure. How can we go on living a normal life knowing that the race we belong to has reached the highest rung on the evolutionary ladder, that it can no longer be perfected by any form of metamorphosis or reflection, and that its most gifted members' painstaking and almost always ambiguous attempts to do good exist only per se, and do not change nature, on which they so absurdly inflict their high-handed rules, by so much as a hair's breadth?

Olga is a woman, I am a man. We no longer feel any sense of wonder or any admiration for these two sexes, and we no longer derive any satisfaction whatsoever from what we are as beings among the whole universe of beings. Thus rather than letting the abyss come to us, we have elected to go to the abyss ourselves.

As he handed the sheet of paper back to her he was saying to himself: It's all a misunderstanding, the mistaken product of disordered minds. But he couldn't help seeing this disorder and its consequences as evidence of the greatness of man. He looked at her sitting there in her wheelchair, so vulnerable and so determined, and a lump came into his throat. He sat down on one of the steps while she was moving the wheelchair a little further away. He could still hear firing over the swallow hole – a monotonous, meaningless sound. Did they each make up their own minds, fully aware of what they were doing, or did one of them put pressure on the other? he wondered. Then he heard the familiar sound of her cigarette lighter and turned towards her. She was holding the pact over the flame. It was burning and turning black and before he could move a muscle there was nothing left in her hand but a tiny triangle of uncharred paper.

'You really are the most appalling coward,' he said angrily, but he knew that her determination had never followed its own logic so unflinchingly. With a single thrust on the wheels she propelled the wheelchair right over to him, her eyes glittering sardonically.

'You've misunderstood me – I shan't kill myself. I don't let history repeat itself,' she whispered in his ear, leaning over the arm of the chair. 'What else could I do but burn it? Now Muller will never have his truth. He doesn't realize it, but that only makes it worse – he'll live in ignorance, without ever suspecting it. That's my revenge. The things you don't know are much truer and much more terrifying than the things you do know.'

In the afternoon she wanted him to take her out round the estate. She was anxious to see how the soldiers were settling in, to make sure they weren't cutting down any trees, but in particular she wanted to reassure herself that it was still her land, that she could move around freely. He settled her into the jeep and they spent all afternoon driving back and forth across the estate. The division wasn't at full strength yet. Colonel B was still expecting an infantry battalion, which was due to arrive that evening. The troops were camping out in the forest, in the clearings, at allegedly strategic points whose justification was far from obvious to the uninitiated. Before very long she grew tired of watching the soldiers rushing backwards and forwards at the double and embarking on all sorts of drill and training exercises that she felt were ludicrous and positively medieval compared to the cataclysm they were preparing to face.

'When I see those soldiers, I feel virtually certain there isn't going to be a war,' she told him on the way back.

Before they reached the fortress they drove past a unit of soldiers and noticed that several of them were signalling them to stop. He recognized some of them – one was the man who'd found a nugget of gold on Bear's Tooth Glacier – and asked where Captain Rollus was. 'He's in prison,' came the reply. 'He's going to be courtmartialled and he may be shot.' Displaying no sign of emotion or resentment, the corporal who'd advised Rollus to abandon the mountaineer's body

301

explained that he'd gone mad. 'He spent too much time with his books,' he said. 'He forgot that what he was doing was real.'

Varlaam's mountain-flying skills were so exceptional that he was entrusted with the twin tasks of transporting the general in charge of the area from one subdivision to another and bringing the troops their post. At least twice a week he and his co-pilot would land the Super-Puma at the heliport. So he was the one who handed the secretary the summons. She was to report to police headquarters at 8.30 in the morning on 22 September, when the case would come up for hearing. She read the summons before lunch, screwed it up and flung it into the fireplace. She was relaxed and there was a touch of derision in her tone. They were in the kitchen. Félicité was preparing lunch and every now and then she would dart a glance at them. Her gaze would occasionally linger on the secretary for a moment or two. This little comedy was repeated several times and before long he felt sure she knew exactly what was afoot, and moreover knew more about it than he did. Sitting with these two women he felt left out. There was something he'd failed to grasp, and his inability to understand was coupled with the fact that he was quite unable to persuade Olga Grekova-Leber to escape.

'We've got two days left,' he said. 'I'm entirely at your service, and so is Varlaam – he's prepared to "borrow" an army helicopter and land us wherever it will be easiest for us to leave the country.'

His words were met by such a stubborn refusal that he decided to say no more. Félicité waited on them as usual, her manner as placid and unsmiling as ever, and they ate their lunch. They ate heartily, but neither of them said a word. Nothing could be said except for the one crucial issue, and that was beyond words now. Félicité sat down at the end of the table and lit her pipe. When the meal was over Olga Grekova-Leber asked him to push her to her rooms. 'I'd like us to have a nap together,' she said. Later on she told him she wouldn't be having dinner and asked him to make sure she wasn't disturbed for any reason whatsoever. 'I'll see you in the library at ten o'clock tomorrow morning.'

Towards the end of the afternoon he came across Colonel B in the courtyard, his plump body smelling of eau de cologne and polish. The colonel told him that a major exercise would take place not the next day but the day after that – a dry run for the evacuation of the civilian population – and that this would result in some minor inconvenience for everyone at the fortress, as several hundred people would be swarming all over it. He apologized over and over again and when the secretary asked him if he seriously believed a nuclear offensive was imminent, for a moment or two he looked thoughtful. 'The point is, you know,' he replied eventually, 'even if you don't want war at any price, you get sucked into it willy-nilly when the other fellow drives you into a situation where if you don't fight, you'll be wiped out or reduced to slavery.'

The secretary deliberately didn't ask him whether he and the thousands of men now serving in the armed forces had any very clear idea of who exactly this 'other fellow' was who was driving the world into war. He returned to his room, flung the windows open and concentrated all his energies on gazing down into the ravine. Darkness fell but he didn't even notice. He could still see as clearly as in broad daylight, as though he was contemplating a huge sunny and shifting space inside himself, with big clouds sailing over it. And he could hear the sound of the torrent, the plaintive murmuring of the torrent endlessly sending its waters rolling on towards the sea.

When he went into the library the following morning it wasn't yet eight, but she was already there. She'd parked the wheelchair behind the desk, on the spot where he'd sat every day for the last thirteen months. He behaved as if nothing had happened, going to sit down facing her, and they stayed like that, looking at one another in silence, for what might have been hours or minutes. But he could tell from the way she looked at him, from her icy expression, that something had happened during the night and that he was back to being just

303

the secretary. She backed the wheelchair slightly away from the desk and crossed her hands over her thighs.

'You haven't drawn your salary since you first started working for me and you've never asked me for it. I opened an account in your name at the Swiss Bank Corporation and I've been making regular payments into it, the sum we agreed at the outset . . .' She broke off, and during the ensuing studied silence he had time to picture exactly what was going to happen next and felt that the wisest course would be to get up and leave the room. 'On top of that, knowing your financial circumstances, I've added to these regular payments a sum that – if as ill luck would have it this war can't make-up its mind to break out after all – should be enough for you to live for a few years without financial worries.'

He didn't answer. Whatever he attempted now, all he could do was play the part she expected of him. He could see the whole intricate mechanism behind her manoeuvring quite clearly, and had the irrational feeling that he'd been manipulated from the start, that he'd never been anything more than a plaything in this woman's hands. He was looking at her and his rising anger was like a dark tide. He stood up, intending to walk over to the door, but his will failed him and he walked over towards her instead. He was moving forward rather slowly, thinking: You're doing exactly what she wants, you've only ever done what she wants. And when he realized that she was backing away, that fear was sweeping over her, he immediately experienced a despicable feeling of satisfaction. The back of the chair banged into the wall. Her hands fumbled on the wheels but there was no chance of escape. She shut her eyes, flung her head back against the wall. He just stood there before her, quite still, his arms hanging limply by his sides, while the tide ebbed away again and his anger turned into a terrible weariness.

'Get it over with quickly,' she whispered. At least that's what he thought he'd heard, because the endless string of curses he'd been hurling at her inside his head ever since he stood up made it difficult to hear properly. He glanced over

304

the rows of books all round them, hundreds of them, all those books containing so much life and so much death. Then this time he really did walk over to the door, feeling – although he hadn't so much as opened his mouth – as if he'd been talking non-stop. Before he left the room he turned round. Her eyes met his. They were huge, the pupils somehow dilated by the outrageous way she'd been treated.

'Get out!' she hissed. 'You're dismissed, fired, like all the others!'

He went straight up to his room, lay down and for the first time on that bed really did fall asleep. Then suddenly a slanting ray of light shone out ahead of him in the depths of the darkness and a secret door – he'd never had any inkling it was there – slowly swung open, revealing a room with lights blazing. The burly outline of a man was silhouetted in the rectangle of light and he recognized him straight away. He wanted to sit up in bed but his body refused to make the slightest movement. He called out, but no sound emerged. The man signalled to him in friendly fashion to come over, and at last he recovered the use of his arms and legs. As he walked over to the door he heard himself say: 'I always thought you were still alive.'

Fra Cosimo nodded in agreement and smiled at him. He took his arm in a fatherly gesture and led him towards a brilliantly lit room that was bare except for a wheelchair sitting in solitary splendour right in the middle of it. He was very familiar with this particular wheelchair. He'd pushed it for years – the bakelite brake handle was broken, one of the foot rests was bent and where the old man's nails had dug into the armrest, the foam padding was sticking out through the torn upholstery. Fra Cosimo was wearing the lightly starched coarse woollen habit he used to put on on Sundays and feast days. He urged him to sit in the wheelchair, his kindly manner seeming so sincere that he complied at once. 'You've done so much, now it's my turn to push you,' said Fra Cosimo, while the wheelchair glided forward surrounded by light. Another door opened with a metallic click. Some reflex made him try to stop the chair by flinging himself against the back of it. Then it came to a standstill inside the goods lift in the shelter.

A tiny jolt made him realize that it was starting on its journey down into the bowels of the fortress. He couldn't see Fra Cosimo but sensed that he was behind him and could hear him wheezing away. 'You must follow that woman, *piccolo*. You'll never be able to live without her,' he said. The door opened, the wheelchair was propelled smoothly forwards by some divine power and he recognized the cave and its underground river. A reddish, flickering light was radiating out all round him. He looked up and the roof of the cave was lost to view in the darkness of a vault arching above him like an unending night-time sky. Then the wheelchair again came to a halt, this time on a rocky platform. Below him was a petrified tree, as dark and glossy as agate, a tree with no leaves on it, but one he recognized. Fra Cosimo whispered right into his ear: 'You must rescue that woman from her appalling life.'

The wheelchair went clattering down a dizzy slope. He tried to twist round to catch a glimpse of Fra Cosimo over his shoulder. I shall never be able to walk again, he thought sadly. She'll have to push me. He'd thought Fra Cosimo was behind him, but suddenly he loomed up ahead of him and pointed downwards to a grey plain bristling with endless rows of tall shapes carved out of stone. 'They're all there, all of them!' he said triumphantly. All round them were rows of tombs – tomb after tomb after tomb as far as the eye could see. Once again he tried to get up, but failed to do so, then tripped and the wheelchair toppled over sideways. Just as he was being flung to the ground he woke up.

A breeze redolent of fallen leaves and chestnuts puffed out the curtains. The jackdaws were drifting like children's kites inside the rectangle of the window, rising up and sinking down again in a series of sudden jerks. He got up, drenched in sweat, took his suitcase out of the cupboard and started putting his things in. Then he remembered the leather bag, which he'd left in the back of the jeep, and decided to go and fetch it and take it with him.

Still dazed by his dream, he found when he reached the courtyard that it was a scene of feverish activity. Colonel B, surrounded by a group of officers, was discussing something with Morel. A little way away a group of about a hundred civilians were waiting impatiently for someone to tell them what to do and he realized he was watching the first phase of the trial evacuation. A sense of expectancy hung over all these people, but there was hesitation too, and the soldiers flanking the pseudo-refugees didn't know what to do with their expressions. It didn't take long to find out what was going on: the mechanism for opening the shelter wasn't working, because, as Morel had been trying to explain to the colonel for getting on for an hour, there was an electronic safety device that could be operated from inside the shelter to seal it off and thus prevent an enemy from getting in. For some unknown reason this device, which was computer-controlled, had been triggered, and this meant the shelter was now impregnable from outside.

Colonel B seemed not so much furious as disconcerted. 'There must surely be some way,' he kept saying, while Morel, who'd now launched into a highly technical explanation, was trying to show that there really wasn't any way, that it was a most unfortunate freak occurrence and one that couldn't possibly have been foreseen. The secretary didn't join in the discussion. He caught Morel's eye for a second, but what he saw there gave him no clues. The colonel was waving his arms about, pulling off his cap to mop his brow, then going on trotting out one by one the various positive arguments as though he would eventually, by the grace of God, stumble on the magic formula that would save the day. When Morel had dealt him one final blow – 'The only possible solution would be to destroy the entrance chamber, but with the technology at our disposal it would take several months' – he looked round helplessly, his glance taking in the whole of the fortress, pointed down to the ground and said: 'But then . . . er . . . then all this is useless, this vast thing that cost thousands of millions isn't any use whatsoever now.'

Morel, his professional pride deeply wounded by the word 'thing', pulled a scornful face: 'None whatsoever, as you say.'

The secretary recovered the bag from the back of the jeep and held it up to his nose. It gave off a very strong smell of leather and sweat, but her own smell had seeped into every fibre. The men in the courtyard were shouting and gesticulating. The civilians were beginning to make a fuss and clamour to be driven back down to the town. Then the colonel's voice could be heard above all the other voices. 'Where's Mrs Leber? Go and fetch Mrs Leber!' Morel pulled himself up to his full height, standing on tiptoe. 'What on earth d'you expect Mrs Leber to do in all this business? Leave her alone!' The colonel's shoulders sagged and that was the last vision of him that remained in the secretary's mind. He could still hear him issuing orders about getting a really top-flight team of engineers together, and before he went back into the fortress he intercepted an ambiguous smile on Morel's face. Then he went straight to her rooms.

The door was bolted from the inside. He spent a long time knocking but no one came, and he went round via the keep and the parapet walk. When he was on the bastion he was anxious to check where the cable car bucket was, but everything seemed to be as usual inside the watchtower. He broke a window to get into her rooms but there was no sign of her. The cupboard doors were open and there was nothing in them, though he caught a whiff of a scent he didn't recognize wafting out of them. Then he went down to the kitchen, but there was no one there either. He called out to Félicité. She couldn't answer his calls, or indeed hear them, but usually you only had to whisper her name and she would appear. He was just leaving when he spotted something – the fossil collection on the mantelpiece had disappeared.

He spent the rest of the day roaming about in the fortress. Then he cleaned his prospecting tools, finished packing and got himself some supper, using what he could find in the kitchen. He was being very sparing with his movements, doing everything slowly, so as not to speed things up or shatter the thin sheet of glass keeping the pain at bay. In the early hours he wrapped himself in a blanket, carried an armchair from her rooms out on to the bastion, facing the ravine, then spent the night there. He gazed up at the stars, sensing that she was somewhere very close to him, yet at the same time further away than the most distant stars.

The day after the date on the summons a helicopter flew up a police inspector and two policemen. They handed him an order for her to appear on pain of arrest, plus a search warrant. 'Mrs Leber has left the fortress,' he said. He let them search the place from top to bottom. The inspector asked how and when she'd left and where she'd gone to. When he said he had no idea, that she'd vanished without even leaving a message for him, the inspector had trouble keeping his temper. 'In that case I shall need to take a statement from you,' he insisted. 'I must ask you to follow me down to the town.'

He had wanted to leave the fortress the same way as he'd come – on foot. But as that didn't seem possible now he asked for a few minutes to collect his luggage.

'What? You mean you're leaving the fortress too?' The inspector sounded uneasy.

'Yes. I was her secretary – I haven't got a job now.'

Before going to the heliport he made a quick detour via the library. The bank slip for the account she'd opened in his name was still lying on the desk. He glanced round at the books, but his mind was elsewhere. Then he slumped into the chair and felt as if he'd never be able to get up again, that there was no point in going on. He opened the drawer where Samuel Leber's revolver was kept, an elderly Herstal spotted with rust, the one he'd always kept in his pocket when he was listening to the screech owls. Why didn't she take me with her? he mused. He tossed the revolver back into the drawer, put the bank slip in his pocket and went out.

The pilot agreed to his request to fly over the fortress so that he could have one last look at that fantastic place that tended to swallow up all those who dwelled there. Then the

309

helicopter plunged down into the ravine and as it flew quite close to the cliff he spotted a flash of light coming from the dense shadow cast by the rock – the chrome skeleton of the wheelchair, dangling from a dead tree.

When he got to the town he took a room at the same hotel as when he'd first come to the fortress, and the innkeeper recognized him straight away. 'It's ages since we've seen you,' he said. 'You haven't been down much, have you?' His tone was clearly intended to encourage the secretary to tell him all about it, but it didn't have the desired effect.

He left his bags at the hotel and set out to stroll round the town. He somehow found himself walking to the cemetery and standing in front of Samuel Leber's grave. It looked as if the marble slab had tilted over even further since the last time he'd been there. A bit further on the gravedigger was working away. The sound of the spade scraping against the stones as it sank into the earth set his teeth on edge. The man climbed up out of the hole he was digging, stuck his spade into the newly dug earth, rubbed his rump and called to him across the graves: 'Did you know him?' He said he hadn't and left the cemetery.

There was a train to the capital only every three days and he decided to go by bus instead. At dinner that evening there were four army officers at the table next to his. He realized straight away that they were engineers and were on their way to the fortress. As far as he could make out from their conversation, they all held different views on potential ways of getting the shelter open. But what was bothering all of them, and prompting them to put forward the most fanciful theories, was the fact that the system had somehow broken down. This unusual incident, the first of its kind, was nudging them down the slippery slope of irrational speculation, and judging by what they were saying, it seemed that the occult could secretly worm its way into electronic circuits and put them out of action, just as a person or animal can be possessed by the devil. When he'd finished his dinner the innkeeper appeared with a glass of spirits, went on standing there by the table, then suddenly ventured a remark.

'I suppose you've handed in your notice. What with everything that's been happening, it can't have been much fun.'

He didn't touch the drink. The officers were speaking much more quietly now and every now and then glancing surreptitiously in their direction.

'Oh, but it was. I enjoyed every minute of it,' he said. 'But I didn't give in my notice. She fired me, as she did all the others.'

The landlord put on a pained expression, shook his head silently and discreetly withdrew. Just as he was walking away a sentence tossed out by one of the engineers could be clearly heard above the general hubbub. 'I'm sure there's someone inside!' The others laughed. He decided to drink the glass of spirits after all, and for a large number of reasons, each more disheartening than the last, very nearly burst out laughing himself.

When he got back to his room it had been dark for some time. He leaned his elbows on the window sill. The room overlooked a paved square and a fountain that was lit by floodlights but wasn't playing. It was a mild evening and various couples and little gangs of soldiers were lingering in the square. He looked out unseeingly on this night-time scene. He wasn't thinking of anything in particular, but any object or living creature his eye happened to fall on reminded him of his own solitary state. Then a woman appeared in the square. She was walking briskly, her heels making a clicking sound on the paving stones, and although he'd never met her, he recognized her. At first he couldn't place her, but when she walked under a street lamp it came back to him – she was the woman who'd been driving the only car that had passed him on the way from the station a year earlier, the day he'd arrived in the town.

He was struck by how clearly that image had stayed in his mind after so long, and how familiar she now seemed because of the length of time that had elapsed. He had a feeling that her reappearance wasn't just chance, or a run-of-the-mill coincidence. Although she wasn't walking as fast as he'd thought at first, so much energy flowed from her that she seemed to be set on spending the night combing the deepest recesses of the darkness to find what everyone seeks, but never finds. When she came on a level with the hotel she suddenly turned off at right angles and he found himself looking straight at her tanned face with its pronounced and regular features, in the white light of the fountain. In a flash of second sight he could see she was one of those rare creatures who live in the purest fire, and who only ever leave their natural home in the depths of all that is inaccessible to mingle with the rest of us when some imminent and terrible danger makes our world seem bearable. She stopped just outside the door into the hotel, seemed undecided about whether or not to go in, then did an about-turn and went back across the square. The way she'd stopped, then hesitated for a second made her seem more like an ordinary mortal, but he went on feeling quite certain, far into the night, that she'd come for him.

He was right. Early the following morning he was brought a message that a lady was waiting for him in reception. The exceptional creature he'd detected in her was still there, but hidden well out of sight, buried deep, as it were, in the sturdy reality of her face.

'I'm Varlaam's wife,' she said. 'He wanted to come himself, but he's been sent off somewhere. I know you're going to leave here and . . .' – she hesitated – '. . . my sister has a son of twenty who's recently been in a bad car crash. His legs are paralysed. Would you be willing to look after him for a while?' She'd been speaking very fast, as though she wanted to get a difficult job over and done with, but her eyes had never once left his face. 'My sister lives in the country,' she added. 'She has a farm with a lot of land.' He asked for time to think it over, but in fact he'd already made up his mind. And as she was leaving the hotel he was thinking, without hesitating for a single second: I'll look after that young man.

Then he set off to walk round the upper part of the town. When the outline of the fortress appeared in the distance at the far end of the ravine, looking more fantastic than ever, he gave it a heartfelt salute. Anguish never becomes a stylistic exercise, he was thinking. Man does whatever's needed to relieve his pain, preferring a bearable existence to greatness, and a little warmth to desolation.

Further Titles Available from Mandarin and Minerva

While every effort is made to keep prices low, it is sometimes necessary to increase prices at short notice. Mandarin Paperbacks reserves the right to show new retail prices on covers which may differ from those previously advertised in the text or elsewhere.

The prices shown below were correct at the time of going to press.

☐	7493 0942 3	**The Silence of the Lambs**	Thomas Harris	£4.99
☐	7493 0134 1	**To Kill A Mockingbird**	Harper Lee	£3.99
☐	7493 0376 X	**Trial by Fire**	Frances Fyfield	£3.99
☐	7493 0732 3	**Mad About Bees**	Candida Crewe	£3.99
☐	7493 9151 0	**Boating for Beginners**	Jeanette Winterson	£4.99
☐	7493 9134 0	**Rebuilding Coventry**	Sue Townsend	£4.99
☐	7493 9916 3	**Zuleika Dobson**	Max Beerbohm	£5.99
☐	7493 9921 X	**An Instant in the Wind**	André Brink	£5.99
☐	7493 9903 1	**Dirty Faxes**	Andrew Davies	£4.99
☐	7493 9112 X	**Hopeful Monsters**	Nicholas Mosley	£5.99
☐	7493 9957 0	**The Joy Luck Club**	Amy Tan	£4.99
☐	7493 9162 6	**Four Bare Legs in a Bed**	Helen Simpson	£4.99

All these books are available at your bookshop or newsagent, or can be ordered direct from the publisher. Just tick the titles you want and fill in the form below.

Mandarin Paperbacks, Cash Sales Department, PO Box 11, Falmouth, Cornwall TR10 9EN.

Please send cheque or postal order, no currency, for purchase price quoted and allow the following for postage and packing:

UK including BFPO	£1.00 for the first book, 50p for the second and 30p for each additional book ordered to a maximum charge of £3.00.
Overseas including Eire	£2 for the first book, £1.00 for the second and 50p for each additional book thereafter.

NAME (Block letters) ....

ADDRESS ....

....

☐ I enclose my remittance for ....

☐ I wish to pay by Access/Visa Card Number ☐☐☐☐☐☐☐☐☐☐☐☐☐☐☐☐

Expiry Date ☐☐☐☐